THE HAUNTING OF HEATHERHURST HALL

SEBASTIAN NOTHWELL

CONTENTS

CHAPTER ONE

Newport, Rhode Island
June 3rd, 1892

L ucinda Coffin strode down the aisle of the church like a princess about to be crowned queen. A white lace veil hid her visage but allowed a glimpse of her swanlike throat, and in no way hid the golden cast of her shining curls. Her wedding gown was likewise worthy of a coronation—gleaming white silk, hand-stitched and embroidered with thousands of perfect pearls. The glorious train trailed behind the bride, the princess-style waistline flattered her figure, and its voluminous shoulders descended into fitted sleeves ending in lace cuffs extending over the back of Lucy's slender, feminine hands.

From her position in the pews amongst the other guests, Kit Morgan recalled the graceful way those slender fingers had held a watercolor brush —and worse yet, the soft clasp of Lucy's hands in hers. Tears pricked her eyes. She forced them down to look at her own stubby fingers and meaty palms. But the sight only brought to mind how it had felt to touch Lucy's golden curls, gently untangling and brushing and braiding hair as fine as silk and shining as the sun. Hair so unlike Kit's own limp, dishwater-blonde locks.

"House of Worth gown," a society matron whispered to her neighbor in the pew ahead of Kit. "The cuffs alone! It's a wonder Coffin could bear to part with the funds."

"He's parting with his daughter," the neighbor whispered back. "Though I suppose he feels the loss of the money more keenly. Quakers, you know."

Kit, who sat between strangers, recalled how she and Lucy had whispered to each other under the covers of a shared bed in the dark of night. Pushing such painful memories from her mind, she lifted her gaze to the altar, where Lucy's soon-to-be husband waited.

John Cabot, a plain-faced man in his mid-thirties, seemed unaffected by the sight of his beautiful young bride. Perhaps her lace veil blocked his view of Lucy's soft lips, button nose, and dancing blue eyes. Kit had gazed deeply into those eyes in the course of a hundred heartfelt conversations in the years she and Lucy had shared at finishing school. No veil could suppress her memories of Lucy's brilliant smile and the light blush that would come to her cheeks as she laughed her merry little laugh—like silver sleigh-bells, ringing easy and free.

He doesn't deserve her.

The uncharitable thought startled Kit, and she pushed it to the back of her mind even as she felt her own strong chin trembling. John Cabot, of the Boston Cabots, had breeding and money besides. He was an excellent prospect for a girl such as Lucinda Coffin of the New Bedford Coffins, herself the inheritor of no small pedigree and a fortune of her own. John Cabot was a perfectly respectable man. Even if he had no hobbies, no humor, and no conversation. Even if Kit could only pick him out of a crowd by his mustache. He made Lucy happy, or so she claimed.

That was enough. To see Lucy happy. It was all Kit ever wanted. She repeated this lie to herself over and over as Lucy climbed the steps to the altar.

Lucy, having alighted the stairs with her aged father's assistance, turned to face her groom. Her father lifted her veil. Kit caught a glimpse of Lucy's beautiful face breaking into resplendent glory with the force of her beaming smile. Then Kit's vision blurred with tears, and she screwed her eyes shut to force them back. It took a strong will to prevent herself from covering her ears against the minister's droning voice reminding the assembled company of their solemn duty to witness the union of two souls in the eyes of the Almighty Lord.

"Should anyone here present know of any reason that this couple should not be joined in holy matrimony, speak now or forever hold your peace."

Kit's heart leapt into her throat. There was every reason not to join Lucinda Coffin in holy matrimony with John Cabot.

Because I love her.

Kit could feel the impossible words drawing together in her lungs and shooting up to escape her lips, blocked only by the lump in her throat, more painful than any she'd suffered in illness. No matter how strong her love, it was nothing compared to that which flowed between the bride and groom. Supposedly. Kit's love was only a schoolgirl crush, the love of bosom friends. Such a love was superseded by the love of a wife for her husband. Such a love would fade as a girl became a woman and entertained the attention of male suitors. Such a love was supposed to become a distant, if treasured, memory.

So why did the resulting heartbreak feel like a knife through Kit's chest?

Kit bit her tongue to keep both words and tears at bay. A true friend wouldn't ruin a bride's special day. Even if it killed her to keep her silence. And Kit was nothing if not a true friend.

It wasn't as though Lucy didn't appreciate her. She did. That only made it worse. Kit had politely turned down countless opportunities to involve herself in the wedding. Lucy had asked her to be the maid-of-honor. Then, when Kit refused, Lucy offered her the position of bridesmaid. Even when Kit declined that, Lucy took no offense, and went on to invite Kit on the cross-Atlantic trip to Paris to see Lucy fitted for her wedding dress. No American heiress worth her father's millions would ever turn down an opportunity to visit the House of Worth. And yet, Kit had. At the time, she thought keeping her distance would help her forget how dearly she loved her friend. Alas, absence only made her heart grow fonder.

The ceremony rolled on, the four-hundred-strong crowd oblivious to Kit's internal struggles. Echoes of the vows reached Kit's ears, warped and vague, as if she were underwater. The burning ache in her chest and throat certainly felt like drowning. Hot tears poured freely down her cheeks, obscuring all sight of the bride and groom as the fateful words, "I do," were repeated by each in turn. And then—

"I now pronounce you man and wife."

A joyous ripple ran through the crowd. Kit clutched her handkerchief over her nose and mouth to suppress her own howl of agony. Through her tears, she caught the barest glimpse of Lucy and her husband coming together and returning down the aisle. A flash of white from Lucy's dress was all she saw. Then her vision swam, and only the stiff whalebone of her corset kept her from collapsing in grief.

"I beg your pardon, Miss..."

The voice, to Kit's left, gave her pause. It was not often she heard an English accent on this side of the Atlantic. She blinked the tears from her eyes as best she could and turned to face the speaker.

Beside her sat a thin man with raven-black hair. Her remaining tears blurred any further detail.

"Are you unwell?" he asked.

Kit gulped down her hysteria to reply, but the moment she withdrew her handkerchief from her mouth, a wail surged up from her throat, and she just barely clamped her hand back over her lips in time to block it. Her shoulders heaved with a single sob as she shook her head violently—the best answer she could manage.

"Here, now," said the man, putting a hand on her shoulder. "Let's find you some fresh air, shall we?"

Kit overcame her bewilderment at his forward nature and nodded her assent. She'd do anything to be out of this wretched church.

Without another word, a strong grip descended on her upper arms, lifting her from her seat and guiding her gently down the pew, away from the center aisle. She overheard guests around them bustling with the business of gathering themselves up to follow the bride and groom out of the church to what would no doubt be a glorious reception at Marble House. A few murmurs of "Pardon me," and "Excuse us, please," from the gentleman, and then the oppressive heat of the church dissipated in the face of a crisp breeze off the bay.

4

Kit took in a few deep breaths of fortifying ocean air, tipping her face to the sun to let gravity stop her tears. Only then did she turn to her rescuer.

Now, with the aid of bright June sunshine, Kit beheld a thin gentleman of no more than five-and-twenty years. From a standing position, she realized he was tall, much taller than she'd expected. She'd grown used to towering over gentlemen ever since she'd shot up like a sapling in her sixteenth year, but this fellow had to be well over six foot, for she had to look up to meet his green-eyed gaze. His crooked nose curved to a point like a beak, as sharp as his cheekbones. And yet, his concerned expression softened his features considerably.

He gazed down upon her for a moment, then his look softened even further into a shy smile. "Better, I hope?"

"Much." Kit clenched her jaw against any remaining trembles and forced a smile of her own. "Thank you, Mr. ...?"

"Sir Vivian Cranbrook," he finished with a very smart bow. "I beg your pardon for not introducing myself earlier."

"The pardon is all mine to beg," Kit blurted, then winced at her own jumbled phrasing. "Do forgive me, Sir Vivian. Miss Morgan, at your service."

"A pleasure to make your acquaintance, Miss Morgan. Is there anything further I might do to assist? I believe my sister has some smelling-salts in her reticule..."

Kit opened her mouth to demur, but a call from the church cut her off.

"Sir Vivian! There you are! Whatever caused you to run off like that?"

The inquiry was accompanied by a familiar giggle. Kit's stomach turned even before she saw the flounce of daffodil-colored skirts bedecked with ribbons.

"Miss Wheeler!" said Sir Vivian, turning to face the lady in question with a friendly smile.

Miss Patience Wheeler trotted out of the church's side door and across the lawn, her auburn ringlets bouncing with every step. She came to a stop beside Sir Vivian and threaded her arm through his with astonishing familiarity. The top of her curls barely crested his shoulder as she looked up at him with an expression probably intended as adoring. Kit thought it looked hungry.

"You dashed out on us all of a sudden!" Patience chided him playfully. "Whatever will you do to make it up to me?"

"A thousand apologies, my dear Miss Wheeler," Sir Vivian began. "May I introduce—?"

"Oh!" Patience laughed. "But we are already acquainted! How wonderful to see you again, Miss Morgan!"

Kit struggled to formulate a socially-appropriate response. She knew she looked a wreck—she'd always been an ugly crier, with puffy eyes, snotty nose, and a crumpled chin. Any fool could tell she was distraught, but Patience especially so, for it was Patience who had caused most of Kit's tears at finishing school. Indecorous comments about clumsy bean-poles in their ballroom dancing classes, or remarks on Kit's square jaw and thick brows in portrait-drawing, or whispers in the dormitory about Kit's supposed monstrous nature at night. Nothing of Kit's was safe from Patience's forked tongue. But Kit had been able to keep her strong chin high, thanks to the soothing nature of Lucy beside her. Lucy, who on many a night had held a sobbing Kit in her arms and told her she was as beautiful and clever as any Athena or Artemis.

Now, with Lucy gone from her forever, Kit felt dangerously close to bursting into tears again.

"Sir Vivian and his sister are here as my guests," Patience chattered on to Kit, squeezing Sir Vivian's arm. To him, she continued, "And Miss Morgan is of the New Bedford Morgans. We're old schoolfriends, she and Miss Coffin and I. Oh, but Miss Coffin is Mrs. Cabot now! I must endeavor to remember that."

"One would suppose attending the wedding would've reminded you," Kit heard herself say in a low, dull tone. "Perhaps the reception will help fix it in your memory."

For an instant, the society smile froze on Patience's face. Ferocity glimmered behind cold blue eyes. Then she laughed it away. "You must be wondering how I know Sir Vivian! My mother and I made his acquaintance on our tour of Italy—his and his sister's acquaintance, that is. They showed us all the finest sights in Rome!"

Kit sincerely doubted it. Rome's finest would be wasted on the girl who considered artistic nudes gauche if not outright grotesque. Still, Kit forced out, "How wonderful for you."

"Yes, it certainly was." Patience's smirk widened. "Have you ever toured the Continent, Miss Morgan?"

"Not yet," said Kit. But of course, Patience already knew that. Just as surely as she knew Kit and Lucy had planned to visit Europe together after they'd finished school. And how those plans were dashed the moment Lucy's mother introduced her to John Cabot, who didn't want his bride-to-be picking up any unsavory Continental notions.

"No?" said Patience, her eyes widening theatrically. "But surely a trip across the sea is the most natural thing for one with such nautical blood in her veins!"

Patience was of course referring to the Morgan family's famous whaling origins. Kit's great-grandfather had made a frankly embarrassing fortune in the industry. The end result, even several generations later, was more than enough to send a young orphan to boarding school. The remainder of her portion was managed by Mr. Enoch Mudge, Esq. All perfectly respectable for an American heiress. But Kit supposed Patience thought an allusion to an ancestry that included sailors and sea-cooks would put off a proper English baronet such as Sir Vivian.

"True enough," Kit replied, her voice dull from her efforts to keep any trace of malice from her tone. "We can't all sail upon oceans of tapioca, after all."

Patience, whose family owned a tapioca plant in western Mass-achusetts, bristled. With a strained trill, she asked, "A beautiful ceremony, wouldn't you agree? It's funny, isn't it? Marrying a Bostonian to prevent a Boston marriage!"

Kit, her eyes darting wildly about for an escape, caught a flicker of movement by the church door. Patience had left it open behind her, and in her wake came a sharp-featured, raven-haired young woman in a gown of deep maroon. The woman looked about as Kit watched. Then she turned to where Sir Vivian, Patience, and Kit had gathered. A pair of steel-gray eyes met Kit's curious look with a glance so severe it stopped her breath.

Sir Vivian frowned and turned over his shoulder to follow Kit's line of sight. "Ah, Alexandra! Do come meet Miss Morgan!"

The woman, Alexandra, strode towards them with smooth, sure steps. Kit couldn't take her eyes off her as she approached. Her face was no less sharp than Sir Vivian's, with a hawkish nose and pointed chin. Her porcelain-pale complexion created a striking contrast against her black hair and rose-red lips. When she came at last to stand beside Sir Vivian's free arm, Kit saw she was of a like height to Patience. This surprised Kit—from the way Alexandra carried herself, she would've sworn she stood eye-to-eye with Sir Vivian. When Alexandra's eyes looked upon Kit, Kit felt as if she faced the judgment of an ancient empress—and might be found wanting.

"Miss Morgan," said Sir Vivian, "may I introduce my sister, Miss Cranbrook. Alexandra, this is Miss Morgan."

Kit curtsied, keenly feeling how her overgrown frame would loom over Alexandra no matter how low she bowed her head. But when she lifted her gaze again, she found the beginnings of a smile flickering at the corner of Alexandra's lips.

"Charmed, I'm sure," said Alexandra, her voice cool and crisp, utterly devoid of artifice. She held out her hand for Kit to clasp.

Kit did so. Her pulse quickened as Alexandra gave her fingers a brief squeeze and released her.

Patience's thin eyebrows knit together tightly enough to push a single wrinkle into her otherwise flawless forehead. "Miss Morgan is of the New Bedford Morgans, you know."

"I had surmised," said Alexandra, gazing into Kit's eyes rather than so much as glancing in Patience's direction. "As Mrs. Cabot is of the New Bedford Coffins. You must be very close friends."

Kit swallowed around the lump returning to her throat. "Indeed."

"And may you remain so for many years more," said Alexandra. "Is your family in attendance, Miss Morgan?"

"Distant relations," said Kit. Though she'd been raised in the household of her aunt and uncle, the only family she felt truly close to was her cousin, Phoebe. They were of a like age and had been raised together by the same nursemaid. But though Phoebe had been invited to the wedding —and indeed, should have occupied a seat in the pews beside Kit—she had sent a polite refusal, with the excuse that she needed to focus upon her studies. For Phoebe Morgan, much to her parents' chagrin, was studying to become a surgeon at Boston University School of Medicine. Kit didn't begrudge her cousin's well-earned ambitions, no matter how lonely it left her at present. "I've come alone."

"A pity," said Alexandra. "In that case, may we accompany you to the reception, Miss Morgan?"

Kit, who had all the while been spinning wheels in the back of her mind to try and invent an excuse to skip the reception, found her train of thought stuttering to a halt. For, as Alexandra had extended her invitation, she had also stepped forward to thread her arm through Kit's as if they'd known each other from the cradle, and looked up at her with a gentle smile.

"I..." said Kit, blinking stupidly down at her. "I would be delighted, Miss Cranbrook."

"Excellent," said Miss Cranbrook, and squeezed Kit's arm.

Kit looked back to Sir Vivian and found Patience had dropped her cheerful facade in favor of a full-blown scowl. Sir Vivian appeared oblivious.

"Shall we?" he asked, holding out his free hand to Kit.

Kit took it, bewildered. Sir Vivian led the three ladies to a waiting carriage.

Marble House, the Vanderbilt's new summer cottage, had been finished just last year. It was aptly named; the front of the house was faced in Westchester marble, while the dining room featured pink Numidian marble, and the front hall's two-story walls and staircase were all of yellow Siena marble, with a gilt bronze railing. Inside, the wedding guests funneled piecemeal into the Grand Salon, which would serve as the evening's ballroom. The Grand Salon boasted walls of gold panels decorated in scenes from ancient Hellenic mythology. Alva Vanderbilt had graciously granted use of the house to the Coffins for the wedding reception. Patience Wheeler blurted all these facts in rapid succession as their bizarre party passed through the massive French Baroque-style doors and entered the crowded front hall. Kit largely ignored her, distracted by the warmth of Alexandra's firm yet gentle grip upon her elbow.

"Refreshments?" asked Sir Vivian.

Kit nodded dumbly. Though Marble House had been specifically constructed to cool the blood on a warm summer night such as this, the heat of hundreds of wedding guests strained its architectural limits.

"Champagne would be divine," gushed Patience.

"Thank you, brother," said Alexandra with a nod.

Sir Vivian smiled and slipped away through the crowd, leaving the three ladies to fend for themselves. Patience turned immediately to Alexandra.

"I was just telling Miss Morgan," she said, "about our holiday in Rome. Wasn't it magnificent?"

"I rather thought so," said Alexandra, again turning to direct her words towards Kit. "Though now that I consider it, it would've been improved by Miss Morgan's presence. Have you ever been?"

"She hasn't," Patience said over Kit's reply.

But Alexandra's gaze never left Kit's face. "A pity. You shall simply have to accompany us when next we visit. Do you enjoy art, Miss Morgan?"

"Very much so," said Kit, ignoring Patience rolling her eyes behind Alexandra's back. While her favorite works were Lucy's watercolor seascapes, she had an appreciative eye for all forms of fine art, from the marble masterpieces of the Italian Renaissance to the modern portraiture of John Singer Sargent. "Do you paint, Miss Cranbrook?"

Alexandra appeared to give the idle inquiry a great deal of thought. "I've been known to produce tolerable watercolors. But I believe my true talents lie nearer to sculpture. And you, Miss Morgan?"

"I sketch from time to time," Kit admitted, not yet bold enough to tell of the hundred-odd sketchbooks she'd filled in her years at school. Still, she found courage enough to add, "Photography is my passion."

A spark of interest flashed through Alexandra's eyes. "Indeed?"

Kit, used to people's patience rapidly draining whenever she spoke of her hobby, felt too mystified by Alexandra's attentions to muster more than a confirming nod.

Alexandra's lips twitched into a devilish little smile. "Perhaps you might be so kind as to take my portrait someday."

"Perhaps," Kit echoed, just as Sir Vivian reappeared over his sister's shoulder and saved her from her own clumsy tongue.

"Miss Morgan was just telling us about her passion for photography," Alexandra told her brother.

"Really?" Sir Vivian appeared delighted by the notion. He handed a glass of champagne to Kit, having dispensed two others to his sister and Patience and kept a fourth for his own consumption. Kit thought he deserved a place in the circus for all his skill at juggling. "How marvelous. Shall we join the throng?"

Under Sir Vivian's direction, the ladies wove their way through the crowd to the Grand Salon. As Patience rattled off the cost of each of the room's furnishings to the dollar, Kit took advantage of the Cranbrook's distraction to toss back her flute of champagne in an unsophisticated gulp. The evening might go easier if her mind couldn't focus quite so sharply on where she was and why. Yet no amount of drink could deafen her. Even now, she overheard countless society dames around her chittering about the wedding.

"—about time she married. Another year and she'd be an old maid—"

"—surprised the Cabots could bear to lower themselves to bring a Quaker into their ranks, though no doubt the money helps—"

"—happy enough, I suppose. She must be used to boredom by now, growing up in New Bedford—"

"May I have this dance, Miss Morgan?"

Kit blinked to rid her eyes of visions of the past and found Sir Vivian before her, holding out his hand.

Kit stared at him. It was the first time in her life any gentleman had ever asked the question. All her previous experience dancing with men had been prompted by matrons whose definition of a perfect ball made no allowances for wallflowers, hissing into the ears of those bachelors not lucky enough to fill the dance card of more becoming girls. Even if she weren't the clumsiest creature on two legs, she towered over most gentlemen, none of whom enjoyed looking up. No one had ever danced with Kit of their own volition—besides Lucy. Lucy had always picked Kit first in their ballroom dancing classes, had gracefully tip-toed around Kit's heavy tread, had smiled through when Kit inevitably trod on her skirt and tore

11

its hem, had let Kit's palm settle on her slender waist and clasped hands with her in rapturous harmony. But Kit wasn't drunk enough to try to dance with the bride on her wedding day.

As Kit struggled to come to terms with the latest unprecedented development in an already turbulent day, she caught sight of Patience over Sir Vivian's shoulder.

Patience's rosy cheeks had gone white with rage—and not entirely without cause. After all, Sir Vivian was her guest, here at her behest to act as her escort. From what Kit recalled of her lessons from finishing school, she felt fairly certain it was a breach of etiquette for him to ask anyone but Patience to the first dance.

However, with her life torn asunder before her very eyes, and love forever flown from her broken heart, Kit didn't have much respect left for the rules of polite society, and still less fortitude to resist the urge for petty vengeance. She put her hand in Sir Vivian's. "I'd be delighted."

Patience looked fit to spit as Sir Vivian gracefully led Kit out to join the rest of the dancers.

"You've danced the waltz before, Miss Morgan?" Sir Vivian asked as they assumed their respective positions.

"Yes." Kit rather liked waltzes. Their steps were simple enough—even a child could manage counting to three—and she felt confident she could execute them competently, if not well. She didn't see fit to impart more information than this to Sir Vivian. He didn't need to know that she was more accustomed to leading the waltz rather than following, and preferred to have her hand upon a girl's waist rather than feel a man's upon her own.

Still, the weight of Sir Vivian's spidery fingers was not so much to bear. He kept his touch light, well within the bounds of propriety, and taking none of the liberties many other gentleman might dare under the excuse of executing the dance.

Kit met his gaze and realized she was, for once, looking up at her dance partner. An anxious weight dropped away. She straightened her neck and shoulders from the slouch she typically assumed to spare the pride of men. She could stand as tall as she liked, and Sir Vivian would continue smiling his friendly smile down upon her. She dared a smile of her own in return.

As Sir Vivian twirled her around the dance floor, Kit caught a glimpse of Patience, puce in the face, arms crossed over her bodice, ignoring the attentions of a suitor inferior to the one she'd lost to Kit. A spark of vengeful satisfaction brought a smirk to Kit's lips. She continued to spin, and saw Alexandra standing near Patience—with her eyes fixed upon Kit.

The smirk dropped from Kit's face. She held Alexandra's gaze for a mere instant, yet it felt as though the world had frozen in place around them, allowing them the luxury of eons. Alexandra's eyes seemed to pierce through her facade, to see past the happy mask she put up to hide the sad little girl within. And more curious still, the wrinkle between her brows seemed to bespeak sympathy for that sad little girl.

Then Kit's range of vision shifted with the spin of the dance and she lost sight of Alexandra entirely. She tried to put that curious sympathy from her mind and focus on Sir Vivian's smiling visage, but as she considered him, she couldn't help noticing the strong resemblance to his sister. The longer she looked, the more similarities she found, from their dark eyebrows to their sharp cheekbones and their beaked noses. Like a pair of ravens, they were.

Then, as if in a dream, Sir Vivian's face transposed entirely with Alexandra's, and Kit imagined she was dancing not with the baronet, but with his sister.

And for the first time in months, Kit felt a flutter of happiness.

The moment she realized what had occurred, she shook her head to clear her senses, but the damage was done. She couldn't look upon Sir Vivian without seeing Alexandra. Worse still, she wasn't sure she minded.

Sir Vivian didn't seem to notice. All throughout the waltz, his easy smile and cheerful chatter never abated. Best of all, he only ever required a nod from Kit to continue his conversation—and unlike most blathering men, he bothered to wait for a response in the first place. Of all the young gentlemen she'd ever encountered, Kit thought Sir Vivian might be the least loathsome. He might even be likable. Kit didn't think it such a chore to agree to a second dance with such a fellow. Or a third. Or a fourth.

By the start of the fifth dance, even Kit's long legs struggled to keep up. The moment she flagged, Sir Vivian took her by the elbow and gently steered her to a chair in the balustrade, where the marble walls opened to the shore and its refreshing sea breeze.

"Thank you," Kit gasped.

"You're more than welcome," said Sir Vivian, standing beside her chair. "I must say, Miss Morgan, you're a very energetic dancer. It's a wonderful change from the company in London."

Kit had overheard society matrons in the past discussing the differences between American and English girls—their talk typically concluding that Americans made for superior brides. But she knew no reply to the compliment but a nod.

Sir Vivian seemed to take it in stride. He smiled out over the crowd. "I wonder where my sister has—ah! There she is! Alexandra!"

Kit jolted upright, her weariness forgotten. In the space of a blink, she spotted Alexandra coming from the front hall, a glass of punch in her hand, Patience at her heels.

"Here," said Alexandra, passing the punch to Kit. "I thought you could use some refreshment."

"Small wonder that you do!" said Patience before Kit could thank her. "Four waltzes in a row is no small feat for a lady!"

It didn't take a particularly conniving mind to pick up on Patience's undertones. But Kit found that, for once, she didn't care what Patience thought or said. It was enough to nod her thanks to Alexandra and sip the punch she'd so kindly provided. It took very little effort to keep her chin high and her eyes upon the Cranbrook siblings—never mind the blazing heat of Patience's pointed glare.

Patience spent another moment glaring at Kit, then rounded upon Sir Vivian and swapped out her indignant tone for a pleading one. "I do hope you're not done dancing this evening, Sir Vivian?"

Kit didn't need to look at her to see the babyish pout she knew accompanied that tone. She'd witnessed the combination a thousand times at finishing school. And yet, for once her heart held no heavy vexation. If she felt anything regarding Patience's behavior, it was admittedly-vindictive amusement. She smiled to herself and took another sip of her punch. It tasted quite good.

All the sweeter for having been delivered by Alexandra's hands.

The thought startled her. She blinked down at the punch, as if it were responsible for her disturbed mind. Dimly, she heard her companions' conversation continuing around her.

"...would be honored, of course," Sir Vivian was saying, "if you would grant me the favor of a dance, Miss Wheeler."

The thought of the simpering look Patience was no doubt serving him in response gave Kit a giggle. In her peripheral vision, she caught another glare from Patience, which only made her giggle more.

A hand alighted on her shoulder. Kit gave a little jump and turned to find a glove of maroon silk, and followed it up to its end upon a lady's pale elbow, and from there the smooth curve of the lady's bare arm to the shoulder of a maroon gown, giving way to a pale neck with raven-dark curls gathered at the nape, and a sharp jaw ending in a pointed chin. Alexandra. It was Alexandra's hand upon Kit's shoulder. Kit didn't know whether to laugh or faint.

"I'll look after our guest," Alexandra said to her brother. "Go on dancing."

Sir Vivian bowed to his sister and took up Patience's hand. They disappeared back into the house, with Patience casting a triumphant smirk over her shoulder at Kit.

Kit didn't care. Kit had Alexandra's hand upon her and had half a mind to swoon from it.

Then suddenly the hand was gone. Kit hardly had time to mourn its loss before Alexandra had pulled up a chair to sit beside her, the hems of their skirts mingling in a swirl of color.

"Are you feeling quite the thing, Miss Morgan?" Alexandra said, reaching out to clasp Kit's knuckles. "Forgive me for saying so, but you seem a bit flushed."

Kit stifled a bark of laughter. She never looked a "bit" flushed. Her blushes took the form of a splotchy strawberry rash all over her face and neck. And she could feel herself blushing now. "I'm fine, but—thank you."

She hoped Alexandra could hear how very much she meant it. The Cranbrook siblings had taken her under their corvid wings when she would have otherwise been bereft and alone. To say nothing of how Alexandra's silk glove now held her hand in a warm embrace.

"I know today must have been a trial for you," said Alexandra. "It can't be easy to watch your friend given away."

And just like that, the warm, bubbly feelings of champagne, dancing, and holding hands with a beautiful lady all fell away with Alexandra's gentle reminder of why Kit was here in this moment. Lucy's wedding. John Cabot. The end of a friendship. Unbidden tears pricked at Kit's eyes once more. She dropped her gaze to her lap and steeled herself against the incoming tide of misery.

"I'm sorry to mention it," Alexandra continued, clenching Kit's hand in hers. "Only—I've some experience in losing a bosom friend. And I wanted you to know you weren't alone."

Kit looked up suddenly. Something in Alexandra's phrasing, in her tone, led her to believe she might know the true meaning behind the word "friend" and what Lucy had been to her.

Alexandra's expression, her dark eyebrows angled inward, softening her gaze, confirmed it.

Kit swallowed the lump in her throat. "Thank you, Miss Cranbrook."

Alexandra smiled. "I do hope you'll forgive my shocking familiarity. But as you've no doubt heard my Christian name on my brother's lips, I wondered if I might ask you yours?"

Kit's mouth went suddenly dry. "Catherine."

Alexandra smiled. "I've had a wonderful evening with you, Catherine."

"My friends call me Kit," Kit blurted. If she'd had a hand free, she'd have clapped it over her own mouth in horror. Until now, the only people to call her Kit were her childhood nursemaid, her cousin Phoebe, and Lucy. It was absurd to think an aristocrat such as Miss Cranbrook would ever want to use such a childish nickname. Though nothing Kit said could take her presumptive comment back, she couldn't stop herself from adding, as if it would help matters, "Close friends do."

Alexandra's smile widened. "Then I hope I may someday earn the privilege."

CHAPTER TWO

K it returned to New Bedford that very night and stayed abed all the next day to recover from the dancing. She stayed abed the day after that, as well, in the hopes of recovering from her broken heart. Her maid, Diana, clucked and shook her head, and Mrs. Teague, the cook, tried to tempt Kit's appetite with all her favorites—squash soup, clam chowder, oven-fresh biscuits cracking with steam—but to no avail.

Mrs. Teague and Diana's efforts proved equally insufficient the next morning. And the next. And the morning after that, as well. Try as she might, Kit couldn't think of any reason to drag herself out to face the new dawn. She awoke each day with a faint hope, the lingering fog of dreams shielding her mind from the cold indifference of reality, only to have the hope dashed as she remembered the wedding.

A fortnight after the wedding marked the end of Lucy's honeymoon and her return with her husband to Boston. Kit read as much in the papers. Despite the society columns' reminder of Lucy's matrimony, Lucy's return to New England lit a spark of hope in Kit's chest. While Lucy had not sent so much as a postcard during her honeymoon, Kit could at least expect a thank-you note now. And, though she didn't dare admit it to herself, the spark of hope in her heart expected far more.

Kit began sitting up straighter in bed each morning, her eyes fixed upon her bedroom door, watching the knob for the rattle heralding Diana's entrance with the breakfast tray—and the silver salver that would hold the morning's mail. For two days the salver held only the *Whalemen's Shipping List* and other newspapers. The third day brought a thick cream-colored envelope with Kit's address in Lucy's beautiful script. Kit's weak hands trembled as her whalebone letter-opener sliced through the envelope. A card fell out. Just a card—no accompanying letter or even a note. The flickering hope in Kit's chest guttered like a candle in a hurricane as she opened the card. Lucy's handwriting looked beautiful as ever. The words she'd written were less so. Beginning with *Dear Miss Morgan*, the card bespoke a perfunctory appreciation for Kit's presence at her wedding, as impersonal as if she'd been some second-cousin thrice-removed, never met before or since. And it was signed not *Your Devoted Lucy*, or even just *Lucy*, but *Mrs. John Cabot*.

The card fell from Kit's limp fingers as a stabbing pain struck her breastbone, driving the breath from her chest. She collapsed back onto her pillows. It felt rather as if she were suffering a heart attack. Kit found she didn't care. So what if she died? If Lucy wouldn't notice, then neither would Kit.

A physician arrived within the hour, apparently called by Mrs. Teague in a fit worry for Kit's health. Kit would've told her to save her concern for someone who thought life worth living, but after a week spent fasting abed, she lacked the conviction to do anything more strenuous than submit to the physician's examination and listen to his hemming and hawing over her pulse and temperature.

The physician prescribed laudanum. Kit left the bottle to gather dust on her nightstand. No medicine manufactured by mortal hands could heal a broken heart. But then Mrs. Teague charged up from her post in the kitchen and said she'd be damned afore she'd let Captain Morgan's daughter waste away to nothin'. According to her, Kit had two options: submit to eating Mrs. Teague's cooking, or submit to taking the laudanum. Kit spared a glance at the bottle and turned to Mrs. Teague to request an invalid diet. Mrs. Teague, satisfied, lumbered back downstairs. Diana arrived not an hour after with a tray of broth and biscuits. Both were as good as everything else Mrs. Teague cooked, but Kit could barely bring herself to swallow the broth, and the biscuits turned to ash in her mouth. She shoved most of the biscuits under her pillow, which earned her praise for her "healthy appetite."

The next day, the twenty-first of June—the first day of summer—dawned with sunshine as brilliant as Lucy's golden hair. Kit lolled her head across her pillow to stare out at the bright blue sky. Occasional seagulls flew past, their shrill calls piercing the otherwise quiet morning.

"Miss Morgan?"

Kit turned towards the sound and found Diana standing in her bedroom doorway with an envelope clutched in her hands. As Kit made eye contact, Diana shuffled closer, as though Kit were an invalid whose condition would turn for the worse at the merest disturbance.

Diana, reaching Kit's beside at last, held out the envelope. "A letter from your cousin, miss."

Kit stared unblinking at Diana's offering. It took a great deal of concentration to muster the will to lift her arm and take the envelope from Diana's fingers.

Diana curtsied. "Mrs. Teague will have breakfast up directly."

Kit nodded vaguely. Diana departed. Kit stared down at the envelope's return address.

Phoebe Morgan
Boston University School of Medicine
Boston, Massachusetts

Phoebe would never stand for such sloth as Kit displayed. And Kit hated to disappoint anyone, much less her favorite cousin.

Kit gathered her courage and sat up. The sudden movement, her first in days, dizzied her, but she anchored her hands to her bedspread and waited out the squall. The seafaring blood in her veins demanded nothing less. When the world stopped spinning, she swung her legs over the side of her bed, heaved herself to a standing position, and staggered to her captain's desk to retrieve her whalebone letter-opener. In one swift slice she extracted the letter from its envelope.

. . .

July 1st, 1892

   Dear Kit,

   Boston is beautiful and bloody as ever. Hope you won't be offended to learn how many of my patients remind me of you—pale things that can't remember the last time they've seen the sun. Of course, they're mill girls, so they've got an excuse. You, however, concern me. I know you must be dreadful lonely in that rattletrap old house, and that wedding can't have improved matters. Promise me you'll step outside at least once per diem. Doctor's orders. I didn't scrape my knees raw teaching you how to ride that damned bicycle for nothing. Hope to visit you soon.

   All my love,

   Phoebe Morgan

A smile twitched across Kit's lips. That damned bicycle, indeed.

   An hour later found Kit astride that very same damned bicycle, Mrs. Teague's breakfast fueling her long legs as they pumped up and down to propel her rapidly down County Street. The captains' houses, their splendid architecture a testament to the triumph of Yankee ingenuity in the whaling industry of old, flew past her eyes in a whirl. The wind in her face made Kit feel like the figurehead of a ship, or a harpooner aboard a whaleboat on a Nantucket sleigh ride, dashing across the ocean, wild and free. It drove all concern from her mind. Not even the rank stench of low tide drifting up from the harbor could touch her at this speed. She easily outpaced the few scattered pedestrians, a farmer's cart, and even a hackney cab.

   Kit's eyes widened and she threw a glance over her shoulder back at the cab. She'd glimpsed two passengers seated atop it, a pair of pale-faced, dark-haired, straight-backed persons, a man in a sober black suit and a woman in a gown of deepest indigo.

   Her second glance confirmed it—she'd just blown past the Cranbrook siblings.

   What the dickens they were doing in New Bedford, Kit couldn't begin to imagine. She steered her bicycle in a wide arc across the street to turn herself around and pedal her way uphill to the cab at a more sedate speed.

The cab had come to a halt in the meantime, and both siblings stared down at her as she skidded to a stop beside it. Sir Vivian looked much as he had at the Cabot wedding; there were only so many ways to wear a black suit. Alexandra, meanwhile, had exchanged her maroon gown for one of deep indigo satin, with puffed sleeves, and a bodice embroidered with indigo thread, lending a rich texture to the fine material which outlined her hourglass figure. Its color accentuated the bone-china white of her skin and cast a blue hue into her steel-gray eyes. Her hat, perched delicately upon her head and fixed in place with an ebony-headed pin, had raven's wings nestled in its indigo folds. Their inky feathers held an iridescence, a kaleidoscope of color whirling and sparkling through the shadows with Alexandra's every breath. Kit, meanwhile, found herself breathless.

"Miss Morgan!" said Alexandra, smiling. "I had no idea you were a New Woman!"

Kit felt the burn of her blotchy blush break out all over her face and neck. "I—I suppose I am, yes."

No doubt Alexandra, being of a respectable, titled Old World family, thought the New Woman a blight upon society. Kit wished she'd been caught walking sedately down the street with a parasol, or even riding. Sidesaddle was a far preferable position to sitting astride a bicycle. Now Alexandra would think the worst of her—a giddy, empty-headed American devoid of grace—and the thought of her disdain withered Kit's spirit.

But Alexandra's smile didn't so much as twitch towards malice. "My brother and I were on our way to call upon you, but alas, it seems you are otherwise occupied."

"Hardly," Kit blurted before her better sense could catch up with her tongue.

Alexandra and Sir Vivian blinked down at her.

"I mean—" Kit swallowed; her mouth had gone suddenly and unaccountably dry. "I'm just riding up and down the street. I'm not running errands or—or anything of that sort. You're more than welcome to call."

It was, without a doubt, the worst invitation anyone had ever been served.

But Alexandra beamed, her eyes glittering. "I can't tell you how happy I am to hear it, Miss Morgan. In that case, and with your permission, may we accompany you back to your home?"

Kit nodded dumbly, disbelief stealing away her meagre powers of speech. She waited in still more stupid silence as Sir Vivian paid the driver and handed his sister down from the cab.

"Do you ride often?" Alexandra asked the moment the toe of her boot touched the cobblestones. "I've never had the privilege myself. It seems tremendous fun."

"It is," Kit said, because it was. And then, because her stupid mouth couldn't wait for her brain to catch up to it, she added, "I could teach you."

Rather than strike Kit down for her impudence, Alexandra's eyes widened in an eager expression. "Could you really?"

A dreamlike image entered Kit's mind, of herself and Alexandra upon a tandem bicycle, flying down the lane. She saw Alexandra laughing for sheer joy. She wondered what Alexandra's laugh sounded like. She very much wished to hear it. "I could certainly try."

Alexandra's lips quirked to one side in a wry half-smile. Kit wished she had her camera to hand. Such an image was well worth preserving. "I very much hope you will, and soon."

Kit's blush blazed brighter in her cheeks, and she ducked her head, using the excuse of dismounting her bicycle to avert her eyes from the intensity of Alexandra's gaze.

Sir Vivian offered to take her bicycle from her, phrasing his suggestion with such grace that Kit saw no course of action but to accept. She released the handlebars to the care of his gloved fingers. The moment Kit's arms were free, Alexandra swooped in to take her by the elbow.

Kit's heart skipped a beat. The heat of Alexandra's arm against her own, even through their respective sleeves, seemed to fly through Kit's veins like strong spirits.

"We've been thinking of you ever since the wedding," said Alexandra, folding her arm more securely into Kit's. "I was just saying to my brother how I'd hoped we'd find you well. You seemed—if I may be frank? — rather downtrodden. I'm so happy to see you recovered."

Kit swallowed away her shame as she recalled the pitiful figure she'd been just this morning, wasting away in her bed. "I'm glad to see you, too."

Which was a stupid thing to say, and Kit regretted it the moment it left her lips, but Alexandra merely squeezed her arm and smiled.

They chatted easily all the way up the street to Kit's house, Alexandra doing most of the talking, and Kit managing a nod here and there. Alexandra spoke of the weather, and the town, and the dozen other inconsequential things people were supposed to say when they met by chance in the street. Kit's mind usually wandered during such talk. But she hung onto Alexandra's every word, marking the way her lips formed each syllable in her mellifluous English accent, so much more sophisticated than Kit's own flat American tongue.

"This is mine," Kit stuttered when they came to the bright-blue captain's house she called home.

"Oh, how delightful!" said Alexandra.

Kit, unable to imagine her modest house could compare to England's hundred-odd castles, was struck dumb anew.

"Vivian, look!" Alexandra continued. "Up there! Is that a widow's walk?"

"Yes," Kit confirmed. "I don't think we've ever had a widow walk upon it, though."

"Probably for the best," said Alexandra with a little laugh, like a splash of water in a bright, babbling brook. "Have you ever walked it, Miss Morgan?"

The correct answer was no. And yet, Kit found herself confessing, "I snuck out onto it a few times with my cousin."

Alexandra laughed again. Kit thought she might say anything to hear her laugh more.

Five minutes later found Kit in her parlor, dispensing tea to the Cranbrook siblings.

"We're staying in Fall River at present," Alexandra explained. "We've spent the whole summer traversing New England and we've just had the most wonderful time—haven't we, Vivian?"

Sir Vivian readily agreed. Kit wondered, privately, if they'd done their traversing in Miss Wheeler's company.

"It's all so very charming, as I'm sure you already know," Alexandra continued. "I particularly enjoyed the budding artists' colony at Province-town. Have you been?"

Kit had, in fact, summered on Cape Cod with Lucy once upon a time, and said as much. Evidently Kit didn't do enough to disguise the melancholy emotional miasma those memories inspired, because no sooner had she spoken of it than Alexandra's severe eyebrows softened in sympathy.

"I'm sorry," Alexandra said, her tone gentle. "I didn't mean to introduce an unpleasant subject."

"Oh, no," Kit blurted, "I'm sure nothing from your lips could ever sound unpleasant."

Alexandra's eyes widened. Kit realized what she'd said and fought the impulse to bite off her own tongue.

Sir Vivian laughed—not so beautiful a laugh as his sister's, but a cheerful sound, nevertheless. "I quite agree, Miss Morgan. My sister can be quite charming when it suits her."

"I do try," Alexandra replied, her dry tone belied by her impish smile.

Kit clapped her fingers to her mouth to stifle her own unseemly bark of laughter.

Alexandra's smile became a mischievous grin.

Conversation continued, the hour grew late, and Kit invited the Cranbrooks to stay for dinner, which they accepted with their customary grace. They departed for Fall River very late in the evening indeed, and Alexandra asked Kit's permission to visit her on the morrow. Kit felt ready to give her permission for anything. Still, as she happily, if clumsily, asked them to call upon her as often as they pleased, she couldn't quite silence the worrisome little voice in the back of her head reminding her that the Cranbrook siblings were merely fulfilling their social obligation. They didn't actually want to be her friends. They were only being polite.

Which is why it very much surprised Kit to hear her doorbell ring at noon the following day, and to find the Cranbrook siblings in her parlor.

"Do forgive my impudence," said Alexandra after she'd greeted Kit with a warm embrace. "But you did promise me a lesson in bicycle-riding."

Kit was only too happy to oblige by leading Alexandra out to her bicycle under Sir Vivian's watchful eye.

"Just sit upon it here," Kit blathered, knowing full well her direction made little sense and provided even less help. "And put your hands upon this bar..."

If such useless instruction annoyed Alexandra, she showed nothing like annoyance in her bearing. Indeed, she seemed almost gleeful underneath her English poise. "And my boots upon the pedals?"

"Yes, but the ball of your foot rather than the heel."

"A fascinating mechanism," Sir Vivian murmured under his breath, his head cocked as he regarded the bicycle.

"You may study it later," said Alexandra. "With Miss Morgan's permission, of course. For now, we ride!"

Alexandra lifted her feet to the pedals. The bicycle wobbled. Before she could think to stop herself, Kit flung out her hands to steady her.

Around Alexandra's waist.

"Thank you," said Alexandra.

Kit hardly heard her. Her mind felt frozen. Her awareness had narrowed to the point where her hands made contact with the bodice of Alexandra's dress. Underneath the satin fabric lay the stiff framework of a corset lending a slender curve to Alexandra's figure—and yet, despite all the layers between, it radiated the warmth of Alexandra's blood. The warmth spread from Kit's palms to the tips of her fingers. She never wanted to let go.

But let go she must, because a lady would never hold another lady about the waist as Kit did now.

Kit released her hold. Alexandra remained upright. If she noticed anything unseemly in Kit's contact, she was too polite to say anything. Far more polite than Kit.

"Push down upon the pedals in turn," Kit recited mechanically, falling back upon routine to keep from relapsing into stunned silence. "It should become easier to balance at speed."

Alexandra did so. Her motions began in jerks and starts, but she took to the exercise—much faster than Kit had—and pedaled away in earnest, until her speed quite rivaled a thoroughbred.

As Alexandra flew down the lane, a note of pride took flight in Kit's heart.

The pride turned to horror as she watched the front wheel jerk suddenly to the left. Alexandra collapsed in a heap, her skirts flying up into the air.

"Alex!" Sir Vivian cried, leaping towards her.

Kit was already three strides ahead of him. "Are you all right!?"

Alexandra sat up. She took heaving, gulping breaths. Kit's heart wrenched. Then, as she reached where Alexandra lay and dropped to her knees beside her, she realized Alexandra was not sobbing, but laughing.

Kit glanced over Alexandra. Her skirts had fallen in a pile around her. But her hat remained pinned to her head, her face looked sharp as ever, and her joints seemed to move freely and easily, with nary a wince.

"How stupid of me!" Alexandra gasped through her laughter. "I can't have made it more than twenty feet!"

"You're not stupid," Kit mumbled, aware as ever that she herself was the stupid one, but Alexandra didn't seem to hear her.

"Is the bicycle all right?" Alexandra asked.

Kit spared a glance for the bicycle. It lay on its side some two yards distant, the handlebars turned in on itself, the front wheel still spinning idly. "It's fine. Are you—?"

"You hit a patch of sand!" Sir Vivian announced, which gave Kit quite a scare, not having noticed his arrival.

"Is that it?" Alexandra started to stand up. Kit hurriedly rose to grasp Alexandra's forearms—she swore she could feel Alexandra's pulse thrumming in her veins even through her satin sleeves—and help pull her to her feet. Sir Vivian stepped in as well, much to Kit's chagrin.

"You see," Sir Vivian chattered away as he picked Alexandra up by her left elbow, "it's a question of friction. Unlike stone or packed earth, the sand—"

"I believe I understand my error, dear, thank you," Alexandra replied, brushing dust from her skirts.

"Are you sure you're not hurt at all?" Kit asked. The first time she'd tumbled from a bicycle, when Phoebe had taught her to ride, she'd skinned both palms catching herself. Now, she attempted a surreptitious peek at Alexandra's gloved hands. What she could see of them seemed frayed, though if the wear and tear were a result of the fall or present beforehand, she couldn't say.

"Positive," said Alexandra. And indeed, from the straight-backed way she carried herself, it seemed no force in the world could touch her. She strode boldly towards where the bicycle lay spinning. Without any hesitation whatsoever, she bent down, grabbed the thing, and hoisted it upright as easily as a fisherman hauling in a net. "Miss Morgan, would you be so kind as to help me mount it again?"

"If—" Kit gulped, her mouth unaccountably dry. "If you're certain we shouldn't retire indoors so you might rest?"

"Nonsense. The thing to do when one falls off a horse is to mount it again straight after, and a bicycle is hardly so high as a horse. Though I would appreciate your assistance in holding the dashed thing steady whilst I do so."

"Of course." Kit rushed to take her place by the handlebars.

Alexandra hopped up onto the seat of the bicycle as easily as a raven alighting a branch. Kit released her hold on the handlebars and stepped out of the way.

And off Alexandra flew once more, zipping away down County Street as if she'd never fallen.

CHAPTER THREE

I t took some hours for Alexandra to tire of her new exercise. When at last she admitted with a gasp that she might require refreshment, Kit was only too happy to suggest they retire to her house for lemonade.

"Do forgive my impertinent curiosity," said Alexandra once they'd all settled into the parlor. "But I recall you mentioning your passion for photography, and I confess I have desired to see your work ever since."

Kit broke out blushing again and excused herself with a stammer to fetch her personal photograph album from her bedchamber. Her stomach flip-flopped as she hurried up the staircase, touching each step with only the balls of her feet, bouncing ever upward. Her heart hammered louder and louder in her ears as she stretched to her full considerable height to retrieve the album from the top shelf of her closet. She clutched it to her chest for the return journey and paused just outside her parlor to gather her courage. She didn't often show off her photographs. At length, she drew as deep a breath as her whalebone corset allowed and entered the parlor with as much composure as she could muster.

"What beautiful binding," Alexandra remarked as Kit handed her the album.

Kit bit the inside of her cheek and dropped her gaze to the carpet. Half of her wanted to watch Alexandra's expression to see what she thought of the photographs; the other half wanted to sink into the floor and disappear. She couldn't remember the last time she'd opened her album to anyone other than Phoebe and, of course, Lucy. Her fingers alternated between crushing her skirts in her fists and smoothing out the resulting wrinkles. The creak of turning pages echoed in the otherwise silent parlor.

As a child, Kit had taken some scattered photographs of the scenery around her, but her primary interest lay in capturing human subjects in scenes illustrative of mythology and fairy-tales. To this end, she enlisted her cousin Phoebe as a model, dressing her up as a faerie queen or a princess of more ancient times. Phoebe would sigh and roll her eyes in between snaps of the camera shutter. She didn't see the point in manufacturing illusions. To her surgical mind, a scientific instrument such as the camera ought to be used to secure definitive proof of actual natural phenomena. In response to such comments, Kit just smiled and kept snapping photographs.

Kit's first double-exposure had been an accident. She had taken photographs of her cousin Phoebe, in Hellenic huntress garb, climbing a hemlock tree. The resulting image showed Phoebe triumphantly perched on a stout limb halfway up the trunk, with her own evanescent twin scrambling up after her. The sight had unnerved Kit in the few moments it took her to piece together what had happened, alone in the dim crimson light of her makeshift darkroom, staring at what appeared to be blood-red proof of ghosts. The realization didn't stop her from showing the resulting photograph to cousin Phoebe, whose eyes went wide with horror for but an instant before her scientific skepticism returned.

When Kit came into her majority, she celebrated with the purchase of a Folding Rochester, which could capture six photographs in a single roll of film. She'd filled roll upon roll with images of herself, her cousin, and her only friend.

Kit recalled this last with a chill. She had forgotten, or forced herself to forget, just how prominent a presence Lucy had in the album. At present, with the Cranbrook siblings carefully paging through the collection, Kit's fixation upon her schoolfriend became more than obvious. Surely the Cranbrooks would notice. Surely they would comment, and that comment would crush Kit's spirit, and the budding friendship between herself and Alexandra would die as swiftly as blooms in a frost.

"Oh, how lovely," said Alexandra.

Kit dared a glance at her face and saw wonder lighting up her marble-carved features.

"Is this Queen Titania?" Alexandra asked, turning the album towards Kit to show her the photograph of Lucy, a crown of flowers upon her head, reclining in a woodland bower.

"Yes," Kit replied, privately recalling the days it had taken her and Lucy to assemble the bower, the hours spent weaving green twigs into the proper shape, and the moment when, at last, the sun had cooperated with their plans and assumed its proper position to cast its golden light through Lucy's effervescent locks, and Kit could place the crown of flowers upon her perfect brow.

"And for her sake do I rear up her boy," Alexandra murmured approvingly. *"And for her sake I will not part with him.* I always loved that passage."

The offhanded comment struck Kit dumb, for those very words—describing the faerie queen's everlasting affection towards her mortal handmaiden—had inspired her to take the photograph in the first place. She and Lucy had interpreted the text as describing a friendship as close as their own. Kit wondered if Alexandra felt the same way towards the bard's words. But all she could force out was, "So do I."

"Really?" A mischievous little smile tugged at the corner of Alexandra's lips. "How fortunate."

And she turned the page.

It was there, over lemonade in the parlor, that Alexandra expressed her fond wish to see Kit again on the morrow, should Kit permit it. They needn't confine their amusement to bicycling—perhaps a picnic would suit, if Kit knew of an appropriately scenic locale for such a thing? And if indeed they found a scenic locale, well then of course Alexandra would bring her sketch-book to capture it, and perhaps Kit would be so kind as to bring her camera for the same purpose?

Kit bid the Cranbrook siblings good-night with her head in a whirl of bewildered happiness.

Around ten o'clock the next morning, Alexandra returned to Kit's doorstep with her brother in tow. Kit met them with a picnic basket prepared by Mrs. Teague. Vivian took it off her hands and helped her up into the carriage.

"And where are we headed?" Alexandra asked her, brimming with evident excitement.

Kit hoped her answer wouldn't disappoint. "To the south-west cemetery, if you please."

A grin stole across Alexandra's lips, her eyes sparkling with delight. "Indeed!"

Vivian relayed the direction to the driver, and they set off. The captains' houses of County Street gave way to boarding houses, then copses of trees and meadows, until they came to a wrought-iron fence with an arched gate. Within its bounds, mausoleums and obelisks dotted the field, with more modest gravestones sprinkled in between, like stars amongst moons. No other living souls remained save their party. The cemetery created a sanctuary of quiet seclusion within the hustle and bustle of New Bedford.

Alexandra, descending from the carriage with her brother's assistance, pronounced it "charming," and congratulated Kit on selecting the perfect location for their picnic. Kit blushed and barely mustered the breath to mumble her thanks.

They spread out underneath a gnarled old oak in a corner of the field as-of-yet empty of graves. Kit remained tongue-tied throughout their luncheon, which left it to her guests to carry the conversation. Alexandra rose to the challenge admirably. She complimented the cemetery itself, noted how one might track the changing fashions of mourning through the decorations upon the graves—the winged skulls of the 18th century gave her particular delight—and even managed to coax Kit into answering a few mild questions regarding the history of the area. Puritans gave way to Quakers, Kit herself belonging to the latter group through her whaling ancestors. Talk of whaling became a digression on the captains' houses they'd passed in their journey, and Kit's house in particular, built by her grandfather. At this point, Kit, feeling more and more self-conscious by the minute, took a bold tactic and turned the conversation around to ask Alexandra about her own house in England.

"Heatherhurst Hall," Alexandra artfully answered the artless inquiry. "It's been in our family for centuries. Parts of the house have stood since the days of Viking invasions. There's a door in the cellar with axe-marks in it which I believe is original. It was a monastery first, then a hunting lodge, then a manor, and now the poor old thing doesn't know what it is. Our home, I suppose."

It sounded frankly magical to Kit. She knew of no American house that could boast such history. Before she could stop herself, she said, "Your very own Camelot."

Rather than chide Kit for her stupidity, Alexandra laughed. "Would that make me Guinevere or Morgan Le Fay?"

"To say nothing of the Fisher King," Sir Vivian murmured, his passive expression dropping into melancholy.

Kit had read *Le Morte d'Arthur* more times than she could count, much to Phoebe's chagrin. And though the Fisher King's story hadn't struck any particular chord with her—nothing like Morgan Le Fay or the Lady in the Lake—she remembered the tale of a withered king whose wounds trapped him in his castle and doomed his lands to ruin.

Before she could ask, Alexandra answered. "We've a particularly vexing family of kingfishers who haunt the grounds and serve us no end of whistles and clicks at inopportune moments. One has been captured and stuffed. He watches over our music room."

"Oh!" said Kit. "How marvelous, to have a specimen so close at hand. For study, I mean."

"Indeed!" Alexandra gave a mischievous smile. "I've drawn him several times. A most regal subject. You should come see him for yourself."

Kit gawked at her in disbelief. An invitation. Unmistakably so. Unprompted, and, unless Kit was very much mistaken, sincere. After all, there was no social obligation surrounding cross-Atlantic voyages to examine taxidermy. So Alexandra couldn't have suggested it simply to be polite. Kit couldn't recall the last time someone had sincerely invited her to visit. Not since finishing school, at the very least. And certainly not from someone so regal, so refined, so effortlessly elegant as Alexandra Cranbrook. Kit felt the familiar burn of her blotchy blush creep up her throat towards her face.

"Your pardon." Sir Vivian stood up, looking very much as if he were about to be ill. "I must stretch my legs."

Kit had an inquiry for his health upon her tongue, but before she could force it past her lips, Alexandra spoke.

"Don't go too far," she called after her brother as he strode off, never once looking back.

"Is..." Kit hesitated, her concern for Sir Vivian at odds with her concern for propriety. "Is he quite well?"

Alexandra sighed not unlike Phoebe had when her mother pitched a histrionic fit regarding grass-stained knees and dirt-smudged cheeks. "Oh, never mind him. He's perfectly well. Every once in a while a mood will overtake him and he has to stride out to stare at the moor like one of Mrs. Radcliffe's villains. You needn't worry. He'll come back. He always comes back."

"Oh," said Kit, unfamiliar with brothers and their behavior. She supposed she'd take Alexandra's word for it.

Alexandra's gaze followed her brother as he wandered off, weaving his way through the tombstones on stilt-like legs. She squinted a little into the distance and raised one gloved hand to brush an errant curl away from her pale forehead. Kit, struck by the sudden urge to smooth Alexandra's hair back for her, and place a kiss upon her brow, all but sat on her hands to keep them still. She turned her focus instead to Alexandra's hand, half-hidden by her black lace glove. Over the glove, Alexandra wore a silver ring upon the middle finger. The sapphire set into it, finely cut, sparkled in the sunshine.

"What a beautiful ring," Kit said.

"Hmm?" Alexandra blinked down at her hand as if she'd only just noticed the ring. Kit couldn't help noticing the length and curl of her dark lashes. "Do you like it? It was my mother's. A little too large for me, I fear. But sentiment wins out."

There was a melancholy aura to her pronunciation of sentiment. Kit knew she shouldn't pry, and yet her wretched curiosity compelled her to lean just a hair closer to Alexandra and ask, "Is your mother...?"

"Deceased," Alexandra declared.

She spoke in the tone of one who'd tired of hearing false sympathies from insincere socialites. Kit knew the feeling well. She'd carried it in her heart ever since her own parents' funeral.

"And yours?" said Alexandra, her voice almost a drawl.

"Deceased," Kit echoed, trying to project even half the world-weary indifference Alexandra exuded. She didn't think she'd managed it. Swallowing away her nerves, she babbled on, pointing further into the cemetery. "She's just there, past the Coffin crypt. Her and Father both."

To Kit's bewilderment, all of Alexandra's apparent cynicism melted away, her arched brows bending into an expression of concern. "Oh dear. I'm sorry."

Kit couldn't bear to look into such a sympathetic face. Particularly a face belonging to one as beautiful as Alexandra. She turned away, her gaze following her own hand towards her family mausoleum. Desperate to fill the silence, she added, "It sounds a bit redundant, doesn't it? The Coffin crypt."

Silence from Alexandra. For a moment, Kit feared she'd offended. Then she heard a bark of laughter, like water spilling over a mill wheel to splash merrily on the rocks below. Kit whirled around to find Alexandra with a lace-gloved hand over her mouth.

Before she realized what she was doing, an answering laugh burst from Kit's throat in helpless, inappropriate mirth.

"Are you quite well over there?" Sir Vivian called across the cemetery, some twenty yards distant.

"Perfectly well, thank you!" Alexandra answered him.

Then, to Kit's astonishment, she wound her arm around Kit's shoulder. Kit's heart leapt for joy.

Sir Vivian, apparently satisfied, wandered further off towards the Quaker markers of Colonial days.

Kit wanted to say something clever to prolong Alexandra's amusement, but she could hardly think with Alexandra's arm around her, the warmth of Alexandra's body so close to her own, Alexandra's breath upon her throat, the scent of Alexandra's jasmine perfume wafting up from her wrists and collar—and so, she said nothing.

Alexandra, when she'd caught her breath, withdrew her grasp upon Kit to pluck the sapphire ring from her finger. "Here—would you care to try it?"

Without waiting for an answer, she took Kit's left wrist—Kit's hand going limp with shock at her touch—and slid the ring onto her ring finger.

Kit could only stare at it in disbelief. It fit as if it were made for her. But more precious than the silver and sapphire combined was the way Alexandra's lace-gloved fingers clasped Kit's wrist. Kit wished it might last forever. She held her breath to keep still, lest she break Alexandra's hold.

"*Vena amoris*," Alexandra whispered as if to herself. Before Kit could ask what she meant, she continued at speaking volume. "It suits you. A pity. I shall have to surrender it to the next Lady Cranbrook."

"Who will that be?" asked Kit.

Alexandra shrugged and slipped the ring off Kit's finger. Kit missed its slender weight.

"Whoever Vivian chooses to marry," said Alexandra, fitting the ring back onto her own hand.

Kit recalled how Patience Wheeler had clung to Sir Vivian's arm at Lucy's wedding. Her stomach twisted. It felt wrong to give something so beautiful to someone so petty. But it couldn't be helped. Unless... "Perhaps he won't marry at all."

To Kit's bewilderment, Alexandra's eyes went wide with horror. "What do you mean?"

"I—" Kit stammered, utterly ignorant of what she'd done or said to elicit such a reaction. "I don't know. I just thought, if he didn't marry, you wouldn't have to give it away. That's all."

The storm behind Alexandra's eyes calmed. "I'm afraid Vivian must marry. Someone has to carry on the baronetcy, after all. If he cannot produce an heir then the estate will fall to some second-cousin or other."

"Oh," said Kit. Then, because she hadn't the first idea what else to say, she added, "I'm sorry."

"It can't be helped." Alexandra shrugged again and glanced out over the cemetery's wide expanse. "It's a pity you haven't found occasion to use your camera yet today. You should capture something before the light fades."

"I could capture you."

Alexandra whirled to face her. Kit clapped a hand over her own mouth. She hadn't meant anything by what she'd said, merely echoing Alexandra's phrasing, but the moment it left her lips and touched her ears she realized how horrible it sounded.

But a gleam came into Alexandra's eye. "Could you, indeed? I should like that very much."

Kit hurried to retrieve her photographic equipment from her bag.

"Should I assume a character?" Alexandra asked.

Kit would've felt more than happy to capture Alexandra as herself. The razor edge of her cheekbones; the strength of her crisp jawline, with her chin like the prow of a ship; the sharp point of her aquiline nose; the elegant arch of her full ebony brows; the flinty spark in her eyes; and her heart-shaped lips. If she must assume a character, Kit thought her well-suited to any part she might care to play, though Lady Macbeth came first and foremost bubbling up from her Gothic imagination. Yet Alexandra seemed to have something in mind already, and Kit, eager to know her thoughts, replied as unconcernedly as she could, "If you like."

Alexandra licked her lips—a gesture so small and slight, with just the tip of her tongue flicking out to wet her plump bottom lip, flushed to the deepest shade of cherry. Kit found herself staring, entranced, at her mouth, and an answering blush came over her face and neck.

"Are you at all familiar," Alexandra asked, "with *Carmilla?*"

Kit, her voice stolen away by Alexandra's casual grace, could only shake her head.

Fortunately, Alexandra took her ignorance as encouragement. "If you're fond of the macabre, I cannot recommend it too highly. It's a tale of a young woman beset by a horrifying monster in the guise of a new friend. Have you heard, perhaps, of vampires?"

"There was a vampire in Rhode Island just last spring," said Kit.

As with most things she said, she wished she could snatch the words back from the air the moment they left her lips. Well-behaved ladies did not gossip about the weird and the wretched.

But Alexandra's eyes, instead of narrowing in disgust or reproach, widened, and took on a gleam of glee.

"Really?" she breathed. "Do tell!"

Kit, unused to encouragement, balked. When she recovered herself enough to reply, her words started with a stammer. "The Brown family of Rhode Island—the wife and most of the daughters had all died of the consumption—and then the son, Edwin, fell ill. The neighbors became convinced the family's misfortune was caused by the deceased relatives— that one among them must be a vampire. They persuaded the father to disinter his wife and daughters."

Most women of Kit's acquaintance would've disdained such a story. Alexandra, however, appeared entranced.

"And what did they find?" she whispered.

"The wife and one of the daughters appeared as..." Kit struggled for a more polite word, then gave up and continued, "decomposed as one might expect from how long they'd lain in their graves."

"But the other daughter...?" Alexandra prompted.

"Mercy," Kit supplied. "Miss Mercy Brown had been buried for months, yet still had flush, full cheeks, and seemed peacefully asleep, with her heart full of blood."

The effect of this revelation upon Alexandra proved better than Kit could've possibly hoped. A wicked grin stole over her features. Her pupils dilated, and her sweet breath came shallow and quick with excitement.

"Then," Alexandra concluded, "she was the vampire?"

Kit nodded. "So the village elders presumed."

"And what did they do?" Alexandra demanded in a hushed undertone. "How did they stop her monstrous feast?"

"They carved the bloodied heart from her chest, and burnt in on a pyre."

Alexandra's sculpted black brows took flight.

Kit, secretly pleased at being the author of such horror, continued. "Then they made a tincture from its ashes... and her brother Edwin drank it."

Alexandra's gasp sounded pure and clear as angels' song to Kit's ears. Unable to restrain her delight any further, Kit let her own smile spread wide and split her mouth in a laugh.

Alexandra chuckled after her, her breathless state leaving her with only quiet puffs, no less enthusiastic for their muffled nature. She recovered herself and asked, "Did it work?"

Kit sobered reluctantly. "No; the boy died soon after."

Alexandra, too, appeared wistful, though none the less beautiful for it. "A pity. It would've been better for him if his sister had indeed been an undead fiend." She paused. "I suppose that's odd."

"I don't find it odd at all," Kit blurted.

A smile returned to tug at the corner of Alexandra's lips. "Even so, you must find it gauche of me to suggest assuming the character of a vampire in a cemetery, after hearing such a tale as that, and so near to us now."

"Not in the least," Kit replied.

Alexandra's secret smile bloomed into a grin, as dazzling as the sun. "You are an extraordinary woman, Kit."

Kit's heart fluttered like a butterfly trapped in a jar.

As they rose to seek out appropriate scenery for their art, Alexandra's hand wound its way through Kit's elbow, linking them arm-in-arm. Even through the sleeve of her dress, the touch felt warm against Kit's flesh, soaking through her skin like a crackling hearth-fire after hours spent in frost-bitten cold. She dared a glance at Alexandra. Alexandra, meanwhile, kept her head up and eyes facing forward, intent upon their mutual goal. Her excitement, evident in her bright eyes and winning smile, felt like a thunderstorm brewing in the air between them, equal parts contagious and electric. Kit could almost taste it on her tongue.

They wandered across the cemetery into the long-abandoned corner of Puritan graves. Kit, with no small feeling of loss, allowed Alexandra's hand to slip out of her arm as Alexandra began winding her way between the markers, seeking the perfect stone. They had a number to choose from, and many with the winged skull engraving Alexandra felt such partiality towards.

"Temperance," Alexandra murmured, reading aloud one of the names.

Her voice could hardly be heard, even in the quiet of the cemetery, but Kit hung on to her every word and watched her lips form every syllable.

"Silence," Alexandra went on, apparently oblivious to Kit's close observation. "Lament. Obedience. Humility. Oh!"

Her exclamation drove through Kit's frame like a bolt of lightning.

"Look here, Kit!" Alexandra continued, turning to her at last with an expression of purest delight. "Come and see!"

Kit hurried to obey her summons. She drew up beside her, relishing the excuse to stand hip-to-hip and peer over her shoulder.

"Thankfull Patience," Alexandra read out with a soft sigh of satisfaction. "How wonderful. This is the one, I think. A marvelously ironical name for a vampire."

Kit heartily agreed and wasted no time in setting up her tripod and camera. Alexandra gracefully lowered herself beside the grave and assumed a pose, lying supine with one arm above her head, her knuckles just brushing the wildflowers at the base of the headstone, and the other hand draped across her slender hourglass waist. The sunlight of the early-afternoon fell over her, bathing her beautiful form in a warm glow. To Kit, it appeared the very picture of perfection. She framed the shot and focused the lens.

"Wait a moment," said Alexandra suddenly.

Kit immediately halted.

Alexandra sat up. She unpinned her hat and set it on the ground beside her.

Then, to Kit's astonishment, she unpinned her hair.

Wave after wave of raven-hued curls tumbled down, spilling over her shoulders in tendrils of purest shadow. The sight stopped Kit's heart.

Alexandra tossed her head and resumed her pose, this time gently spreading her ebony locks over the grave.

"That's better," she announced.

Kit forced her desire down and steadied the camera once more. Still, her voice came out with something of a squeak as she asked, "Ready?"

"Indeed," Alexandra replied—and widened her eyes. Just the slightest movement of her luxuriously long lashes, and she transformed her entire aspect from alluring to unearthly. Her steel-gray irises limned with white gave her the appearance of a predator ready to pounce.

Kit opened the shutter, counted, and closed it with as much composure as she could muster.

But the frantic beating of her heart could not be denied.

They spent the next fortnight in a flurry of daily visits; sojourns to the nearby beaches to gather periwinkles and bird-skulls; bicycle-riding through Buttonwood Park; dozens of photographs of Alexandra as a wide variety of villainesses; and ending each day with a promise to meet again upon the morrow. Kit couldn't recall when she'd last felt so happy. Even with the shadow of Sir Vivian looming as chaperon over all their hours, Alexandra stole moments in which to show Kit certain glances, certain expressions, certain gestures that Kit felt she could not possibly misinterpret. A clasp of the hand. A flutter of the lashes. The biting of her blood-red lip. Each of these sent another dart through Kit's breast, until her heart felt ready to burst with unspoken desire.

Then, one morning, Alexandra arrived alone.

When Diana first announced this, Kit's heart soared with the possibility of an entire day with Alexandra all to herself.

But when she met Alexandra in the morning room, she quickly sobered.

Alexandra looked as elegant as ever in a gown of deepest purple. She sat poised on the edge of the settee, the very picture of feminine perfection. But her expression, in the half-second glimpse Kit had of it as she opened the morning room door, just before Alexandra realized her presence—her expression bespoke pure despair. Faint blue shadows bloomed beneath her downcast eyes, their color hidden by full black lashes. She bit her lips, then drew them together in a thin line, their blood-red hue all the more striking when contrasted against the bone-white pallor of her hollow cheeks.

Then she glanced up at Kit, and the wan smile she offered appeared even more heartbreaking than her evident misery.

Kit hurried across the room to sit beside her. Instinct bid her throw her arms around Alexandra's sloping shoulders—and yet she dared not make so forward a move. Knotting her hands together in her lap to dissuade temptation, she asked, "Whatever is the matter?"

She expected the worst—a death in the family—perhaps even the death of Sir Vivian himself.

Alexandra opened her beautiful mouth and spoke. "We are leaving."

To Kit, those three small words carried tremendous dread. "You and Sir Vivian, you mean? But why?"

"My brother has some investment opportunities he wishes to look over in the western portion of the state."

No one had died, then. Though it seemed all Kit's dreams had. With effort, she managed to put together the proper words demanded by society on such an occasion. "Then this is good-bye."

"With your permission," Alexandra said gently, "I would prefer to think of it as a farewell-for-now."

"Until we meet again?" Kit dared to ask.

"Which, God willing, shall be very soon indeed." Alexandra smiled as she spoke—a wistful one, none the less beautiful for its somber tones.

Kit, feeling hot tears welling up in response, hurried to look away. Her gaze fell upon Alexandra's hands, laid upon her lap. Such elegant hands, the fingers long and well-formed, tapering in perfect feminine shape. Nothing like Kit's own broad palms and round-tipped digits.

Even as she pushed down her bitter reflections upon her own inferiority, Kit noted a discrepancy in Alexandra's hands.

The silver-and-sapphire ring was missing from her delicate finger.

Kit stared at its absence. As if shy of scrutiny, Alexandra's hands curled up to fold in upon each other in her lap. The motion told as plain as words that Kit's attentions had been noticed, and a blush came over her cheeks as she raised her eyes in guilt to meet Alexandra's once again.

A resigned smile still hung upon Alexandra's perfect lips. "Circumstances have forced me to surrender my mother's ring to Vivian."

The true meaning of the news dawned upon Kit. "You mean he has chosen a bride?"

"He has." Most of Alexandra's smile had faded now. "It only remains to be seen if Miss Patience Wheeler will have him."

Silence fell in the wake of this revelation, grim and portentous. The prospect of Patience Wheeler becoming mistress of Heatherhurst Hall did not bode well for anyone's happiness, much less Alexandra's. But even Kit couldn't deny the Wheeler fortune would go a long way towards repairing the Cranbrook family dignity.

"I wish him the best of luck and happiness," Kit forced out.

"Thank you," replied Alexandra.

Kit wanted to say more—to express her condolences to Alexandra on the loss of her ring, and the impending loss of her control over her home. A more selfish part of her also wanted to suggest alternative schemes for Alexandra's happiness, schemes centered around Alexandra remaining in America, perhaps in New Bedford, and perhaps even within Kit's own household. Determined to say something to alleviate Alexandra's pain, Kit turned to her, intending to at least invite her to stay.

Alexandra kissed her.

Kit parted her lips—an unconscious motion, borne of pure astonishment—and Alexandra opened hers in turn, taking Kit's lower lip between them. Her tongue slipped into Kit's mouth. A spark ignited behind her navel, its flames spreading low between her thighs in a wildfire of desire. Her heart threw itself against her ribcage in desperation to be closer to Alexandra.

Then Alexandra broke it off, leaving Kit gasping for breath—and something more.

"I do hope," Alexandra whispered, low and husky, "that I might have the pleasure of calling upon you again, when I return to these shores."

Kit wanted to bring all her hopes into reality, wanted to reassure her that she was perennially welcome in her house, wanted to entice her to return, to stay. But with all breath flown from her, and her heart in her throat, the best she could manage was a whispered, "Yes."

CHAPTER FOUR

July 6th, 1892

Dear Phoebe,

Please forgive my negligence in writing to you these past weeks. My social calendar is quite suddenly and unaccountably full. You have heard stories of Lucy's wedding. You may even have heard that English aristocracy were counted amongst the wedding guests. I have had the good fortune of making the acquaintance of such noble individuals as Sir Vivian Cranbrook and his sister Alexandra. Despite their impressive heritage, they have not a hint of pride in their behavior towards me. Indeed, they are far less standoffish than our Bostonian cousins. They came to call upon me in New Bedford after the wedding and since then we have had a marvelous time together. The city looks quite new through their eyes. I have even taught Alexandra to ride a bicycle, much in the fashion you taught me.

Kit paused in her letter-writing, at a loss for words to describe her feelings towards Alexandra. "Friendship" sprang first and foremost to mind, and yet as ever felt inadequate to describe the depths of her devotion.

"Sir Vivian to see you, Miss Morgan."

Kit looked up from her captain's desk to find Diana curtsying in the doorway. Sir Vivian's name immediately drew Kit's interest, but said interest dimmed somewhat when his name was not followed by that of his sister. "Alone?"

"Yes, Miss Morgan."

Kit furrowed her brow. Most unusual. Still, while no doubt the society matrons would gasp at the notion of an unmarried woman entertaining a bachelor *sans chaperon*, Kit didn't see the harm in receiving a friend. "I'll be down shortly. Please take him to the parlor."

Diana curtsied and departed. Kit signed off her letter, blew the ink dry, addressed, sealed, and stamped the envelope, and set it aside before going downstairs.

Sir Vivian's top hat hung on a hook in the front hall. Sir Vivian himself stood in the parlor, staring at the painting over the mantle. It depicted a beached spermaceti whale, eyes rolled back, jaw hanging open, a particular organ slithering out of its abdomen, and several men taking advantage of its plight by butchering its tail. As Kit entered, he turned away from the painting with a startled look.

"Miss Morgan!" he said.

"Sir Vivian," she replied, not asking why he seemed surprised to see her when he'd called upon her at home for the expressed purpose of seeing her. "The day finds you well, I hope?"

"Tolerably so." He tugged at his collar. "I find you bright as ever."

"Oh." A compliment. Kit never knew what to do with those. She encountered them so rarely. "Thank you, Sir Vivian."

He smiled weakly. "I'm afraid this isn't a mere social call. Do forgive my leaving Alexandra behind. I had to speak with you alone. I have... a particular question."

Kit racked her brain for what that question could possibly be, and came up blank. She wished Alexandra were here. "What is it you wished to ask me, Sir Vivian?"

He opened his mouth, paused on the brink of speech, then closed his mouth and dropped to one knee.

Kit stared at him.

"Miss Morgan," he said, holding his hand out towards her, palm up, beseeching. "Would you do me the honor of becoming my wife?"

Kit continued staring. This wasn't happening. She'd fallen asleep at her desk, and the vapors of whale oil from voyages past had altered her consciousness, not unlike the peculiar effects of wormwood, to bring upon the most unaccountable dreams. It was the only explanation.

Sir Vivian looked up at her, his dark eyes wide in a silent plea. A swallow bobbed down his throat.

Kit surreptitiously pinched her own elbow.

Sir Vivian remained.

Forced to consider him a reality rather than a specter, Kit turned her mind to the gravity of his question. Marriage was not a thing to be entered in lightly. And while she liked Sir Vivian well enough, she didn't suppose herself in love with him.

Still, there were benefits to the arrangement. It would silence all the wagging tongues who called her an old maid. It would certainly set Miss Wheeler's head spinning. And who knew—perhaps marriage would cure Kit of her unnatural instincts as it had appeared to cure Lucy. Sir Vivian was by far the least-objectionable gentleman of Kit's acquaintance, and to date the only one to ever propose. She hadn't even realized he'd been her suitor. He seemed to treat his sister with a great deal of respect and brotherly affection. And his sister…

Once again, as Kit looked upon Sir Vivian's face, she saw Alexandra's finer features imposed upon it. She imagined what it might be like to join hands with her, to have such a sister as she.

"Yes," Kit said to the vision of Alexandra's intriguing gaze and perfect lips.

"Yes?" echoed Sir Vivian.

The sound of his voice brought Kit's imagination crashing back down to earth. "I mean—I do." At least, that's what she thought she was supposed to say.

"You do?" Sir Vivian seemed shocked. Kit wondered if the proposal was as much a surprise to him as it was to her. But he quickly recovered, pulling his gaping jaw up into a smile. "Wonderful! Thank you, Miss Morgan! Or, Catherine, if I may?"

As her fiancé, he had every right to call her Catherine. But, "My friends call me Kit."

"Kit." His smile broadened.

She endeavored to mirror it.

~

July 6th, 1892
Dear Phoebe,
You'll scarcely believe what's happened. Not two minutes after closing my last letter to you, Sir Vivian appeared on my doorstep and asked me to marry him. I accepted. I expect we shall be as happy together as two married people can ever be.
Your cousin,
Kit Morgan

~

July 7th, 1892
Dear Kit,
See Mr. Mudge without delay. More to follow.
Your cousin,
Phoebe Morgan

~

Kit had first met Mr. Mudge when her parents were still alive. He was her father's man of business, and on one afternoon when he departed her father's study, she and her nurse happened upon him in the front hall. The sight of the man, thin as a wraith, with hollow cheeks and deep-set eyes, inspired terror in little Kit. No amount of her nurse's wheedling and scolding could coax her forward to meet this shambling skeleton.

But then his thin lips pulled back into a warm smile that softened the severity of his brow, and he swept the hat from his bald, liver-spotted head and bent his knobbly knees down on the foyer carpet.

"It's a pleasure to make your acquaintance, Miss Catherine," he'd said, his voice nothing like the creaking of a coffin-lid Kit had imagined.

Kit summoned all the courage available to her small frame and stepped out from behind nurse's skirts long enough to dip a little curtsy and mumble how-do-you-do.

Then Mr. Mudge held up one skeletal finger, dipped his other hand into a pocket of his overcoat, and produced a red rubber ball. With a snap of his wrist, he bounced it towards Kit.

Kit's little hands clapped together in front of her and caught the ball between her palms.

Mr. Mudge's smile became a grin as he pronounced her a natural, and Kit had glowed with tiny pride.

Phoebe had met Mr. Mudge after Kit's parents' funeral, when he'd delivered Kit to her aunt and uncle's residence. No word from aunt, uncle, or nurse could loose her convulsive grip on the skirt of Mr. Mudge's coat. Only Phoebe, taking Kit's hand in hers, could lead her away.

Mr. Mudge had given Phoebe a solemn look. "You take good care of your cousin, now."

Phoebe, scarcely seven years old to Kit's four, had served him a grim nod in return, and kept her promise ever since.

At present, in Mr. Mudge's New Bedford office, Phoebe's letter seemed portentous in Mr. Mudge's hands. Kit thought any document would acquire an ominous air if clutched in those gnarled fingers. She had brought the letter to him the same afternoon she received it. She had no idea what it meant, or what more might follow. But she knew Phoebe had a better head on her shoulders than anyone, and Phoebe's directions had never yet steered her wrong.

"Do you have any notion what she might mean?" Kit asked Mr. Mudge as he perused the note.

Mr. Mudge's lips had pursed so tight his mouth seemed like the scar of an old bullet wound in the center of his wizened face. "As a matter of fact, I do. I received a similar missive from your cousin just this morning. She tells me you're engaged to be married."

"I am," said Kit, still bewildered as to what any of that had to do with her cousin asking her to see the family lawyer.

"To a Sir Vivian Cranbrook?" asked Mr. Mudge. "From England?"

"Indeed," said Kit. Mr. Mudge seemed to be waiting for more, so she added, "I met them—Sir Vivian and his sister, I mean—at Lucy's wedding this past June. They've been so terribly kind to me ever since. Perhaps you've seen them around town? They visit as often as they can."

"Haven't had the pleasure," Mr. Mudge murmured. "Miss Phoebe tells me they have an estate in England. Heatherhurst Hall."

"Yes," said Kit, not sure what he expected her to add when he apparently already had all the facts of the case. "In Cumberland, I believe."

"So I've heard." Mr. Mudge raised his wispy eyebrows. "It seems you are on the cusp of becoming an English lady."

"He's only a baronet," Kit hastened to add.

"And when is the wedding?"

"As soon as possible, I should think."

Mr. Mudge's eyebrows rose further. "And whereabouts were you thinking of hosting the ceremony? Here or abroad?"

"Here. Probably. I haven't really given it much thought."

Mr. Mudge's eyebrows vaulted to new extremes of height. "My dear Miss Catherine, every girl dreams of her wedding."

So she'd been told. But Kit had never really envisioned herself as a bride. When she thought of her future, there was a husband, but he remained a vague, ethereal figure in the background, secondary to her dear Lucy. But of course Lucy had gone off and married a definitive, grounded Bostonian. Which left Kit's plans in something of a lurch. Perhaps marriage might cure her as it had apparently cured Lucy. "I suppose."

"Does Sir Vivian have any family of his own who would like to attend?"

"His sister, of course."

"No one else?"

"No. He is an orphan like myself, and not terribly close with his cousins. Which suits me fine. Honestly, the only kin I'd care to invite is Phoebe, and she's far too busy with medical school. So we'll have a very small wedding, in America, as soon as possible. And then I guess I'll be off to England." Kit felt that blotchy blush creep up her neck towards her face. "I really don't see what all the fuss is about. Surely it's better for me to be married than an old maid."

"You're hardly in danger of the latter, Miss Catherine."

"It's very kind of you to say so, Mr. Mudge, but we both know I'm not getting any younger, and twenty-three is more than old enough."

Mr. Mudge stared at her. "You always were a frank young lady, Miss Morgan. If you'll forgive my saying so."

"Of course," said Kit.

"Then forgive my being equally frank in saying you seem to be attempting a surreptitious wedding."

Kit struggled to mount a defense of her actions. "Not maliciously so."

"No, you haven't a malicious bone in your body. But I can't help wondering at your motivations. Does Sir Vivian, too, desire to wed surreptitiously?"

Kit realized she hadn't the faintest idea what Sir Vivian wanted. "We haven't discussed it."

"Haven't—?!" Mr. Mudge caught himself with a cough. "Miss Catherine, this is just about the strangest proposal I've ever heard of. An English lordling happens upon you at your friend's wedding, then the next month you're engaged? With no thought of what or when the wedding will be? Does he intend to settle here afterwards?"

"Oh, goodness, no. I'll be moving to England with him and Alexandra. Miss Cranbrook, I mean," Kit added with haste.

Mr. Mudge's sunken eyes bulged. "And what will your aunt and uncle have to say to that?"

"Rather a lot, I'd imagine. It really doesn't matter. I haven't been their legal ward for five years now." And, truth told, Kit had given very little thought to whether or not they approved of her life since she'd left their household. The only familial opinion she cared for was Phoebe's.

"Fair enough," said Mr. Mudge. "In that case, I'll deal plainly with you. Your cousin Miss Phoebe wrote to me to ask me to convince you to break off your engagement to Sir Vivian."

Kit stared blankly at him, her counter-argument caught in her throat. The prospect of Phoebe's disapproval was no small thing. What Kit had done to earn it, she couldn't fathom. "Whatever for?"

"For the reasons I've laid out before you. It is sudden, it is unprecedented, and it is moving far more quickly than either Miss Phoebe or myself have ever seen you move in all your days."

Kit bristled. "Perhaps I was never so motivated before as I am now."

"Perhaps. Miss Phoebe says you haven't felt yourself ever since the Cabot wedding. Which is understandable."

Kit doubted he understood even a tenth of what she had felt. She stood from the seat Mr. Mudge had graciously offered her at her entrance. "Unless you intend to assist me in the legalities of my upcoming nuptials, Mr. Mudge, I believe our business is concluded."

Mr. Mudge remained seated and silent for a long moment. At last he replied, "I am of course at your service should you require my aid. At the very least I'd like to go over Sir Vivian's estate and draft a pre-nuptial agreement. For your own protection, Miss Catherine."

"Thank you," said Kit, and strode out of his office.

The next morning, Kit wrote to Sir Vivian requesting he call upon her once again, as she had matrimonial matters to discuss with him. He answered her call that very afternoon, appearing on her parlor doorstep rather breathless and flushed.

"I've had a meeting with my family lawyer," Kit began after the how-do-you-do's were done. "Mr. Mudge, Esq. He wants to see some papers before the wedding, and have you sign some, as well."

Sir Vivian didn't seem nearly so shocked as Kit thought he had a right to. "What sort of papers?"

"Something that would tell him how the Cranbrook estate stands." Kit winced. It sounded crass, even to her American ears.

But Sir Vivian didn't so much as flinch. "Of course. I'd be happy to send copies to his office, if you'll be so kind as to provide the address."

Kit retrieved pen and paper from a drawer in an end-table. As she did so, she asked, "How quickly do you think you could get such papers from England?"

"No need. I have copies in my hotel room."

Kit paused in handing over Mr. Mudge's address to Sir Vivian. She didn't think most aristocrats traveled with their accounting in their steamer trunks. Still, Sir Vivian wasn't most aristocrats. With that out of the way, they could get down to what Kit considered the real business. "Regarding our wedding…"

Sir Vivian perked up. "Yes?"

"Do you have any strong opinions regarding where and when it takes place, and who attends?"

"I leave the matter entirely up to you, dear Catherine."

"Kit," she corrected him absentmindedly.

Sir Vivian raised his eyebrows. "Of course. Kit."

The sharp syllable didn't roll off his tongue easily. Kit supposed that would come in time. They had more pressing business to hand. "Would you object to a small wedding held quite soon?"

If Sir Vivian felt surprised by the question, he limited his expression of it to a single blink. "Not at all."

"Excellent. I would like to invite my cousin, Phoebe, and have Mr. Mudge as witness."

"As you wish, Kit."

It sounded a little better the second time. Kit continued. "What guests would you like to have present? Besides your sister, of course."

Sir Vivian's face fell. "Alas, I'm afraid my sister is already on her way back to England. Likely she'll not receive word of our engagement until she arrives in London a week from now."

And another ten days for her to return to America once she'd heard of it. Kit didn't want to wait that long. She didn't want to spend a minute longer in Massachusetts than she absolutely had to. Lucy—Mrs. Cabot—was well-established in Boston society and had no intention of leaving. If Kit stayed, her broken heart would never heal. She could either remain a spinster recluse or fly to distant shores. Her sailor bloodline pulled her toward the latter. Without delay.

Besides, once she and her new husband arrived in England, she could spend the rest of her life with Alexandra as her new sister-in-law. Such a promise made the twinge of Alexandra's sudden absence much easier for Kit to bear.

"Just Phoebe and Mr. Mudge, then." It was the most decisive stance Kit had ever taken, equal parts terrifying and exhilarating. A wicked inspiration struck her. "As for the church… would you have any objection to the Seamen's Bethel?"

She could practically hear her aunt's scream of outrage mingling with the horror of all the society matrons who'd attended Lucy's wedding. Kit withheld a spiteful smile. She had whaling blood in her veins, so why not marry in the sailors' church?

"No objection whatsoever," said Sir Vivian. "It sounds most charming."

"Thank you," said Kit. "Is two weeks too soon?"

"A fortnight?" Sir Vivian seemed somewhat taken aback, but swiftly recovered. "Not at all, if it suits you."

"It suits me fine," Kit declared.

July 9th, 1892
Dear Phoebe,
I understand you have grave concerns regarding my choice of husband, despite never having met him or his sister. You are invited to express these concerns in person by visiting my residence at your earliest convenience, or by visiting the Seamen's Bethel on the morning of July 23rd. Any concerns expressed after that date would be best kept to yourself for both our sakes.
Your cousin,
Kit Morgan

The morning of the twenty-third of July arrived with low-hanging clouds and a distant rumble of thunder rolling in off the sea. Kit paced her front hall from seven o'clock onward. She hardly slept the night previous, finding a few hours' respite between one and four in the morning, and finally giving up at five when the horizon showed the first hint of dawn. Her wedding breakfast was negligible. Her stomach tied itself in knots as she awaited the arrival of Mr. Mudge.

For all his disapproval of the marriage, Mr. Mudge had performed his duties to perfection in the matter of the pre-nuptial agreement. Kit supposed Sir Vivian had impressed him by having all the necessary papers upon his person and by readily signing the agreement Mr. Mudge laid out. But what really seemed to win Mr. Mudge over was Kit herself requesting he give her away at the ceremony. It meant nothing to her when she'd asked, a mere formality, but the shock upon Mr. Mudge's face, and the mistiness that came over his eyes as his knife-slash of a mouth twisted into a small, hopeful smile, bespoke how much it meant to him. His voice had turned hoarse as he agreed, and thanked her for the privilege. Which only made Kit's heart wrench all the harder for the poor old bachelor.

Not only would Mr. Mudge have a role to play in the wedding party, but he would also be the wedding's sole witness. Phoebe had yet to return Kit's last letter, nor had she responded to the wedding invitation. Kit had made out the invitation by hand—partly because she enjoyed drawing the furled banners and filling them in with the pertinent details, and partly because she only had one person to invite. If Phoebe appreciated the invitation's pen-and-ink sketches of songbirds swooping with ribbons in their beaks, she didn't see fit to pass that intelligence along to Kit.

Kit continued pacing her front hall, her steps coming down so hard she feared the heels of her shoes would snap. Twice she tripped over the train of her gown. It was a robin's egg blue morning dress, one she'd been gifted by her aunt upon her graduation from finishing school, and one she'd worn several times on the social calls her aunt had dragged her along to. Perhaps the society matrons would have something to say about Kit not wearing bridal white. Kit didn't much care. It was a dress. That sufficed.

At last, the bell rang. Diana hurried to open the door. There stood Mr. Mudge on the front step in his best gray suit, bowler-hat in hand. Kit's pacing halted as she caught sight of him.

Mr. Mudge appeared equally taken aback at her. A lump traveled down his narrow, knobbly throat as he swallowed. In a hoarse voice, he said, "You look mighty pretty, Miss Catherine."

Kit managed a weak smile in return.

The cab ride down to the Bethel proved uneventful. The stench of dead fish and stagnant saltwater rose higher and higher the nearer they drew to the harbor. Mr. Mudge offered Kit his handkerchief to block the smell. She demurred. As they rattled over the cobblestones, her mind flitted far from her present circumstance, flying with the gulls over the bay and on out to sea. The same sea she'd soon cross to arrive at an unknown shore. She wondered if Lucy had felt similarly detached at her own wedding. She wondered what Alexandra would think when she received word of it. She wondered if Phoebe would arrive in time to prevent it.

At last the cab crested Johnnycake Hill and came to a halt outside of the Seamen's Bethel. Mr. Mudge displayed surprising acrobatics considering his age as he leapt down from his seat and reached up to offer his hand to Kit. She accepted it graciously and alighted upon the sidewalk to stare up at the Bethel.

The Seamen's Bethel was a simple chapel built by the New Bedford Port Society in the hopes of saving the souls of the many whalers who passed through the city on their way to slay leviathan. From what Kit had heard of it growing up, most sailors only visited out of superstition, directly before shipping out to sea. Herman Melville, the travelogue writer, had mentioned it in his book *The Whale*. Kit had started to read her father's copy but found it far more dense than *Typee* or *Omoo*, and so set it down in favor of picking up her camera once again. Kit wondered what Sir Vivian thought of it all, how it compared to the churches of his homeland built hundreds of years ago. And yet, even as she wondered, Kit realized she wasn't curious about what Sir Vivian thought, but about what Alexandra would have to say on the matter. Alexandra would no doubt have cunning whispers about monks walled up in wine-cellars and nuns escaping the weary world of men.

The Bethel's double doors were painted green and arched upward to meet in a point. Mr. Mudge pulled the left door open and ushered Kit inside to a small, dark foyer. The scent of seawater permeated the building. Kit supposed brine had dripped from the boots of a hundred thousand whalers on their pilgrimage to the Bethel in the sixty-odd years since its construction. The doors to the sanctuary proper remained shut. The caretaker, a wizened old man who still looked twice as lively as Mr. Mudge, stood in front of them and greeted Kit with a bow she thought more formal than strictly necessary.

"The groom is ready and waiting at the altar, Miss Morgan," the care-taker said in a voice raw from decades of smoked tobacco.

Kit thanked him and took Mr. Mudge by the elbow. She preferred to get the whole thing over and done with sooner rather than later.

But Mr. Mudge stood firm, his cryptic gaze fixed on the caretaker. "Is anyone else in attendance?"

"No, Mr. Mudge, sir. Just the groom and the parson, sir."

Kit felt simultaneously disappointed and relieved. The adventurous streak in her seafaring soul wanted an audience—sailors on the groom's side, society matrons on the bride's. The wild glee of her imagined sailors would inflame the shock and horror of the stiff old biddies. The thought brought an impish smile to Kit's face. Still, her Yankee pragmatism recognized that it would be for the best if her wedding didn't start a riot.

"Excellent." Mr. Mudge turned to Kit. "Are you ready, Miss Catherine?"

Kit wrested control over her nerves long enough to smile down at him. "Yes."

Mr. Mudge motioned for the caretaker to open the door to the inner sanctum.

Kit's eyes followed the center aisle from the threshold up through the empty pews to the pulpit. It was not, as Melville had written, shaped like the bow of a ship, which disappointed her. It did, however, have a man of God standing to the left of it, and Sir Vivian Cranbrook to the right. Sir Vivian's eyes widened at the sight of her. Then his whole expression soft-ened in something like affection, and his thin lips parted in a smile. Kit endeavored to return it and took her first step down the aisle, bringing Mr. Mudge along beside her.

She'd not hired an organist, so there would be no music to accompany her. The rustle of her skirts and the steady tread of their footsteps echoed up to the distant rafters. With every step, Kit expected to hear the Bethel doors burst open behind her. Lucy, come down from Boston after reading of the marriage in one of her husband's papers. Alexandra, suddenly returned from England, here to witness the happy union of her brother and her friend. Phoebe, acknowledging receipt of Kit's last letter in person.

But no one came. And soon enough, she reached the pulpit.

Mr. Mudge delicately extracted his arm from hers and went to take his seat in the front row of the bride's side. The pastor, a droopy-eyed man who seemed weary of his vocation, began the ceremony in a drone. Sir Vivian didn't seem to notice. His sharp face was all smiles for his bride. Kit mirrored his expression in lieu of inventing her own. It felt easier. Her mind still flew far distant from this moment, wondering if this was how Lucy had felt at her own wedding. Wondering how it would feel to have the love of a husband, and hoping it would drown out the agony of sundered friendship. And even as her mind drifted across melancholy waters, her nerves sparked with anxiety, expecting Phoebe to interrupt at any moment.

"Speak now," drawled the preacher, "or forever hold your peace."

Kit held her breath.

No one spoke.

The preacher let the silence hang before continuing, "Do you have the ring?"

Sir Vivian dipped a hand into his jacket and, from some inner pocket, produced the same silver-and-sapphire ring Alexandra had inherited from her mother.

Kit's heart thrilled to see it again. She recalled how it had sparkled on Alexandra's hand that beautiful day in the cemetery. How Alexandra herself had seemed to sparkle with wit and charm.

If Sir Vivian felt similarly, he kept such feelings to himself. Almost mechanically, he took Kit's left hand and slid the ring onto her ring finger. Not so gracefully as his sister had, but the result was much the same: a perfect fit. The silver, already warm against Kit's skin, seemed to thrum with an echo of Alexandra's pulse. Her heartbeat quickened to match it.

The parson, meanwhile, continued reciting the usual vows. They came to the part where Kit and Sir Vivian had to repeat verses in turn—to have and to hold, to love and to cherish, in sickness and in health, so on and so forth. At last, the parson concluded with, "You may now kiss the bride."

The phrase called to mind all the kisses Kit had bestowed and received in her life. Her nurse had kissed her forehead when she'd been a wee babe. She and Phoebe had shared sisterly kisses on the cheek as they'd grown up side-by-side. Then she'd gone off to finishing school and deepened her acquaintance with Lucinda Coffin. She and Lucy had started off throwing arms over shoulders and around waists, then sharing a bed at night in secret and entangling their legs as well as their arms, and all the while there had been kisses—on the hand, the neck, the cheek, and then, in their last few years of school, lingering kisses between their lips, sweet and soft.

And then, of course, there was the kiss Alexandra had bestowed upon her in the cemetery. Kit's pulse fluttered anew as she recalled it. She still didn't know whether Alexandra had meant it as a mere friendly gesture, or something more.

Perhaps Sir Vivian's kiss would be something like his sister's. Kit held that hope in her mind as she watched her new husband close his eyes and bend down towards her. She let her own lids fall shut and her lips part.

There remained a great resemblance between the Cranbrook siblings. The same raven-black hair, the same thick brows, the same sharp cheekbones and hawkish nose.

But Sir Vivian did not have his sister's lips.

Kit withheld a wince as his thin, dry mouth pressed against hers. Any attempt on her part to encourage a deeper connection rolled off his lips like water off an oilskin. Still, he lingered. Seconds ticked past as the so-called kiss continued, uncomfortable, awkward, and, worst of all, boring.

At last Sir Vivian pulled away. Kit watched his face to discover what he thought of it. If his placid smile were any indication, he'd enjoyed it far more than she had. Kit, meanwhile, was still waiting to feel the spark of the love between husband and wife that would supersede any connexion she felt with another woman.

"Congratulations, Sir Vivian," drawled the parson.

"Yes, indeed," Mr. Mudge jumped in, "congratulations are in order. You certainly have mine, Miss Cath—Mrs.—Lady Cranbrook."

Kit, startled, forced a smile.

CHAPTER FIVE

K it's horse surged beneath her, its powerful legs leaping over brooks and fallen logs to carry her through the dense forest. A black mare, as wild as any stallion, foam flying from its mouth in flecks and its wide white eyes rolling wildly in its skull. Kit rode astride, her bare thighs scarcely covered by her Hellenic chiton. In one hand she held the mare's mane. In the other she held a bow. The howling of she-wolves filled her ears. A full moon hung in the sky, casting a faint silver light upon the scene. The wood loomed dark around her, but she had no fear in her heart. She felt only determination. Alexandra was in these woods, somewhere, and Kit would find her. Whether Alexandra would be a fellow hunter or her quarry, she knew not.

"Catherine?"

The sound of her full name forced her to open her eyes. She sat not astride a charging steed but slumped against the interior wall of a carriage bouncing over an uneven road. And beside her, calling her by her full name, sat Sir Vivian. Her husband. She still hadn't grown used to the notion. Not even after ten days together crossing the Atlantic aboard a steamship, or an entire day sharing a train car from Liverpool to Cumberland, where Sir Vivian had hired a carriage and Kit resolved to spend the ride sleeping off her travel headache.

Sir Vivian smiled and reached across the seat to take her hand. "We're nearly home."

Kit sat up and peered out the carriage window. A wild windswept plain of dead gray grass rolled on under a sky filled with low-hanging clouds. This, then, was a moor. It seemed barren. For an instant, her sleep-addled mind supposed the house must be under one of the rolling hills, like a fairy's brugh. She shook her head to clear it, and then she spotted a hulking shadow on the horizon.

Heatherhurst Hall.

It loomed enormous and proud, quite alone on the barren moor. Its central mass, some three stories tall by Kit's reckoning, appeared crafted of stone, with a brick wing to the east and a wooden one to the west. Kit recalled the hodge-podge tale of its construction Alexandra had relayed to her that wonderful day in the cemetery. Yet as she continued regarding the edifice, she couldn't help but notice how the western wing seemed to collapse in on itself to the south, and how, beyond it, there appeared the ragged remnants of another structure, also of wood, like a barn or carriage-house, its skeletal framework scorched black and splintered.

"You slept through the village," said Sir Vivian, startling Kit out of her self-reflection. "Though I daresay you'll have plenty of time to visit it later."

"Of course," Kit replied automatically. The enormity of the house—her house—had driven all thought of the village from her head.

The carriage rattled closer and closer to Heatherhurst. Kit's gaze fell away from the looming manor and turned to the scenery the carriage passed. The gray grass of the moor was long dead and dried. Occasionally a rock broke up the foliage.

Kit jerked upright and turned her head to regard the road behind them as best she could from the window. There had been a particular rock amongst the grass—but upon reflection, it wasn't a rock at all. It was a jagged piece of metal, its edge torn and pitted with rust, about the size of the carriage door.

"Did you see that?" Kit asked her husband. "Some kind of broken machinery…"

Sir Vivian had a pale face by nature, but Kit would've sworn he turned a whiter shade of pale. "Probably a plough. This area used to be farmland."

Kit had never seen a plough so large or serrated. Of course, she'd never seen a plough at all. Her family made their money sailing, not farming. So she sat back in her carriage seat and turned her attention forward to her new home.

Every lurch of the carriage brought more of Heatherhurst Hall into view. The remains of a wrought-iron gate sat between crumbling stone pillars. It hung open, a state which might've looked welcoming had it been in better repair. As matters stood, the rusted points of the gate seemed more like a bear trap ready to spring shut. The left side, loose in its hinges, creaked back and forth in the wind.

Kit wasn't afraid. As wretched as the gate appeared, she knew what lay beyond.

Alexandra.

Kit's heart thrilled at the thought of her. She'd stood at the bow of the steamship for much of its crossing, taking in the sea air that had soothed her ancestors' souls for countless generations, and letting her mind fly forward to England, where she might meet Alexandra again. She'd pictured it a hundred times; riding up to Heatherhurst Hall with Sir Vivian, Sir Vivian opening the door for her, and Alexandra standing on the threshold. Alexandra's thick dark brows would rise to her widow's peak, and she would bite her lips to suppress a grin, until she could no longer stand it, and then she would throw her arms around Kit's shoulders and kiss her again, as she had in the cemetery. Kit could hardly wait.

Following the road through the gate and up to the house brought them to a carriage circle surrounding a fountain. Once upon a time, Kit supposed, it had been a magnificent triumph. Now, its pool had dried, and a green-gray crust covered the dolphins that used to spout water into the air. The lilies around it had withered and died. The carriage halted between the fountain and the house.

Kit's heart beat in her throat. Mere seconds away from reuniting with Alexandra, and she hadn't the first idea what to say to her. "Good morning" seemed woefully insufficient. She needed something clever, something equal to all the excitement she felt in this moment.

Sir Vivian stepped out of the carriage and reached back to hand Kit down from it. Her booted heel crunched against gravel the color of bleached bone. She looked up at the house. It appeared, if possible, even more imposing than it had at a distance. Windows, doors, gables, every possible point peaked into a Gothic arch, and barbed quatrefoils decorated the top of every one. Even the gutters were ornamented in downward-pointing finials reminiscent of icicles, or perhaps teeth. The wickedly sharp fangs of a vampire ready to devour her.

Still, it couldn't be so bad. It contained Alexandra, after all.

"Home sweet home," said Sir Vivian, his tone blasé.

Kit, whose mouth felt as dry as the stones beneath her boots, could do little more than nod.

Sir Vivian smiled and skipped up the front steps to the double doors— oak, stained so dark they appeared black, and tall enough for Sir Vivian to carry Kit in on his shoulders if he had a mind to. He settled for rapping his knuckles against the ancient wood. The hollow knock resounded through the halls beyond and returned to Kit's ears with a sepulchral echo.

Kit gathered her courage and strode up the steps two at a time to stand beside her husband. There, she began wringing her hands and chewing the fingertip of her glove. Underneath it she wore the silver sapphire ring. She wondered if she ought to remove her gloves to show Alexandra that she wore it proudly. She wanted to tell Alexandra how it reminded her of their connection, how she felt closer to Alexandra than she did to her own husband, and hoped Alexandra felt the same.

A crow's caw echoed across the moor. Kit glanced toward the sound. She saw no sign of any bird. Only the skeleton of the stable and the lumps of twisted metal overgrown with gray grass.

The doors creaked like the opening of a coffin lid. Kit whipped her head back to the house.

There, in the doorway, stood Alexandra.

Kit's breath caught in her throat at the sight of her. The sharp cheek-bones, the aquiline nose, the widow's peak of her raven curls, all were just as Kit remembered. The deep burgundy of her morning dress drew atten-tion to the faint blush in her high cheekbones. A ring of heavy keys hung from her waist. Her steel-gray eyes flew wide, and her heart-shaped lips hung slightly parted in shock.

"Good morning, sister," Sir Vivian chirped.

Kit waited for Alexandra's surprise to give way to elation. Surely Alexandra felt the same joy. Surely the heart that beat beneath her breasts thrummed in time with Kit's.

But no trace of happiness touched Alexandra's features. As her eyes flicked from Sir Vivian to Kit and back again, her expression remained aghast.

Sir Vivian cleared his throat and gestured towards Kit. "May I introduce Lady Cranbrook?"

Kit watched with growing horror as Alexandra's beautiful face twisted into a snarl.

CHAPTER SIX

K it's heart dropped into her stomach. She didn't know what had happened, what she'd done wrong. All she understood was that something had occurred to provoke Alexandra's wrath.

Yet, even consumed by smoldering rage, Alexandra remained beautiful. The flinty fire in her eyes set Kit's heart aflame. The downward swoop of her thick black brows emphasized their magnificent arch, and even her sneer drew attention to her sharp cheekbones and pointed chin. In joy, she looked resplendent. Fury made her appearance truly striking.

And in this moment, all her fury had focused upon Kit.

Sir Vivian let out a quiet cough. "Alex?"

Kit watched a hard swallow travel down Alexandra's pale throat.

"Vivian," Alexandra forced through clenched teeth, her gaze still fixed upon Kit. "Would you be so kind as to speak with me in the drawing room? Privately?"

Sir Vivian balked and turned to Kit. Herself bewildered, she had no answer for him. She barely registered his presence. Alexandra's wrath rose from her like smoke to fill the foyer. She seemed a dragon in her lair, and Kit a woefully-unprepared squire hoping to fill the role of knight.

"Er," Sir Vivian stuttered. "Of course. Your pardon, Catherine."

Kit nodded mutely and watched her new husband follow his seething sister across the foyer to a closed door. The siblings slipped inside. The door shut firm behind them with an echoing thud.

And Kit was alone.

The wind howled across the moor outside and whistled through the house. The very foundations seemed to groan in reply, reverberating against the ribbed vault ceiling some three stories above. This, Kit thought, must have been the nave of the monastery. Where once the soothing chants of the faithful had resounded, now there was only wind. And, in the wind's absence, silence.

Kit stepped further into the foyer. The click of her booted heel against the warped wood cracked like a whip. To her left, a grand staircase of dark walnut swept up from the foyer into the second-story balcony. Its banister looked akin to the back of a church pew, with Gothic arches forming in the negative space between the balusters. She crept towards it, each footstep echoing like a hammer despite her best efforts at taking the small, light, ladylike steps she'd been taught at finishing school.

Putting a hand on the polished railing, she recalled how, as girls, she and Phoebe had taken turns sliding down the banister. Then it had felt like a thrilling dive. But the front hallway of Aunt Drusilla's house in New Bedford seemed closet-sized compared to the enormity of Heatherhurst Hall. Kit wondered if Alexandra had ever slid down this banister. She could imagine her younger, with bouncing black curls, whooping with glee as she swooped down like a falcon on the hunt, leaping off the end to land in a boyish Sir Vivian's arms. Sir Vivian would have to stand just there to catch her...

As Kit glanced towards the floorboards at the base of the stair, she noted a carpet. A small braided thing, hardly three foot by six, obviously handmade. And the only spot of carpeting in the whole foyer. She frowned down at it and gave it a nudge with her toe.

Under the carpet, the wooden floor looked much darker. But the darker portion didn't retain the carpet's shape, as it might've if the difference in coloration were due to sun-damage. Instead, it had the blotchy pattern of spilled wine.

Or something else.

Kit's stomach knotted. She quickly kicked the carpet back into place.

The toe of her boot struck the stair, rending the silence with an echoing crack. She winced from the sound and listened hard as it faded.

As the noise of her clumsiness evanesced, the sound of two discordant voices rose.

Kit turned to the door through which the Cranbrook siblings had disappeared. It appeared not quite so tall as the front doors and lacked their Gothic arch. Evidently a newer architectural addition, post-monastery. More importantly, it hung open a crack. The words of Sir Vivian and Alexandra drifted out into the foyer. Alexandra's voice, though easily recognizable to Kit's ears, was yet too distant for her to make out more than a scrap of phrasing.

"—absolutely ridiculous—"

Kit glanced around the enormous foyer. It remained empty. No prying eyes would see her as she scurried from the staircase to the parlor door and crouched beside the crack to engage in the sin of eavesdropping.

"What," Alexandra hissed, "the Devil happened to Patience Wheeler?"

"I thought you hated her," protested Sir Vivian.

"Of course I did, but—" Alexandra's bosom heaved as she turned away to collect herself, only to round on her brother again an instant later. "I know how to deal with her sort. We had a plan, Vivian!"

"'The best-laid plans of mice and men—'"

"—are torn asunder by idiots with more breeding than sense, apparently! What happened? Did Miss Wheeler refuse you? I cannot imagine why. Lord knows she could never hope to find better. Not with her sickening, simpering—"

"She didn't refuse me," said Sir Vivian. "She didn't have the chance. I never asked her."

"Never asked—!?" Alexandra's eyes flew wide, her lips peeling back into a snarl that reminded Kit of the Furies of old.

"I found I preferred Miss Morgan's company," said Sir Vivian, then corrected himself, "Catherine, I mean."

"Her friends call her *Kit*," Alexandra snapped.

Kit winced at the sound of her own words upon another's lips in anger. It reminded her too much of finishing school, and how Patience Wheeler would repeat anything Kit said in a simpering sing-song tone that never failed to set the other girls laughing at her for no reason Kit could understand.

"Kit, then," said Sir Vivian. The single syllable sounded clumsy and discordant in his deep baritone. "There's hardly a penny difference between their fortunes. And she already liked us, anyhow. Besides, I had to return to Heatherhurst without delay. You know that. This seemed the fastest method. I had no choice."

"You had every choice! Are there not dozens of empty-headed heiresses in Newport alone? Hundreds across America! Thousands of low-born wretches holding out for a title, no matter how penniless its bearer! But no. You had to have *her*." Tears of rage welled in Alexandra's eyes. They flew off, sparkling, as she shook her head to be rid of them. "Any girl in the world, and you had to choose—"

She clamped a hand over her mouth and turned away from her brother.

"Alex," he said gently.

She shook her head again and stepped away from him. Her ragged gasps echoed in the otherwise silent room. Kit's heart pounded against her ribs as she held her own breath.

Sir Vivian watched his sister for a long moment, then drew in a deep breath. "Regardless, she is here now. Would you have me divorce her?"

"No." Alexandra's palm muffled her reply, and at last she dropped her hand before continuing. "No, divorce won't do. Mr. Mudge did his damned work well. If you divorce her, she keeps all her fortune, and we are left with nothing."

Kit's heart dropped. Alexandra had never liked her. Had never considered her a true friend. She'd only ever wanted her money, and had used their friendship and her wretched brother to get it.

And now here was Kit, trapped in a foreign country and bound in holy matrimony to a baronet utterly ruled by his villainous sister, who hated her.

"What should I do?" asked Sir Vivian.

Alexandra straightened, her cold gaze piercing his. "Nothing. Continue as we'd planned. She is Lady Cranbrook now."

"And what will you do?"

Alexandra's gaze drifted to the window and the howling moor beyond it.

Kit, feeling as if a cruel frost had encased her heart, sank to the floor in a hopeless heap.

~

How dare he.

Alexandra's gaze swept over the wild moor surrounding the miserable heap of crumbling stone they called their home. The wind howling across the barren expanse sounded more like a mewl when pitted against the screaming rage in Alexandra's heart.

How very dare he.

When she'd first opened the door to find Kit Morgan upon the threshold, Alexandra's heart had flown in wild hope. Here was her dashing lady knight, come to rescue her from rack and ruin. But rationality quickly dashed those hopes. Kit had not come to her rescue.

She had come as Vivian's bride.

Yet even so, for an instant, Alexandra's imagination veered off into a magnificent flight of fancy in which she turned her back on her brother and fled the room, snatching up Kit's hand in hers as she passed and running full-tilt out of the damned house forevermore. Where they would go, she knew not, but it would be better than this.

As ever, this wild dream broke like a wave upon the rocky shore and dissipated into so much foam. Kit could not take Alexandra's hand, for she'd already given her hand to Vivian in marriage. She had chosen Vivian over Alexandra. She had toyed with Alexandra's affections just to win herself the prestige of becoming Lady Cranbrook. Just like Lizzie before her.

But at least Vivian hadn't encouraged Lizzie's pursuit of him. Now, however, he had sought out the woman Alexandra loved and claimed her for his own.

It wasn't enough for him to waste the family fortune on his stupid machines. Destroying all he loved in the grinding of gears and firing of pistons. Even now, she could hear the echoes of the deafening explosion that had torn their lives apart and doomed them to ruin.

Apparently not sated by this, he had taken Kit as well. Kit Morgan, the New Woman, the refreshingly frank American, the one good thing Alexandra had known since the death of her parents. Who had, like them, chosen her brother over her.

She would never forgive him. But nor could she leave him.

Even if it broke her heart.

"Kit?"

Her name still sounded bizarre in Sir Vivian's clipped baritone. Regardless, Kit hurriedly scrubbed her eyes dry and struggled to her feet. No sooner had she started than she felt his enormous spidery hands on her elbows, pulling her up.

"What on Earth are you doing on the floor?" he asked. "Are you quite well?"

"Fine," Kit hurried to answer him, as she knew she should. Good little American girls were self-reliant and required very little maintenance.

Her husband squinted into her face. If he perceived her lies, he said nothing of them. "I must tend to what I've let go in my absence, but Alexandra will be happy to show you around the house."

Alexandra. The sound of her name sliced through Kit's heart. "No. I mean, I'm just tired. Perhaps there's somewhere I could retire…?"

"Oh! Of course!" If Kit didn't know any better, she'd say her new husband seemed delighted by her exhaustion. "Alexandra will show you to your bedroom. The master bedroom. Our bedroom."

It seemed Sir Vivian struggled almost as much as Kit to recall their new station in life. A weak smile came to her lips. "All right."

"Splendid." Sir Vivian pressed a dry kiss to her forehead and strode off.

Kit, utterly bewildered, watched him cross the hall and take the steps two at a time without ever once looking back at his bride. Then he vanished upstairs. Kit's eyes remained fixed on the upper landing long after his disappearance, until she heard the click of footsteps behind her, and turned to behold Alexandra emerging from the drawing room.

Despite what Kit had overheard, and despite the cold anger still evident on Alexandra's sharp features, there remained a handsome cast to the severity of her thick, dark brows, and even the faint scowl she wore couldn't mar the beauty of her crimson lips. Kit could only stare.

"Do my ears deceive me," said Alexandra, "or did Vivian find you on the floor?"

The blotchy blush flared to life all over Kit's throat and face. "I was tired."

"Apparently." Alexandra wasn't even looking at her, but glancing all about the hall, as if searching for something. "He's run off, hasn't he."

It was barely a question. Kit didn't see the need to answer it.

"Come along, then," said Alexandra when it became apparent Kit had no response. "The master suite is upstairs."

Alexandra turned and began walking away. After a moment's bewilderment, Kit followed.

Their footsteps echoed like gunshots in the empty hall. The house seemed far too quiet. It took a staff of thirty-six servants to keep Marble House in order, and the Newport mansion was hardly a third the size of Heatherhurst Hall. Kit furrowed her brow as she tried to account for it. "The staff...?"

"We have none, save the cook." Alexandra gave Kit a sideways glance. "Surely Vivian told you...?"

"No, he did not." Kit barely had the presence of mind to reply, her thoughts whirling to explain how Sir Vivian could omit such a curious fact in his description of their home. Perhaps he was ashamed. Perhaps that's why they needed Kit's money so badly.

"Typical," Alexandra muttered under her breath. Aloud, she sighed. "You've brought your maid, of course."

"No." Diana hadn't wished to leave her family, and Kit respected that, though it pained her to lose such good help.

"No?" Alexandra echoed. Again, Kit heard overtones of wicked delight. "Then you are quite alone."

Kit swallowed hard and stared down at her skirts. Reminding her of her abandonment seemed particularly cruel, even by finishing school standards.

"Never mind that," Alexandra continued. "This way, if you please."

Kit followed her upstairs to the landing, then to the left, down a narrow hallway whose floorboards warped and buckled to create a path as uneven as broken cobblestones, and creaked under the ladies' tread. They passed several closed doors sinking into their frames, with knobs and locks tarnished black. There were sconces in the walls sprinkled with wax drippings, but otherwise empty. It seemed the Cranbrooks had foregone candles as well as staff. Kit, accustomed to life in the city that lit the world, hoped she might find it within herself to banish the darkness here.

At length, the dark hallway ended in an equally dark door. Like every other door in the hall, it had sunken into its frame, and its silver knob and lock were tarnished. Alexandra removed a ring of keys from a pocket of her gown, selected a silver skeleton key, and wriggled it into the lock. After a moment's struggle, the door creaked open.

"The master bedroom," Alexandra announced.

Kit beheld a four-post bed with deep crimson curtains, matching curtains in the windows on the north and east walls, a hearth empty of wood or coal, and a bare wooden floor. The coffered ceiling put her in mind of a ship's hold. Every wooden piece in the room was stained as dark as the door. Even the wallpaper, once a velvet red, had faded to the color of dried blood. "Sir Vivian sleeps here?"

"He will now." Alexandra stepped aside to allow Kit entrance to the room. "He's master of the house. And you are its lady."

Alexandra didn't sound too pleased about that. Kit winced. Part of her wanted to offer the ladyship to Alexandra. She certainly seemed better-suited to the role. Her ring seemed to hold all the keys to the castle, as it were.

"Do you have keys to every room?" Kit asked.

Alexandra, in the midst of opening the curtains to let the gloom in, paused. "All the ones with locks."

"May I have the key to this room?"

Alexandra dropped her grasp upon the curtains and bodily turned to stare at Kit.

The blotchy blush returned full force to Kit's face. "Or a copy, I mean. So I'm not locked out." *Or locked in.*

Alexandra continued to regard her with the icy gaze of a queen. She wore an expression of flat refusal. But her lips parted to deliver the clipped reply, "Of course."

"Thank you." Kit wished she could leave the matter there, but swallowed her fear and continued. "If we have no staff, how shall I bring my luggage up?"

"Someone drove the carriage, didn't they?" Alexandra said—almost snapped. "If he knows what side his bread is buttered on, he'll stay on long enough to bring your luggage into the house." She paused, her eyes narrowing in suspicion. "What did you bring?"

"Not much." Kit had in fact packed quite light relative to her station. A steamer trunk of clothes, and an old sailor's chest for her books and photography equipment. She'd sold all her New Bedford furniture, save for the captain's desk that had belonged to her father and his father before him. And... "My bicycle."

When Kit had envisioned her arrival to Heatherhurst Hall, she'd planned to divulge the bicycle's delivery in an excited whisper. She imagined Alexandra would grin at the surprise. They would take the bicycle out together, and Kit would resume Alexandra's lessons, until she could ride circles around the fountain in the carriage-yard, her black curls flying out behind her.

In the present reality, Alexandra scowled. "You'll hardly have use for it here."

Kit dropped her gaze. She could barely muster the breath to murmur, "No, I suppose I won't."

CHAPTER SEVEN

August 3rd, 1892

Dear Phoebe,

I have not yet become accustomed to writing the date in the Continental fashion. I haven't had much need to, as you are my only correspondent. Anyone else I might befriend either dwells in this house with me or lives too far distant for us to ever meet. It is not at all like County Street. Heatherhurst Hall is very isolated on the moor. The nearest villager's house is at least two miles off. And the house itself is not so full as one might assume. My husband and my sister-in-law are my only company, and we have but one servant, the cook. Please do not think I am complaining. I merely state the facts of my life as it now stands. Even so, it would do my heart good to hear from my dear cousin again. Please write to me at your earliest convenience. How is medical school? Have you completed your exams? Do you ever find the time to see the sun? I love you dearly and miss you terribly.

Your cousin,

Kit Morgan

Kit finished her signature and lifted the letter to her lips to blow the ink dry. It was a short missive. She hoped it would suffice. She supposed Phoebe would be too busy to read a long one.

As she folded up the letter and sealed it into the envelope she'd previously addressed, it occurred to her she didn't know how to get the letter from Heatherhurst Hall to Boston. Were she still living on County Street, she would have handed it off to Diana to deliver to the Post Office. But she no longer employed Diana. And if there were a Post Office near Heatherhurst Hall, she hadn't seen it.

She stood from her captain's desk—the carriage driver had brought it up to her bedchamber, just as Alexandra had said—and left the room, letter in hand, to seek an answer to her predicament. No doubt Alexandra or Vivian would know how to post a letter here.

Of course, finding them would be easier said than done.

Heatherhurst Hall was massive. Its crooked corridors wound in all directions. Each empty room Kit stumbled across appeared abandoned for years. She began by trying every doorknob in the narrow hallway leading from the master bedroom to the foyer. Two of them opened, revealing rooms with only dust covering the bare hardwood floors. The remainder were locked.

When she came at last to the foyer, she found it empty as well. Her footsteps echoed up to the ribbed vault ceiling.

"Vivian?" she ventured. "Alexandra?"

Her voice wavered with uncertainty and became still more distorted as it reverberated throughout the foyer. She shuddered at the sound and walked on to the east wing.

The first unlocked door she found opened into a dark chamber. Bookshelves in deep mahogany lined the walls, and a matching mahogany desk with forest-green leather blotter sat before the bay windows. The curtains and carpet reiterated the shades of green present in the blotter. This, she supposed, must be Sir Vivian's study.

"Vivian?" she called again, though the room was apparently empty.

Receiving no answer, Kit stepped over the threshold. Curiosity compelled her to peruse the shelves. She expected to find records of the estate's accounts—which she did—and perhaps some literature. But as she skimmed over the spines, she discovered titles like *Chloroform, the Best of Anaesthetics* and *Experiments and Observations on the Gastric Juice and the Physiology of Digestion*. They sounded similar to books Phoebe had collected in

73

her preparation for medical school. Intrigued, Kit pulled the latter off the shelf. The book fell open in her hands.

"The charge, consisting of powder and duck-shot, was received in the left side of the youth, he being at a distance of not more than one yard from the muzzle of the gun. The contents entered posteriorly, and in an oblique direction, forward and inward, literally blowing off integuments and muscles of the size of a man's hand, fracturing and carrying away the anterior half of the sixth rib, fracturing the fifth, lacerating the lower portion of the left lobe of the lungs, the diaphragm, and perforating the stomach."

This, then, was the journal of a surgeon, detailing his apparently successful efforts to save a man brutally maimed by a shotgun blast, and his ongoing research into digestion enabled by the man's wounds. Kit set it aside, making a mental note to ask her husband's permission to borrow it for further reading, and selected another book from the shelves. Like *Physiology of Digestion*, it was a surgeon's journal. Unlike *Physiology of Digestion*, it was handwritten.

13 October, 1889
The patient is a Welshman of some seven-and-twenty years, a steam engineer by trade. He is the victim of a boiler explosion. The accident has severed his left arm at the elbow and caused severe steam burns across the left side of his body. The burn extends from the scalp at the temple down to the left knee. The left ear is entirely melted. Three ribs are fractured; two are broken; one of these pierced the left lung and caused a collapse.

Having reached the end of the page, Kit intended to turn it and continue reading. But as she lifted her hand to do so, she noted a dark stain along the bottom of the page. It seemed to have soaked through the entire text. As she turned the page, the near-black stain cracked and flaked to reveal a more crimson hue.

Kit stared down in horror at what could only be dried blood. She snapped the book shut and shoved it back into place on the shelf.

Her hands shook. She clenched them into fists and scolded herself. Phoebe witnessed far worse gore every day at medical school. If her cousin could carve cadavers as if they were cake, then Kit had no business acting squeamish about a little bloodstain. Particularly when it appeared on the journal of a surgeon. Surely that would be the profession with the most legitimate excuse for spattering a diary with gore. Kit put it from her mind and strode out of the room to continue her search.

Hallway by hallway, corridor by corridor, Kit encountered one locked door after another. Each impotent rattle of a knob only made her more determined to find her sister-in-law and demand a copy of the house-keys. Despite her frustration, her mind kept returning to the handwritten journal and the wounded Welshman described within. The incident had occurred but three years ago. Kit wondered how the journal had come into the Cranbrooks' possession and if they were acquainted with the patient. More likely they knew the surgeon, given the social circle they'd been born into.

Then, at the end of a winding hallway, the house took a curious turn. The floor went up three half-steps, none quite level with the floor, and none at an angle equal to any of the others. After these steps, the hall turned sharply to the right. Kit could see nothing of the room beyond, but she caught sight of the edge of an open door swinging gently in a draught.

Cautious, yet curious, Kit approached. She turned the corner to find a kingfisher perched atop a closed piano lid.

"Oh!" she cried, clutching a hand to her chest in surprise.

The bird didn't react to her exclamation. Not a single one of its feathers ruffled. Nor did its glittering ebony eyes blink. Kit realized the creature was dead and had been stuffed and posed to look as if it were gazing quizzically upon the piano's keys, waiting for a song to begin.

Kit's breaths slowed. Her footsteps echoed up into the rafters as she entered the room. The music room, if the piano were any hint to its purpose. It certainly had the acoustics for it. And the utter emptiness helped. Judging by the dust on the handle of the fireplace poker, no one had used the room in years.

"You must be lonely," Kit murmured to the bird.

She didn't expect an answer, of course, but the stuffed kingfisher was the liveliest creature she'd seen in hours. Its presence emboldened her. She sat down at the piano bench and gazed about the room. The bare floors held scuff marks where other pieces of furniture had once sat. The lily-patterned paper on the walls had sections of vibrant green, which Kit supposed was its original hue, though time and sunlight had faded most of it to a sickly yellow. Some portions had even begun to peel. The tall Gothic windows which had allowed this damage to occur were blocked by velvet curtains. A thick coating of dust obscured their color, though Kit thought it might be blue. The hearth, as she'd already noted, remained empty and cold, like the starved belly of a forgotten beast. And above the hearth hung something hidden by the same sort of curtains that covered the windows.

Kit cocked her head at the curtains above the hearth. Then, setting her letter to Phoebe neatly on the bench beside her, she rose to examine the mystery more closely. A golden pull-rope, frayed by the teeth of long-dead vermin, hung down from the curtains. Kit reached out and gave it a tug. The curtains jerked. She took the rope in both fists and yanked it down hand-over-hand like her ancestors had done with rigging and sails in ages past. The curtains parted to reveal a portrait. Kit's eyes flew wide at the likeness. She staggered back for a wider look.

The portrait, painted in oils by a hand of no small talent, depicted a woman of striking visage. The artist had rendered her in a style reminiscent of the pre-Raphaelites Kit so revered, and in a pose not dissimilar to the *Madame X* which had nearly seen Sargent banished from Paris. Yet still more shocking than her pose was her face. The woman bore the hawkish nose, pointed chin, sharp cheekbones, and swooping brow of Alexandra.

But this woman could not be Alexandra, for there were shadows beneath her eyes and the barest hint of a wrinkle on the brow beneath her widow's peak. Kit would suppose her age some five-and-thirty years. Far older than Alexandra. Though Kit realized she had indeed witnessed Alexandra wearing the same burgundy gown at the Coffin wedding. Kit stared up at the portrait. An elder sister, perhaps? Or Alexandra's mother?

A dissonant chord shattered the silence.

Kit whipped her head towards the piano. Her letter to Phoebe fluttered to the floor. In its wake, the train of a pale yellow gown whisked away from the piano bench and out the open door.

"Alexandra?" said Kit. She snatched up the letter from the floor and started after her.

Upon poking her head into the hall, Kit saw the gown, and the veiled figure who wore it, disappear around the corner. Kit stepped into the hall just in time to witness the veiled figure fly down the hall with astonishing speed. Within the space of a blink, the mysterious woman had ducked down another corridor and vanished. Her absence left Kit gobsmacked.

"Alexandra?" she said again, though she very much doubted it had been her new sister-in-law who fluttered and vanished like the merest spirit. She'd certainly never seen Alexandra in yellow. Such a color would sallow her complexion.

Still, Kit followed where the mysterious figure had led and found herself in an entirely new hallway of the massive house. And at the end of this new hallway stood a door, ajar.

"Alexandra?" Kit called a third time as she approached the door. She had stepped almost within arm's reach of the knob when she heard a response.

"…Yes?"

The voice was unmistakable. Kit pushed the door open with confidence.

A sharp chemical smell made her wrinkle her nose as her eyes swept over the room. It seemed she'd stepped into a flock of birds. Shelves lining the walls abounded with finches, sparrows, swallows, pigeons, magpies, blue-jays, robins, and a resplendent pair of pheasants. All still, all silent, like the kingfisher atop the piano, which Kit supposed must be a sort of cousin to the avian specimens gathered here. Interspersed among the feathered birds sat several sets of bones, some wired together to form a complete creature, others laid out in separate sequence. And besides the bones, there were stray feathers, eggshells, and, in the swallows' case, one whole nest. In one particular corner Kit spied a jar of greenish liquid with a fetal bird suspended within. Its eyes bulged under their thin lids, and its featherless limbs stuck at odd angles.

At a table in the center of the room sat Alexandra. She had turned the table—a beautiful specimen of oak not unsuited to a dining room—into a sort of laboratory bench. Before her she had laid out scissors, tweezers, knives, scalpels, needles and thread, all of which she had evidently put to use dissecting and re-assembling the little brown finch whose bones she had plucked from its body and whose internal organs she had neatly piled onto a piece of scrap paper. Under the table, a burlap sack of sawdust leaned against the legs of her stool.

Alexandra herself had paused in the midst of her task, her shoulders hunched over the table. Her head perked up not unlike a bird's to bestow her steel-eyed stare upon Kit's entrance. Most interesting to Kit, Alexandra wore not a yellow dress, but the same deep violet gown that Kit had seen her in earlier that day.

Kit forced a smile in response to Alexandra's blank stare. "Good morning."

The greeting broke Alexandra's spell of paralysis. She drew herself up to a more ladylike posture and wiped her bloodied fingertips upon a handkerchief. Intent on her task and no longer meeting Kit's gazed, she asked in a cool tone, "I do hope you're not afraid of bones."

"Not in the least," Kit answered honestly. "I could hardly hope to be so, given my cousin Phoebe's chosen profession."

"Ah yes, the medical student." Alexandra's fingers were thoroughly cleansed of blood, but she continued the motion regardless, her eyes now fixed upon her own knuckles. "But bird bones and human bones have a vital difference. Bird bones are hollow. It's why they're light enough to fly. They have their freedom only in exchange for crippling fragility."

Kit thought Alexandra might be talking of something more than birds, but didn't consider this the opportune moment to poke at her new sister-in-law's obviously raw nerves. "You have a beautiful collection regardless."

Alexandra's ablutions abruptly ceased. Her eyes darted towards Kit and held her gaze for a beat of deafening silence. At last, she replied curtly, "Thank you."

"You're very welcome," said Kit, because that was how a polite lady ought to respond. Less politely, she added, "May I ask a few questions regarding the household?"

Alexandra's gaze returned to her bloodied handkerchief. She picked up a knife and began scrubbing at its crimson blade. "You may."

It was the most welcoming thing Kit had heard since her arrival at Heatherhurst Hall. She wasted no time in responding. "I have done a little wandering about the house, and I stumbled across a portrait... I believe it's in the music room? There's a piano, and a kingfisher..." She trailed off, waiting for Alexandra to pick up the fragile thread of conversation.

"There is a room in this house with a piano, a kingfisher, and a portrait, yes." Alexandra's tone had gone, if possible, even icier than when Kit had first entered. "Was that your question?"

"Not entirely. The woman in the portrait—who is she?"

Alexandra placed the now-clean knife down upon the table. She still didn't meet Kit's eyes as she replied, "My mother."

"Oh." Kit thought it best to let that line of inquiry lie for now and used her most chipper tone to change the subject. "I have written a letter to my cousin Phoebe. This probably sounds ridiculous—" Stupid, more like. "—but how do I put it into the mail?"

Alexandra's eyes flicked towards Kit for an instant before they returned to the eviscerated finch. "Leave it in the silver salver by the front door in the foyer. Whoever next goes out will pick it up from there and deliver it to the Post Office in the village."

The particular phrasing of "whoever next" gave Kit pause. "Who else lives here, besides yourself, Sir Vivian, and I?"

"The cook," Alexandra said flatly.

Kit thought back to the ethereal figure she'd followed from the music room. "Does she wear a yellow gown?"

Alexandra's arched eyebrows twisted into an expression of utmost incredulity. "She wears an apron."

Kit, who had only seen the mysterious figure from behind, supposed she might have missed such a detail. "Does she come upstairs often?"

"Hardly," Alexandra snapped. "She has more than enough work to keep her busy in the kitchen."

"Oh." Kit made a mental note to find the kitchen at her earliest convenience.

"Is there anything else?"

The tone of Alexandra's question implied that there should be nothing else at all. But Kit couldn't leave without settling one final matter.

"It's just..." she began, nearly losing her nerve, but drawing upon her store of courage with a deep breath. "Is there somewhere in the house where I might have a darkroom?"

"A darkroom?" Alexandra echoed, aghast.

"For photography," Kit hurried to explain.

"Oh." Alexandra's gaze dropped to the table, and she again busied herself with the work of stuffing the sparrow with straw. She continued coolly, "Still dabbling in photography, then? I'd have thought you'd grow bored of it by now. It seems you're not quite so flighty as I first supposed. You surprise me, Miss Morgan."

Every word that fell from those her lips struck Kit as surely and cruelly as the point of a blade. Reeling from such blows, she could barely muster the presence of mind to riposte. "Lady Cranbrook."

Alexandra's shoulders tensed. "Pardon?"

"I am no longer Miss Morgan," Kit replied in as level a tone as she could manage. "I am Lady Cranbrook now. Though of course you may still call me Kit."

This last she added with what little fondness remained in her from her remembrances of their past acquaintance.

For an instant, the hard line of Alexandra's eyebrows softened. It seemed as though she, too, thought back to those sunny days in New Bedford, when all had been friendliness and ease. Then her jawline stiffened, and she replied with her voice dripping icicles, "As you wish, Lady Cranbrook."

Kit winced.

"I don't know where we'll find room for your little hobby," Alexandra continued, running her fingers through a little bowl of shining black beads resembling birds' eyes.

Kit thought that was rather rich of her to say when in the midst of her own "little hobby," but shrugged the comment off regardless. If they couldn't be friends, she felt determined to at least remain on civil terms. "I only need a smallish space. No bigger than a closet, I should think. And the fewer windows, the better."

"That's the shame about monks," Alexandra muttered. "They're awful fond of letting in the light. I'm afraid you'll not find many dark rooms in Heatherhurst."

"The attic, perhaps?" Kit suggested gently.

The effect of her words upon Alexandra was both immediate and uncanny. Her cool demeanor and faint sneer vanished. Her head snapped up to regard Kit, all pretense of superiority gone from her features. In its place there remained only shock and horror.

"What?" Alexandra snapped, the single word cracking like a bull-whip in the uncomfortable silence.

Kit flinched. "I thought maybe the attic—"

"No." The syllable could not sound more final if it were accompanied by the pounding of a judge's gavel. Alexandra herself had the severe gaze of the most unfeeling magistrate. "Absolutely not."

"Very well," Kit forced out, doing her best to maintain a positive outlook despite Alexandra's impassioned opposition. "Is there a cellar of some kind?"

Alexandra stared at her as if she'd suggested they steer a whaleship towards the moon.

"A root cellar," Kit elaborated. "Or a wine cellar? Something under the house. Someplace dark, which sees little use. I'd be out of your way down there."

She fully expected another flat refusal. Alexandra certainly looked as if she wished to give one.

Instead, Alexandra inhaled sharply through her beakish nose and replied, "We might find a cobwebbed corner in which to keep you."

Kit overlooked the vaguely menacing choice of words and responded with her warmest smile. "Thank you, Alexandra."

"You're welcome," Alexandra said in a voice that implied no such thing.

As Alexandra watched Kit stride off, she was struck by the impulse to scamper after her, grab her shoulders, whirl her around to face her and tell her everything. Of the twisted, unnatural impulse the siblings had inherited. Of Vivian's wretched hubris, and how it had destroyed his truest love. Of what had really happened to Mother, and to Father after.

But as ever, the sheer tangled mass of the truth caught in her throat and choked her. She watched in silence as Kit stepped further and further away down the hall, until she turned the corner and vanished entirely from Alexandra's sight.

Perhaps Kit would understand the truth, if Alexandra were to tell her. If anyone could bear to hear the wretched tale of all the woe that befell the house of Cranbrook, Alexandra thought Kit might. Her steadfast Yankee determination; the straight-backed, strong-jawed way she stood in the face of all the world's torment and refused to bend; these might yet lend her courage enough to listen to the dreadful stories of Heatherhurst Hall without crumbling in horror.

Alexandra had tried to tell another, once. Had been on the brink of confessing all to one she trusted with her heart.

Only to have her heart torn from her chest and thrown onto a pyre.

Perhaps this had been Kit's plan from the beginning. Perhaps she, too, had feigned a friendship with Alexandra merely to secure her brother's hand in marriage.

Just like Lizzie before her.

No, Alexandra would not make the same mistake again. Lizzie had betrayed her. She would never give Kit the chance.

Her mind made up, Alexandra went downstairs to see to dinner.

Heatherhurst Hall, as the estate of a baronet, had once housed a multitude of staff. Alexandra had been raised in a household of no fewer than forty servants. In the last three years, she and her brother had made do with just one—a cook. Tonight, Alexandra descended the servants' stair to speak to this woman in her domain.

Alexandra entered the kitchen to find a hatchet-faced woman of some thirty-odd years, with rail-thin limbs, knobbly joints, and a thin gash of a mouth, plucking a chicken clean with great rapidity and ferocity—so quickly, it fact, that it would've taken a second look for an untrained eye to perceive that in place of a left hand, she possessed an iron hook.

Alexandra had long grown accustomed to the sight of the hook. She and Vivian had crafted it together.

Gertrude had come to Heatherhurst Hall as a young woman with two good hands when Alexandra was just a girl. Hired on as a housemaid, she had stayed on through the death of Lady Eleanor Cranbrook and Sir Ambrose Cranbrook shortly after. Alexandra hardly noticed her then; she'd been just another face in an overwhelming swarm of servants.

Then came the accident.

With the rest of the surviving staff giving notice and fleeing the estate, there were plenty of positions to fill. A more prosperous household might've pensioned Gertrude off. Alexandra offered her a promotion. Gertrude had her choice of lady's maid, housekeeper, or cook, and decided upon the last of these three. Being as clever as she was stubborn, she had quickly learned to compensate for her infirmity and crafted recipes that, if not fashionable, were at least filling. She made the kitchen her domain.

And so life went on at Heatherhurst Hall.

When Vivian had left for America to find a bride, and Alexandra chose to accompany him, they left the house in Gertrude's charge. Alexandra had no qualms in doing so. What Gertrude may have lacked in warmth, she more than made up for in practicality. Upon her return ahead of her brother, Alexandra found the house as safe and sound as she'd left it.

Alexandra tried to take comfort in Gertrude's steadfast nature now, as she gathered herself before saying, "Good evening, Gertie."

"Evenin', Miss Alexandra," Gertrude grunted, hardly looking up.

"My brother has returned."

"So I've heard."

In another time and place Alexandra might have cracked a wry half-smile at her servant's indifference. Tonight, her tone remained grave, her heart like a stone. "He's brought his new bride."

"As we expected."

Obviously. They hadn't gone to America without telling Gertrude the purpose of their voyage. While Alexandra had taken good care of the household accounts, and never once underpaid Gertrude for her services, one had only to glance around the house to see its masters might not be so flush in the pocket as they once were. Most women of Alexandra's station would attempt to hide such circumstances from their staff.

Alexandra had no patience for the sort of subterfuge which would only serve to insult Gertrude's keen intelligence.

Still, Alexandra herself had been surprised by certain aspects of her brother's return, and so she continued, "I thought perhaps you might wish for an introduction to the new Lady Cranbrook."

"Already had it," said Gertrude.

Alexandra choked on the remainder of her prepared speech. Gertrude, apparently unaware she'd said anything out of the ordinary, finished plucking the chicken and set about disemboweling it. Alexandra watched the glistening entrails spill from the fowl, her bewildered mind far off and away.

"When?" she demanded, snapping out of her daze.

This earned her a raised eyebrow from Gertrude, though more likely in response to the sharpness of her tone rather than the meaning of her words. "She came down and introduced herself just this afternoon."

Little Kit Morgan had wandered far and wide in the brief hours since her arrival. Alexandra wondered how many doors she'd opened. How many locks she'd tried. She clutched her chatelaine compulsively, feeling over each and every key hanging from the ring. She'd surrendered none of them yet. But she'd have to soon. She had no excuse for keeping the house-keys from the estate's new mistress. Desperate for distraction, she forced a blasé tone and asked, "How did you find her?"

Gertrude shrugged. "Well enough. About as I expected from an American. No offense intended."

"None taken," Alexandra recited by rote, her imagination still racing.

Dinner was horrid.

Vivian sat at the head of the long table, with Kit at his right hand, and Alexandra all the way down the other end, prohibiting conversation between the two women. Not that conversation seemed likely to occur, with the way Alexandra glared at her whilst stabbing her meal as if her asparagus spears were vampires in their coffins, and the tines of her fork minuscule stakes.

Kit hardly touched a bite. The chicken fricassee tasted like ash upon her tongue. She regretted sending so many plates back uneaten—she only hoped the cook wouldn't take offense. She wondered if she might have the opportunity to introduce herself to this mysterious person. She didn't dare ask Alexandra. She couldn't meet her eyes over dinner. All the more awkward for the lack of staff, without which they were all left to serve the meal themselves. Kit didn't mind, having done much the same with her classmates at finishing school. But Alexandra seemed peeved by it, all the more so when dinner ended and she stayed behind to collect the dishes and carry them down to the kitchen herself, ignoring Kit's feeble protests and mumbled offers of assistance. Her husband appeared content to let his sister do the work, guiding Kit out of the dining room only to abandon her in the upstairs hall—he had some household matters to settle in his study before he came to bed.

And so Kit retired to the master bedroom—her bedroom—alone.

She kept her composure as she undressed, donned her nightgown, brushed her hair, and crawled into bed. Once there, however, with her face pressed against unfamiliar linens that smelled so unlike home, scalding hot tears pricked her eyes. Her attempts to blink them back only forced them down her cheeks in torrents. She gave up all hope of composure and sobbed bitterly into the pillow. Alexandra didn't love her. Alexandra didn't even like her. Alexandra hated her and wanted her gone. All Kit had dreamt of during her Atlantic crossing dissolved before her eyes. She'd been a fool, a stupid little fool, to ever think anyone could love a wretch like herself.

Someone knocked at the door.

Kit swallowed down her last sob and lifted her head from the pillow. Hope, not yet dead despite all she'd endured, gave a feeble flutter within her breast. Her lips parted, a name she dared not utter already on her tongue. *Alexandra*—

"Catherine?" her husband called.

A wave of disappointment washed over her, bathing her in despair. With a last pitiful cry, her hopes perished. Resignation took their place. Kit forced her voice past the lump in her throat. "Come in."

With her engagement, her wedding, and her first kiss inspiring no feelings of butterflies in her stomach or thrill in her veins, she supposed the marriage bed had to be where the solution lay. There, then, Lucy had found the sort of satisfaction that allowed her to forget schoolgirl romance, and God willing, so too would Kit. She knew better than most women what to expect. Her cousin's early interest in medical facts had assured that. No sooner had Phoebe read up on all the mysteries of gynecology than she imparted the whole of it to Kit. The fullness of her knowledge gave Kit a practical view of her circumstances. Seeing to her husband's needs in the bedroom was just another aspect of managing a household as a wife.

Except she'd yet to do it.

She'd expected it on the voyage across the Atlantic—she and her husband had shared a cabin, after all. And they had slept side-by-side in perfect harmony. Vivian didn't snore, nor did he toss and turn through the night. But neither did he do anything more than kiss her cheek as he slipped into bed beside her. Kit, after several days of rumination, concluded he felt discomforted aboard ship and assumed they would know each other more intimately once they returned to shore.

But now that she had come to Heatherhurst Hall only to have her hopes of friendship dashed, she found herself much less amiable towards the notion than she'd felt since Vivian had first proposed. Indeed, all expectation of marital bliss flown from her mind—until now.

In the present moment, Vivian entered the bedroom. He strode smiling towards the bed, then came to a sudden halt as he caught sight of her face. "Good Lord, have you been crying?"

Kit hurriedly scrubbed her eyes with the heel of her hand. "No."

She'd never been a skillful liar, and it was readily apparent she hadn't fooled him. His brow furrowed in concern for an instant before it melted away with a comforting smile. "Homesick?"

It was as good an excuse as any, so Kit nodded, unable to meet his gaze.

She heard his footsteps approach the bed, felt his weight settle upon it. She braced herself.

A dry kiss pecked at her forehead. Then he was up again and off across the room to change into his own nightclothes.

"You'll come to like Heatherhurst," he said over his shoulder. "For all its drafty gloom. Alexandra makes a comfortable little home of it."

The mention of Alexandra's comforts did nothing to soothe Kit. She drew her legs up to her chest and wrapped her arms around them, letting her forehead drop to her knees. Vivian continued extolling the virtues of his childhood home—her home, now—but she hardly listened. She felt quite dead to the world until something patted the top of her head. Glancing up, she found Vivian tucking himself into bed. Resigned, she too slipped under the sheets.

Like every night since their wedding, he kissed her cheek. "You'll feel better in the morning. Everything looks far more handsome by daylight."

She forced a smile.

Apparently satisfied, he turned away from her and fell asleep. Raindrops began to patter against the windows, gently lulling Kit into the same state.

A shattering crash startled her awake. She bolted upright in bed, her eyes snapping open to find only darkness before her. It took her a moment to recall where she lay, and why.

"Vivian—" she said, thinking to rouse her new husband and ask him what the Dickens had caused such a racket, but as she reached out her hand to grasp his shoulder, her fingers moved through empty air and came down upon the counterpane, with only a mattress beneath it. Sir Vivian was gone. She was alone.

A brilliant flash of light blazed through the room, gone as quick as it came, blinding her. Moments later another crash followed. Its echoes rumbled away, and she recognized it as thunder after lightning. A storm raged across the moor. In the thunder's wake, she heard the lashing of rain against the windows.

Her whaling ancestors had sailed a hundred voyages around the legendary Cape Horn, a sea rife with hurricanes in which many a ship simply vanished. A storm on land was nothing by comparison. Kit squared her shoulders against the squall.

Lightning flashed again. As children, Phoebe had taught Kit to gauge a storm's distance by counting the seconds between lightning and thunder. One Mississippi, two Mississippi... The thunder rolled in. Hardly two miles off, by Kit's reckoning. The rumble of thunder faded. Then there was only the rain.

And then, faintly, hardly audible above constant splash of raindrops, she heard a moan.

Kit furrowed her brow at the sound. "Vivian?"

It still felt odd to say his name without putting a "Sir" in front of it. Regardless, he did not answer.

The moan pitched upward into a wail.

Concern drove Kit out of bed entirely. If someone in the house felt ill enough to wail so, she would do her utmost to ease their suffering.

The floorboards felt frozen beneath her bare toes. She grabbed a shawl to throw around her shoulders and rummaged in the night-stand for a match. The blaze of a lit match was nothing compared to the lightning, not even when she set the flame to a candle and raised it to encompass the room. Still, having a little light of her own granted her courage as she crept out of the master bedroom.

The volume of the wailing redoubled once she reached the crooked corridor. She could see nothing beyond the flame of her candle. She wondered if she might almost do better to snuff it out and let her eyes adjust to the darkness.

"Vivian?" she called again.

No one answered her.

The corridor continued until it intersected perpendicularly with another hallway. Here, Kit paused. To the right, she knew, the pathway led to the entry hall. To the left, she hadn't yet explored. And to the left, the wailing echoed.

Kit gripped her candle tighter and turned left.

An empty corridor lay before her. One wall had a tall window with its Gothic arch rising to a pointed peak. The other had a door to a room unknown. Impenetrable shadow cloaked the end of the hall, far beyond the reach of her pathetic candle flame. She held it over her head regardless, peering into the gloom, and called her husband's name.

The wailing fell to a whimper. Kit strained her ears to hear it. She stepped forward, holding her candle out in front of her.

The wind howled, overpowering the phantom whimpers. A draught slipped through a crack in the windows and blew her candle out.

Darkness enveloped her. She stood stock still, blind, helpless, afraid even to move. The wind died down, and in its place, the whimpers rose up. They sounded near the floor.

A vision of something wretched grabbing at her ankles flashed through Kit's mind. With nothing to stand upon to rise above the imagined peril's reach, she faced her fears head-on by sinking to her knees upon the floor. After all, she couldn't be dragged down if she were already kneeling. She set her candle on the floor beside her, leaving the rim of the candle-holder pressed against her knee lest she lose it in the darkness, and began blindly fiddling with her box of matches.

Lightning flashed. For an instant, the whole hallway blazed white.

And in that instant, Kit saw she was not alone.

Something crawled along the carpet. A human figure—or what had once been human—with its limbs shriveled and broken, its back bent, forcing it to jerk and skitter like a spider. Its white nightshirt matched the hue of its pale skin, with its cropped black hair, sunken eyes, and gaping maw the only patches of darkness in all its horrid pallor. Even its hardly-human face had a crooked cast, with the left side melting down into its throat like wax.

Kit caught but a glimpse before darkness fell.

Thunder rolled in the lightning's wake, deafening her as the night blinded her. Yet the after-image of the mangled wraith remained before Kit's eye. She blinked hard to banish it, even as her shaking hands failed to strike a match. The horror of the unknown was nothing to the horror of the certain knowledge that something was there waiting for her, cloaked in storm and shadow, whilst she remained unable to perceive it directly.

As the thunder died down, the howling wind rose up to fill the void. And there, just under the wind, she could hear a piteous whine, near enough to her ears that she felt certain she could reach out and touch the sufferer if she dared.

Then, with a spark of triumph, her match blazed to light. The glow of its minuscule flame in her fingertips felt like the only warm thing left in the cold storm.

And illuminated the creature before her.

What the flash of lightning had made shocking, the flickering of the matchstick-flame turned into a creeping horror. Shadows flitted across the phantom's broken frame, each unnatural bend in its body made deeper and more twisted. Its hollow black eyes reflected two yellow pinpricks, fixed upon Kit.

As Kit stared in mute terror, the half-melted maw wrenched itself open, and a rasping, warbling, eerie voice emerged.

"Pwy wyt ti?" A hacking cough laid the poor creature low, until, with an effort, they continued. "Ble mae Vivian?"

The spark of recognition at the sound of her husband's name overtook Kit's fear for a moment. Not quite believing what she'd heard, she echoed, "Vivian?"

"Vivian!" the spirit cried, unmistakable now, though the accent remained watery and strange.

At school, many of Kit's classmates had become infected with the fever of Spiritualism and had conducted secret ceremonies in the night to try and talk to the dead. Typically, the girls sat around a trunk for a table, lit candles and held hands, and asked the spirits questions, which they were supposed to answer with one knock for yes and two for no. Kit had attended one of these seances and had two hypotheses for the phenomena she witnessed; either the spirits were so far removed from this mortal coil as to render their responses random and incomprehensible to the ears of the living, or the other girls, falling over each other with shrieks and giggles, had made all the answering knocks themselves.

None of their silly games had ever produced a result so tangible as what crawled before Kit's eyes now. Yet as she recalled the seances of her school days, she heard Patience Wheeler's voice explaining in hushed tones how the spirits of the dead communicated with the living in the hopes of resolving whatever unfinished business condemned them to roam the earth bereft of their eternal rest.

Evidently the crawling ghost had unfinished business with her husband, and through resolving this, she might banish it in peace. To this end, she summoned her courage and asked in strong, clear tones, "What do you want with Vivian?"

"Vivian!" the ghost shrieked. With tremendous effort, they flailed their trembling hands, desperately clutching at the man they wanted, the man who wasn't there. "Vivian! Vivian!"

"Tell me what you want with him!" Kit racked her mind for something to say to comfort the wretched thing. Fear blanked out her reasoning. She desperately tried to push past it, fighting her instincts, flailing about for a solution in much the same way the phantom writhed in agony. "I want to help you, I do, but—!"

"Kit!"

Kit whirled towards the sound of her name on a woman's lips and found Alexandra standing in the hall, a candle in hand. Her raven curls tumbled down her shoulders like wings of shadow, sharply contrasted against her pale skin and the paler nightgown which clung to her form. She appeared as much a phantom as the crawling thing—a vision of ethereal beauty to contrast the vision of horror. The shock of seeing her stole all words from Kit's tongue, all thought from her mind. Struck dumb, she could only stare at her.

"Catherine?"

A man's voice now, and behind her. Kit whirled again. Where once the tragic figure had crawled, there was no sign of it now. Only her husband, upright, clad in a nightshirt, regarding her with an expression of total bewilderment illuminated by his sister's candle.

CHAPTER EIGHT

"Vivian!" Kit cried, never so happy to see him before in her life.

He continued staring at her. "What on earth are you doing out of bed?"

She hardly knew how to begin. "I heard—I saw—!"

With furrowed brow, he strode towards her, bent down, and, grasping her by the elbows, lifted her upright. He snuffed out her matchstick with an effortless pinch of his fingers.

"They asked for you!" Kit babbled, painfully aware of how incoherent she sounded. "They called your name!"

"Who did?" Vivian asked, bewildered.

"A ghost! Bent and broken—they must have died horribly—crawling down the hall, and—!" Kit choked back a sob. "They wailed so piteously— they were in so much pain—!"

Vivian appeared shocked, not by her description of the spirit, but by her reaction to it. He began patting her arm awkwardly. "Must've been the wind. It moans through the eaves, you see."

"It wasn't the wind!" Kit insisted. "Whoever it was, they spoke to me —or tried to—I couldn't understand them, some ancient language—not Latin, I don't think, but—"

"The wind," Vivian continued as if he couldn't hear her, "must sound very strange to you, I know, but I assure you it's quite usual for a house so old as this, and situated upon the moors as we are."

Kit gaped at him incredulously. "Does it create *visions?*"

"No," Vivian admitted, "but the flashes of lightning through the windows and the fluttering curtains—"

"—do not recreate the image of a broken person crawling across the floor!" Kit cried.

Her husband remained unmoved. As did his sister, for as Kit cast a despairing glance at her, Alexandra rolled her eyes at him.

"It must have come through there!" Kit blurted in desperation, flinging her arm towards the door at the end of the hall, just barely visible in the reach of her candle in her husband's hand. "Where does that passage lead? What lies beyond it?"

"The attic," Alexandra said in lifeless tones.

Kit glanced back at her—saw only cold indifference in her face—and returned to her husband. "Come with me—through there—I'll show you—!"

Vivian paled. His wide eyes stared deeply into Kits as he clamped his hand around her shoulder and held her firm. "Catherine—darling—you must never go near the attic."

Kit blinked back at him. Where talk of ghosts and spirits hadn't fazed him, the mere mention of the attic turned his whole aspect grave. His grip upon her arms felt as if it would bruise. Bewildered, she replied, "Why not?"

Vivian's brows raised in shock—clearly, he'd never expected his wife to question his orders—and his mouth opened, but no sound emerged. He turned to his sister with a look of mute desperation.

"Tell her, Vivian." Alexandra's bared teeth made her words a challenge. "Tell her why she cannot go into the attic."

Vivian's features underwent a curious transformation, flitting from fear to shock to—for the briefest flicker—anger, eventually deciding upon wistful resignation. This last expression he turned upon Kit. With a pained smile, he said, "The roof."

Kit cast a confused glance between the siblings, and repeated her husband's words as a question.

"Yes." Vivian seemed pleased she'd caught on so quickly. "You may not have noticed when we arrived, for the carriage drive faces the south-east, and the worst damage is to the south-west, but the roof is in a sad state. Parts of the attic are already open to the elements. I should hate for any broken beams to collapse upon your head, or for the floorboards to give way beneath you, should you set foot up there."

Kit stared at him. "Then we must repair it."

Vivian's pained smile vanished in a flash of unmistakable alarm. "Repair it?"

"Of course," said Kit. "Have you had the damage assessed? How much will it cost to repair? Not more than we could afford, surely. Even if we must tighten our belts, it would be very false economy to live in a house without a roof. And if it cannot be repaired—well, then, we must simply sell the house and move on."

Both siblings gawked at her.

"Sell the house?" Vivian echoed incredulously.

"I know it would pain you dearly to part with the family estate—" Kit began.

"Do you, now?" asked Alexandra.

The rest of Kit's counter-argument died in her throat at the sound of Alexandra's inquiry, so quiet and yet so sharp, cold and quelling. Even Vivian appeared unnerved by it.

Alexandra's steel-gray eyes fixed upon Kit and Kit alone, her stare piercing her heart. In that same soft and frozen tone, she continued, "You have no idea what it means. This house has been in our family for centuries. Our ancestors were not fishermen. Our grandfather didn't come by his money in a whale-oil windfall. We did not purchase our property in living memory. This house *is* our family. It is all we have left of them."

The references to fishermen and whale-oil were as pointed as harpoons. Kit, the hot flush creeping up her neck, swallowed down the lump in her throat and blinked away the burning in her eyes. She didn't know what she'd done to make Alexandra hate her so. But she refused to rise to the bait. Crying wouldn't solve the issue. Instead of bursting into tears, she replied, "Then we won't sell it. But the roof must be fixed. We cannot live in a falling-down house."

"Many better families have," Alexandra muttered.

Vivian, visibly uneasy with the growing tension between his sister and his wife, cleared his throat. "Very well. I'll see about having the damage assessed."

"Thank you, Vivian." Kit forced a smile and pecked her husband's cheek in gratitude.

Alexandra whirled away with a loud scoff.

As she watched her brother put an arm around his wife's shoulders and lead her meekly back to bed, Alex's own blood boiled. She'd nearly had him.

Of course Kit had questioned the forbidden attic. It was absurd to live in a house with a ragged roof and rotting beams. And wasn't that the whole point of marrying an American heiress? To bring in the money so desperately needed to prevent the walls from crumbling down around them? If only Kit had pressed him. If only her Yankee determination extended to peeling back her husband's veneer, and revealing the corrupted decay within.

But that didn't matter now. Vivian had deftly evaded confrontation, as always.

Her bitter disappointment stung all the more for the knowledge that the cause of Kit's latest distress was even now putting his arm around her shoulders, walking her back to their shared chambers, slipping into bed beside her, holding her close, perhaps even kissing her, and...

Jealousy surged through her veins like a viper's venom, poisoning her mind against her brother even more than before. Such bitterness hurt less than the knowledge that Kit preferred his attentions over hers. Unbidden memories of another time when Kit Morgan had all-but-collapsed in tears, and Vivian carried her away from the crush of the wedding crowd, delivering her into Alexandra's arms. How the sight of one so regal as Kit, crumbling from heartbreak, had stirred up sympathy and anger within Alexandra—sympathy for the well-known agony of watching one's beloved freely give herself into the arms of another, and anger at anyone who would dare upset such a beautiful creature. Alexandra felt compelled to reach out, to hold her, to comfort and console her.

But now Kit sought solace in Vivian's arms.

Kit—with her golden locks tumbling down her shoulders to catch the flickering candlelight and bloom into brilliance amongst the encroaching shadows, and the delicate gauze of her white nightgown clinging to her curves—preferred Vivian's embrace over Alexandra's.

And once again, Alexandra's heart wrenched itself in twain.

Her tight-clenched fists dug her nails into her palms. Then, with a sharp inhalation, she forced her hands open, her fingers spreading wide, knuckles cracking under the strain.

Her brother and his wife had vanished into the night, safe behind their locked door.

Which left Alex free to turn away down the corridor and begin climbing the attic stair.

CHAPTER NINE

For all his failure to believe her, Kit couldn't fault her husband for lack of tenderness. He guided her back to their bedroom and tucked her in with all the fond care of a beloved nurse. Exhausted by her ordeal, she fell asleep before he got into bed beside her. When a raven's croak roused her the next morning, he'd already gone.

Kit sat up blearily blinking at her unfamiliar surroundings. The stormclouds had thinned to a mere gray blanket over the sky, and what light penetrated their cover washed over the room. What had seemed claustrophobic and oppressive last night looked merely unfashionable and abandoned by day.

Her husband's side of the bed had been made up as if no one had ever slept in it. Kit assumed the maid had done so, until she recalled they had no maid, and then she attributed the making of the bed to her husband's fastidious nature, no doubt either the result or the cause of his fascination with engineering. That trait had made itself readily apparent on their Atlantic crossing. He'd brought her down to look at the boilers in the belly of the steamer, where shirtless men shoveled fuel into a raging fire day and night, caked with coal dust and streaked with sweat. She'd humored him, calling the boiler "interesting" and the whole experience "educational," while she waited nearly an hour for him to grow tired of staring at the machine and the men who worked it. But once they returned to their quarters, he'd made it all right by brushing every trace of coal from her dress, which otherwise would've been quite ruined, and escorting her to the deck so she could sketch the ship and the sea.

The chimes of a clock echoed from somewhere deep within the house, striking ten. Kit bolted out of bed—she'd never slept so late before in her life; a captain's daughter knew better—and dressed for breakfast, expecting her husband to come check on her at any moment. But a knock never sounded, and a door never opened, and a quarter-hour later saw her out the door of her own accord, taking her first steps into the hallway since the horror of last night.

Like her bedroom, the hallway appeared far less menacing in morning light. She strode on down to the intersection, where a right-hand turn would take her to the front hall, and from there on downstairs to the breakfast room.

Yet here, she paused. She couldn't help glancing to the left, her heart beating just a little faster as she recalled her nightmare.

There was much the same about the left-hand path by day. The arched Gothic window, with the crack in a lower corner through which the wind had blown out her candle, showed the wild moor rolling on as gray as the clouded sky. The door in the opposing wall remained closed. But the end of the hall, where neither lightning nor candlelight had penetrated the previous evening, daylight showed plain. The hallway terminated in another closed door.

Kit, already late for breakfast by several hours, supposed a few more minutes wouldn't matter, and turned down the left-hand path.

First, she examined the floor. Some rain as well as wind had come in through the window-crack, creating a small spot of damp on the wall and floor nearby. Apart from this, the carpet and floorboards appeared undisturbed. She moved on to the first door.

No sooner had her fingertips alighted upon the knob than the door itself swung inward with a creak.

Kit, who'd fully expected to find the door locked, withheld a gasp at the sudden motion, then allowed herself a bitter snort at her own cowardice. Her nerves did no justice to her nautical ancestry.

The door hadn't swung far, leaving the merest gap. Kit peered through, squinting at the room beyond. It appeared totally empty.

Emboldened, Kit laid her palm upon the door and gently pushed it open.

Before her stood a small chamber, windowless, empty of furniture and people alike. Perhaps it had once been a nursery. Or a servant's quarters. Thick gray dust covered the floorboards, and motes of the same drifted through the air.

As she crossed its threshold, she realized the floorboards were not so completely covered as she had first supposed. The area immediately in front of the door was swept clean, as if by a broom, or a lady's skirts. From the doorway, the sweeping pattern swirled outward in a disjointed fashion, as though unskirted limbs had flown wildly. Following the trail to the center of the room, the sunlight trickling in from the hallway illuminated a single bare footprint in the dust.

Kit stared at the footprint. Too small to be her husband's, and too large for her sister-in-law. Perhaps her own foot might fit into it—but though Kit remembered many curious things from last night, she didn't recall stepping into this room.

She did, however, recall the sudden disappearance of another figure.

Her heart flew into her throat. She spun and fled the room, slamming the door behind her and holding it shut. Her pulse pounded in her ears as she gasped for breath. She waited for she knew not what. A minute passed like an hour. As the seconds ticked by, her pulse slowed, her breathing evened out, and she berated herself for her foolishness. Jumping at shadows in the night was one thing. Jumping at footprints in the day was quite another. Perhaps she hadn't even seen a footprint. Perhaps it was a trick of the light. A bizarre stirring of dust.

Kit cracked the door open and peered inside just to be sure.

The footprint remained plain in the center of the floor.

She slammed the door again and fervently wished she had a key to lock it behind her. Still, at least she had proof now. She hadn't imagined the previous night's vision. There was someone—or something—creeping about the house. Her husband might disbelieve her eyes, but not his own.

She would show him the footprint and see what his scientific mind had to say to that.

Kit shrugged away the crawling feeling on the nape of her neck and forced herself to release her hold on the doorknob, half-expecting it to fly open.

But it didn't move.

Kit stepped away, keeping her eye on the doorknob all the while, as she retreated until her back pressed against the opposite wall. She dared a glance down the hall to the other door at its end. A mere stone's throw away, and yet it took considerable gathering of her courage for her to inch along the wall towards it. When she had it just within reach, she stretched her arm out to its fullest and tried the knob with her fingertips.

Locked.

Kit tempered her disappointment with the comforting thought that at least one door in this house wouldn't surprise her by flying open. She turned her back upon it to stride down the hall—though she did press quite close to the opposing wall as she passed the first door—and go down to breakfast.

The breakfast room at Heatherhurst Hall was just off the foyer. Its eastern-facing windows should have filled the room with light, were it not for the natural clouded gloom of the moors. As matters stood, Kit walked into a grim chamber with a smaller table than the dining room and a massive sideboard that made the few plates upon it look smaller still. Kit hardly glanced at the food, her attention arrested by the presence at the table. While her husband was missing, Alexandra sat hunched over her own breakfast, alone and evidently deep in thought.

Kit stumbled to a halt on the threshold. In the instant she had to observe her before she was herself observed, Kit perceived shadows of deep indigo beneath Alexandra's eyes. It seemed her sister-in-law had slept as poorly as herself, if not poorer. Such bruising would be considered a mark against a beauty in society. But as Kit looked upon Alexandra's exhausted visage, the weariness therein seemed to her like the green scaling on a copper weather-vane, or the black streaks down the cheeks of a marble angel in a cemetery. A mark not of ugliness, but of having endured the trials and tribulations of the world, and emerged all the more beautiful for it.

Then she realized Alexandra was staring right back at her.

"You're late," Alexandra snapped.

Kit supposed it'd been too much to hope for a friendly greeting or an inquiry into how well she'd slept after her dreadful fright. She put aside her disappointment and forced a polite smile. "Good morning, Alexandra."

"There's bacon on the sideboard," Alexandra replied, not returning the smile. "It's burnt. The eggs have probably gone cold by now. The tea most certainly has."

"Thank you," said Kit, pitching her voice as if Alexandra had just offered her a sumptuous feast. "I'm sure it'll do for me."

Alexandra stared at her in disgust for another moment, then dropped her gaze to her own breakfast without a word.

Kit helped herself to burnt bacon, rubbery eggs, and cold tea, setting her own place on the opposite end of the table from Alexandra, to the right of Vivian's seat, or where he would've sat, if he hadn't already finished his breakfast and departed on his own way.

"Where is Vivian?" Kit asked.

Alexandra flashed her a look of suspicion. Kit couldn't imagine why. What possible underhanded motive could she have in wondering where her own husband had gone?

"I'm sure I don't know," Alexandra answered in a tone which plainly showed her resentment at being asked. "I suppose he's in the study, writing to see about having the roof repaired, just as you wanted."

Kit didn't think wanting the roof repaired was such an absurd desire. Still, she continued smiling. "I'm glad to hear it."

Alexandra had already turned away.

Kit finished her breakfast in silence. She didn't dare bring up the footprint. Her composure wouldn't bear much more of Alexandra's scorn.

As Kit stood up from her place setting, she wondered who, in the absence of a maid, would clear away the dirty dishes. She turned to Alexandra, the question already on the tip of her tongue.

"Leave it," Alexandra said without looking up. "I'll see to it."

Her response surprised Kit for reasons beyond her rudeness. Alexandra was the sister of a baronet. Surely it was beneath her to act as a scullery-maid. And yet, Kit supposed it was also beneath herself, now that she'd married the same baronet and ascended to the position of Lady Cranbrook.

Kit put on her best finishing-school smile and asked, "Where is Vivian's study?"

She'd braced herself for another withering glare, but Alexandra merely sighed and stood from the table.

"Follow me," she said.

Kit, relieved to have such a quick and easy answer to her inquiry, trotted into the foyer after her. Their twinned footsteps echoed up to the arched ceiling so many floors above. What would've been an awkward silence in a closed corridor became unbearable in the vast empty expanse. By the time they reached the bottom of the grand staircase, Kit felt desperate to break it.

"About last night," she blurted.

Alexandra halted. Slowly, as if moving in a dream, she turned just far enough to catch Kit in the corner of her eye over her shoulder. In a quelling tone, she replied, "What about it?"

"I've found proof," Kit continued, though even as she spoke she began to doubt her own words. "Of what I saw."

Alexandra said nothing for a long moment, still not looking directly at Kit. "I'm afraid I don't recall."

"The ghost," Kit said. "In the hallway. The one who called for Vivian."

"Oh," Alexandra said coolly. "You mean your sleep-walking."

Kit stared at her. "I wasn't asleep."

"I understand it often feels that way, when one is under the influence of a malevolent incubus," Alexandra continued in an almost maternal tone. "But I assure you, you were dead to the world before Vivian and I found you and awoke you."

The air went out of Kit's lungs. She could voice no objection, though her mind screamed vehement denial.

"The first few nights in a new house are often uncomfortable," Alexandra went on, apparently warming to her subject. "I can't imagine the storm made such unfamiliar surroundings any less intimidating. It's no wonder your mind took in these feelings of uneasiness and, guiding your unconscious body through the halls, gave you the vision of a tangible horror to explain your emotions."

Kit, her fists clenched tight in her skirts, replied through gritted teeth. "Nightmares do not leave footprints."

She fully expected Alexandra to laugh her off once more. But this final detail caused Alexandra to turn and face her at last. And what a face she had. Ivory white, drained of all color save her blood-red lips and her steel-gray eyes. Like Snow White, Kit thought, if at the fairytale's end the narrator revealed that Snow White and her wicked queen were one and the same. Kit's pulse quickened with fear—and with something else, too.

"Footprints?" Alexandra echoed, the word encrusted with frost.

"Just the one footprint," Kit blathered, her resolve crumbling under Alexandra's hard gaze. "In the empty room, off the hallway junction where I saw the phantom."

Alexandra's unblinking stare burned into Kit. "And when, pray tell, did you discover this... footprint?"

"This morning. Before breakfast."

"How curious." Alexandra turned around again, as if Kit had never spoken, and resumed walking. Without bothering to speak over her shoulder, she added, "I suppose Vivian may find it amusing, if you care to tell him."

Kit had cared far more for Alexandra's opinion. Her failure to convince her sister-in-law of the truth was a crushing blow. She doubted her husband could say anything to help her recover from it. But perhaps he would be able to reach Alexandra where Kit had failed. Kit took this small hope and allowed it to buoy her up and carry her down the winding corridors in Alexandra's wake.

In the east wing, Alexandra stopped in front of a closed door, and knocked. Not a light rap of fingertips, either, but hitting her knuckles against the wood with such force that, were she not wearing gloves, she might well fear breaking her skin.

"Yes?" came Vivian's voice from within.

Rather than give a verbal answer, Alexandra shoved the door open.

Dark mahogany paneled the study walls, occasionally breaking out into shelves holding thick leather-bound volumes and intermittent curiosities —a human skull, or a clever imitation, among them. Green velvet curtains, moth-eaten enough to pass for lace, hung on either side of the single bay window. In front of the window stood a mighty mahogany desk, the crest carved into its front bearing a dragon rampant, and its scaled legs ending in enormous clawed talons to match, putting Kit's own captain's desk to shame. At this desk sat her husband, with papers spread out before him, a compass in one hand and a carpenter's pencil in the other. Interrupted, he blinked up at the two women, all his features wide with undisguised astonishment.

"There he is," Alexandra declared.

Then she turned on her heel and left, brushing past Kit in the doorway.

It was the nearest she and Kit had been ever since Alexandra had left New Bedford. Kit held her breath, but still caught the sweet notes of her jasmine perfume. The scent brought back all the memories she'd worked to repress from the moment of her arrival to Heatherhurst Hall. Memories of bicycle rides and cemeteries, of photographs and a silver-and-sapphire ring. The very same ring Kit now wore upon her finger. She felt its metal grow hot in her hand, as if it still thrummed with Alexandra's pulse, so near to her vein and so deeply connected to her heart.

And then, in a rush of faded blue silk, she was gone.

In her absence, Kit remained dumbstruck upon the threshold, staring down the now-empty hallway. The sound of shuffling paper from within the study roused her attention, and she turned to find her husband standing from his desk and striding towards her, an affable smile upon his thin lips.

"Good morning, my sweet!" he said, kissing her forehead with greater ease than any man had since she'd stopped growing. "I hope you'll forgive me for missing you at breakfast. Urgent matters demanded my attention."

Kit endeavored to return his affection but couldn't keep her curiosity from drawing her eyes away from his face towards the papers on his desk. "Writing to see about having the roof repaired?"

"What?" Vivian's brow furrowed. "Oh, yes, that. I suppose I should, though I don't know if I'll get to it today. Tomorrow, perhaps."

Kit, bemused, wondered what he'd been working on so diligently at his desk if not the roof. But she had more pressing matters to hand. She steeled her nerves and forced herself to remain calm, to imitate the cool and reasonable tones of her sister-in-law's voice. "Vivian, would you come with me, please?"

Vivian blinked at her. "Where?"

"To the hallway where you found me last night." If Vivian shared his sister's interpretation of events, Kit didn't want to give him the chance to dismiss her. She'd say nothing to him of ghosts or spirits. Not until she could show him the tell-tale footprint. She almost looked forward to hearing what the Cranbrook siblings would have to say to that.

"To what end?" Vivian asked.

Kit, desperate, grasped his hand. His spidery fingers felt cold and clammy in her warm palm. "Vivian, please! It'll only take a moment!"

Her sudden handclasp startled him, but he recovered with the grace suitable to his station and smiled indulgently down at her. "Very well. Lead on."

And so, trailing him by the hand like a schoolgirl, Kit led her husband away from his study, across the foyer, and towards the very spot of her nightmare. As they neared the place, she felt his hand clench in hers.

Kit came to a halt between the window and the door, standing precisely where the wretched white wraith had writhed and wailed. She turned to face her husband, never releasing her hold on his fingers, and asked, "Do you remember what I saw last night?"

Vivian appeared pained. "I recall my sister and I found you wandering the halls, sleepwalking, until she roused you, at which point you became inconsolable. Bordering on hysteric."

Kit bit back her instinctive rebuttal against his accusation of sleepwalking. "I saw a poor broken thing, crying your name."

"You had a nightmare," Vivian said gently.

"Nightmares," Kit insisted, losing the last shred of her patience, "do not leave footprints!"

If her behavior had confused her husband before, now he looked truly bewildered. "What?"

Kit leapt past him and shoved the door open. It swung inward easily, revealing the empty room, same as before.

Except for the gleaming floorboards.

Kit stared in horror at the pristine room.

Vivian glanced at it, then returned to her. "Are you feeling quite the thing, Catherine?"

"We don't have a maid," Kit murmured in disbelief.

"No, we do not," Vivian concurred, somewhat bemused. "Would you prefer if we hired one?"

"If we don't have a maid," Kit said, raising her voice over her husband's suggestion, "then who swept this room?"

This question didn't appear nearly as unsettling to Vivian as it felt to her. He merely shrugged. "Alexandra, probably. She handles most of the housekeeping. Beneath her station, of course, but needs must. I can speak to her about hiring staff, if you wish it."

Kit said nothing. Her proof had vanished as completely as the phantom who'd left it behind.

CHAPTER TEN

Vivian kissed her forehead and returned to his study. Kit watched him go in stunned silence. She didn't dare ask him where the door at the end of the hall led. It seemed entirely possible he'd deny the door's existence as well.

Instead, she put her mind to the mystery of who had swept up the footprint. Perhaps Vivian's had guessed correctly in naming his sister as the culprit. Though Kit struggled to account for how swiftly Alexandra had acted. It'd been mere minutes between Alexandra departing the study, and Kit leading her husband to the scene of the crime.

Ghosts moved swiftly.

The thought came unbidden to Kit's mind. She struggled to cast it aside. Spirits, it was said, could pass through walls, could drift silent and unseen where'er they willed, could create such a draught as might whisk away the dust and the footprint with it.

Kit shuddered and slammed the door shut on her latest folly.

As she retreated down the hall towards the master bedroom, she couldn't help wishing for proof of the spirit to show her husband and sister-in-law. Neither had seen the wraith itself. And the footprint was erased as thoroughly as if, left in the sand of a beach, a rising tide had come to wash it away. If only she could have fixed it in place, like the chemical processes of her darkroom fixed a photographic print to paper.

The idea brought her to a sudden halt. A phantom or a footprint could be waved away, but a photograph would prove difficult for even the Cranbrooks to deny. She'd need a darkroom in which to develop the photographs, but that could be arranged afterward. First, she required film worth developing.

Kit scampered into her bedroom and opened her trunk. She'd yet to unpack most of her belongings, and upended them all over the floor to dig out the photographic equipment securely nestled beneath and between her clothes, the soft cloth acting as padding to prevent breakage of more delicate pieces. With relief, she discovered that everything had survived her Atlantic crossing. Camera in hand and tripod under her arm, she wanted only a ghost to capture on film. She emerged from her bedroom and began her hunt.

Trouble was, she mused as she wandered the winding corridors of Heatherhurst, the circumstances most conducive to ghosts were least conducive to photography. Ghosts required midnight storms with howling winds and guttering candles. Photographs required brightest daylight, or, lacking cooperation from the weather, ignited magnesium. But even with chemical assistance, unless she had enough luck to time the snap of the shutter precisely with the flash of the lightning, any photograph she attempted to take in a storm would turn out as black as thunderclouds.

Still, perhaps a ghost or two might be brave enough to come out into the sunshine.

Arming herself with her familiar photography equipment leant Kit enough courage to return, once again, to the curious hallway with the empty room and the locked door. No evidence remained for the human eye, but perhaps the science of photography could perceive what Kit could not. She took up her position at the juncture, screwing her tripod into place where the two hallways converged, and placed her camera upon it facing the locked door at the end.

"Steady as she goes," she muttered to herself and removed the lens cap to expose the plate to the light.

Eight seconds passed without incident.

Kit replaced the lens cap. Though she herself had perceived nothing, perhaps the camera had seen something more. She began scribbling the date, time, and location on the back of the plate.

A muffled thud sounded from above.

Kit jerked her gaze up to the ceiling. She saw nothing overtly amiss, but heard something like a hundred claws scraping for purchase against the eaves. Her imagination supplied the crawling specter of last night, scuttling in frantic circles just above her head. A chill ran through her.

Then it moved.

The sound traveled over her, past her, behind her, scrambling away down the hall towards the grand foyer.

Kit whirled to follow it, her eyes fixed upon the ceiling. She dashed after the sound, always just ahead of her, prickling in her ears. That horrible scratching, like a host of spiders, or something worse.

Her foot came down upon air.

Kit flailed to catch her balance, hardly knowing where she stood. Instinct threw her arms around the nearest object—a wooden post, as tall as herself, sharp with Gothic carvings. She embraced it like a lover and hung all her weight upon it, kicking to find the floor again. For one perilous moment, she felt herself floating. Then her heels came down upon solid ground at last.

She stood at the top of the grand staircase in the foyer, wrapped around its banister like a sailor clinging to the mizzenmast. A vast expanse yawned beneath her. In her desperate pursuit of the phantom sound, she'd nearly plunged to her doom.

No sooner did she realize where she stood then she flung her gaze upward again, straining her ears to hear the horrible scratching noise. Only her own gasps reached her ears. She sounded as if she were drowning.

Kit let go of the banister and turned in a slow, hopeless circle, still staring upward. Her neck ached. Her heart pounded.

"Hello?" she whispered.

"Kit?"

Startled, Kit clung to the banister again and whirled towards the voice. It had come not from above, but beneath.

There, at the bottom of the staircase so far and away below, stood Alexandra. The train of her sapphire blue gown swirled over the floorboards in a continuation of the staircase's turn, creating a spiraling fractal like the center of a whirlpool in a maelstrom, revealing the ocean's treacherous depths. One delicate white hand clutched the dark mahogany railing as if she'd clawed her way out of the storm to reach Kit. Her pale face turned upwards, her swanlike throat bared, her lips parted, her eyes wide and rimmed with white. Her swooping black brows furrowed in what almost looked like, but could not possibly be, concern.

How long she had stood there, Kit knew not. Shame flushed her cheeks as she considered what Alexandra might have seen—what a fool she must have looked—

"I heard something," Alexandra said.

Kit's heart fluttered in her throat. "So did I! Something scratching in the ceiling…"

She trailed off as Alexandra's look of concern shifted into annoyance.

"I heard a thump," Alexandra continued. "As if someone had almost fallen down the stair and caught herself at the last moment."

The back of Kit's neck burned. She swallowed against the lump in her throat, but no words came. She had nothing to say in her own defense.

Alexandra sighed. "Do be more careful."

Kit didn't have time to reassure her, to promise anything she wished, before Alexandra turned and strode away across the foyer, disappearing into the dining room.

With her went Kit's last shred of dignity. She sank to the floor, her shoulders slumped, the back of her skull thudding dully against the banister, her legs splayed beneath her skirts like an awkward gosling. No matter how small an action she took, it inevitably lowered Alexandra's opinion of her. She couldn't even walk down the hall without nearly plummeting down the stairs. Such a clumsy wretch as herself had no place within the elegant halls of Heatherhurst. Certainly no place beside a woman so stunning as Alexandra.

Self-pity dropped Kit's gaze to the floor. There upon the carpet she discovered a flat square piece of coated glass. Her photographic plate. Fallen. Forgotten. Much like herself.

With a surge of effort, she lurched forward and just barely caught the corner of the plate between her outstretched fingers. She flipped it over between her knuckles, her unseeing eyes fixed on the undeveloped image. There might very well be nothing upon it but the long empty hallway and the closed door at the end. Perhaps the phantoms she chased were just figments of her fevered imagination after all.

Or, perhaps, if she persevered, her photographs might reveal something after all. Something she could show to Alexandra to explain her own bizarre behavior, to redeem herself in her sister-in-law's eyes.

Setting her jaw with renewed determination, Kit tucked the plate into her pocket and dragged herself up from the floor. No scraping sound came from overhead as she re-traced her steps. No phantoms flickered in the corner of her eyes as she reached the crossway and moved beyond it to where she'd left her photographic equipment. There stood the tripod with her camera balanced upon it. Unmoved. Untouched. A still and silent witness to the empty hall and the locked door.

With practiced precision, Kit collapsed the tripod and tucked it under her arm. Putting her mind to where else a ghost might wander within Heatherhurst Hall, she recalled the mysterious veiled figure she'd chased out of the music room on her first day in the house, and strode there with purpose. Down the winding corridor, up the three curious half-steps, around the sharp right corner, and through the open door. She struggled somewhat to get her tripod over the threshold, tucked as it was under her arm, but at length, she stood within the silent chamber.

Kit crossed the room, past the stuffed kingfisher upon the closed piano lid, to the thick velvet curtains blocking the arched Gothic windows. Tugging them aside dislodged plumes of dust, but no hacking cough could deter Kit from wrestling them into submission as her ancestors had restrained wind-filled sails. Sunlight bloomed through the window, highlighting the thousands of swirling dust motes. More importantly, it provided the vital illumination for her photographic experiment.

Setting up her tripod beside the piano, Kit aimed her camera at the portrait over the hearth. The late Lady Cranbrook depicted therein might very well be the spirit who haunted these hallowed halls. A photograph would prove a more portable point of reference than the painting. Once developed, Kit could carry it around in her pocket for quick comparison with any phantoms who might cross her path.

Kit focused the lens, capped it, slid a fresh plate into the camera, uncapped the lens once more, and counted to eight. As she counted, she found her gaze compelled upward to meet the eyes of Alexandra's mother. She wondered what had become of her. What cruel fate befell her. How old Alexandra had been when she found herself orphaned. What must she have felt. Kit knew her own feelings upon the subject of her parents' demise, but for Alexandra... She didn't dare pretend she had the barest inkling of what turmoil surged through Alexandra's heart.

Six, seven, eight. Kit re-capped the lens. In tall, awkward script on the back of the plate, she wrote, *Lady Cranbrook, Music Room.*

Gathering up her equipage once more, Kit considered where else in the house a ghost might dwell. She carried her photographic equipment down the hall, her lips pursed in thought, her eyes upon the carpet before her. The puffed shoulders of her dress-sleeves brushed the walls on either side of the narrow corridor leading away from the music room. They filled her ears with a soft shuffling sound, ebbing and flowing in time with her steps.

Then the shuffling became a scratch.

Kit stumbled to a halt. For a half-second, she believed her sleeves had caught upon the wall somehow, snagged a loose nail and begun to tear. But though her forward progress stopped, the scratching continued. Indeed, it only grew louder as she stood stock-still in the hall. A scraping, scrabbling, desperate sound, inches from her ears, with only the wainscoting separating her cheek from whatever wretched creature scratched so. Whatever had scuttled above her head now crawled right beside her.

Terror stopped her breath. Only her frantic heartbeat pulsing in her ears rivalled the horrible scraping sound. She knew she ought to set up her camera once again, to take what chance she could at capturing the source of the nightmare noise, but her arms clenched compulsively around her tripod, taut muscles trembling with fear. She didn't even dare look, couldn't force her eyes to slide towards the blank wall.

What felt like hours later, but couldn't have been longer than a few seconds, the scratching stopped.

And in its place, right beside Kit's ear, came a ragged breath. The unmistakable hollow gasp of a single, dreadful inhalation. Like a draught in a tomb.

Kit bolted.

CHAPTER ELEVEN

Kit fled down the twisted halls of Heatherhurst, clutching her photography equipment to her chest. She had no heading, no idea of where she might end up. Only a desperate desire to be anywhere other than where she was. Anywhere away from that wretched scratching and bestial breath.

The corridor ahead of her crossed another. She took advantage of the juncture to make a sharp left turn. Doubtless whatever infernal phantom chased her wouldn't be fooled by such childish tactics, but it was the best her terrified mind could conjure.

Until she caught sight of a long-limbed shadow lurching into her path.

There wasn't enough room to dodge in the narrow hall, nor enough space between her and it for her to stop herself from crashing into its lanky form. She screwed her eyes shut and braced herself for the impact.

Rather than a cold darkness enveloping and consuming her, skeletal hands grasped her shoulders, their iron grip halting her in an instant. She was caught. The horrible scratching thing from the walls had emerged to take her as its prisoner.

"Catherine, are you all right?"

Sir Vivian. Her husband. She had, for a few hours, quite forgotten she had a husband. Her ears burned with shame. She opened her eyes.

114

She'd gotten turned around and faced the grand foyer again. The top of the staircase lay just down the hall behind Sir Vivian. He'd been backlit by the high-arched windows in the southern wall. She squinted to make out the expression on his face. Bewilderment, probably.

"Whatever is the matter?" he asked.

"There's something in the ceiling," she blurted. "Something in the walls."

He stared at her. Then, gently, he took the tripod from her arms. She forced her tight-clenched fists to relinquish it. He set it aside, leaning against the wall. He moved so slowly, as if afraid of startling her. As if she weren't already in a full-blown panic.

"There's something in the walls!" she repeated, willing him to listen to her. "I heard a horrible scratching noise, and—"

"Rats," Vivian muttered.

"—and someone *breathing!*" Kit insisted.

"Rats," Vivian said again, louder and more matter-of-fact. "They've plagued us for generations. I suppose they must consider Heatherhurst Hall as much their ancestral home as ours, at this point."

Kit didn't think rats had lungs large enough to draw in the dreadful rattling gasp she'd heard in the wall beside her ear.

"Alexandra told me a bizarre anecdote once," Vivian continued, apparently oblivious to Kit's disbelief. "Have you ever heard of a rat-king?"

Kit shook her head.

"Rather grotesque, I'm afraid. Supposedly when too many rats cluster in an enclosed space, their tails become entangled and grow together, and they must live the rest of their lives all knotted up as one. Those that die are dragged along by the surviving remainder, until, presumably, we are left with a single living rat trailing however many corpses of its fellows behind it. This creature is called a rat-king. According to Alexandra," he added, citing his source as an afterthought.

Kit stared at him.

Vivian coughed. "It's dreadful to think on, but I suppose such a creature must be what you heard scratching in the walls."

"Then we must exterminate them," said Kit.

Vivian's mouth opened and closed wordlessly as he stared at her in what she supposed must be disbelief, though she thought it unwarranted.

"Poison," Kit prompted him. "Or traps. Is there a neighboring farmer who might sell us one of his barn-cats? Perhaps we could hire a rat-catcher to send his terrier through the walls."

This last suggestion seemed to galvanize Vivian. He shot up straight and looked down upon her with a forbidding gaze. "Absolutely not."

Kit, no less bewildered by his refusal, couldn't stop her mouth from asking the most childish of questions. "Why?"

"Why would I refuse to trap a dog in the walls of my house?" Vivian replied. His voice never went quite as arch as his sister's, and thus he couldn't truly be said to scoff, though he still managed to communicate how absurd he found Kit's inquiry.

Kit hadn't thought of that. A poor little puppy, who only wished to please its master, forced into the cramped eaves to do battle with the wretched rat-king... She shuddered. And while she supposed a barn-cat would have a fairer chance in the same place, she didn't wish to condemn any creature to such a fate. "Poison, then. Is there a chemist in the village? Could we procure some arsenic from him?"

Vivian appeared reluctant to consider even this mild solution. It took him a moment to admit, "There is a chemist. Alexandra could procure the poison from him. I'll notify her that you wish to do so."

Kit knew this concession should ease her mind. She contrived to feel relaxed. "Thank you."

A wan smile appeared on Vivian's thin lips. "Forgive my curt answer. As I mentioned before, parts of the house are in dangerous disrepair— particularly the upper floors, where I suspect the rats make much of their home. It'd be a terrible risk for anyone to delve there, even a rat-catcher. Or his dog."

Kit nodded her agreement. Her eyes fell upon the camera she still clutched to her bosom.

Vivian followed her gaze. "What were you photographing, if you don't mind my asking?"

"The music room," Kit said. She didn't think he'd take well to her idea of photographing the haunted hallway.

He cocked his head curiously. "Whatever for?"

"I admire the portrait of..." Kit stopped herself, all-too-late realizing her error. She had no wish to remind him of old wounds, particularly not now, when they'd just come to an understanding.

If the allusion to his late mother bothered him, Vivian disguised it with the stiff upper lip for which his countrymen were famed. "I see."

Desperate to avoid another awkward silence, Kit let her stupid tongue run on. "It's very skillfully painted."

"It's a fair likeness," Vivian admitted, though no light reached his eyes.

"I wanted to photograph the grand staircase next," Kit went on. She had no intention of it before this moment, but the lie felt necessary, if only to move along from a topic painful to them both.

Vivian looked visibly grateful for the change of subject. He picked up her tripod and held out his arm to her. "In that case, may I have the privilege of escorting you down to the foyer?"

Kit forced a smile and wound her hand through his elbow.

They descended the staircase together, arm-in-arm, just as they would for a dinner party or ball. Kit wondered what sort of balls Vivian's ancestors had thrown here in years past. Perhaps Alexandra herself had played hostess to one such party on her brother's behalf. Kit herself had no love of balls; the crushing crowds, the deafening murmur, the unbearable heat of a hundred bodies, the humiliation of never being asked to dance. But then again, she'd never been the hostess. Things would be quite different at a ball held in her honor, at her behest, in her house. If the throng grew too thick, she could retreat at her leisure, her own private bedroom a mere staircase away. And every gentleman guest would vie to fill her dance-card, if only to be polite. She imagined a crowd in the foyer now, the four hundred faces of the Cabot wedding reception turned up to watch her come down on Sir Vivian's arm. Patience Wheeler would stand at the front, boiling over with impotent rage, tongues of jealous flame flying from her cheeks. Everyone would look up at them and wish to be in their place.

And yet, it didn't make Kit happy.

Certainly, there was still some small part of her left over from her boarding school days that wished to see Patience Wheeler get her just desserts. But to have a grand country house and an aristocratic husband didn't fill the hungry void within Kit's chest. Nor would a ball. Who would she even invite if she held one? She didn't have Mrs. Astor's four hundred friends. Lucy had left her. Alexandra despised her. She had no friends at all. Not one.

Perhaps, said a treacherous little voice within her mind, if she were to descend not upon Vivian's arm, but upon Alexandra's...

Kit stumbled. Intent on her own morose thoughts, she hadn't realized the staircase had ended, and, putting her foot down in the expectation of another step, she found floorboards about six inches sooner than antici- pated. Vivian caught and steadied her. She apologized. He demurred.

"Forgive me," Vivian said. "I don't mean to abandon you, only I have pressing business to which I must attend."

"Hiring workmen to repair the roof?" she guessed.

"Yes, of course, that—amongst other things. But to the point, will you be all right if I leave you here alone?"

Kit didn't particularly wish to be alone in the house with the rat-king skittering through the walls. Yet she didn't particularly wish for Vivian's company, either. If, on the other hand, her sister-in-law had offered to remain as her protector... but such an occurrence seemed highly unlikely.

"Yes," Kit lied. "I'll be fine."

Vivian gave her a paternal smile and, with another dry peck to her fore- head, left her alone with her tripod and camera.

Kit forced her fears of the rat-king down to the back of her mind. Again, she set up her tripod, screwed her camera into place upon it, facing the staircase and the shadowy void beneath it. Focusing the lens framed the swooping curve of the staircase. She capped the lens, inserted the prepared plate, uncapped the lens and counted to eight. Each number echoed up to the vaulted ceiling in a chant far less musical than she supposed the monks had delivered in a darker age. Then she capped the lens, removed the plate, and lightly sketched the words *Grand Staircase* on its reverse side.

She turned the plate over again in her hand, considering. It was the last of the plates she'd prepared before she left New Bedford. She'd require glass and chemicals to prepare more, and a whole darkroom besides if she ever wanted to see what the lens of her camera had detected. For the moment, she had none of it. She did, however, have her sketchbooks, her pencils, her charcoal, and her watercolors. More than one way to skin a cat, as Phoebe so grotesquely put it, and more than one way for an artist to capture an image.

It took a quarter-hour for Kit to stow away her camera and tripod in her sea-chest, and another to come down to the foyer again with her drawing materials and her little camp stool. The camera lens had a more limited scope than the human eye. While space permitted barely allowed Kit to get the whole staircase into the camera's frame, she could, through the panoramic lens of her own gaze, capture not only the grand sweep of the stair, but also the foyer floorboards spreading out beneath it, and the vaulted ceiling high above, to give a truer sense of its breathtaking architectural scale. She sat down and began to draw, beginning with the areas where the sun moving across the sky seemed most likely to change the light as the hours passed. The vast expanse of the room amplified the scrap of her pencil against the parchment.

An unearthly growl broke the silence.

Kit bolted upright. Her pencil, clutched in her compulsive fist, scraped a thick black line across her sketch. Her eyes darted wildly about the room.

Another gurgling growl sounded. Not from above her, but from beneath her. Within her.

Her stomach.

Kit dropped her pencil in disgust. Not only was she foolish enough to forget luncheon, but doubly foolish enough to mistake her own digestion for a monster. And she'd ruined her own drawing as a direct result.

Her stomach gurgled again, demanding attention. She pulled her watch from her pocket and realized she'd spent more than two hours absorbed in her craft. The minuscule hands now showed half-past one.

From her childhood to her school-days and on into her life as a grown woman, Kit had become accustomed to being told when to eat. A servant, if not a friend, would come and prompt her, telling her such-and-such a meal was served, and would she please put down her paintbrush or her bicycle or her book or her camera and come to the table?

But at Heatherhurst Hall, she had neither servants nor friends, and as such, with her stomach growling, she found herself at a loss for what to do about it. She hadn't the first notion where she might find the kitchens. She did, however, know where the breakfast room and dining room lay. With any luck, one of these would contain luncheon.

The breakfast-room was empty. Even the sun had long since abandoned the eastward-facing windows, leaving the table and chairs in cold shadow.

In the dining room, she found her husband just tucking into his own repast. Cold meats were laid out on the sideboard, with a single plate and glass already dirtied and set aside for removal to the kitchen.

Vivian, caught with his fork halfway to his mouth, lowered it to greet her. "Catherine! You've just missed Alexandra."

Kit's heart sank unaccountably. She had no reason to regret arriving too late to dine with her sister-in-law. Particularly when arriving too late to breakfast with her own husband had caused her no such consternation. And yet, here she stood, the weight of her disappointment anchoring her to the threshold.

Vivian rose to get her a plate and, when she showed no inclination to take it from him, proceeded to fill it with cold meats on her behalf and set it down beside his own. When he went so far as to pull out the chair for her, what else could she do but sit down? She did so with her mind still whirling with self-reproach. Her appetite suffered in consequence, though she managed at length to clear half of her plate of the heaping portions her husband had handed out to her. Another one of his little idiosyncrasies—unlike most gentlemen, he seemed to believe his wife had a stomach equal to his own. Something to be glad of, surely, for Kit had often gone to bed hungry based on others' assumptions of her appetite. Few correctly estimated the amount of fuel her considerable frame required. At present, she thanked him with a smile. He returned it, though the exchange did nothing to slow down his own consumption, nor did further marital feeling stop him from abandoning her once he'd finished his own meal.

"Business," was all the explanation he gave her as he strolled out of the dining room.

Kit, left alone to poke at her chicken with her fork, found she had no desire to finish it, and set her plate back on the sideboard, stacked atop her sister-in-law's and her husband's dishes. Presumably the cook would come to fetch them. Kit would've happily carried them down to the kitchen herself, if she knew where within the winding halls it lay. Perhaps later she would find both the opportunity and the bravery required to ask Alexandra.

At present, she returned to the foyer. Her sketchbook and stool sat precisely where she left them. She picked them up and resumed her drawing.

Shadows shifted all around her, growing longer, their edges blurring. She entered into the pleasant trance of her craft, a place where she needn't consider what horrid creatures stalked her in the walls, or what hideous phantoms lurked around every corner, or how her sister-in-law hated her. There was only the pencil and the parchment and the beautiful sweeping stair. She hunched over her drawing, her nose inches from the page, and squinted against the growing darkness.

A hand came down upon her shoulder.

CHAPTER TWELVE

Kit shrieked. She leapt up—her sketchbook clattered to the floor, the camp stool flung aside, her pencils scattered—and whirled towards her assailant.

Alexandra stood before her, one hand still outstretched, her eyes wide with astonishment.

They stared at each other for a long moment. Plenty of time for Kit's mind to begin berating her for her own idiocy. What a child she must appear, to scream and shrink from something as simple as a hand on her shoulder. The blotchy blush rushed to her cheeks as she considered what Alexandra must think of her now.

At length, Alexandra recollected herself. "Dinner is served."

"Thank you," Kit replied automatically.

Another awkward silence fell. Kit almost wanted to invite Alexandra to touch her a second time, to prove she would not display such cowardice twice, to show how in fact Alexandra's touch should delight her—but ladies did not say such things aloud. Unable to bear further scrutiny, she dropped her gaze to her hands. She found her fingertips gray with lead, and her skirts flecked with pencil-shavings. New shame washed over her. Surely Alexandra must despise her slovenly appearance almost as much as she despised her skittish overreaction to innocent stimulus.

"I should change," Kit blurted.

Alexandra blinked at her. "Then Vivian and I shall await you in the dining room."

Belatedly, Kit realized changing her dress would mean forcing her husband and sister-in-law to put off their meal. Yet neither could she go in to dine as she was. She felt trapped between two equally wretched solecisms.

"Do you require assistance?" asked Alexandra, motioning towards the mess of Kit's drawing supplies.

"No," Kit hurried to reassure her, stooping to pick up the scattered pieces as she spoke. "I can manage by myself. Thank you."

Alexandra appeared unconvinced, but said only, "Very well," and departed.

Kit quickly snatched up her belongings and retreated upstairs to the master bedroom. She scrubbed the lead from her fingertips and threw on a gown more appropriate to the evening. Then she descended the grand staircase alone.

To Kit, going down to dinner for the second time in her new house felt no less terrifying than it had the first night. Indeed, rathermoreso, now that she knew spirits haunted the halls and both siblings seemed set against her.

Despite this, as she entered the dining room, she tried to cheer herself with the reminder that Alexandra had come to find her, rather than eat another meal without her. Probably at her brother's behest, yet still she had come. Kit resolved to continue being as cheerful as possible and give no reason for Alexandra to dislike her further.

Kit took her seat at her blithely smiling husband's right hand. Alexandra exiled herself to the other end of the table. The meal commenced in silence and continued on in kind. Kit flinched from the clinking of her own knife and fork; they reverberated so loud through the sepulchral atmosphere. Neither of the Cranbrook siblings seemed to notice.

The first course gave way to the second course. As Vivian carved the roast, Kit balled her fists in her skirts and willed herself to be courageous, to find the scrap of will left to her by her whaling ancestors and speak. Her grandfathers could sing out for a whale. Surely she could find her voice in a dining room.

"Alexandra," Kit forced out. "Perhaps you would accompany me down to the village tomorrow?"

Vivian paused in the midst of dispensing a slice of the roast onto Kit's plate.

Alexandra turned her piercing gaze upon her. In icy tones, she replied, "Whatever for?"

"I'd like to begin inquiries for hiring staff," Kit answered. She managed to keep her voice from wavering, though she couldn't help the white-knuckled grip she kept upon her knife. "Interview some of the village girls and see if they might be willing to become housemaids."

"Housemaids?" echoed Alexandra, as if the concept were purest absurdity.

"Or scullery-maids," Kit hastened to add. "Or—or whatever post you think we ought to fill first."

Alexandra gave her a slow, catlike blink, then rolled her eyes towards her brother.

Vivian coughed. "You shall have to work this out between yourselves. I don't intend to involve myself in household matters."

Alexandra's jaw clenched as she turned back to Kit. "And who, pray tell, is to pay the wages of this staff?"

She pronounced the word "staff" as if it were foreign to her and tasted bitter upon her tongue.

Kit steadied herself and answered, "I am."

Both siblings stared at her.

"I've a considerable independence," Kit continued, feeling as though she were babbling. Nothing she was saying could possibly come as a surprise to the Cranbrooks. If Vivian hadn't married her for her money, then Kit hadn't the first idea why he'd bothered bringing her here to this ramshackle old house. A house which could be beautiful, if... "It will pay for the tradesmen to fix the roof and for the staff to keep the property in order."

Alexandra broke her dumbstruck stare with a dismissive cluck of her tongue. "I'm afraid you sorely underestimate the expense of servants."

"And I'm afraid," Kit replied, "you sorely underestimate the depths of my coffers!"

The instant those words left her lips, she regretted them. Only a crass American would be so gauche as to brag about her bank accounts. Such behavior might suit Patience Wheeler, but Kit felt a hot flush blooming from her throat to her ears. She dropped her gaze to her plate, not wanting to see what expressions of dismay or disgust might cross Alexandra's face in response to her brash *faux pas*. Silence fell in its wake and stretched out for an unbearably long moment.

Surely Vivian or Alexandra would say something—anything—but what broke the tension wasn't words. Instead, Kit heard the clink of knife and fork against porcelain. Under her lashes, she glanced towards her husband and perceived he had resumed his meal as if no solecism or harsh speech had ever interrupted it.

Bewildered by his indifference, Kit dared to raise her head and see what on earth Alexandra thought of it all, if anything.

The instant she lifted her eyes, she met Alexandra's gaze, burning into her heart like a brand.

Kit quickly dropped her head again, to the much less intimidating sight of her own knuckles clenched white around her fork. Bracing herself, she forced out, "It is for your sake as much as my own, Alexandra. I know how much work it must be for you to keep this house in order. You shouldn't have to—it's too much for any one person—so perhaps if we had hired help..."

She trailed off, once again surreptitiously peering through her lashes to gauge the effect of her words. As much to her astonishment as to her relief, she found Alexandra's expression had softened. Just a touch. Enough to make her seem less like an ancient goddess sitting in judgment of a lowly sacrifice, and more human.

The moment their eyes met, Alexandra dropped her gaze to her plate and resumed carving her roast. In lofty tones, she replied, "I see no reason why we might not take our exercise tomorrow by going down to the village.

Kit's heart soared. She bit her lip to contain a gleeful smile—the first to strike her ever since her arrival to Heatherhurst Hall.

Vivian fetched wine from the sideboard and refreshed his own drink. He then bent the bottle towards Kit's half-empty glass.

"Husband," she said impulsively. "Is there any place within the house where I might set up a darkroom for my photography?"

Vivian, holding the wine bottle poised to pour, stopped as if he himself were captured mid-gesture by a camera. He exchanged a speaking glance with his sister. A single drop fell from the bottleneck into Kit's glass.

"I need only space," Kit added, desperate to fill the void. "And very little of it. Anywhere without much natural light. Perhaps there's a cellar...?"

Vivian chortled, softly, breathlessly, and without mirth. "I'm afraid my mechanical hobbies have quite filled every corner of the house below-ground."

Not the basement, then. Kit didn't dare ask about the attic. But she needed somewhere to develop her photographs. To bring proof of her nightmares to light. In pleading tones, she replied, "Any cupboard will do, really."

Vivian hesitated, another look flashing between him and his sister, before he responded. "I'm sure we may find someplace suitable on the morrow."

An affirmative, in so many words. A yes. A victory. Kit flashed a genuine smile at her husband, then settled down to drink her wine quietly like a good little girl. She could be a suitable wife if she applied herself. No matter what her finishing school classmates had grimly foretold.

Alexandra retrieved the pudding from the sideboard and passed it on to her brother to dispense. Kit felt like a child enjoying a high treat. For once, the sweetness didn't turn to bitter ash upon her tongue. She could enjoy herself. Perhaps even relax. The silence didn't feel nearly so oppressive as it had at the beginning of the meal. Now it seemed almost companionable.

Alexandra, having delicately polished off her pudding, set her spoon down upon her empty plate with an echoing clink. "Vivian, would you be so kind as to remain with me after you've finished?"

Flying high on her successes, Kit couldn't stop herself from blurting,

"If you require help in clearing the table, I'm happy to render my assistance."

The moment the words left her lips, she wished she could snatch them back.

Both siblings jerked their heads towards her, like twin ravens, blinking in astonished inquiry.

Alexandra's voice cut through the deafening silence like a knife. "I wish to speak to my brother alone."

Icicles dripped from her words, sharp enough to pierce Kit's heart. Like a dove struck mid-flight by cruel arrows, it plunged into her stomach, sinking like a stone, dragging her spirit down with it.

Vivian gave her a tight smile. "Go on upstairs. I'll be along shortly."

Sent to her room like a disruptive child. Hot shame burned all over her face and neck. She blinked back the tears pricking her eyes, nodded, and darted from the room, fleeing as much from Alexandra's fuming rage as from her own folly.

Alexandra had the opportunity for bitter regret as she saw the effect her words had upon Kit. To watch tears prick those deep brown eyes, to see her scamper away like a frightened child, to know that her own false tongue had caused such a beautiful creature so much pain—it brought a surge of rage to Alexandra's heart, which she unjustly turned upon her brother. Never mind that he had dismissed his bride at Alexandra's own request, and couldn't have possibly spoken any gentler to her. She rounded upon him with renewed self-righteous fury.

"I'm not doing it again," she declared.

"Doing what?" Vivian asked in a tone of total bewilderment.

Of course he hadn't noticed. All her efforts were beneath his notice. Just as the strain of a steamship's boiler was beneath the notice of the first-class passengers who strolled across the upper decks, and only noticed how smooth their passage had been when choppy waters disturbed it.

Alexandra clenched her teeth. "Lying to her. Pretending not to know what she means when she speaks of a wraith haunting the halls. Telling her she's seeing things or going mad, or that she's forbidden from the attic because of falling beams, and not because—!"

"Enough!"

Alexandra had begun in a whisper, but each word had risen in volume despite herself, until, by the time her brother cut her off, she had come very near to screaming. Even she had to admit he'd done right in silencing her. Voices carried through empty halls.

Yet in silencing her, Vivian seemed to have spent all his reserves of courage, for now that she'd held her tongue, he brought his hands up to his face and covered his eyes like a child, as if he could escape her notice if only he couldn't see her. He shook his head in his palms, his shoulders shaking with repressed sobs.

Alexandra might've pitied him, if he hadn't exhausted her sympathies years ago. "I'll not lie to her again. If she asks me direct, I will tell her the whole. You may keep your own secrets. I want no part of it."

"Please," Vivian whispered through his fingers.

Years of repression and silence boiled over in Alexandra's breast. Now that she'd finally confronted the subject, she found her tongue could not be stopped. "I'll tell her about Mother and Father—about your machine— about your failures—!"

"—and see me clapped in irons!" Vivian jerked his head up at last to confront her with wide, wet eyes. "Is that what you want? Two years hard labor and a disgrace that can be wiped clean only through self-destruction!?"

Alexandra choked on her own taunts. No, she didn't want that. For all his faults—all his sins—she knew she couldn't bear the sight of her own brother, her only living family, sent down to serve a prison sentence for the least of all his crimes.

Vivian pressed his advantage. "If not for my sake, then for the sake of—!"

She stopped him with an upraised hand, warding off the name. They'd not spoken it aloud in years. They dared not. No matter how empty the halls of Heatherhurst. She didn't need to hear it now. Not with her brother's bride in the house. They knew of whom they spoke. Alexandra suffered enough guilt without the invoking of a name. She steadied herself with a shuddering breath. "For all our sakes."

Vivian sighed in unmistakable relief and gave her a wan smile.

Alexandra did not return it. "I will keep my silence, if you become a better husband."

Confusion overtook Vivian's features once more.

Alexandra had already wasted many hours wishing her brother might become as adept in understanding people as he was in understanding machines. She didn't waste another minute on it before explaining her demands. "Tomorrow, I will humor her by accompanying her to the village. While we are gone, you will clear out a room in the basement for her photography."

"You mustn't think I begrudge her anything," Vivian began, "but my work—"

"—will contrive to take up less space than it does now. All she wants is a little room for her chemical processes. A cupboard will do. And you will give it to her."

All attempt at levity had flown from Vivian's features. He replied stiffly, "Will the wine cellar suffice?"

"It will."

"Then she may have it," Vivian concluded, his words clipped.

A good little sister would thank him and bid him good-night. Alexandra merely turned on her heel and retreated to her own chambers without once looking back.

All the while, her mind raced.

She had, of course, considered the problem before she and Vivian had ever set out for America to find an heiress. She'd prepared their lies, ironed out all the wrinkles in their story. But she hadn't accounted for the pangs of conscience that would come with imparting such lies to Kit. She hadn't accounted for Kit at all. And how could she?

How could she have predicted falling in love with her brother's bride?

She could have lied to Patience Wheeler easily—would have relished in doing so—because she despised Patience Wheeler. One did not live with such a person; one lived around them, and managed them, and bore their annoyances with stoicism, soothed by the knowledge that one was superior.

Alexandra had full awareness of her own hypocrisy. Which only made it that much harder to bear. Love had made her stupid. Love had frayed her steely nerves to the point of snapping, had forced her to question her own behavior, had made her look within herself and realize she had grown as much a monster as any malevolent spirit lurking within the crumbling edifice of Heatherhurst Hall. Her own selfishness had made her unworthy of Kit.

And it only made her love Kit all the more.

Stalwart. Resilient. Refusing to buckle under the weight of the Cranbrook family's sin. Always working to better not only her own circumstances, but Vivian's and Alexandra's—no matter how hard they used her. Ever searching for the solution. Never once giving in, no matter how she might fail, but scrambling up again with a new thought, a new idea, a new hope for compromise and peace.

If Kit could keep her efforts up without faltering, even the tight-knit lies of Heatherhurst couldn't withstand her assault for long. She'd unravel everything. Alexandra almost hoped she would.

But if Kit did succeed—if she took up her righteous sword and cut through the Gordian knot of deceit—then what she found amongst the resulting wreckage would turn her away from Heatherhurst Hall forever.

CHAPTER THIRTEEN

As she had every morning since her arrival to Heatherhurst Hall, Kit awoke alone.

More curious still, she'd fallen asleep alone as well. She didn't begrudge Vivian his work—from the state of his study, he seemed to have plenty of it—but she had thought he might rouse her when he came to bed some hours after her.

No doubt Vivian, acutely aware of his new bride's misery, whether or not he discerned its true cause, had elected to give her space and time to heal before he made marital demands upon her. Or perhaps he simply didn't want children so early in their marriage. The result suited her well enough regardless, so she expended no more thought in pondering the mystery, and instead turned her attention to her toilette.

Through her years at finishing school, Kit had grown accustomed to dressing herself. She missed Diana's assistance, of course, and her company as well, but unlike some young ladies of her station, she was not rendered helpless for lack of a maid. Her artist's eye, or so Lucy had said, allowed her to pick her wardrobe with more care than certain persons whose taste might charitably be described as shocking—Patience Wheeler, for example, whose complexion was not at all shown justice by the vivid pinks and yellows she insisted upon for her dresses.

This morning, Kit selected an olive green morning dress with a brown lace shawl. Muted earth colors, sober and inoffensive. Nothing flashy, no bright jewel tones or sparkling satins or enormous stuffed birds precariously balanced on preposterous hats. Nothing like the American New Woman. Nothing to offend Alexandra. Though, Kit supposed, Alexandra might not mind the fashion of stuffed birds upon hats. Indeed, if what Kit had seen of her workroom proved any indication, were Alexandra not the daughter of a baronet, she might make a very capable milliner.

These thoughts saw Kit out of the master bedroom—her bedroom—down the halls to the foyer, where she descended the grand staircase with little incident but, so she imagined, far less grace than any of her predecessors. She'd never yet mastered the delicate feminine step. Her long feet clomped like the hooves of a goat, a noise she knew must be muffled by her skirts, yet nevertheless sounded loud as a thunderclap in her own ears, a sensation not alleviated by the echoing emptiness of the front hall, with its vaulted ceiling towering above her.

She reached the ground floor under a cloud of self-loathing, and, with her gaze focused upon the floorboards, caught a flicker of motion in her peripheral vision. Instinct turned her head towards it.

There, by the opposing wall, stood a woman.

"Oh!" Kit cried, startled.

The woman appeared likewise astonished, even going so far as to put one hand upon her breast in alarm just as Kit did. Not only that, but she had on a strikingly similar olive green dress, and her own brown lace shawl. Furthermore, her square jaw and pointed chin…

Kit's self-loathing redoubled as she realized she'd come face-to-face with her own reflection, and in the most telling symptom of her own stupidity yet, failed to recognize it.

She approached the mirror, hardly able to bear the sight of her own figure drawing nearer and nearer, and cursing herself under her breath all the while. Her failure to notice it before now did not long remain a mystery. On the floor beneath it lay a crumpled pile of moth-eaten velvet, the remains of a curtain that had just yesterday hung on the gilt rod above the mirror. The true puzzle was how such a frail remnant of cloth had stayed up so long in the first place. Kit made an attempt at re-hanging the curtain, but the velvet disintegrated in her fingers, and she dared not try further, lest her clumsy efforts destroy some precious heirloom of the estate. She dropped the remainder onto the floor where she'd found it.

As she straightened, the mirror again caught her eye. She'd dressed in her own mirror upstairs—her husband's mirror, really, a full-length piece probably older than the both of them combined—but couldn't resist the siren song of self-doubt that demanded she look over her presentation once more. She locked eyes with her own reflection, critically examining her square jaw, her snub nose, her stringy hair. Every piece of her person that Patience Wheeler and the rest had torn to shreds at finishing school.

Feeling herself spiral down into dark memories, she forcibly wrenched her mind away and turned her gaze to her wardrobe. The olive green dress —drab, but unobjectionable. Its cut had nothing in it to offend even the most prudish of mothers. The brown lace shawl—lace was extravagant, but brown a suitably sober shade. Again she found herself hoping Alexandra would approve. Even mere approval seemed an unattainable goal. She dared not hope Alexandra might enjoy the sight of her, no matter how she was attired.

It occurred to her that not since Lucy's wedding had she put so much effort into her appearance for the sake of someone who cared so little. Heartbreak compounded upon heartbreak, and yet she couldn't stop herself. She was compelled again and again to try and mold herself into something more pleasing. Something that someone could love. Tears pricked at her eyes. She blinked them away.

And as she blinked, she saw a flicker of movement in the mirror.

Kit jerked her head up to look over her reflection's shoulder. There, behind her twinned image, was a veiled woman walking across the foyer, from the base of the stair to the dining room door.

Ashamed to have a witness to her foolish sorrows, Kit whirled around, an apology already on her lips.

No one was there.

Kit blinked stupidly at the empty foyer. She'd seen someone. She felt sure of it. The figure had even appeared familiar, had reminded her of the woman she'd glimpsed in the music room the other day. The same yellow dress. The same veil.

"Who's there?" she called, her voice cracking.

Her inquiry echoed up to the vaulted ceiling without answer.

Unbearably conscious of how much noise she made with every foot-step, Kit crept across the foyer to the dining room, towards which the apparition had seemed to head. She arrived at an empty room, holding only the long table and its matched chairs, the little-used sideboard, and utterly bereft of life, human or otherwise. Nevertheless, Kit made a full circuit of the table, peering into every possible nook and cranny. She found only cobwebs.

Forced to admit defeat, she departed the dining room for the breakfast room, her head in a whirl all the while. Perhaps the dim light reflecting in her own tears had created the illusion of someone else in the mirror. A weak hypothesis, she knew, but the best she could manage with her own talents. Try as she might, she didn't have her cousin's scientific mind. Other possibilities seemed weaker still. Alexandra didn't wear veils indoors—Kit might not know her sister-in-law as well as she'd like, but she at least knew that—and Kit doubted the cook wore a veil at all. Nor did Vivian wear veils or dresses, at least not to Kit's knowledge. Besides, the figure in yellow had been far shorter than her husband's six-foot frame. Shorter than Kit herself; closer to an average woman's height.

Kit arrived in the breakfast room still bewildered. Vivian had gone, his empty plates the only hint of his former presence. Alexandra remained, doubtless waiting for Kit to join her before their walk down to the village. The sight of Alexandra sitting down to breakfast alone, in a blue gown without a veil, confirmed Kit's assertion that the figure in yellow had not been her sister-in-law. Nor did Alexandra appear in any way winded or unkempt, as one might expect from a person who'd just dashed around the house to change all her clothes in secret. She did, however, appear vexed. Kit immediately apologized for coming down late to breakfast, in the hopes that such an offering might appease her sister-in-law. Instead, Alexandra curtly informed Kit that she had nothing to apologize for. Kit chose to focus on the meaning of the words themselves rather than the implications of the tone in which they were delivered and sat down to another silent breakfast of rubbery eggs and burnt bacon. She ate her share with ladylike haste, eager to get on the road—though whether she hurried in desperation to escape the haunted halls or in eagerness for the opportunity to prove herself to Alexandra, she couldn't say.

The grandfather clock chimed quarter-past the hour. Alexandra stacked the dirty dishes on the sideboard and marched out into the foyer. Kit followed cautiously, her eyes flicking back and forth across the empty expanse of the front hall. But no veiled figure appeared.

A dreadful creak tore through the air. Kit flinched from the sound and whirled to find Alexandra opening the front door. She turned an inquiring glance upon Kit but said nothing, merely walking out in silence, leaving the door open behind her. Kit passed through in her wake and, with some effort, tugged the door shut. The muffled echo of the impact resounded through the thick oak.

As she stepped out into the courtyard, her heels crunching on gravel like crushed bone, Kit thought of her bicycle lying forgotten in the master bedroom beside the rest of her luggage. How foolish her daydreams seemed now, her hopes of teaching Alexandra to ride and turning circles 'round the fountain together. How childish to suppose that a lady such as Alexandra would consent to sit upon her handlebars and whoop with glee and wild freedom.

Still, it seemed ridiculous to expect a woman of Alexandra's station to walk the two miles to town. Her consequence required a carriage, or at the very least, a horse. But the stables, or what Kit could see of them from the front of the house, appeared half-collapsed. Her imagination ran on regardless, granting her a vision of Alexandra on horseback. How graceful she would appear in a riding habit and top hat, a crop in one hand and reins in the other. Kit's mind went further still, picturing the top hat flying off in the course of a frantic chase, and Alexandra's wild raven locks flying behind her as her steed leapt ahead.

"Will you be coming presently?"

The inquiry jolted Kit from her reverie. She found herself standing stock-still in the middle of the courtyard, and Alexandra already some yards ahead, having paused in the walk to turn over her shoulder and question Kit's dawdling. The severe arch of Alexandra's magnificently-sculpted brow made Kit's heart stutter in her chest. She blurted some excuse and trotted to catch up. Alexandra waited until the instant they stood neck-and-neck before setting off again.

Wind whistled across the vast empty moor. At first Kit kept her eye upon the landscape, but the bleak expanse turned her eye inexorably towards her traveling companion. Amongst the monotonous grays and browns of land and sky alike, Alexandra's blue dress stood out as a sparkling sapphire, appearing all the more precious for its dull surroundings. To say nothing of the noble figure clothed within it.

Alexandra's eyes glanced her way, and Kit realized she'd been staring.

"I like your dress," Kit blurted.

Alexandra's footsteps stuttered to a halt, and she turned to face Kit with a look of bewilderment. After a moment, in which Kit had ample opportunity to berate herself, Alexandra replied, "Thank you."

"You're welcome," said Kit, the words automatic, as if she read her script directly out of an etiquette manual.

Alexandra resumed walking but continued looking at Kit. At length, she said, "Your dress brings out your eyes."

Kit, who knew her eyes to be as dull a brown as her lace shawl, took the comment as the subtle insult it was doubtless meant to be. Still, she refused to give in, and said only, "Thank you. I unpacked it this morning."

A single line creased the space between Alexandra's thick-sculpted eyebrows. "I didn't realize you hadn't yet unpacked."

Kit blushed. A few more steps passed in silence.

"Do you require assistance in unpacking?" Alexandra asked.

Kit's blush deepened. She couldn't decide which was worse; that Alexandra considered her incompetent in something so simple as unpacking without a maid, or the prospect of Alexandra going through her sea-chest and judging each and every article her perfect fingertips touched. With great effort, Kit forced out a quiet, "No, thank you."

Alexandra appeared to take this refusal in stride.

Not looking forward to another prolonged and awkward silence, Kit blurted, "It's probably in my blood."

Alexandra's flinty eyes widened.

Kit hurried to explain her bizarre comment. "My ancestors lived out of their sea-chests for years at a time. There's no such thing as unpacking on a whaleship."

A curious tremor passed over Alexandra's face. The corners of her mouth seemed particularly affected. At length, she replied, "I hope you need not feel driven to such extremities here at Heatherhurst Hall. We are quite land-locked."

So Kit had observed. She had to admit it felt somewhat eerie to hear no calling of gulls. Though even the most homesick daughter of New Bedford couldn't miss the stench of low tide.

Turning to the surrounding landscape to keep the conversation going, her eye fell upon a patch of crimson in the otherwise brown moor. What-ever-it-was lay just a few yards off the path, and drew closer with every step. It seemed, at first, the outcropping of an underground boulder, but as Kit squinted at it, she realized its mottled texture and curious color were both borne of rust, and the object itself must therefore be of iron, or steel. Grass and scrub grew over, around, and through it, making its already unfathomable shape all the more twisted and inscrutable.

"What is that?" Kit asked, pointing at the undefined hulk.

Alexandra glanced at her, followed the gesture to its terminus, then snapped her attention back to the road ahead, her movements as rapid and precise as if commanded by clockwork. In clipped words, she replied, "I don't know."

Kit dropped her arm to her side again and declined to press the issue further. She caught sight of more bizarre rusted remains on the moor— two even further off than the first, and one quite near to the road—but turned her eyes away in a pale imitation of Alexandra's blind deter-mination.

At length, the village itself came into view. The quaint collection of cottages and storefronts had hardly held her attention when her husband had brought her through it on her way to her new home; her focus had been solely upon the future, in eager anticipation of seeing Alexandra again. Now, with Alexandra by her side, and knowing full well how little regard Alexandra held for her, she saw it all quite clearly. Kit imagined it might've passed for picturesque in earlier times. Now, the weathered wood and thatch had turned the same shade of gray as the stones, and all seemed about to buckle under the weight of the oppressive gloom.

Alexandra strode on. If she perceived the dark atmosphere hanging over the village, she did not pay it any heed. Kit hurried after her. If nothing else, the buildings offered some small protection against the howling wind of the moor.

People did not flood the streets as they might in Boston or even New Bedford, but neither were Kit and Alexandra alone in their excursion to the village. Farmers and townsfolk alike bustled from storefront to storefront, their eyes flickering in faint recognition as they alighted upon the ladies, then hurrying on their way.

Kit had expected stares. She'd certainly caught eyes on her first trip through the village, despite Vivian's efforts at expediency. Everyone wanted a look at the baronet's new bride. She could hardly begrudge them that much.

But she had not expected whispers.

Whispers followed them through the village, some behind weather-beaten hands, and more hissed between clenched teeth just barely after she and Alexandra had passed out of earshot.

Alexandra, meanwhile, appeared to take no notice of the sparks of gossip catching wind and flaring across the village like wildfire. She moved through the village like a bark through a tempest, plunging forward with quick, sure-footed strides, and her sharp chin held high as a ship's figurehead cresting over the waves.

Kit could only attempt a pale imitation of her sister-in-law's evident confidence. Her eyes betrayed her, flicking across her unfamiliar surroundings in desperate search of recognizable landmarks, whilst deftly avoiding meeting the gaze of any passers-by. She recognized, or thought she did, a butcher shop, a bakery, a general store, and a bar—or rather, a public house.

Above one particular door, a cast-iron hand protruded, holding an elaborately decorated key as long as its own arm. The trade sign was beautifully crafted, though weather-beaten and spotted with rust.

"Is that the locksmith?" Kit asked softly, hardly daring to draw Alexandra's attention.

"Indeed," Alexandra replied coolly. "Our sojourn is at an end."

Kit entered the locksmith's shop in Alexandra's wake. Behind the counter stood a mountain of a man, whose bulk blocked the smithing half of his business from view.

"Good morning, Miss Cranbrook," said the locksmith, with a curious glance at Kit.

Alexandra returned the greeting and, with a gesture at Kit, announced, "Lady Cranbrook."

The locksmith's eyes widened for an instant before he resumed a more professional expression to direct a deferential nod towards Kit.

Kit stammered out an appropriate response. She'd not heard her new title aloud since the Atlantic crossing, and she hadn't grown any more used to it in the interim. She didn't feel like a Lady Cranbrook. She hardly felt like a lady. Her American independence recoiled from the concept of aristocracy, and quite apart from that, she had not a drop of blue blood in her veins. It seemed absurd that she, who had a title only as a courtesy from her marriage, should be treated with more deference than Alexandra, who not only had a hereditary connection to it, but also far more regal carriage than Kit could ever hope to possess. And yet, as matters stood, Kit was addressed with all the ceremony of a queen, and Alexandra greeted with all the regard of a schoolgirl.

"Lady Cranbrook," Alexandra continued to the locksmith, "will require a copy of the housekeys."

So saying, she detached the ring of keys from her chatelaine and laid it out upon the counter. The locksmith picked them up—they looked particularly delicate when clenched in his meaty fist—and promised her they'd be done in little over an hour, if she cared to wait. Alexandra demurred, saying they had other errands to attend in town and would return for the keys afterwards. Kit barely had time to murmur farewell before she found herself dragged from the locksmith's shop, not by any physical assertion on Alexandra's part, but by the wake of her parting, as a whaleboat would be pulled into the wake of its ship.

They next stopped at the post office—or depot, as the English termed it. Other small details stuck out to Kit as incongruous, reminding her how she stood on unfamiliar shores, in a place to which she never would and never could belong.

"Miss Cranbrook," said the clerk in a monotone.

Alexandra bid the clerk good-morning and introduced Kit once again as Lady Cranbrook. Kit murmured a politeness in response to the clerk's deferential nod.

"Any mail for Heatherhurst Hall?" Alexandra asked, her self-possessed speech in no way altered by the cool reception.

The clerk shook his head. "No, miss."

Kit's heart sank. No one had written her. Not even Mr. Mudge. All her letters to Phoebe remained unanswered. Doubtless her cousin remained far too busy with medical school to write. Or perhaps she did not understand Kit's new address. It had taken Kit herself several attempts to grow accustomed to the idea of shires in place of states, and living in a house without a number, or even a real street.

"Is there a letter addressed to Miss Morgan?" she asked. "Miss Catherine Morgan," if Mr. Mudge had been the one to write, "or Kit Morgan?" For Phoebe always called her Kit.

The clerk's bushy eyebrows rose, as did Alexandra's sculpted ones.

A blush came to Kit's cheek, but she swallowed her discomfort to elaborate on her point. "It's my maiden name. My family haven't quite got used to..." The phrase "my title" felt wrong on her tongue, so she amended her explanation. "...to calling me a Cranbrook."

No sooner had the words dropped from her lips than she saw, from the astonishment evident in both Alexandra's face and the clerk's, that what she'd said was worse than what she'd avoided saying. The corners of Alexandra's lips twitched, as if she repressed open-mouthed shock, or worse, a laugh at Kit's stupidity.

"I'm afraid not, my lady," said the clerk, drawing her attention away from Alexandra's face. "Though I'll be sure to keep an eye out for any such letters addressed as you describe."

"Thank you," Kit forced out around the shameful lump in her throat.

"Yes, thank you," Alexandra echoed tightly. Then, in a gesture Kit couldn't help interpreting as merciful, she added, "Good-bye," and, taking Kit firmly by the elbow, steered her out of the post office.

The wind off the moor chilled Kit's flaming cheeks. Instinct told her to turn to Alexandra and apologize for her solecisms, her awkward nature, her total inability to carry on a normal human conversation in public. But she knew even this would be a wrong move. Polite society didn't acknowledge mistakes in public. They would, however, rake them over and over again in private, hissing behind fans or closed doors how, yet again, that little blonde idiot had said something which could not be believed. She could almost hear those whispers now, the tiny hairs on the nape of her neck standing straight at the thought of the infernal hisses of gossip. No, Kit couldn't say anything to dig herself out of the grave her own words had buried her in. The only thing she could do going forward would be to button her lips and bite her tongue.

Alexandra led the way across the street to the chemist. Kit followed a few steps behind, wishing a runaway carriage would take the corner on two wheels and smash her to pieces where she walked. She had no such luck, arriving at her destination safe and sound, with Alexandra waiting for her upon the threshold. Alexandra served her a quizzical look before going inside. Kit ducked in after her.

The chemist's shop at least offered a facsimile of familiarity. For Kit, the sharp tang of concoctions and components brought forth memories of her earliest experiences procuring the necessary supplies to develop photographs, with Phoebe by her side, and Phoebe ordering a few more questionable ingredients of her own for the purposes of home experimentation. Even the chemist himself appeared much like his American counterpart, down to his bottle-brush mustache and the garters of his shirtsleeves.

"Miss Cranbrook," he said, as everyone else they'd met that morning had done.

Alexandra greeted him by name, introduced Kit as Lady Cranbrook, and wasted no further time in making her request in the plainest possible speech. "Rat poison."

The chemist blinked at her, then flicked his beady eyes towards Kit, as if in warning.

"Arsenic green, if you have it," Alexandra elaborated, as if a misunderstanding were what prevented him from fulfilling her order. "It worked well enough for the Parisian sewers. I suppose it should serve for Heatherhurst."

After another moment's pause, the chemist informed her that, regrettably, he had none of Paris green, but he did indeed have more conventional arsenic compounds which would do just as well, if not better. Alexandra assented to the substitution. As the chemist turned to begin carefully counting out the grains of poison, she turned to Kit.

"Did you know," she said in an offhanded fashion, "there are some people who call arsenic 'inheritance powder'?"

Kit, glancing past Alexandra, saw the chemist behind her pause in his measurements, turn to look over his shoulder at Alexandra, and then, very slowly, resume his task.

Stifling an unseemly snort of laughter—surely not the reaction Alexandra hoped to invoke—Kit replied, "I did not know."

Alexandra seemed unaccountably disappointed in Kit's response, but before Kit could beg her forgiveness, she shrugged and said only, "Well, now you do."

With that, she turned away from Kit to watch the chemist at his work.

Kit wondered, but dared not ask, if Alexandra were a regular customer of the chemist. She supposed she must be, if only for the sake of her status as an amateur taxidermist. Formaldehyde was not so easily concocted in the home. At least, she didn't presume so.

"Is there anything else, my lady?" the chemist asked.

"Yes," Kit blurted, pushing down the discomfort of being addressed by a title. "Do you have any developing solution? For a photographic darkroom?"

The chemist seemed relieved for the opportunity to dispense something other than bare-faced poison. He gathered together the necessary components, all the while uttering instructions as to their use, and warnings as to their mis-use. Kit nodded along, forcing a smile as she listened to the litany she had known by heart for years. At length, he finished both his recital and his dispensing. Alexandra tucked their purchases into her basket and, bidding good-bye to the chemist, indicated Kit should follow her out into the lane once again.

It was a matter of minutes to turn their steps back to the locksmith's shop. More villagers passed them on their way, and Kit found her gaze lingering upon what little she could glimpse of their faces as they turned away.

Alexandra, meanwhile, strode straight towards the locksmith's door.

Kit hung back. Alexandra stopped on the threshold and turned back with an eyebrow gracefully arched in expectation.

"Perhaps," said Kit, struck with inspiration and attempting to disguise it, "I might wait outside whilst you conduct your business. The village is quite beautiful, in its own way. I should like to sketch a little of it if time permits."

Alexandra's arch look softened. Kit expected her to scoff, or to demand her presence within the locksmith's shop. But Alexandra merely nodded and slipped inside without another word.

Alone, Kit turned from the locksmith's door to the rest of the village. She took out her memorandum book and a pencil and drew a few idle lines to represent the cast-iron hand and key. Her attention, however, was not on the drawing, but on the villagers wandering past. As they stared at her, she cast surreptitious looks back at them. A few noticed and hurried on. Most did not. One particular cluster looked promising; a man and his wife with their two daughters, between fourteen and nineteen by Kit's guess. They had just emerged from the general store and walked by the locksmith, presumably on their way home. As they passed by Kit, she lifted her head from her sketching and attempted to catch the wife's eye.

The moment their gazes locked, the wife ducked her head, and, catching her daughters by their elbows, made to hurry them along past Kit. The husband, however, stopped before her and doffed his cap. Kit wondered if he intended it as a sacrificial gesture, to distract the predatory aristocrat from her prey.

Kit introduced herself as best she could, pronouncing the words "Lady Cranbrook" with only the barest hint of a stammer, and inquired as to the farmer's name.

"Brown, my lady," he replied.

"Mr. Brown," said Kit, perhaps too quickly in her eagerness to establish a rapport with her tenants. "I am looking for girls to work as maids at

Heatherhurst Hall. Would perhaps your daughters, or anyone of your acquaintance, be willing to fill these positions?"

Mr. Brown appeared abashed. "Beggin' your pardon, my lady, but I'd lief as not send any o' mine up to the big house. Precious few ever came back."

Kit's response died on her tongue. Unless she very much mistook him, the farmer had just implied that other villagers had gone up to work at Heatherhurst Hall in the past. Yet now, none remained. Where had they gone, if they hadn't returned home to their families? The image of the wailing wraith flashed through her mind. Perhaps it had once been a villager. And perhaps it wasn't alone.

Never apt at disguising her emotions, she knew some of her fear had shown in her features, for she found her trepidation mirrored in the farmer's face.

"I meant no offense," he hastened to add. "Weren't nobody's fault what happened. But after such an accident as that, folks're bound to shy away from givin' o'er their children for work up there."

Kit, her heart seizing with fear, forced out the words, "What accident?"

The farmer's eyes widened. He opened his mouth, began his answer in a halting stammer—then his gaze flicked towards something over her shoulder, and he shut his mouth so sharp and quick she feared he'd bite off his own tongue.

Kit turned around to find Alexandra standing behind her.

"Good morning, Mr. Brown," Alexandra said to the farmer in a far warmer tone than Kit had heard her use in all her time at Heatherhurst Hall. And yet there remained a wistfulness to her words, a sorrowful tinge to her greeting, as if she knew it wouldn't be returned in the spirit in which it was offered.

And indeed, like every other villager they'd encountered in their excursion, the farmer, Mr. Brown, held his mouth in a firm line as he bowed his head, tugged at his forelock in reply, and continued on his way.

A curious look flickered across Alexandra's features. For an instant, Kit thought it might've been regret, or sorrow. But she quickly assured herself it could be nothing more than resignation.

There wasn't much time to ponder it, as cold indifference once again settled upon Alexandra's face as she turned to address Kit.

"Your house-keys," Alexandra said, brandishing a jangling ring of new-forged implements.

Kit held out her trembling hand, and Alexandra dropped the keys into her palm.

"Thank you," said Kit.

Alexandra turned on her heel and began leading the way up the road again, clearly expecting Kit to follow. Kit, desperate to meet if not exceed Alexandra's expectations, dashed after her.

CHAPTER FOURTEEN

The swift pace set by Alexandra brought the two ladies back home to the Cranbrook estate within hours. Though Kit's legs were longer, given she stood nearly a head taller than her sister-in-law, she struggled to match Alexandra's furiously swift strides. Such a pace kept Kit short of breath, which damped down any attempt at conversation on her part.

Heatherhurst Hall, when the high crags of the roof came into view at last, appeared at first unchanged from when they'd left it that morning. The distant tower, eaves, and gables reminded Kit of a doll's house. Step by step, the house grew, until new details, previously hidden, became exposed. Details such as a matchstick-doll man scampering to and fro across the lawn between great iron lumps of machinery. At length, the machines began producing cotton-wad clouds of steam, to the great excitement of the little matchstick man. And it became undeniable to Kit that this little matchstick-doll man was, in fact, her six-foot-tall husband, rendered miniature by distance. In the hours the ladies had spent in the village, he had harvested mechanical abundance from the barren fields: bushels of cogs, grease, and steam.

"Vivian!" Kit called, waving to catch his eye.

It took longer than she expected—long enough for her to wonder if

146

waving across a field would be considered appropriate behavior for a baronet's wife—but he noticed her at last and took a break from fiddling with his machines to return her gesture.

Kit trotted up to him, glad for the sight of a friendly face after her day in the dreary village accompanied by her dour sister-in-law. As she approached, he gestured widely to the mechanical maze around himself.

"This is my engineering!" Vivian expostulated, beaming with delight.

Kit hadn't seen him so happy since he'd shown her the boiler-keepers in the belly of the steamship. She strove to match his enthusiasm. "How wonderful! It looks dashed clever."

"Spent all day hauling it up out of the cellar," Vivian continued. "To make room for your photography, you know."

Kit, genuinely touched by his efforts, felt also a pang of remorse for demanding he go through such trouble to find space for her darkroom. She opened her mouth to apologize.

"All day?" Alexandra interrupted in skeptical tones.

Kit hadn't noticed her following along behind to meet Vivian and jumped a little at this announcement of her presence. Turning towards her, she saw her sister-in-law was seething. Kit wracked her mind to think of what she'd done, what she'd said, to upset Alexandra so. But Alexandra wasn't looking at her. She was too busy glaring daggers at her brother.

"Yes," Vivian replied affably, as if his sister weren't practically breathing fire. "All day."

"Then I suppose," Alexandra continued, her voice tightly controlled, "you could find no time in which to hire tradesmen to fix the house."

Vivian looked at her blankly. "I rather thought you'd see to that while you were in the village."

Alexandra's jaw clenched.

Alarmed at the conversation's turn, Kit drew upon her courage and stepped between them. "How silly of me to forget! Please forgive me, Vivian, for being so absent-minded. And after you went through such pains to clear the cellar! I cannot thank you enough. I hope you're not vexed."

Throughout her improvised speech, she kept her pitch high and a smile plastered over her mouth, just as finishing school had taught her. Every inch the meek, sweet, chipper little wife all men desired.

To her relief, Vivian responded in kind with a disbelieving chuckle. "Vexed? Hardly! We'll simply have to try again on the morrow. But first, I really must finish my work whilst I have daylight."

"Of course!" Kit replied, her smile turning more sincere, her honeyed words having to all appearances produced the desired result. "I'll not bother you any further until dinner."

She paused there, wondering if she ought to punctuate her stated affections with a handclasp, or perhaps even a kiss on his cheek. If he had any such expectations of her, she wished he'd state them outright.

But he simply smiled at her and turned back to his machines.

Kit supposed he didn't want to indulge in any displays out-of-doors. Or perhaps simply not in front of his sister.

Said sister, meanwhile, continued to fume silently. With a final glare at her brother, the likes of which would've sundered Kit's spirit had it been cast in her direction, she stormed off into the house without another word.

Vivian, intent upon his engineering, didn't seem to notice.

After another moment's indecision, Kit went into the house. Though Alexandra had long vanished, Kit felt keenly aware of following in her wake. The air seemed to crackle with the remnants of her rage. The thought sent shivers down Kit's arms, the tiny hairs prickling beneath her satin sleeves.

With the day's errands done, Kit was left to her own devices. She stood in the foyer brimming with possibility, her basket full of photographic chemicals on her arm, and her new ring of house-keys in her pocket. With-drawing the ring, she ran her fingertips over the keys, tracing their elegant shanks from stem to stern. She was now truly mistress of Heatherhurst Hall. Every door would open to her.

Every door.

The thought struck her like a thunderbolt—though the spark had been building in her mind ever since she first suggested to Alexandra that she might need a copy of the housekeys. The door at the end of the hall would remain locked no longer. She could open it at her leisure. She would know what lay beyond its forbidden portal.

Kit forced herself to take small, quick steps across the foyer and up the grand staircase. She wanted to hike up her skirts and run outright, take the stairs two or three at a time, and dash down the crooked corridors towards her prize. But if either her husband or her sister-in-law should catch her in the act… The thought made her shudder more than the phantoms she knew lurked in the walls.

At length, she reached the fateful fork in the path, the one branch leading to the master bedroom, the other to the forbidden door. Her pulse quickened as she entered the haunted hall. The click of her heels against the floorboards sounded loud as the cracking of bones in the emptiness. Nevertheless she pressed on, until she stood before the locked door. Her fingers, clenched around her chatelaine throughout her journey, trembled as they released their hold. Kit selected a key and slid it into the lock.

It would not turn.

Undaunted, she tried again with the next key in the ring.

It wouldn't turn, either.

The third key produced the same result. The fourth key wouldn't even fit into the lock, its teeth far too large to gain entrance. But the fifth key slid in easily.

Too easily.

Kit could feel it the instant it entered—the lack of resistance, how its slender shank and stubby teeth clattered against the interior of the lock like stones tossed down a well. Dreading the result, she turned the key. It spun over and over in her fingertips, the teeth not even touching the tumblers, much less pushing them aside.

The first key, then. Or the second. Or the third. She must have done something wrong, have been too rough or too gentle upon the mechanism. She tried the keys again.

None would turn.

Frantic, feeling as though she would burst into tears, she sank to her knees in front of the door and peered into the keyhole directly. Something had gummed up the lock. A piece of dust, or gravel, or clay, had somehow got inside and blocked it.

But she beheld no obstruction.

What she saw instead, through the worn narrow passage of the keyhole, was a dark wet spot surrounded by a white ring.

A curious sound reached her ears as she looked. It reminded her of a dog's panting, the same harsh and ragged breaths, only far slower.

And she realized she was staring into a human eye.

CHAPTER FIFTEEN

K it fell back from the keyhole, landing in a heap of skirts on the floorboards of the abandoned hallway. She scrambled further backwards on all fours. Her shoulder hit something. She flailed away from it instinctively. Only by glancing back in absolute terror did she realize the hallway was empty, and the solid mass that bruised her shoulder had been, in fact, the outer wall. Her blind backwards path had curved just enough to bring on the collision.

The moment she realized the wall for what it was, it transformed from foe to friend, and she hurried to press her back against it, to have the solace of at least one quarter from which she need not fear an ambush.

The solidity of the wall—horsehair plaster over stone, cold and hard—only emphasized the shudders that ran through her own weak frame. The horrible vision still flashed before her. A human eye. Or what had once been human. She strained her ears for any sound of the creature on the other side of the door, but could hear nothing above her own panicked gasps.

How long she sat paralyzed with terror, she couldn't reckon. Her gaze fixed upon the carpet, not daring to look anywhere near the door again, for fear of what fresh horrors she might witness.

In the midst of her fit, a single point of clarity emerged, coalescing into a thought which came to her in her cousin Phoebe's voice.

You can't very well stay in this hallway forever, can you?

Kit wished Phoebe were here now, to comfort her, to reassure her, to confirm what she'd seen, to mount a rational defense against the unknown and unknowable. But Phoebe was an ocean away. Phoebe was saving other young women now, through her surgery, and Kit had to fend for herself.

Even alone, Kit knew what Phoebe would say to her. Science required evidence to support hypotheses. Evidence gathered through repeated experiment. The data Kit had collected just now, peeking through the keyhole only once, wouldn't be sufficient to prove anything. The sight of the eye in the keyhole would be but a mere anecdote if the experiment could not be repeated.

She had to look again.

Kit poured all of her will into forcing her trembling limbs to move, to crawl towards the danger rather than away. Inch by inch, she slid along the wall, keeping her back to it as she approached the locked door. No sound reached her from the other side of the door, not even when she pressed herself into the corner beside it, her eyes level with the doorknob. She steadied herself with a deep breath, then, even more slowly than before, left the security of the wall behind and peered through the keyhole.

Again, all was dark. But where before it had been the liquid pool of a human pupil, now it was only dry shadow. She squinted against the darkness and thought there might be stairs, their wood warped and ancient.

Apart from that, there was nothing at all.

Kit stared harder in disbelief. It brought nothing more to her sight. Her ears picked up only her own shuddering breaths and the thudding of her heart against her ribcage. Her pulse slowed as she looked into the darkness, her breathing evened out, her legs ached from kneeling so long, and still, she saw nothing of the creature. The cramping grew too painful for her to maintain her position, and she fell back into the corner, defeated.

It must have been her imagination, for all it had seemed so real. Like every other apparition she'd encountered within Heatherhurst Hall.

She knew the litany well, could recite it as easily as breathing: *It must have been your imagination*. She'd heard it a hundred times if she'd heard it once, all throughout her childhood. Her vivid imagination was infamous amongst family, friends, and enemies alike. It had given her a host of nightmares. Phoebe had soothed them in their shared girlhood; then, as Phoebe began her medical career and Kit went off to finishing school, the task of reassuring Kit fell to Lucy. Kit knew full well it was no small task. Nightmares ripped her out of slumber to wake shrieking, or sobbing, or paralyzed in the night, with an unseen incubus upon her chest, freezing all her limbs in place, despite all her will to move. Most of her schoolmates found her night terrors an inconvenience at best. Patience Wheeler sneered at them, and at Kit by association. But Lucy put her arms around her shoulders and held her safe until the fear, like the tide, ebbed in due time. And as she'd grown up, the nightmares themselves had faded altogether, from a nightly occurrence to a weekly or monthly one, and then to but a few times a year, leaving them all-but-forgotten.

Yet Kit's imagination remained. She supposed wiser minds than hers would consider the nightmares just punishment for such flights of fancy as she indulged. The Puritans, as Phoebe had helpfully informed her, had considered imagination to be a sin, and had named their children in remembrance of it, as they named them Desire or Lechery. Kit and Phoebe had found more than one ancient gravestone carved with IMAGINATION in their youthful adventures into wooded and abandoned cemeteries. Kit had supposed she might be whipped in the stocks for it, had she been so unfortunate as to live but two centuries hence—until Phoebe reminded her they both came from Quaker blood, and would have already been banished from the Massachusetts colony for religious reasons.

Regardless, imagination—her gift and her curse—must have been the cause of the eye in the keyhole. There was nothing else for it. As disturbing as such a notion might feel to her raw-scraped nerves. It gave her no comfort as she turned her back on the locked door and, ignoring the prickling sensation on the nape of her neck, strode away.

She retreated down the hall without any real idea of a destination and found her fearful feet had taken her to the master bedroom. Her bedroom, such as it was. The only place in all of England she could even feign to call her sanctuary. She tried to summon a feeling of safety as she rushed inside and shut the door behind herself.

It came easier as her trembling fingers found, at last, a key that would fit the lock. At least one key in her new chatelaine would be of use to her. She turned it and felt immeasurable relief as she heard the bolt slide into place. Whatever lurked in the corridors of Heatherhurst Hall, it couldn't follow her here. Not unless it, too, possessed a ring of keys—and Kit felt fairly confident it possessed no such thing, else it would have released itself from its prison at the end of the hall. Furthermore, she sternly reminded herself, though without conviction, it didn't exist at all, and was only the product of her own over-active imagination.

She ran her fingers over her keys again as a physical reminder of her defense against the metaphysical. She might not have a key to the attic, but she at least had a key to her own bedroom.

Then she remembered Alexandra had the very same ring of keys.

Her breath caught in her throat as a vision flashed before her mind—a vision of herself, asleep, alone in her marriage bed, a full moon hanging in the sky outside the high-arched window, throwing off just enough illumination to reveal the turning of the doorknob, the slow inward creak of the door, and a shadow sliding across the floor with supernatural ease, rising up beside the bed in the form of the raven-haired Alexandra, looming over Kit, helpless and utterly ignorant of the danger—until Alexandra swooped down upon her, and—

Kit snapped out of the waking nightmare, her heart pounding with new fear—or perhaps some other, more unspeakable emotion.

She shook her head to clear it. Alexandra was no monster. At least, she was no more monstrous than Kit herself, and very likely less so. She was just a normal woman, with normal instincts, and no unnatural passions to speak of. Try as she might, Kit couldn't quite consider that a relief.

For an instant, she considered telling her husband or her sister-in-law about the eye in the keyhole. She banished the notion almost as soon as it arrived—for, if she told them of the apparition, she would first have to confess to peering through the keyhole herself like a nosy child. The best she could hope for was her husband's bewilderment. The worst, which she feared almost as much as the apparition itself, would of course be her sister-in-law's scorn.

Yet she couldn't hide in her bedroom forever—not from ghosts nor from Alexandra. She would have to leave it eventually. Flee it, most likely, if the phantoms found her here. She would prefer to leave it on her own terms, for her own determined purpose. Telling tales of ghosts without any material proof would undoubtedly lead to humiliation at best—and thus, if she gave up cowering, as she must, she would then have to go in search of evidence. She'd returned from the village with a ring of keys, yes, but she had come back with something else as well. Something that might do even better than keys to prove her phantoms real.

She had the chemicals required to develop her photographic plates.

And, thanks to her husband, she had a darkroom in which to perform the process.

Kit threw all her efforts into her self-made distraction and hurriedly gathered up the photographic plates she had exposed just yesterday, tucking them into the basket with her darkroom supplies. Then, gathering her courage, she left the master bedroom.

The halls—empty, dark, and labyrinthine—contained more than enough shadows to startle one of Kit's nervous constitution, but she heard no more scuttling in the walls and saw no spirits as she journeyed across the house to the foyer, descended the grand staircase, and pushed open the massive oak doors to the outside world.

She found her husband just where she'd left him: out-of-doors, surrounded by his experiments in engineering. She called his name softly at first, not wishing to startle him with her interruption, but quickly realized she'd have to repeat the call at much greater volume if she wished to obtain his attention. On the fourth repetition, he raised his head from his work.

"I'm terribly sorry to intrude," she began, "but when you have a moment to spare, would you mind showing me the room you cleared out for me in the cellar?"

He complied with all the friendly ease she'd come to expect of him in their short acquaintance, leading her back into the house, across the foyer, past the dining room and down a narrow hall towards what she assumed, from the sounds of chopping, splashing, and the thud of blades against wood, to be the kitchen. She saw none of it, however, for he steered her to an alcove off to the left and through a plain, unassuming door.

Before them loomed stone steps spiraling downward into a black abyss. A suffocating cloud of hot, stale air rose from it. Kit's heart leapt into her throat.

Vivian, meanwhile, struck a match. It threw a faint flickering light into the darkness, which did little more than put the already-imposing shadows into eerie motion.

"Just down here," he chirruped, leading the way without looking back to see if she followed.

Kit hesitated on the threshold.

Vivian continued without her, oblivious, taking his match-flame with him.

Kit dug her nails into her palms. Vivian wasn't afraid. He'd lived all his life in these haunted halls. Just today he'd traversed this very staircase, up and down, over and over, all alone, to bring his machines out into the sunshine, to clear out a space for her. She'd requested a darkroom, and now she refused it for her fear of the dark.

Self-loathing motivated her where courage could not, and she stepped down after him.

Walking within the spiral staircase felt like traversing the inside of a ball of yarn, or a fist, ever turning inward and growing more and more cramped and confined. Kit braced one hand against the outer wall. The rough wood gave way to stone beneath her fingertips as she sunk deeper and deeper beneath the house. Ahead of her, she could see nothing save her husband's match-flame and his long silhouette made even taller by the flickering light.

When Kit thought she could stand it no longer without giving way to a scream, the staircase ended. Vivian stopped moving down and began moving simply forward. The match-light made it look as if he were gliding rather than walking into a hallway barely large enough to admit the top of his head and the breadth of his shoulders. Kit followed in his wake, her ears pricked for the scuttling of rats. Or worse.

Vivian halted suddenly. Kit drew up short to keep from running into him.

"Here!" he announced, no less cheerful for his sepulchral surroundings.

He raised his lit match in front of him, throwing its fluttering light into another dark alcove. The door within appeared unspeakably ancient, yet plain, its warped surface holding no decoration save several deep gouges carved apparently at random into the wood.

Kit stared at it, curious, then with a start recalled what Alexandra had told her on their cemetery picnic in New Bedford, about the axe-wounds in the door from the Viking raids upon the ancient monastery. The conversation felt as long ago and far away as the monks and Vikings themselves.

Vivian pushed the door open and stepped inside. Kit followed.

At last, they had reached a place where the feeble match-light proved almost sufficient. They stood in a tiny antechamber, its ceiling so low Vivian had to stoop to fit inside, and Kit herself had but a few inches between the cobwebs and the crown of her head. If she flung out both arms to their full length, her fingertips would scrape the walls. A low counter ran along one short wall. The whole room might have passed for a crypt, undisturbed for centuries, except one modern touch—a sink in the corner, with a water pump, which couldn't have been more than a decade old.

For the first time since she'd tried her keys upon the locked door in the abandoned hallway, Kit smiled.

"It's perfect!" she declared, turning to thank her husband.

The match-light turned his benevolent grin into a ghoulish grimace. "Splendid! Put down your basket and we'll go fetch a lamp."

"No need," said Kit, pulling out her ruby lantern and holding it up for him to light.

Vivian blinked, puzzled, but nevertheless reached out to touch the flame of the match to the lantern's wick.

The pathetic match-flame blazed to vibrant life. Its flickering yellow light, strengthened by the lantern and tinted by its scarlet screens, turned into a blood-red glow, bathing the tiny chamber in crimson.

Now able to see the whole of her husband's face, Kit noted that, for the first time since he'd led her into the sepulchral cellar, he appeared unnerved. She attempted a winning smile to comfort him. He made the same effort in returning it. Kit thanked him for his assistance, and he made a speedy retreat upstairs.

The ruby lantern flung out a hellish glow. Kit nonetheless found it comforting. The familiar red light would reveal the fruits of her labors, as it had a hundred times before. She'd long since grown accustomed to the sight of developing solution and water turned crimson as blood. She poured out both into their appointed trays and put her photographic plates in the water to soak.

After a few moments, she removed the first plate and immersed it in the developing solution. Before her eyes, the image bloomed in negative. All light became shadow, gradually resolving into the inverted shape of the long hallway with the door at its end. No phantom flitted across its expanse.

Kit tried to restrain her disappointment. It was a good photograph regardless, clear and crisp, with an aesthetically-pleasing balance of light and dark. She washed it off with water and put it into the fixing bath. It took no small measure of patience for her to wait until the opaque yellow color had completely disappeared from the back of the plate. A quarter of an hour seemed a lifetime when she had two potential ghost photographs yet to develop. She washed it again and laid it out to dry—then pounced like a vampire upon the next plate.

The second development only increased her impatience. She gently rocked the tray until all milky-white parts of the plate had turned to dark gray, revealing the portrait of the late Lady Cranbrook. Again, it proved a perfectly acceptable photograph, but revealed none of the spectral evidence she'd hoped to capture. Withholding a disappointed sigh, she fixed the image and left it drying beside the first plate.

The third and final plate held little hope for her. Heart in throat, she immersed the plate in the developing tray. Like frost creeping over a windowpane, the lights and shadows emerged in reverse. There, in vivid white, was the vast shadow under the grand staircase.

And there, just underneath it, stood a stark black figure.

Kit stared at the blot on the plate. An error in her photographic process, surely—some trick of double-exposure, or some sort of finger-print smudge in the delicate chemical coating.

But this shadow had the unmistakable outline of a woman's silhouette, and its face, veiled, appeared as a hideous ebony skull beneath its gauze.

A ghost.

CHAPTER SIXTEEN

A scream grew in Kit's throat. She didn't dare release it. Her horror remained a silent one as she stared down in disbelief at the plate now held in her trembling fingertips. As terrifying as the sight before her appeared, another emotion overwhelmed her fear.

Relief.

She had her proof at last.

All the nights spent in lonely terror—all the days spent jumping at shadows—all the wondering whether she was going mad, or had been mad all along—it was over now. At least one of the ghosts was real, and she had the photograph to prove it.

She studied the image, squinting to perceive details in the dim red glow. The curious drape of the gown, several decades out-of-date, and the way its hem trailed across the floor... It seemed familiar, somehow, and not simply because she'd glimpsed it out of the corner of her eye more times than she cared to admit. It looked, in fact, very much like a photograph she'd already developed. Kit snatched up the other plate to compare. A glance confirmed her suspicions.

The ghost was Alexandra and Vivian's mother.

Her elation faded at this revelation. What had once been terrifying was now simply tragic. A mother who couldn't bear to leave her children, who had to stand by and watch herself replaced by an American interloper, taking her son and her title from her in one fell swoop. No wonder she haunted the new mistress of Heatherhurst Hall. Kit supposed she would do the same in her place.

Kit carefully replaced the plates in the cleansing bath. She'd make prints of them once they were ready, but for now, her proof required just one more ingredient to make it real. One she couldn't bear to wait for.

A witness.

Kit strode boldly from her little antechamber into the darkness of the corridor. Leaving the door open behind her allowed the faint glow of the ruby lamp to light her first few steps. Beyond that, she found she didn't care. What were shadows now, when she knew not only the truth behind her ghost, but its identity and motivations? The unknown frightened her. The known, however, she could confront with relative ease. She braced her hands against the walls to mark her path, and when they gave way to the circular tower of the spiral stair, she felt for each step with her toe before alighting. Then her boot struck a wooden door, and she pushed it open to enter the sunlit hallway of the house once more.

She intended to fetch her husband—she knew precisely where to find him, out-of-doors amongst his machines—but as she hiked up her skirts and trotted into the foyer, she smashed headfirst into someone coming the other way.

"Oh!" Kit cried, more startled than frightened for once. The physical crash was proof enough she'd encountered a living person rather than a phantom. And furthermore, the person she'd crashed into had been—

"Oh!" Alexandra echoed in much the same tone. Her eyes flew wide in astonishment, and her sculpted black brows soared to her widow's peak before swooping down again to knit in something like concern. "Are you all right?"

The question surprised Kit as much as the collision. She shook it off. There were other matters to hand—matters far more important than whether or not Alexandra's inquiry was genuine. To that end, she grabbed Alexandra's wrist.

Alexandra's expression transformed from concerned to alarmed.

"Come with me!" Kit begged, forcing herself to ignore Alexandra's evident discomfort. Just a moment, and it would all be over. "Please! There's something I must show you! Something you have to see!"

Her words were a child's words, inelegant, pleading, wheedling. She fully expected Alexandra to shake her off.

But to her surprise, Alexandra grabbed her wrist in turn.

In the same moment, Alexandra's face hardened into determination, and in a low tone which bespoke all the urgency Kit wished to express, Alexandra demanded, "Show me."

Kit, not foolish enough to question the first streak of luck she'd experienced since coming to Heatherhurst, wasted no time in beginning to drag her back to the hallway. Almost as an afterthought, she said, "It's in the cellar."

Her forward progress stopped short with an implacable tug on her wrist. She turned to find Alexandra had halted.

"We'll need a candle," Alexandra explained. "Wait here."

Waiting was the last thing Kit wanted to do in that moment. Still, not wishing to do anything that might upset Alexandra, she bit her lip and nodded, dropping her hold upon Alexandra's wrist.

Alexandra gathered her skirts and set off across the foyer towards the morning room. She vanished inside. Seconds ticked past on the grandfather clock, echoing up to the rafters, out of time with Kit's rapid pulse. Kit clenched her own skirts in her fists, worrying the fabric between her knuckles. Two minutes passed like two hours before Alexandra reappeared in the foyer. She hurried towards Kit with a box of matches in one hand and the promised candle in the other.

Kit led her without delay to the cellar door, down the spiral staircase, and through the catacomb corridor. She stopped in front of the door with the axe-marks.

"You must snuff your candle," she told Alexandra apologetically. "The photographic plates have not yet fixed, and may yet be destroyed by even so much light as this."

If Alexandra thought ill of this request, she said nothing of it. Without a moment's hesitation, she licked her thumb and forefinger and pinched the candle-flame out. It gave a sharp hiss as it died. Darkness swooped in to take its place. All that remained to Kit's eyes was the outline of the darkroom door limned in hellish red.

Kit pushed it open and strode into the antechamber, Alexandra quick on her heels. She went to the bath and plunged both hands into the cold, crimson water. Her fingertips found the sharp edges of first one plate, then another. One plate in each hand, she lifted both and held them up to the light. In her right hand she held the photograph of the portrait in the music room. In her left hand she held the photograph of the empty hallway and the locked door.

Setting the plates aside with a disappointed *tsk*, she plunged her hands into the bath again, aware of Alexandra's eyes on her. She swept her hands back and forth, creating waves and currents in the tray as she searched for the third and final plate. Her fingertips ran the whole length and breadth of the tray. They felt nothing save smooth enamel.

A seed of anxiety took root in Kit's mind. She ignored it, trailing her hands through the tray again. And again. Still, she came up with nothing.

And all the while, Alexandra watched and waited just behind her.

Humiliation and panic swirled together in a maelstrom within Kit's mind. Her chest felt tight. Her heart leapt into her throat. She gave up on the bath. Regardless of what her memory told her, she had not left the plate there. She must have put it on the counter. She whirled, just barely avoiding another collision with Alexandra as she swept over the counter in search of the plate.

But it was not there, either.

Kit spun again, and again, her eyes flicking from one scarlet corner to another in search of something, anything, that might tell her where the precious plate had gone. Several times she almost met Alexandra's eyes, but quickly averted her gaze, her cheeks growing as hot and red as the ruby lamp.

For a third time, she plunged both arms into the bath, up to the elbows this time, heedless of her dress sleeves. Again, she came up empty handed. She stared at her palms, bereft. Her scattered mind came to a conclusion too horrible to face, yet too rational to deny.

The plate was gone.

~

Alexandra hated lying.

She held nothing but contempt for anyone who thought her stupid enough to believe a falsehood, and had given the cut direct to many a girl at school for daring to cross her in such a way.

As much as she despised lies on the lips of others, she loathed tenfold to drop them from her own lips. Her skin crawled at the thought. Her mind shied from the sound.

Which made the matter of Kit Morgan all the more unbearable.

She relished the few moments in which she could tell her the truth. For example, the matter of the photograph. Alexandra hadn't the faintest idea where it had gone. When first she'd heard of it, she doubted it had ever existed.

But as she looked into Kit's earnest face and read the plea writ plain upon her beautiful visage, Alexandra beheld no lies.

And her stomach turned even as she told the truth. She had not seen the photograph. She certainly hadn't touched it. And she had no answer as to its current whereabouts.

The tears in Kit's eyes as Alexandra denied her truths made Alexandra's own eyes burn with tears she couldn't allow to gather.

Nor could she allow herself to follow Kit back to her chambers, to kiss the tears from her cheeks, to take her in her arms in the firmest embrace to shore her up against the horrors of the house surrounding them.

So she watched, helpless and stone, as Kit fled.

Every fiber of Alexandra's being begged her to chase after her. Her legs even went so far as to take two steps, quite without her permission, towards that purpose. But she threw out her arms in the doorway and halted her forward progress. She couldn't allow herself to follow Kit. She couldn't answer for what she'd do—what might happen—if she did. She listened to Kit's retreating footsteps, waited until they echoed away into silence.

The darkroom, with its blood-red lantern and ample shadows, was not a welcoming place. It was even less so alone. Alexandra forced herself to wait a full minute, and not a moment longer, before she herself escaped its crimson confines.

She climbed back up into the house using the servants' stair, which terminated near the kitchen. As she stepped out of the staircase into the hall, something yellow fluttered in her peripheral vision. Something like the train of a gown vanishing around the corner ahead.

"Gertie?" Alex called—even as her memory supplied the fact that Gertie still dressed in the black-and-white uniforms she'd worn as a housemaid, and even if she did own a more colorful dress, she certainly wouldn't wear it in a place so prone to staining it as the kitchen.

Regardless, no one responded to her call.

Suspicion grew in Alexandra's mind. She shut the door to the servant's stair with a quiet click, then crept forward, following the path that the fluttering yellow skirt had taken. In a swift and singular motion, she rounded the corner.

There, at the end of the hall, walked her mother.

Alexandra stumbled to a halt. She gaped with open-mouthed disbelief at the apparition before her. She couldn't make out its face—its back being turned to her—but neither could she mistake the gown. The gauzy white muslin had yellowed with age, yet retained the cut and style of the very dress Lady Eleanor Cranbrook had worn in her bridal portrait.

As Alexandra stared, the specter of her mother continued on, until it reached the end of the hall and turned another corner, out of her sight.

While it appeared before her, Alexandra remained paralyzed. The moment it disappeared, all her feeling rushed back to her at once. She found herself gasping for air, having held her breath all the while. She didn't wait to catch it, instead launching herself forward down the hall, all-but-tripping over her own skirts like a child as she chased her mother. She turned the same corner, and found—

—nothing.

Only the empty foyer loomed before her. Grand. Imposing. Bereft.

"Miss Alexandra?"

Alexandra whirled towards the voice and discovered, at the end of the hall which she'd just left, Gertie. The cook stood at relative ease, her hook by her side, and one scarred eyebrow raised. Alexandra's disappointment was beyond words.

"Gertie!" she snapped, even as she knew full well it wasn't Gertie's fault she'd been fool enough to chase a phantom. "Where have you been?"

Gertie withstood the interrogation with commendable stoicism. "In the kitchen, miss."

"Have you seen anyone?" Alexandra demanded.

"No one save my lady, miss."

Alexandra's heart stopped for an instant—until she recalled that her mother was no longer "my lady" to Gertie, now that Kit had married Vivian and supplanted her place as the mistress of the house. She supposed Gertie could hardly have avoided seeing Kit in her desperate flight.

"Beggin' your pardon, Miss Alexandra," Gertie added. "But would you mind terribly asking Sir Vivian to return my hatchet at his earliest convenience?"

Alexandra stared at her.

"I don't need it urgent-like," Gertie continued, apparently assuming Alexandra's silence stemmed from confusion rather than disbelief. "I can wring the cockerels' necks as well as anyone. Only I find the blade makes for a much cleaner business."

As Gertie spoke, her familiar matter-of-fact tone washed over Alexandra, soothing her nerves. By the time her explanation had finished, Alexandra found her voice again. "Yes, of course. I'll ask him."

"Thank you, miss."

Alexandra nodded, and Gertie took herself off around the corner, back to the kitchen from whence she'd come.

It was just like Vivian, Alexandra reflected as she crossed the foyer, to take someone else's instruments without asking, and fail to return them in a timely fashion. She forced all her nerves down and instead poured the same energy into resenting her brother's selfishness. Inconsiderate Vivian was as normal as stoic Gertie. Everything was normal, after all. She'd seen nothing that couldn't be explained. The apparition must have been a trick of the light. Dust particles in a sunbeam. A reflection off a spotted mirror.

Something normal. Anything normal. Nothing like what Kit had claimed to capture in her photograph.

She found Vivian precisely where she'd left him, surrounded by his blasted contraptions. He had his shirtsleeves rolled up to his elbows. Black grease streaked across his forehead. If he took any notice of her approach, he didn't give any sign of it. His attention remained wholly focused upon the gears of something Alexandra didn't recognize. It wasn't the boiler, that much she knew. Nor was it the stoker. Though it did have a similar system of pulleys and teeth.

"Vivian," she called, standing well back from the machines, though none seemed in motion. She repeated her call twice more before he deigned to answer.

"Oh!" he said, lifting his head from his tinkering at last. "Dinner already?"

Alexandra forced her clenched jaw to open. "No. Gertie would like her hatchet returned."

Vivian furrowed his brow. "Returned from where?"

"From here," Alexandra replied with no small measure of frustration. "From you."

Vivian glanced around, then faced her again. "I don't have it."

No doubt he had simply mislaid it amongst his countless bits and bobs. Regardless, Alexandra had no more patience to spare this day. "Whenever you find it, return it to her. Please."

Vivian blinked. "As you like."

Already having turned away and begun walking back to the house, Alexandra paused. It was nothing her brother had said, only a whisper in the corner of her own mind. She considered herself a rational woman. Phantoms and apparitions were all well and good for novels. But they had no place in her waking life, miserable though it might be. And while she could not bring herself to confide in Gertie, much less Kit, she could not herself deny what she had seen. She required outside aid. Another rational mind to help her close the gates and bar the door against the threat of the supernatural.

She turned to face her brother. "Vivian."

"Yes?" he replied, more quickly than she'd expected, though he didn't lift his head from the work he'd resumed.

Alexandra licked her lips. "I saw something."

Vivian made a noncommittal sound.

"Something that looked like mother."

She felt a bitter satisfaction seeing the effect of her words upon his person. He at once stopped turning a bolt, but was much slower to put down the wrench and straighten up to face her.

"Pardon?" he asked. A pinch of fear had wound its way into his features.

"I was coming up from the cellar," she forced out, not daring to pause, lest she reconsider her words, "and I saw something in the hall. Walking away from me."

"A ghost, you mean?" Vivian chuckled uneasily. "You're letting Catherine's fancies get the best of you."

His attempts to dismiss her testimony had precisely the effect she required—her temper flared, giving her words conviction as she replied, "Ghost or no, I saw it."

"What makes you think it was..." Vivian swallowed. "...who you think it was?"

Even now he couldn't speak of her. Alexandra could blame him for many things, but she could hardly blame him for that. She attempted to soften her tone as she justified herself. "It was wearing Mother's wedding gown."

Vivian furrowed his brow. "That's just makes it all the more nonsensical. She didn't die in her wedding gown."

"I know that!" Alexandra snapped.

Vivian winced. Alexandra thought he deserved it. She knew better than anyone what Mother had worn the moment she died. She alone had been there, perched on the upper landing in the foyer. She alone, just five years old, watched helplessly as Mother tumbled down, down, down the grand staircase, the train of her gown flying up in her wake. Its scarlet hue had hid much of the resulting damage from Alexandra. But nothing could disguise the owlish angle of her head and neck when she at last struck the floor of the foyer and lay still. How she had stared back up at her daughter with blank, lifeless eyes.

Nurse had arrived soon after, and everyone else soon after that. Staff swarmed the foyer and upper landing, crowding around the corpse like flies until Father came. Nurse spirited Alexandra away up to the nursery, where Vivian still waited, utterly ignorant to what had befallen their mother.

Everyone said Mother had fallen down the stairs.

Only Alexandra knew she had jumped.

CHAPTER SEVENTEEN

Kit fled her new darkroom—sullied as it was by her most recent humiliation—and dashed upstairs in retreat to the only other refuge she might hope to have in all of Heatherhurst Hall.

To no small relief, she found the master bedroom empty. She whisked herself inside, pausing only long enough to lock the door behind her before flinging herself face-first onto the mattress and soaking the pillow with the torrent of tears she'd just barely held back throughout her escape. Disappointment and shame overwhelmed her. She felt little more than a child beneath their crushing weight. To have held proof in her hands, proof that her nightmares were real, proof no one could dare deny, not even Alexandra—only to have that proof vanish as suddenly as the phantom it represented—no words could express her grief. Only a mournful howl she muffled with her pillow, heard by no one but herself.

And yet, even as the cacophony of her own misery faded away with her spent breath, another sound met her ears.

Thump, thump, thump.

Kit's sob caught in her throat. Her heaving shoulders stilled. Her nerves, raw with emotion, now strained to pick up the noise.

Thump, thump, thump. Persistent. Rhythmic. It came not from beneath her, where the cook would tread, nor from out-of-doors, where

Vivian toiled with his machines, nor from the hallway, where Alexandra might even now be approaching to comfort her. But such a comfort was mere childish fancy. The reality was quite different—a steady thud—coming from nowhere but above her.

Kit lifted her head from her pillow and trained her red-rimmed eyes upward.

Thump, thump, thump. Like the beating of Poe's hideous heart, coming from above the ceiling rather than beneath the floorboards.

Kit slipped off her shoes and dropped them beside the bed. Balancing herself with one hand on a bedpost, she stood up, craning her neck to bring her ear as close to the ceiling as possible. Her considerable height brought her nearer to her goal than most women in her position might've hoped, but still left her some six or seven inches short of pressing her ear against the very timbers.

Still, she heard the slow and steady trod of footsteps above her. Someone—or something—pacing back and forth, back and forth, towards and away from her, as mindless and repetitive as a metronome. Thump, thump, thump. Kit held her breath, lest her own fearful gasps overpower the sound.

And then, on one particular walk away, the footsteps failed to return.

Kit strained her ears as the echoes faded, the steps themselves growing softer and softer as they departed, until they vanished entirely, and she fancied she half-imagined their continuing on. As horrible as their presence had been, she felt sorry to hear them go.

Until they came back.

Thump, thump, thump. Starting soft, growing louder and louder with each step. No longer above her bed, now coming from the doorway, and the hall beyond. Coming closer. Coming for her.

Kit dug her fingers into the carving of the bedpost, the iron grip the only thing keeping her upright in her terrified state.

Thump, thump, thump, directly behind the door.

She wanted to cry out, to demand who or what tormented her so, and for what purpose. But her throat closed tight with fear, and not even the weakest word could escape her lips.

The door opened. A wraith stood on the threshold, tall and thin, its spidery limbs swathed in a black suit, and its face...

...belonged to her husband.

Kit's held breath escaped her in a yelp. "Vivian!"

Vivian blinked at her. "Catherine, what the deuce are you doing up there?"

His tone was merely quizzical, without a trace of chiding or reproof, yet Kit's face and neck colored in shame regardless as she considered her ridiculous position upon the bed. She opened her mouth to stammer a defense of her actions.

Just as a thump resounded from the ceiling above. Followed by another. And another.

Kit allowed herself a panicked glance up at the sound, then fixed her eyes upon her husband's face.

His gaze flicked to where she'd looked for but an instant before meeting her own, steady and unchanging. "Are you feeling quite the thing?"

"Do you hear that?" Kit hissed, keeping her voice low and wishing he'd do the same, for even as they talked the thumping never abated. It kept on, back and forth, over and over, a lighter tread than she'd heard previously, but nevertheless present, persistent, haunting. Again she searched his face for dawning comprehension. Again she encountered only bewilderment.

"Hear what?" he said.

She gawked at him in frank disbelief. The thumping continued overhead.

Vivian stepped towards her, holding his hands out up to her. "Won't you come down?"

"Do you not hear the footsteps?" she demanded.

Vivian paused in his approach, his arms still suspended in midair. "Footsteps?"

"Up there!" Kit pointed, her fingertip grazing the ceiling.

His eyes tracked her gesture, but no gleam of understanding lit them. He returned his gaze to her face and reached for her again. "Do come down, Catherine. I'm rather afraid you might fall."

Kit fixed her wide-eyed look of horror upon his uncomprehending visage. How could he not hear it? Was he going deaf? Was she going mad?

Thump, thump, thump. The footsteps fell in and out of time with the frantic beating of her terrified heart.

Perhaps Vivian was lying. Kit recalled stories of mad wives kept locked away in attics. *Jane Eyre. The Woman in White.* Perhaps the sound of footsteps upstairs came as no surprise to him, because he knew who dwelled up there. Perhaps he knew to whom the horrible eye in the keyhole belonged. Perhaps he had put them there.

Vivian took her hand, his fingers long and thin, yet soft.

Or perhaps, she thought with no small measure of misery, she had imagined the footsteps and the eye alike.

She bent to take his other hand and allowed him to help her down. In short order she stood upon the floor once more. As she looked up into her husband's face, the noise of the footsteps faded away, confirming her suspicions. All it took was a small distraction, and the phantoms of her mind dissipated like so much mist over the moor.

Vivian smiled down at her. "There, now, that's better, isn't it?"

Kit forced a smile in return.

August 17th, 1892

Dear Phoebe,

You will think me mad when you receive this, but if I do not tell someone what I have seen, I shall go very mad indeed.

There are ghosts within the walls of Heatherhurst Hall. The first is a pale, twisted creature, hardly human, which crawls the uppermost floors and wails in agony. The second is the woman in yellow, who patrols the hallways in silence and seems to take far less notice of me than I do of her.

I know not what to do about what I have seen. I have told my new husband and sister-in-law. They tell me I am over-imaginative, that I am dreaming. You doubtless remember me as a dreamer, but I assure you these visions are as tangible as you or I. I even managed to capture one on with my camera, and developed the photograph as proof, only to have it snatched away the moment I left my darkroom to fetch a second witness. I suspect my sister-in-law may have stolen it. Or perhaps the ghost itself.

Please write back to me. I am sorry for my hubris in leaping headlong into this marriage. But I could not have spent another moment in New Bedford without going truly mad. As terrified as I am at Heatherhurst Hall, it is a relief compared to the sheer misery I felt at home. If nothing else, I feel alive, which is more than I could say before.

Your loving cousin,

Kit Morgan

It had been two weeks since Kit had placed her first letter in the silver salver in the foyer, per Alexandra's instruction, where it had disappeared as if spirited away by faerie hands. It seemed foolish to entrust yet another letter to this bizarre system. Still, Kit stamped and sealed the envelope and stood from her desk to do what she had done with her last missive.

She walked, as she had done before, out of her sitting room, down the long, dark, narrow hall towards the grand staircase. The warped floorboards creaked and groaned with every step. She reached the hallway's end, where the cramped passage opened up into the vast foyer. Rather than look up into the weathered rafters and cracking plaster, she turned her gaze to the ground below and the staircase that would lead her there. She placed one hand upon the dusty banister to steady herself. Her other hand clutched her final letter tight.

She descended without incident. Her crossing of the foyer to reach the silver salver by the door proved equally unremarkable. She placed her letter in the silver salver with a hand that trembled only slightly.

Then she turned her back upon it and strode off towards the drawing room with nary a backward glance. Shoulders down, neck long, chin up, head high, she walked with long, sure steps, as if she cared not a whit for the letter's fate, as if she'd already forgotten it ever existed. She reached the drawing room and shut its door behind her.

Leaving only the barest crack through which she could watch the foyer.

The grandfather clock in the drawing room kept slightly different time from the grandfather clock in the foyer. Seconds ticked past out of sync with each other, making it difficult for Kit to keep track as she stood behind the door, peering through the gap. She thought perhaps a quarter-hour had passed when she beheld a flicker of movement. Something by the staircase. Something faintly yellow, like the edge of an old newspaper. She narrowed her focus to the stair.

And before her eyes, the woman in yellow appeared.

By the light of day, Kit could see her dress was older than she'd originally supposed. Its empire waistline bespoke the Georgian era. Its gauzy skirts had once been white, and yellowed over time. Her skin still held the milky white hue of death. And as before, a veil covered her face.

Kit watched as the woman in yellow bent forward and arched her neck, peering out from under the staircase. Her head twitched back and forth with unnatural speed to survey the foyer. For an instant, her veiled visage faced Kit's position hidden behind the drawing room door, and Kit feared she'd been caught. But then the woman's head twitched away again, and after a few moments more, her focus seemed to settle upon the silver salver.

Kit's breath caught in her throat.

The woman in yellow slowly slid one foot forward. Then another. It took her ages to emerge fully from under the stair, like some slithering thing that feared the touch of sunlight. The moment her entire form crawled from the shadow into the dim sunlight, she sprang into motion, skittering across the foyer floor to the end-table by the front door where the salver lay. She snatched the letter from the salver as she passed and scampered on towards the dining room.

Kit burst from the drawing room. "Wait!"

The woman in yellow halted. Her head whipped towards Kit, her veil trailing ethereally in her wake. For an instant, they matched stares.

Then the woman broke into a run.

Kit bolted after her.

It took mere seconds for Kit's long strides to cross the foyer. Yet those few seconds were long enough to allow the woman in yellow to disappear into the dining room. The door swung shut behind her.

Kit slammed bodily against it, throwing her weight behind her shoulder as both hands fumbled for the knob. It turned freely once she had it in her grasp. The door itself budged an inch or two, then slammed shut again. As if someone were trying to hold it shut.

Some might suppose their mortal strength would prove futile against such supernatural forces, and give up.

Kit threw her shoulder into the door again.

The weight on the other side of the door gave way with a lurch. The door swung inward. Kit tumbled over the threshold after it.

As she fell, she caught a glimpse of a pale yellow skirt disappearing through the wall.

Kit scrambled to her feet and ran to the wall. Unlike a ghost, she had to maneuver around the long table rather than simply passing through it. Still, she made it to the wall in good time regardless. Again she stopped her forward momentum by slamming her hands against the wainscoting.

An echoing thud resounded.

Kit's eyes flew wide. If she didn't know better, she'd say it sounded downright hollow. She balled her right hand into a fist and slammed the side of it into the wainscoting.

A definitively hollow knock echoed away into nothingness.

Kit spread the fingers of both hands wide and ran them lightly over the wainscoting, starting with small concentric circles and branching further and further out, her fingertips seeking cracks, loose panels, anything that might grant her passage through the wall. She forced herself to be patient and thorough in her search, though with every passing moment she knew the woman in yellow drew further and further away, her trail growing cold as her grave.

Then, unexpectedly, she felt a draught against her palm.

Her fingers flew over the area again, and this time her nails caught in a hairline crack in the wall.

Kit would've crowed in victory had her heart not been in her throat. She traced the crack up the wall to the end of the wainscoting and down to the baseboard. Having discerned the outline of the secret door, she set her shoulder to the task of forcing it open. With a sound like the scraping of old bones, a two-foot section of the wainscoting swung inward.

Heedless of danger, Kit immediately poked her head inside.

She found a stonework tunnel. Dust hung in the air and covered the floor. And in that dust, Kit could see small, faint footprints.

Kit bounded after them.

The light from the dining room windows did not penetrate far into the darkness of the secret tunnel. After three yards or so it dissolved into pitch black. Even the keenest eyes couldn't tell where it led. Kit, undaunted, put her hands to the walls on either side of her. The rough-hewn stones were cold against her fingertips. She felt her way forward, creeping as best she could in the cramped tunnel. The air around her remained stale and silent—until her foot touched down onto something with more give than slate, which responded with a wretched creak.

Kit flinched, but grinned even as she did so. The stone slabs had given way to wood. And, as she swept her foot back and forth, she found a wooden barrier. Tracing upward with the tip of her toe, she found it stopped some six inches up, continued horizontally six inches forward, and then repeated the pattern.

She had found a secret staircase.

Kit bit back a whoop of joy and bounded upward to meet her ghost.

Further forward and up, she heard the pitter-patter of phantom foot-steps. She was gaining on the woman in yellow. She was sure of it. Any moment now she would catch her and, at last, find out what had become of all her letters home. She would discover why this phantom haunted the halls of Heatherhurst.

Then, as her boot struck triumphantly down in the hopes of propelling her up, something cracked underfoot.

Kit glanced down, which showed her nothing, because all remained dark. But she felt the board beneath her splinter and give way. She scrambled to brace her hands on the stones to prevent her fall even as her leg plummeted into the void, her shin scraping against the stair ahead, and her ankle twisting against whatever architectural contraption held the staircase up in the first place. Whatever it was, it proved more solid than her flesh, which bent at an angle she didn't think it had ever bent at before. A whirlwind of pain shot up from the point of contention, and she bit her lip to keep from screaming. Her other leg knelt against the remaining stairs, twisted under her in a way which she might have considered uncomfortable if she had any nerve endings to spare after whatever she'd done to her ankle.

Something cold and wet dripped from her shin. She thought she might be bleeding.

But even worse, she would never catch the woman in yellow now.

How foolish she must look, trapped in a forgotten corner of the house —and to have trapped herself by chasing after a ghost, only to be left behind without any material proof of her quarry. Her husband would be ashamed to see her like this. And Alexandra would be livid.

Kit groped for the staircase, clenching the lip of the step ahead in a white-knuckled grip and pulling with all her might, as she pushed against the step behind with her one good leg. Her vision went white as her injured limb flared in agonizing protest. She lurched out of the broken stair and collapsed onto the steps above with a shattering crash. New pains bloomed down her side where she'd landed. Her wounded leg continued throbbing, burning, wrenching, and bleeding. She lifted her head to the sensation of the staircase spinning around her. Then everything went dark.

CHAPTER EIGHTEEN

K it awoke to an atmosphere of softness and light, quite at odds with the unforgiving darkness in which she'd fallen. She lay on her back, blinking up at the familiar indigo curtains of the four-poster bed in the master bedroom. Tilting her strong chin forward, she discovered sunbeams—thick and bright, a rarity on the stormy moors —sending broad strokes of light across her body, creating patches of warmth in an already-cozy environment, thanks to the blazing hearth fire she could just glimpse beyond the foot of the bed, over the lumps of her toes beneath her counterpane.

Rolling her head across her pillow, Kit took in the sight of the nightstand, with a tea-tray set upon it, the familiar bone-china tea-set assembled, with a thin plume of steam yet curling from the teapot's spout, and a few scones left on a plate. A bottle of laudanum sat rather incongruously amongst the teacups. Kit's eyes drifted away from it, and in doing so, she realized she was not alone.

In an armchair pulled up next to the bed sat Alexandra.

Kit's breath caught in her throat.

Alexandra, meanwhile, seemed not to have noticed Kit's waking. She had a writing desk upon her lap and had bent over it to scribble furiously into some manner of diary. The scratching of her pen as it flew across the pages mingled with the crackling of the hearth. Her look of intense concentration, with raven-black brows knit, her sharp jawline clenched, her lips alternately pursed and bit, and her keen eyes darting back and forth to follow her feverish writing, all seemed of particular beauty to Kit, like a pacing panther threatening at any moment to break out of its iron cage.

Suddenly, the pen halted, and the spark of Alexandra's flinty gaze flicked in Kit's direction.

Kit, lying abed with nothing to hand, had no means with which to pretend distraction, and so could only stare back.

To Kit's astonishment, Alexandra seemed likewise dumbstruck. Their eyes locked. Seconds ticked past whilst both women remained mute.

Then Alexandra shut her diary and set the writing desk on the floor. She smoothed out the wrinkles in her sapphire skirt and, turning towards Kit once more, opened her mouth to speak.

"Did you see her?" Kit blurted.

Alexandra stared at her with an expression of total bewilderment.

Such a look would have quelled Kit before, but now, she found her reticence unaccountably gone. "The woman. The veiled woman. In the yellow dress. I chased her through the foyer, into the dining room, and up the secret passage. Did you see her?"

"I did not," said Alexandra with total sangfroid.

"Oh." A minor setback—Kit refused to let it drag her down. "Who found me, then? Vivian? Did he see—"

"I found you," Alexandra cut her off.

Kit frowned. "How curious, then, that you did not see her. But why didn't you tell me about the secret passage? Or didn't you know about it? There's a staircase. In the dining room. Perhaps for the staff..."

"We have no staff save our cook."

"But you found me in the stair—!"

"I found you halfway down the grand staircase in the foyer," said Alexandra, her voice mechanical. "You had Vivian's silver letter-opener in your hands. Evidently you fell upon it."

Kit stared at Alexandra, who still wouldn't meet her gaze.

"A letter-opener...?" Kit murmured in disbelief.

"Yes. Quite sharp. It tore through your skirts and pierced your shin." A faint blush brought the lightest shade of pink to Alexandra's high cheekbones. "You nearly bled to death."

That part Kit remembered. But the details were off. "No, my foot broke through a rotten step in the hidden stair, and the splinters—"

Alexandra slammed her palm down on the nightstand, rattling the tea-things. "There is no hidden stair!"

Despite her outburst, Alexandra had yet to look Kit in the eye.

Kit bit her tongue. If Alexandra refused to admit the staircase existed, she had every right to do so. But Kit knew the truth. She would hold that truth close to her breast and never let it go. "You're right. I'm sorry."

Alexandra flinched as if Kit had struck her.

Kit swallowed past the dryness in her mouth. "Alexandra?"

Alexandra made a sound. If Kit didn't know better, she would've called it a sob. In the same moment, three drops fell from Alexandra's face onto the tea-tray. They sparkled like sea-spray in the candlelight.

Before Kit could remark upon any of this, Alexandra threw her head back and drew in a deep breath. She exhaled slowly, blinking at the ceiling all the while. At long last, she turned to face Kit.

"Thank you," she said. "For being reasonable."

Reasonable. Alexandra could have laughed at her own absurdity, were her heart not brimming with bitter shame. There was nothing reasonable in Heatherhurst Hall. Least of all herself. If she'd ever had a reasonable thought in her head, the events of the past twenty-four hours had driven it out.

She had been tending matters in the attic when she heard a bizarre scampering sound, the patter of feet and the slam of a door. Alarming, to say the least, for whoever had made such noise sounded nothing like her brother, and nothing like Gertie, either. The steps were too quick, too light, too rapid. As for the slamming of the door, Gertie had better sense, and Vivian wouldn't dare.

Alexandra crept away from her business to investigate the mysterious noise. Raising her candle high revealed no one hidden in the shadowy corners of the attic. The staircase down to the house remained locked, just as she'd left it.

The servants' passage, however, was open.

And as she stretched her arm out to banish the gloom with candlelight, the flickering flame revealed a human figure sprawled upon the steps. A woman, her long arms stretched above her head, and her golden hair coming loose to sparkle in the light.

Kit.

Cold dread seized Alexandra's heart as she flew down the steps. The house had killed her forbidden love as surely as it had killed her mother.

She had fallen to her knees beside her, had screamed for Vivian's aid, had blindly traced her fingertips over her pale swanlike throat in desperate search for a pulse—and to her mingled disbelief and relief, had found one, deep and strong, as indomitable as Kit herself. Hope sprung anew in her chest.

A low moan issued from Kit's throat, and her eyes fluttered open. "…Alex…?"

Never had Alexandra felt such joy at the sound of her voice. "Yes, it's me, I'm here. Did you strike your head?"

Kit furrowed her brow. "I don't think so. No, I struck the step with my shin and my heel went through… I don't know. But it's only my leg that's hurt, I'm sure."

"You can feel your legs?"

A strangled laugh came from Kit. "Yes, though I rather wish I couldn't feel the one in particular. It's cut upon something. I'm sorry to be so much trouble."

This last she murmured, trailing off into another swoon before Alexandra could recover enough to tell her she was worth all the trouble in the world.

Without thinking, Alexandra pulled Kit's insensible body to her lap and cradled her head, stroking her golden locks back from her ivory brow and murmuring comforting nonsense until Vivian arrived.

What he thought to find his wife in his sister's arms, Alex didn't know, and hardly cared. She wanted him only for the strength of his shoulders and ordered him to lift his bride from the stair. He obeyed her without question. Jealousy flashed through her as she watched him raise her beloved with ease—how she wished she could be the one to carry Kit away from danger, away from here. Heart in her throat, she followed him down through the dining room, then up again to the master bedroom, where Vivian laid Kit out as sweetly as if he actually loved her, and didn't merely find her convenient.

When it came time to dismiss him—for, marriage vows or no marriage vows, Alexandra couldn't bear to have him watching as she dressed Kit for bed—it felt as much a relief as if, in going, he'd opened a window to let a cool breeze into a chamber which had been shut up for centuries. She sent him away to alert Gertie to the accident and to have boiling water, fresh linen bandages, and *Cassell's Household Guide* brought up. On *Cassell's* recommendation, she had Gertie fetch the nitrate-bath from Kit's photographic darkroom.

Not even Gertie was immune to her jealousies. Alexandra opened the bedroom door long enough to retrieve the requested articles from her cook's hands, then locked the door again, shutting out the rest of the household.

Then, at last, she turned her full attention to the fallen angel lying still and senseless upon the bed.

And realized she would have to undress her.

Shame and fear warred within her as she stared, helpless, at her all-too-beautiful patient. Fear won out. She pushed her sleeves up to her elbows and scrubbed her hands as if she could cleanse her mind of sinful thoughts by scouring her knuckles. Then she returned to the matter at hand.

From dress to camisole, crinolette to petticoats, corset and stockings, drawers to chemise—she stripped her patient with single-minded determination, forcing herself to forget who she doctored. It proved difficult, particularly the corset, with its whalebone boning and whale-ivory busk, such as only a daughter of New Bedford would wear in this age of steel. The sight of blood helped sober her. It had soaked through the petticoats, drying to near-black rust, and flaking as she peeled back the stiff layers of gory cotton. Drawers were likewise ruined, cut away to reveal the wound itself; a jagged slash in the left shin, red and raw and angry, scattered splinters still sticking out from the edges. Her heart stopped the moment she saw it. She forced herself to keep working, to cut away the remnants of the stocking, laddered in both directions from the point of injury and drenched in crimson. Further down, the ankle had swelled; a sprain, if they were lucky.

Alexandra rolled up the ruined petticoats and slipped them underneath the wounded leg. Kit gave a soft moan. The sound reached Alexandra's ears like a shriek of agony and wrenched her heart in two.

The worst was yet to come.

Alexandra reached for the bottle of nitrate solution, pulled the cork from the neck, and poured its contents over the wound. It hissed as it struck the gory mess and flowed down, now tinged copper with blood, to soak into the ruined petticoats. Vapors stung her nose.

Kit's leg twitched. Alexandra dropped the bottle and put both hands on her knee to keep it in place. Yet no hold, no matter how secure, could prevent another moan from Kit's throat. Nor could anything be done to stop her eyes from fluttering open.

"Alex...?" she murmured.

"Hush," Alexandra replied softly, one hand flying to smooth the fine blonde hairs back from Kit's forehead before she could stop herself.

Kit, evidently too exhausted by her ordeal to resist the command, relaxed. Her eyes fell shut once more. Her brow burned beneath Alexandra's fingers. Alexandra tried to take comfort in it. A fever would help burn out any burgeoning infection. A fever would do her good.

Still, it was with a heavy heart that Alexandra cleaned the excess nitrate solution from Kit's leg. With silk thread and a silver needle, she stitched the wound shut, then bandaged it with clean linen. The ruined petticoats—now soaked with silver nitrate as well as blood—she removed to the door for later disposal by Gertie. A fresh pillow replaced them, keeping the injured limb elevated.

Having dealt with the gash, only the sprain remained. Trivial by comparison to the bloody wound. Alexandra wrapped it tight in bandages soaked in cold water. Elevated as it was by the pillow, the swelling would diminish, and there was nothing more to do for it but wait.

Which left Alexandra without distraction from Kit.

She glanced over Kit's body, searching at first for further injuries. She found none. Kit's Amazonian figure appeared no less formidable without the armor of her bodice and skirts. Long, shapely legs stretched across the bed; the ever-so-slight crest of her hipbones contrasted against the soft curve of her belly; fine blonde curls covered the mound of her sex; and her perfect teardrop breasts rose and fell with each sweet breath. Her head had fallen to the side against her pillow, exposing her slender throat and accentuating its long and graceful sweep from her strong chin down to her collarbone. Even in repose, her face had the quiet elegance of a born queen. Her full, soft lips hung barely parted, as if waiting for a kiss to wake her.

Alexandra realized she was not only staring, but had leaned over the bed to peer into Kit's sleeping face, and her own lips were now dangerously close to performing that service.

She recoiled, her stomach churning, and quickly covered Kit's nude form with the bedclothes.

She could not, however, throw a similar cover over her own shame.

Night fell. Alexandra remained awake and vigilant. She half-expected Vivian to attempt to come down and sleep in the master bed—it was his before it was his wife's, after all—but as the hours ticked past without his arrival, Alexandra had to concede she'd underestimated him. Doubtless he remained in the attic. There was almost as much up there to retain his attention as there was out in the yard amongst his damned machines. Things far closer to his heart than his wife. Truthfully, Alexandra felt glad he kept his distance, yet she couldn't quite dismiss her own bitterness at his failure to appreciate a woman such as Kit.

Morning came, bringing with it uncharacteristically bright sunshine which seemed to mock Alexandra's own inner darkness. She turned her attention upon her patient once more. The wound, when she checked it, appeared no worse. The sprained ankle looked much better, much of the swelling having receded, proving the injury a minor one.

Alexandra caught herself staring again at the long blonde hair flowing over her patient's pillow. Like molten gold, yet far finer and softer. Like the golden fleece, then. Tantalizing. Tempting. Cursed.

Still, Alexandra couldn't help noticing the faerie knots in the tresses, brought on by her patient's turning her head back and forth in the course of her slumbers.

Alexandra turned to her patient's dressing-table and took up the ivory-handled brush—no, she realized, whalebone-handled, an appropriate instrument for a daughter of New Bedford. Ever so gently, she brought its bristles to Kit's flowing tresses. The fine blonde hairs parted easily under the brush, their silky strands sliding through Alexandra's fingers like quicksilver.

Like Rapunzel, she thought, the comparison coming unbidden to her mind. A beautiful young woman, with long golden locks, trapped in a tower by a hideous witch. Which, Alexandra supposed, made herself the witch. She certainly felt no less villainous. A wicked sister-in-law, rather than a wicked stepmother, but the story remained the same. Vivian had acted as her cruel henchman, luring Kit under false pretenses, capturing the princess and dragging her back to their haunted ancestral halls, to wither away in anonymity. Unlike the fairy tale, there would be no knight, no prince, no one to rescue Kit from Alexandra's clutches.

Self-loathing bubbled up in Alexandra's heart and boiled over through her veins, brackening her soul. Kit slept on oblivious.

Setting aside the hairbrush, Alexandra cast about the room for something else to distract herself from her own unnatural instincts. Finding nothing that did not remind her of her all-too-beautiful patient, she went to the door, yanking the bell-rope as she went.

The air in the hall could not be accurately described as fresh, but it was nevertheless cooler than the air of the sick-room. Alexandra gasped in great lungfuls of it, willing the flush away from her face. Gertie arrived in short order.

"My journal," Alexandra asked of her. "From the attic."

Gertie fetched it without hesitation and handed it over without comment. Alexandra thanked her and waited until she'd gone to retreat once again into the sickroom. Even now, she couldn't bear to have anyone else gaze upon Kit in her most vulnerable moments.

With her journal clenched tight in her hands, Alexandra returned to her post at Kit's bedside. Kit remained asleep, apparently unaware of her abandonment. Still no excuse. It was a poor nurse indeed who disregarded her patient. Alexandra resolved to remain, delaying only long enough to drag a chair over to the nightstand, and dig up her brother's writing desk from a forgotten corner. She settled into the chair with the writing desk on her lap and opened her journal.

18 August, 1892

Patient is a young woman, aged three-and-twenty years, American.

Reducing Kit to such anonymity felt like treason, yet Alexandra knew it as the only remedy for her own sick obsession. She could not continue if she treated her as Kit. For her own sake as much as for Alexandra's, she would have to become merely another patient. Alexandra grit her teeth and wrote on.

Patient suffered a fall down a staircase.

Alexandra pushed down the remembrance of her own mother. If Kit had jumped rather than fallen… Alexandra would never forgive herself.

Patient's left foot broke through wooden step, resulting in a gash about three inches long on the shin, and a sprained ankle. Patient collapsed due to blood loss and pain.

The thought of Kit's pain seared Alexandra's mind. She set her jaw against it and dug the tip of her pen into the parchment. She wrote on, and on, and on, filling pages with description of the patient's wounds, the treatments rendered, the expected prognosis. This last, at least, proved a light-hearted end to an otherwise bleak tale. Kit would likely recover within weeks, and without anything worse to show for it than a thin scar.

Alexandra, meanwhile, would remain monstrous forever.

A knock sounded upon the door; Gertie with the breakfast-tray. Alexandra took it from her in the hall and locked the door against her gaze. With her own stomach still in knots, and her patient yet asleep, she set the tray on the night-stand and returned to her journal. Minutes ticked by uncounted.

Then, even as she scribbled, she felt a prickling sensation at the nape of her neck.

As if she were being watched.

Alexandra stopped writing, turned her head…

…and locked eyes with her patient.

Kit stared at her. Awake. Aware. Fever broken. Well on the road to recovery.

All this brought Alexandra closer to happiness than she'd felt since her return to Heatherhurst Hall.

Then Kit opened her perfect lips and spoke the words to send a chill down Alexandra's spine.

"Did you see her?"

Thus set off the wretched spiral of deceit to cover Alexandra's own horror. All told, after a day spent in constant panic over the fate of her beautiful patient, not sleeping for fear of being missed when most needed, and without any appetite left after her nerves tied her stomach in knots, Alexandra could by no measure be deemed a reasonable person, much less in a fit state to judge the reason of another soul.

Yet here she sat, praising Kit for being "reasonable" in her acquiescence to Alexandra's lies.

Did you see her? A woman in a yellow dress and a veil. A woman in Mother's wedding gown. A woman on the stairs.

Alexandra could hardly admit to herself what she'd seen. To admit it to Kit was unthinkable.

Yet Kit deserved to know it, and to know far more. The surety of it clawed at Alexandra's heart. It burned her like a brand at her breast, down to the bone. Her nerves strained to the point of snapping. She needed to release some of the truth, lest, in its eagerness to escape her, there should be a second accident.

As Alexandra dared another glance at Kit, bewildered and innocent, a dangerous thought occurred. Perhaps her situation was not so impossible. Perhaps she could afford to give Kit a grain or two of all the truth she so richly deserved. And for once, she knew just how to begin.

"I'm sorry," she said.

How sorry she was she could not now fully explain, lest she arouse Kit's suspicions—but she could confess a fraction of her sincere regret for all she'd done.

Kit furrowed her brow in confusion. Even this appeared becoming upon her sweet face. "It's all right."

It most certainly was not all right, but Alexandra knew it would be useless to argue. She looked away from Kit's face as she spoke on, unable to meet her innocent gaze. "It gave me something of a fright to find you on the stair. I was frantic with worry."

This, too, was altogether factual, though more painful to admit.

Alexandra forced herself to continue. "It reminded me of when I found my mother."

Merging the two truths—that her mother had died upon the grand staircase, and that the sight of Kit bleeding and insensible had brought all the horror of her childhood rushing back—allowed Alex to craft a more believable lie, one that flowed like honey rather than molasses. Yet it still tasted like ash upon her tongue.

"She had fallen," Alexandra heard herself say as if from a great distance. "Broke her neck."

"Oh!" Kit gasped. "You poor thing! I'm so sorry!"

Alex, who did not often suffer to be called a "poor thing," dared to look up at her then.

The wide-eyed expression of purest sympathy she found upon Kit's regal features broke her heart.

A sob tore itself from Alexandra's throat, bubbling up from the brackish pool in her chest. She clapped a hand over her mouth and turned away, unable to bear the sight of Kit's undeserved kindness for another instant. That her victim should feel so tenderly towards her captor—the knowledge felt like an anchor tied around her neck, dragging her down to the twisted and unfathomable depths.

For the greatest truth of all still weighed upon her mind:

Kit deserved better.

CHAPTER NINETEEN

E ven through the haze of laudanum, Alexandra's confession left Kit with much to consider. First and foremost, it confirmed her suspicions that the ghost was, in fact, the late Lady Cranbrook. Of course Kit had captured her image by photographing the staircase—she had died there. It made perfect sense.

However, she didn't think it prudent to inform Alexandra of this revelation. Particularly without the photographic plate to support her claim.

So Kit kept her silence upon the subject.

Alexandra continued writing in her diary for several moments. The only sound came from the crackling of the hearth fire. Kit's attention faltered. She drifted off, returned to find not much changed save the angle of the shadows across her bedspread, drifted off again, and awoke on what must have been another morning, because Alexandra had a fresh tray of tea, toast, and broth.

"You need to eat something," Alexandra said.

Kit struggled to sit up so she might obey her command. She'd hardly started to move when Alexandra swooped in, cradling her shoulders in one arm and sliding a pillow behind her with the other, a motion so smooth and well-practiced it was half over before Kit knew it had begun. No sooner had Kit realized she hadn't the strength to raise her hands then

Alexandra had a spoonful of broth ready to bring to her lips. Kit, her face hot with shame as well as fever, had only to open her lips. Alexandra slipped the spoon between them. Kit swallowed. The broth slipped down her throat with silky ease.

"There you are," Alexandra murmured, as if to herself.

It could hardly be considered praise, yet Kit felt a glow of satisfaction as warm as the broth. She consumed all her breakfast in much the same manner, determined to do credit to her beautiful nurse. With the meal ended, Kit assumed Alexandra would return to her diary.

"Is there something I might read to you?" Alexandra asked instead.

Kit considered the question gravely. No one had read to her since her girlhood. She'd left all her books behind in New Bedford, with the intention of sending for them when she arrived in England. Events following her arrival had quite driven them out of her head. Now the only books which came to mind were tales of Gothic horror, Poe and Radcliffe and the Brontës. None of which would prove any particular comfort in this moment. She pushed herself to think of others.

Her father had favored Melville's *Typee* and *Omoo*, while her mother had cherished Dickens. Despite her whaling ancestry, Kit found Melville thick as mud. Dickens, however, had certain merits for her, though not the same as for her mother. Her mother had enjoyed *A Christmas Carol* and read it annually aloud at the appropriate season, as reverently as if it were among the canon of Christmas hymns sung in New Bedford's myriad churches. Kit, meanwhile, felt drawn towards Dickens's later works, particularly *The Mystery of Edwin Drood*. Though it wasn't the titular Edwin Drood nor his Mystery which compelled her attention, but the dark and brooding Helena Landless, one half of a pair of mysterious twins, who had dressed in boy's clothes to attempt an escape from her cruel stepfather, and who defended the guileless Miss Rosa Budd with such courage and vigor. Dickens had died before he could finish the novel, which meant his pen could do nothing to contradict young Kit's wild imaginings. Perhaps Helena would take up boy's garb once again and carry Rosa away from the terrible Mystery.

Moreso than Dickens, though in a similar theme, Kit enjoyed Thackeray's novel of social-climbing, *Vanity Fair*. It would've been an entertaining but ultimately forgettable piece of literature, were it not for the character of Rebecca Crawley, who stirred unspeakable emotions in Kit's breast as she read, and demanded the title of heroine despite the author's insistence that his novel had none. The fluttering of Kit's heart was encouraged by one particular phrase. "Rebecca kissed her." Such a small, insignificant sentence, and yet Thackery or his editor or some enterprising printer had contrived to put it on its very own line, a three-word paragraph separated from all the rest of the text, so its minuscule form might not be lost amongst larger phrases. Indeed, to Kit, it had seemed to fly off the page and pierce her heart like an arrow. *Rebecca kissed her.* How she wished to meet a Rebecca of her own, a fierce and cunning woman who would gently guide her upstairs to some hidden chamber, far from the prying eyes of the world, to kiss her. She had hoped Alexandra might fill such a place. Those hopes were ashes now.

"Kit?"

Kit glanced up from her lap, found Alexandra gazing at her with some concern, and realized she'd quite forgotten to answer her original question.

"Do you have…" Kit trailed off, the opium haze obscuring which tome she considered a particular favorite. Then, in a rush, the true answer sprang from her lips quite without her permission. *"The Goblin Market?"*

A book of children's poems. Of course, Kit reflected with no small amount of bitterness, her foolish tongue would run on and request a reading fit only for nursery-room babes. By now Alexandra probably expected nothing less of her. Certainly nothing more.

Yet, as Kit scolded herself for her childish impulses, she saw no corresponding disdain in Alexandra's elegant features. Her aquiline nose didn't turn up at the suggestion, nor did her eyes glare in disapproval. No frown marred the graceful arch of her full brows. No sneer twisted her lips. If anything, Alexandra's expression bespoke concern. Pity, Kit quickly corrected her assessment, for Alexandra couldn't possibly feel anything so warm as concern towards her idiot American sister-in-law.

"Of course," Alexandra said, the full tones of her voice no less rich for the soft manner in which they left her rose-red lips.

Before Kit had time to blink at the unexpected answer, Alexandra had risen from her seat and gone to the door. She paused upon the threshold and looked back.

"I'll only be a moment," she promised in that same soft, rich voice.

Then she vanished down the hall, shutting the door behind herself with a muted click.

Laudanum left Kit with very little of the mental acumen required to reckon the passage of time. Every minute without Alexandra beside her felt like an eternity. She stared into the roaring hearth. Her mind turned to the little matchstick girl, though the anodyne in her veins twisted the story until the matchsticks, rather than leaving the little girl frozen to death, blazed up into an inferno, wherein the little girl danced and laughed in rapturous joy.

A sudden creak jolted Kit from her bizarre reverie. She jerked her head towards the doorway, where Alexandra now stood. Alexandra had returned after all, and with a well-worn volume tucked under her arm. Kit met her gaze. Alexandra looked quite unlike herself—uncertain, hesitant, worried. Not an imperious note in all her features.

"Did I wake you?" Alexandra asked.

"I don't think so," Kit replied.

Alexandra's expression shifted again, into something Kit couldn't quite decipher, though had she seen such a look on her cousin Phoebe's face, she would've interpreted it as weary bemusement, as one might feel for a beloved friend who'd done or said something nonsensical.

Before Kit could come to any conclusions regarding Alexandra's peculiar expression, Alexandra had shut the door, crossed the room, and sat beside her bed once more. She set the book upon her lap. Kit glimpsed the familiar title—*The Goblin Market and Other Poems*. Her own copy remained in New Bedford. The Heatherhurst Hall copy appeared just as careworn, if not moreso, with the fabric of the cover worn down on the corners, and scuffs on the leather binding.

Without prompting, Alexandra opened the book. To Kit's eyes, it seemed to fall open in her hands, not at the beginning, but somewhere towards the middle, as if the book itself knew which poem she wanted from it. Indeed, it opened to a page with dog-eared corners and stitches which had begun pulling away from the spine. Whoever had added this particular volume to the Heatherhurst Hall library, someone had loved it well, and often. Kit wondered who.

"*Morning and evening*," Alexandra began. "*Maids heard the goblins cry...*"

Her voice, low and smoky, leant a rich fullness to the words. It drew Kit in, down the winding garden path of the poem, to the goblin market itself. She saw it all before her eyes more vividly than ever before. The forbidden decadence of the faerie fruit, the little house where dwelled two sisters independent of society, their intimacy, their devotion.

When, as a child, Kit had first heard the poem, it had felt somehow forbidden. And not, she thought, in quite the way the publisher had intended. Children were supposed to fear the goblin market, terrifying and tempting in equal parts, and learn a lesson about straying from established paths. But the parts which spoke to Kit, the parts that drew her attention and kept it fixed upon the same lines, over and over, and thrilled her girlish heart, were the lines regarding "*Golden head by golden head... Folded in each other's wings... Like two blossoms on one stem...*" and other such implications of the inseparability of Laura and Lizzie. To say nothing of where such closeness lead.

As Alexandra went over these lines now, in her siren's voice, the words seemed to fall from her lips like drops of nectar. Soothing. Familiar. Kit worried a pinch of her coverlet between her fingers as she stared at Alexandra's lashes, and how very long and full they looked with her eyes downcast towards her book.

Her book. Was this, in fact, Alexandra's personal copy? She certainly seemed familiar with its text, the words rolling off her tongue with surety and precision. Had she, too, cherished it in her girlhood? Read its lines over and over with shivers of illicit pleasure? Kit clenched the coverlet in her fist.

Alexandra read on, the poem's rhythm building, steady as waves falling upon the shore and bringing in the tide, over and over, ever increasing. "*Did you miss me? Come and kiss me. Never mind my bruises; hug me, kiss me, suck my juices...*"

And there it was. More terrifying than the assault of the goblin-men, more forbidden than the market, was Lizzie offering her body up to Laura, and Laura drinking her fever's antidote from her flesh. Perhaps Kit's own fever would break if Alexandra offered herself up. She imagined Alexandra crawling into bed beside her, twining limbs around her, her lips pressed against her ear, imploring. *"Eat me, drink me, love me."*

If their places were exchanged, and Alexandra thrashed about with fever, tangled in her sheets, beads of sweat shining on her skin, Kit would have no hesitation to join her, to hold her, to implore Alexandra to eat of her flesh, to drink of her blood, to love her.

"She kiss'd and kiss'd her with a hungry mouth," Alexandra continued, oblivious to Kit's wild fantasies.

And oblivious she would remain. For, even as Kit's fever peaked, and a different sort of flame kindled beneath her navel, she knew it must be snuffed out. Alexandra didn't know. Alexandra couldn't know. How desperately Kit wanted her. How she pined. How it sickened her.

"Swift fire spread through her veins, knock'd at her heart, Met the fire smoldering there And overbore its lesser flame; She gorged on bitterness without a name."

Bitter and nameless indeed were the secret hopes of Kit's heart, forever unfulfilled.

Her desire ebbed as the poem closed, its fever-pitch cooling as it described the girls' recovery from their shared madness, how they grew up and parted to become mothers, as all good girls ought, and warned their children away from the goblin market and its twisted fruit.

"...To strengthen whilst one stands," Alexandra concluded, and fell silent.

She remained silent for a long moment. Kit half-expected her to shut the book. But at length, she turned the page, and began anew.

As Alexandra continued on to the other poems in the collection, Kit failed to follow. Her mind stuck upon the goblin market, Laura and Lizzie, the unfathomable bond that was their salvation, but which had brought Kit only disappointment and heartbreak. Eat me, drink me, love me. For women to lie together and nourish each other. Nothing less would satisfy. Kit longed for nothing more than the opportunity to show Alexandra how she could, if permitted, nourish her. How the fruits of her body could soothe her, revive her. How the blue-black bruises under her eyes would fade, and her pursed lips spread into a free and easy laugh, if only she would let Kit nourish her.

Kit drifted off in the midst of the next poem. She dreamt of her own little cottage by a babbling brook, and of going to the water's edge and peering over at her reflection. She beheld not her own face, but Alexandra's marble-carved visage. Impulse seized her and she plunged in to grasp her beloved. But the water proved far deeper than the little creek belied, and she found herself drowning alone in darkness. Fierce and desperate kicks brought her to the surface at last—her wet hair streaming into her eyes, water burning her throat, coughing—and as she clutched at the mud and reeds of the bank to pull herself out, she looked up into Alexandra's face. For Alexandra sat upon the bank now, grinning down at her with pointed teeth like a fox. Kit reached for her, and Alexandra rocked back, laughing at her plight. Again and again Kit attempted to leap from the stream and catch her. Over and over Alexandra danced out of her grasp.

Kit awoke gasping for breath. She whipped her head to-and-fro across her pillow in search of Alexandra. She half-expected to find her gone, and herself left alone in the vast and lonely bed.

But Alexandra remained right beside her, already wetting a cloth and pressing it to Kit's forehead. Her free hand grasped Kit's hand.

"It's all right," she said. "You're safe. I'm here."

"Alex," Kit mumbled, the syllables familiar to her tongue. She wondered if she'd called for her in her sleep. She burned with shame as well as fever.

Alexandra didn't seem to notice the difference. She only repeated, "I'm here."

Her crisis quelled, Kit lay quiet, her heart split between secret enjoyment of Alexandra's tender ministrations and self-loathing for the same. At length Alexandra seemed satisfied with Kit's state of health, and she withdrew to measure out another dose of laudanum. Kit swallowed it without complaint. Alexandra picked up *The Goblin Market and Other Poems*.

"What sort of books do you like?" Kit asked.

Alexandra stared at her. Kit realized she'd wondered aloud and wished she could draw the curtains around the bed to shield her shame from Alexandra's view.

"I remember," Kit blurted, desperate to break the growing silence, "you said you enjoyed *Carmilla*."

"I do," Alexandra admitted after a moment.

"I started reading it," Kit confessed. "In New Bedford. But I haven't had the chance to finish it. I'm sorry."

Alexandra said nothing.

Kit racked her brain for something to offer up in penance. "What I did read, I quite enjoyed."

Alexandra, who had stared fixedly at her in something like bewilderment all the while, spoke at last. "Would you like me to continue reading it to you?"

The tale of a cursed monster feeding off of an invalid lady was hardly appropriate bedside reading for a convalescent. But where concern over the propriety of her own speech and actions had ruled Kit's life, now etiquette seemed the laws of a distant land, inapplicable to her current position. Perhaps the laudanum had dulled these senses as well. It left her with no power to stop herself from giving the answer which felt truest in her heart. "Yes."

Alexandra rose from her chair and did something Kit had never yet seen done in Heatherhurst Hall.

She pulled the bell-rope for a servant.

Kit watched in stunned silence as Alexandra then went to the door, opened it just enough to slip out into the dark hallway beyond, and shut it behind her. A lonesome and silent quarter-hour passed before she returned, book in hand, and took her seat as if she'd done nothing out-of-the-ordinary at all.

Evidently a servant had come, for who else could have brought the book, and yet Kit would not be more astonished to hear that one of the house's phantoms had passed through walls to retrieve the book on Alexandra's behalf.

Oblivious to the leaps and bounds of Kit's wild imagination, Alexandra opened her book and began to read aloud.

The next day, Kit felt stronger and required more occupation than listening to Alexandra read. Not that the sound of Alexandra's voice alone didn't hold Kit's full attention, but Kit felt anxious not to appear as if she hung onto Alexandra's every word quite so much as she did. At a convenient break between chapters, Kit ventured to request her sketchbook and pencils, and Alexandra wasted no time in dispensing them. Alexandra resumed reading, and Kit began to draw.

Her artistic education had taught her to reference reality whenever possible. In absence of inspiration in her sick-room, she turned her mind inward and drew from imagination. Such behavior would've earned her scorn from her finishing-school tutors. Yet the images her pencil produced now—towers covered in wild vines, medieval princesses rescued by knights, fairy queens attended by nymphs—came direct from her laudanum dreams. Perhaps that same laudanum clouded her artistic judgment, but Kit thought her years of training through life-drawing had leant realism to her penciled renditions of these visions.

"Remarkable," Alexandra murmured.

Kit, whose attention had narrowed to her art, and who had not noticed Alexandra's approach until she'd spoken, froze like a startled deer. Her focus shifted at once from her sketchbook to Alexandra's overpowering presence, her head inches from Kit's own as she peered over her shoulder at the watercolor page. Warmth radiated from her face and throat, striking Kit like rays of brilliant sunshine. Kit's pulse pounded in her ears. She dared not look at Alexandra directly. The sight of her in her peripheral vision was enough to stop her breath.

Desperate for distraction, Kit returned her gaze to her own drawing. Alexandra's scrutiny forced her to consider it with new eyes. And as she did, she realized a fatal error in her sketch. Switching so rapidly between damsels in distress and their chivalrous rescuers, she had grown confused, and now...

...now, in her hands, she held a drawing of a raven-haired princess rescued by an undeniably feminine golden-haired knight.

Kit stared in disbelief at her own handiwork. The lady-knight's long blonde tresses streamed in a fantastical wind, flying like a victorious banner above a battlefield. One might say she'd depicted Sir Galahad, or some other pure and boyish knight of the Round Table, but she knew, in the darkest and most shadowy corners of her own heart, what she had done.

And Alexandra couldn't possibly be blind to it.

"Your photography is wonderful," Alexandra continued in breathless tones. "But this—!"

A flush broke out all over Kit's face and throat. Her ears and neck burned. "It's nothing."

"It's certainly not—" Alexandra began, but then her eyes flicked from the sketchbook to Kit's face, and she abruptly stopped.

Kit dropped her gaze to the blanket, worrying it between her fingertips. An awkward silence ensued. It lasted until Alexandra returned to her chair.

"What would you like me to read next?" she asked conversationally, as if she'd never seen the drawings.

Kit fought against the laudanum to produce a coherent answer. "Do you have *Vanity Fair?*"

They did, as a matter of fact. In short order the book was retrieved—in the exact same manner as *Carmilla* had been.

That night, Kit awoke to hushed voices. Peering through the candlelit gloom, she spied a shadow at the door. Her heart leapt into her throat. Then she recognized the shadow as Alexandra. Still, her pulse remained rapid. She strained her ears to hear the whispered conversation.

"You may tell Vivian," Alexandra said, "that while I appreciate his efforts to give his wife privacy, it might behoove him to at least make an appearance at her sickbed."

Kit hadn't noticed her husband's absence until that moment. Now that she thought of it, she marveled at it. Where had he been sleeping these past few nights, if not in the master bedroom? Perhaps he'd returned to the rooms he'd occupied as a younger man, before his father passed. Or perhaps he'd gone to a room beyond the reach of Kit's own chatelaine.

Perhaps he spent his nights on the other side of the locked door.

The thought sent a chill down Kit's spine. She shivered.

"Are you cold?" asked Alexandra.

The question broke over Kit like a bucket of ice-water. She hadn't realized Alexandra had returned to her bedside until she'd spoken.

"A little," Kit lied. It was a better explanation than the truth.

Alexandra stoked the fire to a blazing roar before returning to her book.

The third day dawned. Kit felt well enough to leave her bed. Alexandra helped her take exercise by walking up and down the room.

To have Alexandra's hand entangled in her own was intoxicating enough. To have Alexandra's other hand settle onto her waist, with nothing but a nightdress between them, was exhilarating. And then to hear Alexandra's low voice in her ear, bidding her to lean against her, to settle her head upon her shoulder—that was pure bliss.

It took a conscious effort for Kit to remember that Alexandra hated her.

At the end of the exercise, she returned to her bed, and Alexandra tucked her in with startling tenderness. Kit reminded herself it meant nothing, other than Alexandra's particular determination to be a good nurse.

"You're very nearly better," Alexandra observed as she drew the bedclothes up to Kit's chin and smoothed them out. "Soon you won't have any need for me."

But I still want you.

Kit bit her tongue, just barely catching the words before they escaped her lips.

Thankfully, Alexandra had turned away to measure out her laudanum and hadn't noticed anything amiss. Kit took her medicine in silence like a good girl and drifted off to sleep with Alexandra reading beside her.

When she woke, daylight remained.

But Alexandra's voice had stopped.

Kit looked towards her chair, puzzled. She found Alexandra sitting in it, precisely where she'd left her, but the book had fallen from her hands to the floor—doubtless the resulting noise had woken Kit—and Alexandra herself had fallen asleep.

Only then did Kit realize that in all her convalescence, she had never yet seen Alexandra sleeping.

Alexandra's corset kept her upright, but her head had lolled to rest against the back of her chair. Her carved-marble features relaxed in repose, like the aftermath of Saint Teresa's ecstasy. The blue shadows beneath her eyes contrasted the ivory pale shade of her sharp cheeks. Her sculpted ebony brows had only their natural arch, rather than the twist of disdain or the knit of concern. A few raven curls had come unpinned from the rest of her hair and tumbled down over her smooth forehead. Her bosom rose and fell with each gentle breath. For the first time in all the while Kit had known her, she appeared something close to vulnerable. Kit found her weakness as beautiful as her strength.

A light clinking sound reached her ears. Something akin to a wind-chime, but fainter, somewhat muffled. Kit glanced about for its source. Her eyes traced the length of Alexandra's sleeve, down to the cuffs, to her perfect hands with their tapered fingers lying loosely curled...

...and the chatelaine at her waist, with its ring of keys softly clinking together as she breathed.

Kit's own breath caught in her throat. Alexandra had pulled her chair right beside the nightstand, as near to Kit's pillow without climbing into her bed. Kit could reach out and touch her with hardly a stretch.

Which left the ring of keys well within her grasp.

Kit's heart threw itself against her ribcage.

She couldn't just snatch the keys from Alexandra's waist. She needed to think. She needed a plan. Kit forced her brain to work against the soporific laudanum. Her eyes flitted over the room in search of something to aid her in her quest.

And fell upon her own ring of keys on the nightstand.

The spark of inspiration kindled flame in Kit's mind. With a hand which trembled far less than she'd expected, she slowly reached out and touched her own keys. With absolute gentleness, she wrapped her fingers around them, between them, preventing them from clanking against each other, forcing them to be silent. She raised the ring of keys into the air and brought it back to herself, stuffing it under her pillow.

All the while, Alexandra slept.

Kit reached out again, this time towards Alexandra. Her fingertips ghosted over the chatelaine. It radiated the warmth of Alexandra's blood. Slowly, she worked her fingers into the folds of Alexandra's skirts, warmer still, and unhooked the chatelaine. It dropped into her waiting palm with the lightest clink.

Alexandra slumbered on.

Shaking now, Kit closed her fist around the chatelaine and withdrew her hand, clenching her prize to her bosom. With her free hand, she retrieved her own keys from under her pillow, then set to work with feverish urgency, removing Alexandra's keys from her chatelaine, and replacing them with her own. Every few moments her eyes darted to Alexandra to ensure she still slept.

When she'd finished, she returned the chatelaine to Alexandra's skirts, her heart in her throat as she hooked it back into place.

Alexandra remained oblivious.

Kit celebrated a private victory—but her exuberance died away as she realized she had still harder labor to perform yet.

She had to get up.

Again, she carefully planned her movements before she made them, sliding sideways between the bedclothes, to the side of the bed opposite Alexandra. Ever-so-slowly, she peeled back the blanket, the bedsheets, folding them back upon themselves and revealing her own withered form, clad only in her nightgown.

Then, with clenched jaw, she sat up.

Her arms supported her weight, which surprised her. But the true test would be upon her injured ankle. Braced for pain, she swung both legs over the edge of the mattress. A sharp twinge shot up from her wounds. She grit her teeth against it, refusing to cry out. She had not come this far just to ruin her own plans now. She counted to three and stood.

Agony.

Her knee buckled. She winced and clutched the bed-post for support. Her weak leg wouldn't carry her down the grand staircase, across the foyer to the dining room, and up the secret passage.

The abandoned hallway, however, lay far closer to the master bedroom. And if any key would fit its locked door, that key would be found upon Alexandra's chatelaine.

Kit bent forward, bracing her hands against the mattress rather than the bed-post. It made for poor security, being far softer and giving way too easily to truly support her weight, but she shuffled on regardless, until she reached the foot of the bed and the next post. And the next. She dared glances at Alexandra throughout and rejoiced to find her still sleeping.

But the third bed-post was not the end of her journey. Now she braced against a chest of drawers—now against the wall itself—and at last, she could settle her weight against the door-frame. Her hand shook as she grasped the doorknob in her fingertips. She cast one final look over her shoulder at Alexandra.

Alexandra did not wake.

Kit turned the knob—the door swung open—she darted through it—slumped against the wall of the corridor outside—flung a hand back to quiet the sound of the door thudding shut.

Freedom. The hall felt cold in comparison to the warmth of her sickroom, the floorboards like ice against her bare feet. With her back to the wall, she crept along, keeping her weight off her injured leg as best she could. It'd begun to ache even in the moments when she didn't aggravate the wound with her movement. Adrenaline helped her push it from her mind. Her progress might be slow, but it was progress, nevertheless. Every sideways step brought her closer to the object of her quest.

She reached the fork in the passage. The locked door was within sight now, though it stood so far distant. She kept going, determination guiding her every movement. She passed the window. Then the corner.

And then, with one palm braced against the wall beside it, she stood in front of the locked door.

One by one, she tried the keys, just as she had with her own key-ring. Most didn't fit. Some slid into the lock, only to fail in turning. Soon she had only five left to try, then three, then one. One final key. One last hope.

The key slid into the lock. She attempted to turn it.

No, she *did* turn it.

She turned the key, felt the tumblers give way, heard the click of the lock.

And with a faint creak, the door swung open.

CHAPTER TWENTY

Not far—perhaps an inch—but it swung freely. Kit held her breath, hardly able to believe in her own victory. She'd found a key to fit the locked door. At last, the solution to all Heatherhurst Hall's mysteries lay within her reach.

Kit raised a shaking hand to its edge and pulled it out as carefully as one turning the page of an ancient manuscript. Slowly yet surely, it drew back, revealing what had been concealed to her from her first night in Heatherhurst Hall.

A dark and narrow staircase stood before her.

Kit stared into its gloom. It appeared rather like the secret staircase in the dining room. There was hardly space enough for a person to crouch between the door and the first step. Whoever she had seen through the keyhole—if, indeed, she had seen anybody—must have been a very slight figure indeed.

As she peered up into the darkness, she saw, at its peak, a shaft of light. Sunlight. Somewhere up there was a window, allowing precious illumination to pierce the attic's mysteries.

Kit braced her hands against the bare wooden walls and began to climb.

The air she pulled into her lungs as she dragged herself up tasted musty, of dust and medicine. She knew the taste of medicine well after so many days spent in convalescence.

At last her head crested the top of the stair, and she took in her first sight of the attic.

A long, low passage stretched out before her. Bare rafters. Bare brick chimneys. Bare floorboards. A few windows—not just the one—let in the sunlight. Motes of dust drifted through it, as carefree as butterflies. The rest lay in shadow. At the far end she could just glimpse two rows of wooden bedframes. Small. Rickety. All barren. Abandoned.

This, then, must be the old servants' quarters.

Kit stepped up into the room, easily grasping one of the rafters overhead to hold herself upright. Her clumsy footsteps echoed throughout the empty space. She spared a glance at her own feet, not wanting to add a nasty splinter to her collection of injuries, and realized she had erred in her assumptions of the dust.

For, while the floorboards were dusty indeed, a clear path swept through it, leading off around the corner of one of the brick chimneys.

A path much like what might be left in the wake of a lady's skirts.

Kit swallowed down her fear and followed in the footsteps of the unknown. She rounded the corner of the chimney.

Enormous white shapes loomed in her path.

Kit clenched her knuckles against the rafters and stifled a scream. A half-second later, she realized she had happened upon discarded furniture, covered by sheets to protect it from the dust. Berating herself for her foolishness after she'd come so far, she forced her eyes away from the furniture and to the floor, finding the path again. It snaked between the chairs and tables. She followed it with her eyes.

Right up to a door.

Kit stared in disbelief at the obstacle. It stood in shadow, the sunlight from the windows not reaching this far back into the attic. She could not yet tell if it were locked.

She clutched her ring of keys tight in her fist and stepped forward. She braced herself against the vague outlines of settees and ottomans, bending, stooping, grasping, lurching, moving ever onward towards the door. As she reached it, she laid her palm against it.

It swung inward beneath her touch.

Kit caught her breath in her throat. A spot of luck at last. Hardly daring to make a sound, she gently pushed the door fully open. Light spilled out across the threshold. She squinted against the brightness.

When her eyes adjusted, she beheld a bedroom.

Her first impression was one of comfort. It seemed as if someone had plucked a cozy little cottage out of the countryside and gently laid it within the attic of a haunted manor. The walls were papered in robin's-egg blue, and a braided rag carpet adorned the floor. Not a speck of dust flew through the air here—and the air itself smelled of lavender. Another chimney stood at one end, with a charming little fire crackling in it. An overstuffed ottoman sat in front of a bookshelf filled with tomes beside a bed.

And there, in the bed, lay the wretched broken thing from the night of the storm.

But it wasn't crawling now. By the light of day, it reclined almost peacefully, sprawled under a counterpane, its head resting upon a pillow, its cropped hair the only spot of black in the sea of white. The whole face appeared much different, no longer contorted by screams of pain, though the skin of the left side still melted down the throat into the hollow of the jutting collarbone. The large eyes had closed, and its lips barely parted for the long breaths of sleep. It seemed almost peaceful.

Kit's horror turned to wonder as she stared. Had the poor creature perished in this very bed? The room looked very well-kept, without a single cobweb in its eaves and not a spot of dust to be seen. Perhaps this was the ghost of a beloved relative, and the Cranbrook siblings had taken care of the bedchamber in their loving memory. No wonder they guarded the attic so jealously, if it brought them such comfort and pain in equal measure.

Watching the sleeping figure gave her no clue to its identity. The poor creature's rail-thin frame made it androgynous—while the shoulders appeared broad and the Adam's apple prominent, Kit had seen the very same attributes in women as well as men, and both or neither might appear in a body so wracked by time and decay as to become mere skin stretched over bone. The black-and-white shades of the hair and flesh could hint towards Cranbrook ancestry, but while the colors were right, the shape was all wrong—the ghost lacked the distinctive beak both Vivian and Alexandra possessed. Kit wished she'd thought to bring her sketchbook—or better yet, her camera—to capture the ethereal image.

Then the ghost's eyelids fluttered.

Kit held her breath and watched, frozen, as the long dark lashes parted to reveal eyes of deepest brown, like two wells whose water glittered fathoms below the surface. They blinked, and then, ever-so-slowly, rolled towards where she sat, and fixed upon her face.

Not knowing what else one might say to a ghost, Kit said, "Good morning."

The ghost looked blankly back at her. Its mouth opened, and a weak voice emerged. It spoke in the same tremulous, lyrical words she'd heard on the night of the storm, but far softer. Its message sounded far less ominous without wind and thunder roaring behind it. Though it remained incomprehensible.

"I'm sorry," Kit said, pitching her voice low to match the ghost's. The room itself, so soft and quiet, seemed to defy any speech louder than a whisper. "I don't understand."

The ghost furrowed its brow. Then its lips twitched, and the unmarred corner pulled back. A low huff of air emerged from its throat, and Kit realized it was chuckling at her. She had no time to absorb this new intelligence before it spoke again.

"English, eh?"

Kit, astounded, took a moment to reply. "I am American myself, but—yes, I speak English."

The ghost laughed again, in short huffs, apparently all the breath its spectral lungs could gather. "Who are you?"

Kit couldn't help gawking at the ghost. Its accent sounded like nothing she'd ever heard in all her days, yet its inquiry was in the plainest English. She stammered, "I am Catherine Morgan—Lady Cranbrook—my friends call me Kit."

The ghost's expression changed from curiosity to surprise. "Forgive me, my lady. I didn't recognize you."

"I shouldn't think you would," Kit babbled. It struck her as curious that the spirit who roamed the halls of her husband's house would fail to know her identity—for, according to Patience Wheeler and her spiritualist ilk, the dead knew all the business of the living—though she supposed with such a large house to wander, perhaps the ghost had not often run across evidence of her occupation. "We've not been introduced, I don't think. Though we have met before."

"Have we?" The ghost furrowed its brow again. Kit suppressed the urge to press her hand to its forehead, knowing her fingers would only pass through its phantasmal form, which seemed to her the rudest possible thing for a living person to do to a ghost. The ghost spoke again, startling her out of her introspection. "You'll forgive me, I hope. My memory's not what it was."

"No, of course not," Kit rushed to reassure it. "At least, I shouldn't think so, after so long." She wondered idly how long the poor thing had been dead, though she didn't dare ask. Yet, as she contrasted the serenity of her present moment against the nightmare of the past, she recalled the lingering inquiry raised by the events of that night. "Pray, don't take offense, but I must ask—what did you want of Sir Vivian?"

The ghost's dark eyes widened. "Sir Vivian?"

"Yes." Kit wondered if spirits considered the mention of past hauntings a solecism. "When last we met, you cried out for him. In the thunderstorm."

A tinge of pink came to the ghost's cheeks. Apparently the dead could blush. "I confess I hardly remember it. I was not at my best."

The poor creature seemed so ashamed of forgetting that Kit hated to press the issue, and so changed the subject. "What should I call you?"

The ghost blinked at her, then raised a trembling hand and tugged at a lock of dark hair hanging over its forehead. "Evans, my lady. Gareth Evans."

A man, then. And not a Cranbrook after all. "How did you come to Heatherhurst Hall?"

"Sir Vivian hired me on to see to his machines. I'm an engineer by trade. Or I was."

So he knew he was deceased. Kit relaxed somewhat, no longer in dread of revealing the horrible truth to a poor unsuspecting soul. Furthermore,

he had died within living memory, after Vivian had gained his majority—
for Vivian couldn't have hired anyone as a child and would hardly have
hired on a corpse at any age. Such answers raised only more questions. Kit
opened her mouth to voice them.

Before she could speak, there came a scrabbling sound from within the
walls.

Kit whipped her head towards it. In the time it took her to do so, the
noise stopped, but her unease did not. It sounded exactly as what she'd
heard before—scratching, shuffling, rattling, so loud and covering such
ground that no one creature could make it, but only a swarm of some-
things unknown. The vision of the rat-king rose unbidden from her imagination. She shuddered.

"Are you cold?"

The inquiry, in such a small voice, yet spoken with such gentle
concern, startled Kit as much as the scratching in the walls. She turned to
the ghost—Evans—for it was he who'd spoken. Her face must've shown
something of her fear, for Evans's expression mirrored it the moment they
locked eyes.

"Forgive me, my lady," he said. "I meant no offense."

"None taken," Kit blurted. "It's only... did you hear that?"

His dark eyes rolled towards the spot in the wall where the sound had
originated. "They claim it's rats."

So he listened to the conversations of the living. Kit, seized with the
idea that this spirit might have knowledge of all that passed under this
roof, pressed on. "Is it, though?"

"Don't know. Can't say."

His answers grew shorter, his words fainter. Kit had a sudden terror of
his fading away before her eyes. She'd pushed him too far in her eagerness. Remembering the childish seances of her finishing school days, Kit
endeavored to release him, so he might regain his strength in the spiritual
realm. "You must be tired. You should rest."

Unmistakable relief flashed through his pained features as he
murmured, "Thank you, my lady."

Without thinking, Kit reached out to grasp his hand. Gently, as one
might do for an ill relative, a gesture of the merest comfort, one drilled

into her head through hours of instruction in etiquette and propriety and Christian duty. She forgot, for a moment, that her touch could dissolve him.

But rather than passing through his hand, her fingertips touched flesh as cold as the grave.

She jerked back from the frostbitten reminder of death, cursing herself for her absent mind even as she shivered in repressed horror.

In a small mercy, the ghost's eyes had already fluttered shut, and he lay still, utterly insensible to her presence.

Kit crept away from his bedside and let her gaze drift away from the sleeping ghost, sweeping over the room's smaller details, many she'd missed before. Someone had pinned pictures to the sloping ceiling above the bed, including fire-engine diagrams and hand-tinted seaside postcards. A low bookshelf sat beside the nightstand. She stooped to examine its contents. Stacks of magazines—*The Engineer, The Strand, Household Words*—intermingled with penny dreadfuls and dime novels.

One particular book had a leather-bound cover and blank spine, quite unlike the rest. With absolute stealth, Kit slid it off the shelf and opened it to find handwritten pages. She recognized the tall, thin, looping letters instantly as the customary Cranbrook script, like Vivian's and Alexandra's and the unknown surgeon's.

This must be the patient, she realized. Gareth, the poor dead engineer. In her hands she held a chronology of his final days, the terrible circumstances leading to his death.

Her nerve failed her and she snapped the book shut in her palms. The noise echoed off the slanted walls. She flinched from it and stole another glance at the ghost. He slumbered on, his otherworldly rest impervious to mortal sound.

Setting the journal aside, Kit continued on down the shelf. Buried under a dozen issues of *Household Words* lay a plain cigar box. Curiosity compelled her to shift the magazines and retrieve the humble box from its hiding spot. Its lid opened with a creak of protest, revealing its trove: a sheaf of letters, held together by a faded lavender ribbon.

In no small wonderment, Kit lifted the letters from the box. Beneath them lay a lock of strawberry-blonde hair likewise tied in lavender ribbon.

A horrible scratching noise filled her ear, as if a wretched creature sat upon her shoulder and attempted to claw its way into her skull.

Kit dropped the box. Letters scattered across the floor, the faded ribbon no match for the impact.

She paid them no heed, whipping her head towards the terrible sound. Her gaze fell upon the wall. The sound had already ceased, but doubtless it had come from within the eaves, as before.

Kit shuddered and began re-gathering the letters into the box, and, when done, stacking the surgeon's journal on top for good measure and tucking all beneath her arm. She would read them and within them find the solution to all Heatherhurst Hall's mysteries. But not here, in this sepulchral chamber, haunted by a benign wraith as it was. The rat-king did not wish her here, and she would, for now, heed its warning. She crept away towards the stair and down into the house again.

CHAPTER TWENTY-ONE

To Kit, the journey back through the attic felt far less fraught than her initial expedition. Though the treasures tucked under her arm presented new obstacles in finding ways to take the weight off her injured leg, the fluttering of hope in her bosom buoyed her up so she might as well have been weightless. She practically floated as she weaved her way through the abandoned furniture, around the chimney, and down the narrow stair.

Only when she once again stood in the long hallway with its single window did she consider the difficulties she faced in sneaking back into the master bedroom. She had enjoyed unprecedented fortune in making her escape. She didn't dare hope to find her return marked by the same streak of luck.

With her back pressed to the wall, she inched her way along, creeping not unlike a phantom herself. Her heart fluttered in her throat at the thought of her impending discovery.

Yet, as she slowly made her way, she encountered not her husband, nor her sister-in-law, nor the lady in yellow. No footsteps echoed through the empty and sepulchral halls, save her own.

Her anticipation only heightened as she rounded the final corner and glimpsed the door to the master bedroom, its long silhouette limned in gold from the combined illumination of the sunlight and the hearth fire on the other side.

Ten more steps. Five more. Two. She reached one shaking hand towards the ornate knob and turned it with the barest touch of her fingertips.

The door swung open, slow and steady as a morning glory opening its petals to the dawn, and revealed the master bedroom in all its warm glow.

There, beside the empty bed, sat Alexandra, asleep, precisely as Kit had left her.

Kit caught her sigh of relief before it ever left her, lest even that soft sound should awaken Alexandra. Noiseless as a mote of dust floating through the air, she slid into the room, shut the door behind her, crept across the carpet, and climbed back into her bed. To any observer, it would appear as though she'd never left it. Only one difference existed—she had slid the cigar box under the bed, where the overhanging bedclothes would hide it from view.

Her quest complete, she had only to close her eyes and feign the same sleep that had overtaken Alexandra.

Feigned sleep quickly became true slumber. Kit didn't realize this until she awoke to the sound of someone stirring. She opened her eyes to find Alexandra standing and stretching. Even her yawn appeared beautiful to Kit's eyes, like the silent roar of an ethereal lioness.

Alexandra turned towards her. Kit let her eyes fall shut again and endeavored to imitate the easy breath of sleep. She listened to the soft swish of silk skirts as Alexandra moved about the room, to the clinking of the laudanum bottle, and the clatter of the tea-tray. It seemed Alexandra had a hundred odd chores to perform in the sickroom. Kit waited for an opportune moment to feign her awakening.

Then, to Kit's astonishment, she heard the unmistakable rattle of a turning knob, and the coffin-lid creak of the door opening. One final swish of skirts, and the door clicked shut. Only the crackling of the fire remained.

Kit dared to open her eyes.

An empty room stood before her. Warm. Bright. Bereft. Alexandra's absence loomed like a ghost in her wake.

Kit hesitated an instant longer—then threw off her bedclothes and dived under the bed for the cigar-box. She knew not how long she had until Alexandra's return. She was determined to make the most of every second. Throwing open the lid of the cigar-box, she snatched the bundle of letters up and stashed the box back under the bed. Letters, she reasoned, could easily be stuffed under her pillow or her own body if absolutely necessary. A few sheaves of parchment were none so telling as a box.

The letters felt crisp between her fingertips. She untied the ribbon, selected the first letter from the bundle, and opened it to read.

~

5th of September, 1882

Dear Miss Cranbrook,

I write to thank you for your kindness. The friendship you, the sister of a baronet, have shown me, a mere vicar's daughter, is far beyond noblesse oblige, *and I cannot begin to express my appreciation for it. I do hope we might continue our acquaintance for many happy years.*

Your obedient servant,

Miss Elizabeth Hopkins

~

Dear Alexandra,

Your invitation to visit your ancestral home was most gracious of you to extend. The kindly condescension you have displayed in doing so is simply beyond compare. I am equal parts humbled and delighted to accept.

Sincerely,

Elizabeth

~

Dear Alex,

I cannot thank you enough for permitting me to spend the holiday with you and your most noble brother at Heatherhurst Hall. What a joy it was to roast chestnuts over the roaring hearth fire of your ancient home!

Sincerely yours,

Lizzie

~

My dearest Alex,

This holiday stretches far too long without you. How dearly I wish I could have joined you at Heatherhurst Hall, but Mama insisted upon having me at home. She and Father are so terribly boorish compared to the exquisite company of my darling Alex and your most noble brother. Every night my pillow is freshly damp with tears at the thought of our parting and the long, long hours until we might see each other again. My only comfort comes from gazing up into the night sky, on what few clear nights reach us in town, and hoping your eyes might find the same stars as mine. I hope you might think of me as often as I think of you, though I'm certain it pains us both, and my heart wrenches at the thought of your pain.

Please pass along my well-wishes to Sir Vivian.

Affectionately yours,

Lizzie

~

My dearest darling Alex,

I received your gift just this afternoon. It gladdened my heart to an inexpressible extent. I only wish I could have shown you my gratitude in person, though I understand from your note that your emotions, as heightened as my own, would not allow you to delay a moment in sending it off to me. I am gratified not only to carry your miniature in the cunning silver locket which now rests upon my warm bosom, but also to know you crafted this portrait especially for me with your own clever hands. I shall wear it always and think of you just as often. I can hardly wait to see you again at school. In the meantime, I only hope I may think of something suitable to give you in return.

Do say "good morning" to that noble brother of yours on my behalf. I am thinking of him as well.

Devotedly yours,
Lizzie

~

Miss Cranbrook,

It demeans me to address you directly. A wiser woman than I might address you only through the services of a solicitor. However, with respect to the acquaintance developed through our shared years at school, I feel it is only fair I write you this final letter.

Whatever I did to vex you, I do not deserve the ruin you have brought to what should have been my happy future. I know you poisoned your brother's mind against me. Why, I cannot fathom. Perhaps it is jealousy—though of him or I, I cannot say, and it repulses me to contemplate it further.

I know not what I did to give you such an unnatural impression of our friendship, but rest assured I do not share your abominable instincts. I have put up with your advances thus far out of Christian kindness and pity for your disturbed mind. But it has gone quite far enough. Should you attempt further contact with myself or anyone associated with me, I will be forced to act. The headmistress should be only too happy to hear of your sins. If you wish me to keep my silence, you will heed this warning.

Sincerely,
Miss Elizabeth Hopkins

~

The final letter fell from Kit's trembling fingers.

She knew not what to think. There was nothing in the letters' text— not one word she could point to and declare here was the key to their hidden meaning—and yet, she knew with every singing heartstring what had occurred between Alexandra and her Lizzie. It had been the same between herself and her Lucy. It was the incident obliquely referred to at the reception for the Cabot wedding—the loss of a bosom friend—the reason Alexandra had sought her out and told her she was not alone.

Ever since her arrival to Heatherhurst Hall, Kit had told herself she must have misinterpreted Alexandra's meaning, had put too much weight upon such slender words.

But now...

The coffin-creak of the door interrupted her thoughts. Kit jerked her head up to regard Alexandra standing upon the threshold.

"Good morning," Alexandra began.

She started forward before Kit could answer her, approaching the bed with steps so swift yet so sure that she appeared to be gliding rather than running, like the vampire of *Carmilla*.

There was no time to do anything, certainly no time in which to hide the letters that lay scattered all across the bed, so Kit made no attempt. She merely sat very still and quiet, like a fawn, alone in a secluded glen, surprised by a panther.

Yet when the fatal collision came, it was Alexandra who recoiled.

"What is—" she had begun, glancing over the papers. Then her steel-gray eyes flew wide, and all the fury left her in an expression of purest horror. Her face drained of color. Her heart-shaped lips, once blood-red, now palest pink, hung parted in shock. She looked from the papers, then to Kit, back and forth, and seemed powerless to move any part of her save her eyes.

"I've read them," Kit confessed, unable to bear the suspense for another second. "I've read them all."

Without raising her eyes from the letters, Alexandra sat down hard in her chair by the nightstand. Silence fell with her. Still, she would not meet Kit's gaze. Kit waited for her to speak, to shriek, to scold her for her impertinence, her insistence upon prying into things she had no right to know. To read private correspondence was beyond the forgiveness of any sister-in-law, never mind one who bore her such hatred as Alexandra.

And yet, as the seconds ticked past into minutes, Alexandra remained silent as stone.

The silence had a curious alchemical effect upon Kit's nerves. Her fear of discovery faded, her heart unable to keep up the frantic beating of butterfly's wings and settling instead into a more reasonable tempo. The absence of fear left a void waiting to be filled. And to Kit's own surprise, the emotion that surged in to take its place was anger.

"Did you love her?" she heard herself ask, as if from a great distance. She could hardly discern her own voice above the pounding of blood in her ears.

Alexandra stared at her. Her lips parted. No sound came.

Kit filled the silence. "You loved her. I know you did. You loved her, as I am sure—" Kit choked, tears welling in her eyes. "—as I am sure you once loved me!"

Still Alexandra stared and said nothing.

"Why do you hate me?" The words poured from Kit's heart like a tide of blood. "What did I do to turn you against me? You loved me, once! I know you loved me! Why did you stop? What have I done to turn your love to hatred? Tell me, for God's sake!"

Alexandra opened her mouth again, only this time, a weak and croaking voice emerged from her bloodless lips. "Nothing."

Kit stared at her in disbelief. "What."

"You've done nothing to turn my love for you to hatred."

"Then why—"

"I haven't stopped loving you." Alexandra staggered towards her. "I've tried—I've made every effort—but I cannot."

Kit could hardly believe her ears. "Why!? Why in God's name should you choose to make such an effort?"

"Because," said Alexandra, "you married my brother."

And all at once, Kit realized her mistake.

Alexandra's love for Lizzie had not been the only romance hinted at in the correspondence. Lizzie's constant asides—giving her regards to Alexandra's "noble brother"—culminating in the accusation of sabotage by Alexandra against her desired match. Lizzie had set her cap at Vivian and used Alexandra to get to him. She had failed.

But Kit had succeeded.

Kit, who had spent all that time in New Bedford courting and being courted by Alexandra, had shown up without warning on her doorstep, arm-in-arm with her brother, the fated silver-and-sapphire ring gleaming on her finger.

She had to explain her actions, and quickly, before she lost Alexandra forever. She required eloquence—all possible powers of oration.

What actually left her mouth was, "I only married him to be closer to you!"

Alexandra could not possibly look more shocked than Kit felt at her own words.

Speech had failed them both. Only action could save them now. Kit surged up from her sickbed, grasping Alexandra by the hand. Pulling herself up even as Alexandra bent down, she closed her eyes and tilted her head—

—and met Alexandra's open mouth with a kiss.

CHAPTER TWENTY-TWO

"I love you," Alex whispered. "I have loved you from the moment I first saw you. I have tried with all my heart to stop loving you, but—"

She cut herself off with a gasp and her lips returned to Kit's with renewed passion.

"Don't stop," Kit murmured when they parted for breath. "Never stop."

Alexandra looked down upon her with a wicked smile. "I intend to begin."

So saying, she withdrew from the bed and began to undress.

After all, it hardly seemed fair for Alexandra to remain clothed, whilst Kit had nothing more than a sheer muslin nightgown to garb herself. Though Alexandra had to admit she quite enjoyed the view the nightgown provided—the tantalizing veil of softest cotton, like dew-drops on spider-webs, clinging to every curve and swell of Kit's magnificent body, draping delicate folds over secrets Alexandra could hardly wait to discover.

Even with the considerable distraction of removing her own bustle, gown, and petticoats, Alexandra couldn't help noticing the rapt attention with which Kit watched her every move. Deep brown eyes followed her hands as they untied ribbons and undid buttons, tugged sleeves and tossed aside skirts.

Then Alexandra, beginning to untie her corset, paused.

A gleam had come into Kit's eye, the unmistakable glimmer of desire. Evidently delighted at all she'd seen thus far, her expression had lit up further, 'til it shone as bright as her golden tresses. She bit her lip as her eyes traced the hourglass outline of Alexandra's hips and waist.

Alexandra knew that look well. It seemed Kit particularly enjoyed the sight of a woman in a corset. And far be it from Alexandra to deny her what gave her such pleasure.

Rather than untie her laces, Alexandra slid her hands around to her sides, running them up and down the boned curve of her waist. The silk made a soft shushing sound as her fingertips ghosted over the material. She watched Kit's eyes widen, the pupils growing deep and dark.

"You like that," Alexandra mused aloud, unable to repress her own satisfied grin. "Don't you."

It wasn't a question, but Kit answered anyway, with a shy little nod. The strawberry blush blooming all over her face and throat bespoke still more.

Alexandra reached out, gently plucked up one of Kit's hands by the wrist and pulled it to herself, laying Kit's palm against the swell of her hip beneath the silk and steel of her corset.

Kit gave a breathless little gasp. Her eyes darted between Alexandra's face and her own hand.

"Go on," Alexandra purred.

She released Kit's wrist.

Kit looked as though she could not believe her own good fortune. First, she ran her thumb over the curve of Alexandra's waist. Then she traced a line of steel boning down to the garter straps. Her touch felt delicate, hardly noticeable, yet Alexandra couldn't help but notice. Indeed, Kit's touch absorbed all her attention. Her own heart threw itself against her ribs as she watched.

Then Kit slid two fingers beneath the garter strap and Alexandra's thigh, and Alexandra felt as if lightning struck her where fingertips met skin, branding her, leaving her glowing in its afterimage, white-hot and half-melted.

Kit, apparently oblivious as to the effects of her actions, continued toying with the garter strap, rolling it between her fingertips, running her fingers up and down its length, tracing the buckles, and ultimately snapping it against Alexandra's thigh, by purest accident, and leaving a red mark blooming on milk-white skin.

Alexandra recognized the repentant look upon Kit's face and swooped down to kiss her before she could open her mouth to apologize. Thus distracted, she offered no resistance as Alexandra caught her hand, bringing it up. She broke the kiss—leaving Kit gasping for breath and something more—and applied her mouth instead to the inside of Kit's wrist. Kit gasped. Her pulse thrummed against Alexandra's lips, rapid, frantic, desperate. Alexandra opened her mouth and let her teeth scrape lightly over the throbbing veins. Kit's gasps became moans. Alexandra felt her own thighs grow damp in response.

Unable to restrain herself another instant, Alexandra pounced onto the bed and straddled Kit's hips. The armor of her corset held her erect as she gazed imperiously down at her captive lover, clothed only in the sheerest nightgown, translucent, vulnerable. In a flash of inspiration, Alexandra wondered how Kit might look with a riding crop pressed against her throat. Magnificent, most likely. And, judging by the wide-eyed, open-mouthed look of breathless desire upon her face now, absolutely delighted.

One final touch remained. Alexandra reached up and unpinned her hair. Raven waves cascaded down her bare shoulders as she shook her hair free of all restraints. When she finally returned her gaze to Kit's face, she found her entranced. Moving as if in a dream, Kit reached up to touch an ebony curl, brushing the strands back and forth in her fingertips.

As much fun as it was to watch Kit in all the delight of new discovery, Alexandra had more pressing needs. She made them known by rolling her hips against Kit's.

Even through the muslin nightgown, such contact had the desired effect. Kit gave a full-bodied shudder, beginning beneath the soft mound of curls covering her sex and radiating outward, rumbling down through her thighs and up her spine, her back arching, her belly alternately concave and convex with her stuttering gasps.

Between her legs, Alexandra felt a wetness to match her own. The muslin had soaked through, rendering transparent what had moments before appeared merely translucent.

To not only want, but to find herself wanted in turn—

Alexandra, wild with desire, adjusted her stance to bring her knee between Kit's thighs, which opened eagerly to receive her. She descended upon Kit again, ravenous with unnatural hunger. Her lips found her throat in the same instant Kit's thighs clenched tight around her own, drawing her in, tangling them together. The barest movement brought her quim to Kit's, and to feel her pulse echoing through her own sex felt like coming home. Her hips bucked without her realizing, moving with pure instinct, rolling against her, between her, into her, with her—for Kit, too, had caught upon the same tide, and wave after wave rolled through them, building and building, each crest breaking only to reform into something greater, something grander, something that made Kit's eyes flutter shut, and her mouth fall open in wanton moans, and the whole of her writhe into Alexandra, who could hardly contain her in her arms, who thrashed against her, soft curves with sharp bones.

Alexandra fought to keep her eyes open. She wanted to bear witness, to see the very moment the final wave broke, to watch as Kit shattered in her grasp, to witness the expression of unrestrained ecstasy flow over her beautiful features—

And the sight brought Alexandra crashing down with her.

CHAPTER TWENTY-THREE

K it couldn't recall the last time she'd felt so content. To have Alexandra's arms around her, their legs entangled, her head upon her bosom, hearing her heart beating in her breast and the sound of it mingling with her own pulse in her ears... and to know, to be certain, that Alexandra loved her in precisely the way she'd always hoped. She felt she could die of happiness.

And as the wonderful languid afternoon stretched on, Alexandra began whispering into her ear. Sweet nothings, endearments, the ghost of her breath over her cheek as delicious as her words. Soon Kit began to whisper back—though her own speech turned away from the insignificant and towards the shadows that had lurked in the back of her mind ever since her arrival in England.

"I have so many questions," Kit confided. "About Heatherhurst."

After all, as Melville would have it, there was no place like a bed for confidential disclosures between friends. And Kit felt certain she and Alexandra were friends indeed.

"I want to tell you everything," Alexandra whispered, her hushed voice as much confession as confidence. "But first... I must introduce you to someone in particular."

Kit's mind lit up with curiosity. "Someone within the house?"

"Indeed," Alexandra answered, and, with a quick kiss to Kit's forehead, left the bed to dress.

Kit watched her without bothering to disguise her interest—she had no need to, not now, after everything—and found the process of covering up just as enticing as the disrobing. The transformation from wanton to pristine proved fascinating. Tangled black curls tumbling down in wild abandon became a tight and intricate knot at the back of Alexandra's head. The flushed red flesh, streaked with sweat, was washed and brushed into smooth ivory once again. Watching her lace her own corset, buckle her garters, pull on her stockings... Kit felt ready to tear them all off her again. Yet she only bit her lip and let her eyes do the feasting.

Soon enough, Alexandra returned to the bed to help Kit dress as well. Kit didn't think she cut half as elegant a figure as she hobbled around on her wounded leg. But her beautiful assistant more than made up for her own clumsiness. Alexandra laced her corset more delicately and tenderly than any lady's maid, and slipped her shoe over her stocking in a manner which would have put Cinderella's prince to shame. The addition of a feather-light kiss to her calf as she pulled away made Kit's knees weak.

All too soon, it ended, and Alexandra took her hand and led her from the sickroom.

"Where are we going?" Kit dared to whisper as they left the master bedroom behind.

"To the attic," Alexandra murmured in return.

A spark of realization told Kit she might already know the person to whom Alexandra wished to introduce her. After all, she'd been to the attic just today and met but one soul.

The ghost of Gareth Evans.

Kit's mind raced as Alexandra led her ever-so-slowly down the sepulchral corridors. If, indeed, Alexandra meant to introduce her to Gareth, then it meant Alexandra could see him—knew he was as real as she—and would then, therefore, have to believe in ghosts as much as or more than Kit.

Yet Kit held her tongue, lest, in speaking her suspicions, she open herself up to unbearable disappointment.

Kit found her second sojourn into the attic far more comfortable than the first. She thought ascending arm-in-arm with Alexandra might have something to do with it. Alexandra led her up the stairs, around the corner, through the cache of abandoned furniture, and up to the door she'd shut herself scant hours before.

Alexandra put her delicate fingers upon the doorknob, then turned to Kit.

"I would ask you to brace yourself for what you are about to see," said Alexandra. "While you may find the sight distasteful, I assure you there is no danger, and I would hope that you might..." She shook her head. "I know you will feel compassion for what lies beyond."

Beyond. Kit shivered. Alexandra knew, then, that a ghost dwelled here. Had known all along, without telling Kit, for how could she tell the new bride that the ancestral halls were haunted, and expect to be believed?

Kit almost opened her mouth to confess she'd already witnessed what Alexandra intended to show her, but Alexandra had returned to the door. The knob rattled as it turned. The hinges creaked as the door opened.

The bright little room remained much as it had when Kit left it. The ghost of Gareth Evans lay in the bed, his twisted frame relaxed in repose, his narrow chest rising and falling with shallow breaths.

"Don't be afraid," Alexandra whispered.

"I'm not," Kit replied.

She meant to say more, explaining what she already knew, but the ghost of Gareth Evans stirred, distracting her. His breath quickened, his limbs shifted, and his eyes opened. At first he appeared insensible to their presence. Then his head rolled across the pillow, and his eyes fixed upon the two women. Another moment later, they focused, and recognition brightened his features.

"Good morning, Miss Alexandra," he said.

"Gareth," said Alexandra, "this is Lady Cranbrook."

Kit stepped closer, intending to perform the appropriate how-d'you-do's and assure Evans that all her friends called her Kit, and he, as a spirit, might feel welcome to the privilege as well.

Evans, meanwhile, said, "You can see her, too?"

Kit's comforting speech died in her throat. She choked on whatever she'd meant to say and turned to face the spirit—the man—in the bed.

But the man had eyes only for Alexandra.

And Alexandra, never once taking her mournful gaze off the man's face, replied, "Yes, Gareth. I can see her, too."

Kit glanced rapidly between them, unable to decide which to confront. At last she settled on the man in the bed and choked out, "You—you're not a ghost at all, are you?"

Evans blinked at her. "Aren't you?"

Kit's mind whirled. The memory of her first stormy night in Heatherhurst Hall rushed to the surface. The inexorable realization that she had not encountered an apparition, but a living, breathing, flesh-and-blood man, crashed upon her. She thought she might faint. Clutching Alexandra's arm to steady herself, she managed to answer, "No."

Alexandra, meanwhile, seemed only to have just understood the grave misunderstanding both parties had operated under up to this point. She squeezed Kit's arm in a reassuring manner, unspoken apologies filling her eyes.

"I'm glad you're not a ghost," Evans added. "Not that I've anything against ghosts, mind, but you're far too kind to be dead already."

"Likewise," Kit managed to force out. She cleared her throat and wished dearly for something to wet her whistle.

Evans smiled and turned to Alexandra. "Now that we've solved the mystery of Lady Cranbrook, perhaps you'd like to tell me about the woman in yellow?"

Kit's heart dropped into her stomach. She stared at Evans in wide-eyed horror. Her gaze flicked towards Alexandra. She expected to see skepticism. Instead, she encountered an expression of alarm to match her own.

Evans glanced between the two of them. "The woman in the yellow dress. She visits me from time to time. And she's not so nice about it as Lady Cranbrook is, I can tell you that."

Cold sweat beaded on Kit's forehead.

"My dear," Alexandra replied in a tone Kit recognized as forced control, "do you perhaps mean Gertie?"

"No, I do not mean Gertie! God's bodkins, if I don't know Gertie by now then I'm about as sharp as a ball-bearing. There's Gertie, and you, and Vivian, and the woman in yellow. So far as I know. If you're hiding anybody else under the stairs, I wish you'd give me some forewarning of it."

Alexandra stared at him in disbelief—no, not quite disbelief. Horror. Horror borne of recognition. Her lips parted for speech.

"She's real," Kit blurted before Alexandra could answer.

Both Evans and Alexandra stared at her. Again, as ever, she felt the familiar burn of her blotchy blush, but put it from her mind. The sheer horror of her realization helped.

"The woman in yellow is real," she repeated, as much for her own benefit as for theirs. "I have seen her. I have photographed her. Thank you, Mr. Evans, for confirming it."

"Call me Gareth," he said offhandedly, as if they'd been in the midst of discussing the weather. Then he furrowed his brow. "I didn't realize there was any question as to her veracity."

"Things have been strange of late," Alexandra said, her voice carefully controlled. "But we've solved one mystery at least. Thank you, Gareth."

Gareth appeared no less confused by this speech. He nodded regardless. "Happy to be of service, Miss Alexandra."

CHAPTER TWENTY-FOUR

K it watched and waited as Alexandra gave Gareth another dose of laudanum from the nearly-empty bottle on the nightstand. Bidding him good-bye and wishing him well, the ladies left him to catch what much-needed rest he could.

Alexandra remained quiet as she led Kit back downstairs to the master bedroom. Kit didn't press her for words. She'd already revealed so much, and to pry seemed like rubbing salt into her wounds.

Yet no sooner had Alexandra settled Kit upon the bed—sitting up, rather than reclining—and locked the bedroom door than she turned and said, "You require more explanation."

It wasn't a question. Kit didn't dare contradict her.

Alexandra took a deep breath and exhaled it through pursed lips. Her gaze had fallen to the floor, and she kept it there for a long moment. When she met Kit's eyes again, she did so with a look of grim determination. "I have seen the woman in yellow."

Everything Kit had thought she'd known fell away.

Evidently something of this showed on her face, for Alexandra looked away again, this time sideways, towards the clock ticking upon the mantle. Kit wished to reassure her, to tell her she believed her, that she knew she told the truth. But she knew not how to begin.

Alexandra spoke again. "I believe... I may know who she is."

Another silence fell. If only Alexandra would come away from the door, would come closer to the bed, within Kit's reach, then she needn't struggle so to find the right words to comfort her. She could hold her in her arms and clutch her to her bosom, kiss her, console her.

Alexandra finally released her hold upon the doorknob, but only to grasp her chatelaine instead. Her fingers ran over each key, one by one, clinking them against their fellows, a gentle sound.

Then, in a voice so small and quiet Kit struggled to hear it above the jingling of the chatelaine, Alexandra said, "I think she's my mother."

"I think so, too," said Kit.

Alexandra jerked her head up to look at her then.

Kit held out her hands in mute entreaty.

Alexandra rushed across the room into her arms.

They held each other for a long moment, with Alexandra taking shuddering breaths in Kit's ear, and Kit running her hand through Alexandra's hair and on down her back, caressing her, comforting her as best she could. She pressed a kiss to her neck, her cheek. Alexandra clutched her tighter.

At length, Alexandra pulled away to look seriously into Kit's eyes. "I'm afraid I've not yet satisfactorily explained Gareth's presence in the attic."

"I've met him already," Kit hurried to confess.

Alexandra raised her eyebrows.

"I could hardly have avoided it," Kit forced herself to continue, "in retrieving those letters."

At the mention of the forbidden correspondence, Alexandra bit her lip in chagrin. "Of course."

"And I saw him before," Kit added, carefully watching for Alexandra's reaction. "On my first night here. The night of the storm."

"Yes, you did." Alexandra closed her eyes as if pained. "I'm sorry for my part in deceiving you then. And after."

Kit forgave her instantly. "But why was such deception necessary? Why didn't you—or Vivian—tell me about him?" A thought struck her. "Does Vivian know he's here?"

Alexandra gave a bark of the bitterest laughter. "Oh, he knows, all right. Vivian is the reason Gareth is here in the first place."

Kit stared at her. "Then why...?"

"Perhaps," said Alexandra, "it would be best for me to start from the beginning."

Kit heartily agreed.

Even so, it took Alexandra a moment to gather herself and begin her tale. "You have wondered, perhaps, why it is that my brother does not often share your bed."

A blush bloomed in Alexandra's sharp cheeks. Kit wanted to kiss it, to feel its warmth beneath her lips, but restrained herself.

Alexandra continued. "Vivian is as fond of the company of men as I am fond of the company of women."

It took Kit a moment to parse this, but once she had, her blush rivaled Alexandra's. "Oh."

Alexandra nodded. "Precisely. After my mother... passed on, Vivian and I were sent away to school. You already know what became of me there, from the correspondence. Unfortunately Vivian's time at school proved no less infamous. One particular incident caused the headmaster to contact our father." She paused. "Our father perished in a shooting accident shortly after receiving the headmaster's letter."

The implications of such a coincidence couldn't be ignored, even by Kit. Her heart broke anew for the bereft siblings. She grasped Alexandra's hand.

Alexandra returned the gesture and spoke on. "Vivian and I finished our respective educations and returned home. I settled into the role of managing the household. Vivian, meanwhile, had taken up amateur engineering." She rolled her eyes towards the window. "Hence his machines."

Kit recalled his great interest in the boiler room of the steamship that had carried them across the Atlantic on their honeymoon... and his great interest in the shirtless, muscular men who shoveled coal there.

"Eton," Alexandra continued, "had not given Vivian sufficient training to be an engineer on his own, so he sought outside help. Professional aid for his amateur pursuits. He ended up hiring a promising young Welshman who'd studied engineering as it pertained to the coal mines and had been the stationary engineer on-site at a particular mine for some years."

The connection came like lightning to Kit's mind. "Gareth Evans."

"Precisely. He and Vivian began working together on repairing an old threshing machine one of the county farmers had discarded. They found they got on well." Alexandra leveled a knowing look at Kit. "Very well."

"Ah," said Kit.

Alexandra smiled wistfully. "Their affection for each other was rivaled only by their affection for their machines. They repaired the thresher, but had no means by which power it, and therefore no way to test it. In the interest of economy, Vivian purchased a steam engine from a textile mill in Manchester that was replacing its equipment. When it arrived, he and Gareth assembled the machinery, filled the boiler with water and the furnace with coal, and set the whole thing working. They discovered, to their dissatisfaction, that the boiler leaked. Not to be deterred, they set about repairing it. Vivian hit upon the notion of keeping the boiler running, so they might more easily perceive the holes through which the steam escaped, whilst they stopped up the leaks." Alexandra's tone grew still more bitter as she met Kit's eyes. "Perhaps you have already found the flaw in this scheme."

Kit, her throat tight with suspense, mutely shook her head.

Alexandra dropped her gaze again with a sigh. "Such boilers are typically tested with water—cold water. They are filled, and then, should any leaks be present, water will drip from them, and the engineers testing the boiler may mark them with chalk for later repair. Vivian," a note of bitterness entered her voice, "thought he had found a more efficient method in using steam instead of water. For, after all, water expands greatly when it becomes steam, and so while it would take ever-so-many gallons of water to fill the boiler cold, it would take far fewer gallons of water if they were first turned into steam. Furthermore, by repairing the leaks as they became apparent, he and Gareth could have the boiler fixed far faster than if they simply marked the leaks with chalk and repaired them later once the mechanism was stopped."

Kit furrowed her brow at this explanation. It all seemed rather technical. Doubtless a more mechanically-inclined mind than her own would understand it in an instant, and already be nodding along with Alexandra's words. But to Kit's more artistic brain, something about the change in method sounded as if it boded ill.

"At first," Alexandra continued, "it all proceeded according to plan. But what they failed to understand was that with each leak they stopped, pressure rose in the boiler."

Belatedly, Kit realized the inevitable result. She stifled a cry of horror, knowing nothing she said now could prevent what had already happened.

"When they'd nearly finished," Alexandra continued in the same low, expressionless tone, "it burst."

Kit's imagination likewise exploded, showing her a vision of what must have occurred to bend and break Gareth's body so to reduce him to the poor wretch she found in the attic—a horrible conflagration of scalding steam and steel.

"The sound carried for miles," Alexandra went on. "The blast rent the boiler in twain—cast iron three inches thick torn asunder. Like ripping the wings off of a butterfly. The pieces were blown hundreds of yards away. You've seen some of them, on the road to the village."

Kit recalled the twisted hunks of rusted iron and how unwilling Alexandra had been to acknowledge their existence. Her reluctance came as small wonder now that she knew they were the remains of such disaster.

"One portion of steel plate struck the stables," said Alexandra. "It killed two horses outright. The remainder had to be destroyed—their injuries were too great to survive. Their screams…"

She broke off with a shudder. Kit clasped her hand. Alexandra looked at it, startled, then brought her gaze up to meet Kit's for the briefest instant before her eyes fell again and, with a shaking breath, she continued her tale.

"A smaller piece struck Vivian in the side—broke his ribs and scalded his flesh. Perhaps you've seen the resulting scars. As for Gareth… I know you've seen some of his. His face melted by the steam. I can tell you the rest of him fared no better. He survived by miracle."

And the assistance of the unknown surgeon, Kit thought.

Alexandra spoke on. "Another, larger portion struck the house. It hit the roof of the south-west wing and fell through to the cellar. The collapse killed one housemaid outright. Abigail. Others were injured. And Gertie— Gertrude, rather—barely escaped with her life. That's how she lost her hand."

"Who is Gertrude?" asked Kit.

Alexandra frowned puzzledly at her. "Our cook."

"Oh." Kit supposed it was rather silly that she, as the lady of the estate, didn't know the name of the only servant they employed.

To Kit's relief, Alexandra continued on as though no solecism had occurred. "When the dust had settled and I realized the extent of the disaster, I sent for the surgeon with all haste. He arrived and immediately began attending to my brother. Vivian's injuries, while grave, were hardly the worst, but when one is called to the country seat of a baronet, one naturally attends to the baronet's needs first." A poorly-concealed sneer tugged at Alexandra's lips. "Thus it fell to me to tend to the other survivors. Gareth, in particular, proved a frightening case—the surgeon had dismissed him as a lost cause—but as you have seen, he survived, despite the odds against him. Vivian would've never forgiven me had I let him perish."

"Then it was your diary!" Kit gasped. "The one on the shelf in the attic!"

Alexandra looked at her strangely. It took her a moment to recognize her expression as bashful. "Yes, that one—and others, too. His condition has remained stable for years, for better or worse. Though, since Vivian's return, I have noticed a decline."

Ever since he returned with his bride, Kit thought, with no small amount of guilt. Seeing Lucy wed to John Cabot had left her bedridden for weeks. She could imagine the effect upon Gareth, already an invalid, to see his beloved come home with a feminine interloper on his arm.

"Gertie, too," Alexandra continued, oblivious, "is not so much the worse for the loss of her hand, to hear her tell it. But for the rest, we are well ruined. All the other surviving staff quit without notice and dispersed to parts unknown. The villagers, farmers, and tenants were already suspicious of Vivian's experiments. The accident confirmed all their worst fears and turned the whole county against us once and for all. Even if we could afford to hire new staff, no one in all Cumberland would dare come to Heatherhurst."

Kit clasped her hand tighter.

"And now," Alexandra said with no small measure of bitterness, "Vivian has decided to renew his experiments. Despite their decided failures, and despite his own failure to improve his knowledge of their workings since his last self-made disaster."

A cold chill crept over Kit's flesh. She pushed down her fears to voice the foremost question in her mind after Alexandra's confession. "What in the Dickens possessed Vivian to lock his lover away in an attic?"

Alexandra sighed. "Are you familiar with English law?"

"Not terribly," Kit confessed. "Is it illegal to hire Welshmen? Or to experiment with steam engines?"

"It is illegal for men to lie with men," said Alexandra. "Or kiss. Or hold each other in too much regard. The law is very loosely written. They call it the Blackmailer's Bill, and with good reason. Affection between men is punishable by two years' hard labor."

Kit stared at her. "...Oh."

"And so we are all trapped within Heatherhurst Hall." Alexandra's voice caught, and fresh tears sparkled in her gray eyes. She blinked them back with ferocity, though the gaze she turned upon Kit looked no less mournful. "And now, through Vivian's wretched scheme of marriage, so are you."

Kit furrowed her brow. "How so?"

Alexandra served her a blank look.

"Really," Kit babbled, as much to fill the awkward silence as to assuage Alexandra's misery, "I should think leaving the house altogether would prove the most practical solution. You do not like the isolation, nor the reminder of..." She struggled for a polite phrase to cover both Vivian's folly and the previous Lady Cranbrook's suicide. "...past misfortune. You were happy in Newport—in New Bedford—in America in general, I think. At least, you seemed so to me."

A faint smile flickered across Alexandra's lips. "I was."

"Then why not return?" What had begun as mere fancy now took the shape of a real plan, startling no one as much as Kit herself. "We've money enough, thanks to my inheritance. My connections there are small and few, but they are connections, nonetheless. We could all move to a new house, make new friends, forget all the horrors—"

"What of Gareth?" Alexandra asked.

Kit stared at her in frank disbelief. "Bring him with us, of course!"

Alexandra's eyes flew wide.

"I don't doubt his debilitation is great," Kit hastened to elaborate. "But a cruise in a steamship would not do him too much harm—aside from the seasickness, which, while I won't pretend isn't miserable, would at least be temporary. And then he'd be in America, and we could get him all the best surgeons. My cousin Phoebe, for one! I'm sure she could do wonders for him. And if not herself, she would know someone better, and while perhaps his injuries may be beyond cure, we could at least offer him the best comfort the medical profession could possibly provide. And a change of scenery is good for everything! I don't doubt a fresh sea breeze, or the sight of a few green trees instead of the lonely brown moor—no offense intended—"

"None taken," Alexandra replied tonelessly.

"—would brighten his prospects considerably!" Kit finished with triumph.

"But the law," Alexandra began.

Kit frowned. "The English law is abominable, yes... but to my knowledge, there's no equal to it in America. At least not in Massachusetts. I'd have to ask Mr. Mudge about it—in circumspect terms, of course."

Alexandra continued staring at her, but the expression in her wide gray eyes had turned from shock to wonder. "You really would do it."

"Of course I would! It'd be the best thing for everyone!" Kit hesitated. "Unless... unless you don't agree?"

"On the contrary," Alexandra replied. "I agree wholeheartedly. But I'm afraid we'll require Vivian's assent above all else."

Kit, emboldened, declared, "Then we should ask for it without delay!"

"And your ankle?" Alexandra asked

The simple inquiry dampened Kit's fervor somewhat, but she soon enough discovered a solution. "If Gareth is to travel in his condition, I can hardly do less with a mere sprain!"

"Still," Alexandra replied, "we should do as little as possible to aggravate it in the meantime. Wait here."

Without further explanation, she practically leapt from Kit's side and flew to the window. In a swift and well-practiced motion, she threw it open, and stuck her head and shoulders out into the crisp air.

"Vivian!" she cried at the top of her voice, clear and carrying as far as any church-bell.

CHAPTER TWENTY-FIVE

E ven with the considerable power of her voice, Alexandra had to call for her brother twice more before Kit heard something like a muffled reply. Alexandra waved at something or someone below. Kit watched and waited, entranced.

"Come inside!" Alexandra shouted, one hand to the side of her mouth to aid in the amplification of her command. "I must speak with you! It's terribly urgent!"

She paused a moment longer, then, apparently receiving an affirmative reply from her brother below, dashed back to Kit with the grin of a giddy schoolgirl. Alexandra threw her arms around her and pressed a kiss to her cheek as they waited for Vivian to arrive.

Some minutes after, there came the heavy tread of his footsteps in the hall—quicker than expected, as if he were running. Kit clenched Alexandra's hand. The door swung open, and Vivian stood upon the threshold, panting with exertion.

"What is it?" he gasped, looking from Alexandra to Kit and back again. "Are you all right?"

Kit blinked at him. "I'm quite well, thank you."

This answer appeared to bewilder him, but he replied with restraint,

"Oh. I'm glad of it." He turned to Alexandra, a furrow marring his heavy brow. "I thought something had happened."

"Oh, but something has happened!" said Alexandra, laughing lightly. "The most wonderful thing in the world has happened! Do tell him, Kit!"

Though the plan was of her own contrivance, when put on the spot thusly, Kit hardly knew where to begin.

"Alexandra has told me," she said haltingly, "who lives in the attic."

Vivian's face drained of color. His eyes flicked from Kit to his sister, and back again. He licked his thin lips. "How much has she told you, exactly?"

Kit couldn't stand the suspense another moment.

"I've met Gareth!" she blurted.

"It's not what it seems!" Vivian cried out.

Kit, startled, asked, "What's not what it seems?"

"He's not—" Sir Vivian seemed on the verge of an apoplectic fit, he struggled so to get his words out. "I'm not—!"

"Of course not," said Kit in her most soothing voice.

A long, miserable groan hung in the air. Vivian had covered his face in both hands.

"Oh God," he wailed, kneading his forehead with his knuckles. "What have I done?"

"It's all right," Kit began, but Vivian interrupted her.

"Don't—" He dropped his hands from his face and looked at Kit with the face of a man buried alive. "Catherine, please—"

"You and he are—" She stopped, her tongue lacking the vocabulary for the concept she knew to be real and true, more so than anything else in this world, and she fell back upon the only word she knew, as inadequate as it seemed to describe the depth of what she felt. "—friends!"

Vivian, apparently struck dumb, nodded.

"Not just friends," Kit babbled on. "But as Lucy and I were, and as Alexandra and I—" Kit stumbled to a halt, her mouth having run far ahead of her mind. As she and Alexandra were? Would be? As she hoped they might become?

Vivian appeared equally confused by this sudden detour in her conversation. "Pardon?"

"She means lovers," Alexandra replied in a matter-of-fact tone.

This did nothing to ease her brother's evident distress.

"Please," whimpered Vivian, "for God's sake, stop talking."

"This isn't about you, Vivian!" Alexandra snapped.

The expression he turned upon her appeared aghast.

With a sharp inhale, Alexandra recovered her composure. "This is about Kit's new plan for our future."

She turned to Kit with a smile intended to encourage her to elucidate their scheme. Vivian, too, looked to her, with an expression of purest despair. Kit only hoped her plan would alleviate it.

"I would like," Kit said, her words halting despite Alexandra's support, "to return to New Bedford. And I would very much like to bring Alexandra, yourself, and Mr. Evans with me."

She waited for his face to brighten, for him to smile as he realized the hope such a journey would bring to their bleak future.

She waited in vain.

"Impossible," said Vivian. "He's not well enough to travel."

Alexandra gawked at him. "His condition won't improve if he remains, either!"

"Be that as it may, I will not drag him from his sickbed."

"Drag him!" Alexandra scoffed in disbelief.

"I believe," Kit interrupted, "that 'assist' may be the more appropriate verb. As in, we shall all together assist Mr. Evans in leaving his sickbed in Heatherhurst Hall and seeking medical advice further afield. I mean to cast no aspersions upon Alex's skills—"

Alexandra laughed bitterly. "It's not an aspersion if it's the truth!"

"—but surely," Kit continued, the ghost of a wistful smile at the corner of her lips, "a qualified surgeon would do Mr. Evans a great deal of good."

But Vivian's thin-lipped expression remained despite her reasoning. In steely tones, he replied, "I will not leave Heatherhurst Hall."

Fresh horror bloomed in Alexandra's bosom. Evidently she had overestimated her brother's love for his Welshman. Perhaps she had even overestimated his humanity. The man who stood before her now, the man she called her brother, seemed to have no more feeling or sympathy than his machines. If he had a heart at all, it'd been cast in iron.

Vivian turned his gaze upon her. "Heatherhurst Hall has been in our family since the dissolution of the monasteries. It is all that remains of our ancestry. All that we have left of our family. You said so yourself, the very night I brought Catherine home."

So she had. Alexandra could've murdered her past self for giving Vivian the fuel for the argument he made against her now. She wanted to scream at him, but the lump in her throat blocked her voice.

Taking her silence as assent, Vivian returned to his wife. "It is your home now as well, Catherine. I cannot abandon it."

"Fine," said Kit.

Alexandra whirled on her, aghast. But as she looked to her beloved, she saw that her brother's icy demeanor had met its match in the burning passion of his wife. For Kit's cheeks were aflame, and her strong jaw set tight, and her words lower and harder than Alexandra had yet heard from her lips.

"You will stay," Kit continued in that same commanding voice. "Mr. Evans, Alexandra, and I shall go."

Alexandra hardly believed her ears. Her heart soared. Her lady knight had stormed the castle and broken the chains of its prisoners. Now, Kit stood firm before the dragon, determined to bring it to heel and rescue them all.

The dragon, meanwhile, appeared incapable of understanding its defeat. Vivian gaped at his American bride. "What?"

"I am going back to New Bedford," Kit replied matter-of-factly. "And I am bringing your sister and Mr. Evans with me."

Vivian's eyes bulged. "You can't."

"I can," Kit said, unmoved by the building rage evident in his features. "And I will."

"I won't let you!"

Vivian advanced a step towards them, his hands in fists at his sides. Alexandra gripped Kit's arm, prepared to thrust herself in front of her as a living barrier against her brother's anger.

Kit never wavered. "Mr. Mudge has seen to it that our divorce will be quite clean of any legal difficulties. I will retain my inheritance; you will retain your house. I hope it may serve you well."

Vivian appeared not to hear her, his face white with fury. "I won't let you take him!"

Blood pounded in Alexandra's ears. So long they had remained trapped here, festering in their ancestral halls, haunted by their sins, confined with the ghosts of their pasts. And now, at the very instant the hope of escape appeared, Vivian refused to leave. Alexandra had never felt such rage towards him in all her life. Not when his hubris had destroyed their home. Not when he'd taken her lover for his bride. Not when he'd taken his bride for granted, refusing to acknowledge the sacrifices she'd made to follow him to his wretched house. Not 'til now had he tried Alexandra's patience to its breaking point. And now, her patience snapped.

"Yes, you will," Alexandra declared. Her rage gave her a cold tone of perfect sangfroid, and she used it to her full advantage. "Because if you attempt to stop us, I will inform the authorities that you have kept a man imprisoned in your attic for nigh-on three years for your own indecent purposes."

For Kit's sake, she could threaten what she would never have considered doing for her own benefit.

And yet, as both Kit and her own brother stared at her in silent horror, she began to think she might have gone a step too far.

Vivian found his voice first. "Prison will kill him!"

"Whether he dies in gaol or under this roof," Alexandra declared, "he dies imprisoned regardless!"

The shocked silence resumed. Alexandra knew she ought to feel ashamed of her words, yet she couldn't muster such a feeling now.

Within the silence, a phantom noise came to her ears, something like the opening of a door in the far distance. And something like a voice, as well, echoing up through the halls. Alexandra almost questioned it, then Kit opened her mouth and drew all her attention.

In a quiet, soothing tone barely above a whisper, Kit began to speak—to Vivian.

"The law of England is against you," she said. "But I believe you'll find

American law far more forgiving. At least, the burden of proof is far higher, and prosecution far less common. No one will question a gentleman living quietly with his invalid friend. The crossing of classes will be a mere eccentricity, not social ruin. And the question of inversion will never arise. No one will know. No one will care. You may live free from persecution. You could be free from fear."

Vivian cast a look of wide-eyed disbelief at her, then turned it upon Alexandra. Surely, she thought, now that Kit had softened the blow, he would see the wisdom of their words.

Yet he said nothing.

The moment stretched on, and in it, Alexandra came to her final decision.

"We will not remain," Alexandra added, never taking her gaze from her brother's face. "Nor will we leave Gareth behind to suffer and die. You may leave with us. Or you may remain alone. The choice is yours. But we are leaving regardless."

Vivian opened his mouth to retort, but stopped before he began, as if interrupted.

Alexandra was about to question him when she heard it, too. The same sound as before. An eerie call echoing through the empty halls of the sepulchral mansion. Except now, unlike before, it seemed almost to resolve into human speech.

"Halloa!"

The hair on the nape of Alexandra's neck prickled. Vivian opened his mouth to continue their argument. She motioned for his silence, but he seemed resolute upon breaking it.

"Quiet!" she hissed over him. "Someone's here!"

"Is anyone there?"

The voice again. Louder. Stronger. More resolute. More real. It came not from the walls or the rafters, but from, Alexandra supposed, the front hall.

A glance at her lover and her brother's faces told her they, too, heard it. The color drained from Vivian's cheeks. But Kit's eyes sparkled with delight.

"Is that—?" she began in an eager whisper, then stopped herself.

But the voice would not wait. "If there's anyone at home, I should very much like an explanation, if you please!"

Alexandra would've asked for the same. For, while she did not recognize the voice, she thought it sounded distinctly American.

"Phoebe!" Kit cried, and dashed from the room without another word.

CHAPTER TWENTY-SIX

lexandra ran after her. Down the corridor, around the corner, onto the landing, coming to a halt against the railing at the top of the grand staircase, and peering below to find—

"Phoebe!"

Kit, embracing an unknown figure in the foyer.

Alexandra stared down at the tender scene. The stranger looked to be a barrel-shaped young woman, Alexandra's age or perhaps a little older, in a powder-blue morning dress and sensible hat. A steamer trunk stood on its end, almost as tall as the newcomer herself, and a black leather surgeon's bag lay on the floor beside it—but there was no one else in the foyer save the women.

Kit pulled away from the stranger at last and spun to regard Alexandra upon the staircase.

"Alexandra!" she cried, her joy writ broad across her features. "Come down! It's Phoebe!"

And all at once, everything made sense.

Alexandra descended the staircase at once and crossed the foyer to approach the ladies, sizing up Phoebe Morgan as she went. Both cousins possessed strong builds, though where Kit had the frame of an Amazon, Phoebe's sturdiness put one in mind of an anvil, and where Kit's figure was long and willowy, regal and statuesque, her cousin stood almost a full head shorter than her. Yet in the strength of their jawlines and in their pointed chins, one could clearly see the Morgan bloodline ran through both women.

"Alex!" Kit's fingers remained around her wrist even as she reached out her arm for Alexandra. "This is my cousin, Miss—"

The cousin coughed. "Doctor."

"Oh!" Kit blinked, her beautiful eyes wide and round, shining with delight. "Of course! Dr. Phoebe Morgan!"

Dr. Morgan nodded to Alex. "How d'you do."

Blunt, perfunctory, and graceless. Such an introduction would never do in high society. Alexandra, instantly charmed, felt a grin creep over her face as she held out her hand. "Miss Alexandra Cranbrook."

Dr. Morgan had a cast-iron handshake, which Alexandra heartily approved.

"And this is my—my husband," Kit said, motioning over Alexandra's shoulder. "Sir Vivian Cranbrook."

Alexandra turned to regard her brother, who'd followed her down the stairs as silent as a shade, and with as grave a face.

"Charmed," Vivian grunted. He had not yet bothered to recover his manners following their heated argument.

Dr. Morgan stuck out her hand for him to shake as well. It took him rather longer to return the gesture than Alexandra would've liked.

"I beg your pardon for being so poor a host," Vivian spoke through clenched teeth, "but I'm afraid there are urgent manners to which I must attend. Please excuse me."

And, without waiting to be excused by anyone, he strode off, mounting the grand staircase with unexpected speed and vanishing into the upper floors of the house.

Alexandra permitted herself precisely three seconds of self-indulgent indignation at his behavior. Then, with a deep breath, she cleared all thought of him from her head and turned to her guest. "Shall we have your luggage brought in?"

Dr. Morgan raised her black leather bag in one hand and rapped the knuckles of the other against her trunk. "Already done."

Alexandra had to admire the practicality of a woman who could cross the Atlantic with only a single steamer trunk. Apparently it ran in the Morgan bloodline. She turned to Kit to comment upon it.

Kit, her hostess duty done, hung back with the unmistakable expression of the shy child who, having introduced her dearest friends with the highest expectations, experienced the creeping horror of doubt.

Alexandra, determined to put those fears to rest, turned her most brilliant smile upon Dr. Morgan. "I confess myself delighted to make your acquaintance. Kit has sung your praises from the moment she and I met. Come into the morning room, won't you? Some tea and light refreshment —you must be exhausted from your journey."

"On the contrary," said Dr. Morgan. "Train rides invigorate me. But I'll take you up on that tea, if you don't mind. Thanks much."

Alexandra wondered how Kit had endured even a moment in Heatherhurst Hall, with its crumbling edifice held together by cobwebs of deceit, if this were the level of honesty with which she had been raised.

Alexandra led Phoebe and Kit to the morning room, and, after seeing them settled comfortably, departed for the kitchen to see about tea. She clasped Kit's shoulder as she passed out of the room—gently, briefly—and Kit couldn't help watching her go with some small measure of loss, though she knew she'd shortly return.

The moment Alexandra left the room, Phoebe turned to Kit and plucked at the cuffs of Kit's sleeves.

"It's my wedding gown," Kit said, assuming Phoebe's interest derived from disapproval. "Your mother bought it for me to pay my morning calls in some years back; the cuffs are a little frayed, true, but nothing you need worry yourself over."

Phoebe, meanwhile, had pushed the sleeves up Kit's arm and begun examining her bare wrists.

"No ligature marks," she muttered to herself before pulling the cuffs down again in two swift and precise tugs.

"Beg pardon?" Kit asked.

Rather than answer, her cousin put a hand to her cheek and gently turned her face towards the light. "Are you wearing powder?"

Kit blushed, but affirmed she was not, in fact, painted up like an actress.

Phoebe ran her stubby fingers over Kit's cheekbone and traced the outline of her eye socket. "No visible contusion. Does this hurt at all?"

"No," Kit replied, still wondering what on earth her cousin meant by her surreptitious examination, but content to wait for an answer. Phoebe always had an answer, delayed or not.

Phoebe prodded Kit's other cheek and eye for good measure. Apparently satisfied, she dropped her hands to her lap once more.

"Is there anything amiss?" asked Kit.

Phoebe raised an eyebrow. "I was about to ask you the same question."

Kit struggled to answer. Yes, something was amiss—everything was amiss—but they were closer than ever to a solution, and it all depended upon absolute secrecy. Yet surely Phoebe of all people could be trusted.

"I don't mean to worry you, Kit, but..." Phoebe cast a wary glance at the doorway. "How much do you know about your husband and sister-in-law? About their family?"

Kit shrugged. "Practically everything now."

Phoebe blinked at her with an expression Kit only belatedly recognized as surprise—for Kit had never said or done anything to astonish Phoebe in all their years together, until now. Recovering herself with a cough, Phoebe asked, "You are aware of what became of their parents?"

"You are referring to their suicides?"

Kit realized she'd spoken perhaps a bit too casually as Phoebe's eyes went very round indeed.

"Sir Ambrose's supposed suicide, yes," Phoebe continued. "I'm glad I've not shocked you with it. But I'm afraid what else I have to say will shock you very much indeed. You must brace yourself, Kit."

Kit, curious as to what her indefatigable cousin might consider more shocking than suicide, returned her handclasp firmly. "What is it?"

"I believe the suicide of the late Sir Ambrose and the death of Lady Cranbrook would more correctly be termed double-murder."

Kit stared at her.

Phoebe patted her hand. "I warned you it'd be a shock. And that's the least of it."

Kit, utterly bewildered and at a loss to explain how or why her cousin had come to such conclusions, squeaked, "There's more?"

"Indeed," Phoebe continued, her tone grim. "For I believe the murderer—or murderers—to be none other than your husband and his sister."

Dumbfounded, Kit could only ask, "Why?"

Phoebe squeezed Kit's hand in a manner more bracing than comforting. "To cover up their own incestuous affair."

Kit's jaw fell open. "What!?"

"Doubtless you do not believe me," Phoebe went on. "I cannot blame you. It is an outrage, to be sure. But it is not so unthinkable as you might at first suppose. Consider how mysterious the circumstances of the late Lady Cranbrook's demise—particularly the circumstance of Miss Alexandra Cranbrook being the first witness upon the scene, and the only one to see her fall."

The suggestion of incest had astonished Kit. Now the initial shock had given way to indignant rage, and upon this further slur to Alexandra's character—that she would lie about what she had seen, about that which had forever colored her life, about her deepest agonies—Kit felt a surge of true anger on Alexandra's behalf.

Phoebe, perhaps assuming Kit's change in color came from horror rather than wrath, continued. "Consider also the sudden nature of Sir Ambrose's suicide, when none thought him capable of such an act. "

"I have never considered it," Kit said, surprising herself with the strength of her own voice. "And I do not believe now is the time to start."

"If not now, when?" Phoebe urged.

"After I have informed you of the true solution to all this mystery," Kit declared. "And I can assure you with perfect serenity that it is far, far simpler than your wild imaginings have led you to believe!"

Phoebe raised her eyebrows. Kit realized, belatedly, it was the first time in all their lives she had ever raised her voice to her cousin.

"Then I beg of you," said Phoebe without a trace of sarcasm in her voice. "Enlighten me."

Kit hesitated. "Have you ever heard of—that is to say, are you at all familiar with—the phenomenon of men who..." She searched her mind for an appropriate phrase. "...prefer the company of men?"

Phoebe blinked. "Inversion, yes."

"Oh." Kit supposed one could learn of anything at medical school. "Good. That will make this all very much easier."

And with that, she told all. Beginning with Alexandra's mother throwing herself down the grand staircase, and ending with the most recent discovery of Gareth Evans being quite alive, and confirmation that the apparition of the woman in yellow was not, in fact, a delusion Kit experienced alone, but a phenomenon witnessed by no fewer than three distinct persons. Very little of the history seemed to surprise Phoebe. Even when it came to the affection between Alexandra and Kit, at which Kit herself blushed and stammered, Phoebe remained nonplussed.

"I've read—well, never you mind what I've read," Phoebe told her, "but I assure you I've studied the science behind sexual inversion and only a fool would try to cure it, much less condemn it. Though—and I mean no offense—I'd just as soon my cousin hadn't gone and married one."

"How could I do otherwise," Kit asked, "when I am one myself?"

Phoebe conceded that point. Yet one point she refused to concede.

"Ghosts, Kit?" Phoebe asked. "Really?"

"Just the one ghost," Kit corrected her.

Phoebe remained unconvinced. "I believe that you are sincere when you insist upon its existence, and that you have certainly seen something, but as to it being the late Lady Cranbrook... It seems hardly scientific."

"But Alexandra and Gareth—!"

"—have witnessed the same phenomenon, which only proves that it is not your own hallucination. It does not necessarily prove that the phenomenon, whatever it is, is a ghost."

Kit gave the matter up. "I'm glad you've come regardless. After you sent the note about my marriage, and I went through with the wedding anyway, I thought you'd be awfully disappointed in me. And when you didn't respond to my letters..."

"What letters?" Phoebe interjected.

Kit supposed the ghost had stolen more of her correspondence than previously suspected.

Phoebe dismissed the notion with a wave of her hand. "I'm sorry I missed 'em, no matter what happened to 'em. I thought you weren't writing to me because you weren't allowed to."

Kit blinked at her. "Not allowed to?"

"I thought the whole marriage happened in such a rush for all the worst reasons," Phoebe said without the slightest hint of apology in her tone. "Figured Sir Vivian needed your money, and badly. Badly enough to lock his new bride away in his secluded family seat. And I'm still not entirely convinced I'm wrong. Don't think I didn't notice you limping as you hurried down the stairs," she added dryly.

"Because of the secret passage," Kit reiterated, even as she recalled her cousin's examination the instant they were alone, searching for all the signs of an ill-used wife.

"Forgive me," said Phoebe, "but from the moment I received the announcement of your engagement, I expected the worst. The description given by Mr. Mudge didn't help matters. I confess myself surprised by his decision to participate in the wedding, given all he knew of the Cranbrook estate. And then the business with the Bordens…"

"The Bordens?" Kit furrowed her brow. She'd heard of the family, certainly—one could hardly grow up next-door to Fall River without knowing all the mill-owning bloodlines—but they'd never mixed, socially. Kit supposed they considered themselves too far above her ilk. "Whatever do you mean? What's happened?"

Phoebe's eyes widened. "Do they not have newspapers in Cumberland?"

"I haven't read any, no," Kit admitted, somewhat miffed at her cousin's sarcasm. "I've been rather preoccupied."

"Regardless," Phoebe continued, "it's enough to make anybody suspect anything might be going on behind the closed doors of even the best families."

Kit opened her mouth to demand her cousin speak plainly once and for all—but just then, Alexandra returned with a tea-tray in her arms, and Kit quite forgot the matter.

CHAPTER TWENTY-SEVEN

Dinner began better yet than any meal Kit had attended since her arrival to Heatherhurst Hall. Even Vivian's belated arrival, with storm-clouds still evident upon his brow, couldn't dampen her spirits. She spent an instant wondering where he'd been and what he'd been doing since her cousin's arrival—perhaps discussing their imminent departure with Gareth upstairs—then returned her attention to the light and easy conversation flowing between Phoebe and Alexandra.

There were few greater joys, Kit thought, than introducing the two people dearest to one's heart and finding them as amicable to each other as to one's self. Phoebe had a host of horrible stories from her experience in medical school and her work in surgery thereafter. Most genteel persons would shy away from such tales. But Alexandra, her eyes glinting, listened eagerly to every shocking word and pressed Phoebe for more details, which Phoebe was only too happy to provide.

Vivian stopped this conversation by clearing his throat and serving the first course.

Alexandra spared him only the most flickering glance before smoothly steering their talk towards the arts and asking Phoebe's opinion on Kit's own photography. Kit blushed to hear it, but Phoebe had no such reservations, taking the opportunity to praise her work to the fullest extent allowed by her scientific mind.

Kit shyly dropped her eyes to her plate and took her first bite.

The unmistakable burn of ginger filled her mouth and set her eyes to watering.

She hurried to chew and swallow her portion, which only spread the burning sensation down her throat, and quickly took a gulp of wine. Milk would've served her better, she knew from experience, but didn't wish to appear even more immature for requesting a child's drink at dinner.

"What's the matter?"

Kit jumped at the question and turned to Alexandra, who'd asked it.

"Nothing," she lied.

Phoebe, who'd managed to sneak in a bite in between words of their conversation, answered for her. "It's the ginger."

For once, Kit wished her cousin didn't know her quite so well.

Kit had hated ginger since her infancy. Her parents, nursemaid, aunt and uncle all marveled at it, but made allowances for her diet. Finishing school was another story. With the content of her meals now totally beyond her control, she had to carefully pick around the burning spice when it occurred in meals—or, in cases where ginger made its way into the base of a soup or sauce, somehow avoid eating entirely. Her habit could hardly remain secret for long under such circumstances. Word travelled through the school like wildfire, and it became yet another way for her peers to torment her. Ginger was surreptitiously added to her plate at meals. Ginger was stuffed into her pillowcase. Ginger was rubbed onto her toothbrush. Patience Wheeler had even gone so far as to give Kit a box of candied ginger for Christmas at finishing school, as her idea of a grand joke. Propriety had forced Kit to publicly and sincerely thank her tormentor for her troubles, yet another humiliation in a long list of humiliations. Patience had accepted her gratitude with a simpering smile and "encouraged" Kit to try a piece. Kit couldn't manage it without tearing up. She then offered the box to Lucy, who came up with the grand idea of sharing the treat with the whole dormitory, a plan which did much to increase Kit's popularity with the other students—though Patience had certainly never intended such a result from her schemes. The popularity had lasted only until the next semester, but the humiliation had lasted years, right up to the present day.

"Do you dislike ginger?" Alexandra asked.

"She can't stand it," Phoebe told her.

Kit braced for Alexandra's scorn.

"Well, this won't do at all," Alexandra declared. "Vivian, would you be so kind as to ring for Gertie so we might have her send something else in for Kit to eat?"

Such tender solicitude was worse than disdain, Kit thought, particularly when she felt so unworthy of it.

Vivian pulled the bell-rope. Kit hunched down in her seat, mortified.

Alexandra clasped her hand. "You needn't be ashamed. It's hardly your fault."

Kit couldn't help feeling it very much was.

Footsteps sounded from the far door leading to the kitchens—a passage Kit had never yet traversed, save to go down the spiral staircase into the cellar. She felt more than ever like the worst mistress of any household that ever was, to have never once looked in on her kitchen, or introduced herself to her cook.

The footsteps drew nearer and stopped just outside the door. The door creaked open. Kit, who'd fixed her gaze upon her plate, dared a glance upward.

A woman stood upon the threshold. Thin, wiry, hatchet-faced, with her hair held back in a kerchief, and an apron over her black dress. She had one hand yet upon the doorknob. The other—

Kit's eyes widened, for the other hand was an iron hook, planted on the woman's hip as well as any palm.

"Aye, Sir Vivian?" the woman said.

"Gertie," Vivian replied. "Would you be so kind as to prepare something without ginger for Lady Cranbrook?"

The woman—Gertie—raised an eyebrow and cast her beady gaze over the gathered party. She lingered on Kit and Phoebe—no surprise to Kit, as they must have been absolute strangers to her—before returning her attention to Vivian.

"Beggin' your pardon, sir," she answered, "but it was Lady Cranbrook who especially requested ginger in the first place."

Four pairs of eyes fixed upon Kit, which was four too many for her liking. The blotchy blush broke out over her face and throat. She felt as if her whole head were ablaze.

"Catherine," said Vivian, his formality failing to cover his evident confusion. "Did you ask Gertie to prepare a dish with ginger for dinner?"

It felt useless to deny it—it would be her mere word against that of a long-standing servant—but she could hardly claim to have done what she had not, and so Kit replied, in a very small voice, "No, I did not."

Vivian furrowed his brow. "Then how—?"

"With all due respect, Sir Vivian," said Gertie, "I can honestly say I've never seen this woman afore in all my life."

Relief flooded Kit's veins. A shocked silence settled over the rest of the party.

"Gertie," Alexandra said slowly, in a tone Kit now recognized as forced patience. "You told me with your own lips that Lady Cranbrook introduced herself to you on her first day in this house."

"Aye," Gertie conceded. "The day Sir Vivian returned, a woman came down to my kitchen and told me she was Lady Cranbrook."

Kit, who'd never done any such thing, grew only more bewildered.

"But," added Gertie, "that lady was not this lady."

"This is absurd!" Vivian burst out. "Who was it, then, if not Lady Cranbrook?"

Kit, a horrible conclusion coming together in her mind, pushed down her natural hesitation to speak. "Is it at all possible the lady was... the previous Lady Cranbrook?"

Alexandra's eyes flew wide in horror. Kit bitterly regretted having brought it up, but it had to be done. She had to be certain.

Gertie, meanwhile, chortled. "Beggin' your pardon, ma'am, but I'd know my old mistress anywhere, God rest her soul. This lady was not she. Though she did wear her gown."

"What," said Alexandra, the single syllable equal parts deadpan and sharp.

"My late mistress's wedding gown," Gertie elaborated. "Wears it most days. I'd supposed Sir Vivian had given her his blessing to do it. Not my place to question his judgment," she added, with a twist to her lips suggesting she had often questioned it privately.

Alexandra's knuckles clenched white around her knife. "She wears Mother's wedding gown?"

"Alex," Vivian began, but Kit as well as anyone could tell Alexandra paid him no heed in this moment.

Gertie eyed her mistress's cutlery warily, but said only, "Aye, Miss Alexandra, she does."

"What does she look like?" Phoebe broke in, startling Kit. "This false Lady Cranbrook? Short? Tall? Young? Old?"

The barrage of blunt questions did nothing to ripple Gertie's steady nerve. "About the same height as yourself, ma'am—"

"Short, then," Phoebe concluded.

"Yes. But rather younger, I should think," Gertie went on. "Not long out of the schoolroom by my guess. Reddish hair. Blue eyes. Pink cheeks."

Kit felt as if she'd been kicked in the stomach. Breathless with fear of what seemed impossible, yet became truer and more undeniable with each word of description, she forced out, "Does she have thin brows, and a small nose that turns up at the end?"

"Aye," Gertie conceded. "I'd say her features are smallish. Bit pinched."

The whole party stared at Kit in wonder.

"Kit," Alexandra said slowly. "Do you know this woman?"

Kit thought she did but dared not say. The idea was too outlandish, bordering on the ridiculous. And yet…

A noise came from behind her. From behind the door to the foyer, now closed. The thick oak had muffled the small, high-pitched sound, but it rang in Kit's ears like the shrillest scream. It was a sound she'd heard in all her worst moments, the sound that haunted her hours both waking and sleeping all throughout finishing school, the sound that brought her shoulders up to her ears and had her whirling around to face its source.

A giggle.

Kit tore her gaze from the closed door to glance once around the table —to gauge whether or not the rest of the party had heard the horrible noise—but could read nothing in their shocked faces, and had no time to question further. She burst up from her seat.

Her chair clattered to the floor behind her as she bolted to the door and flung it open. Alexandra—Vivian—Phoebe—even Gertie—Kit had never had so many witnesses to hand. If she could only convince them to follow her, if she could only make them see what she feared to witness now—

She flew into the foyer and stumbled to a halt at the sight of the veiled woman in yellow.

The veiled woman stood just a few yards distant from the dining room door, half-crouched with one arm behind her back, as if she'd been interrupted in the midst of eavesdropping with her ear to the keyhole, and had hardly time to scamper away from the scene of her crime. She seemed far less ethereal now, in her all-too-human pose.

Their gazes locked for an instant—then, in a rush of heels upon hardwood, the rest of the party arrived at Kit's back.

Kit, not daring to take her eyes off the veiled woman, lest she vanish again, called out, "Alexandra!"

"Yes," came the answering hiss.

Kit's heart soared to hear her beloved's voice beside her when she needed her most. "Do you see her?"

"I do," Alexandra immediately replied.

"As do I," came Phoebe's voice.

"And I," Vivian added belatedly.

The veiled woman continued staring at them all. As they spoke amongst themselves, she slowly drew herself up from her crouched position, until she stood at her full height—a height which left her a good head shorter than Kit. Her right hand remained behind her back, like a child hiding a forbidden toy from its nurse.

"Gertie," Alexandra said. "Is this the woman you know as the lady of the house?"

"Aye," said Gertie, in a tone of far less wonder than Kit thought appropriate.

Kit, meanwhile, kept watch upon the veiled woman. Her pose shifted, her sheer skirts flowing with every twitch, and a portion of her hidden arm came into view. She had something in her hand, something clenched in her delicate fist, a long wooden handle, and at its end... a blade.

With a start, Kit recognized it as a hatchet.

"Explain yourself!" Alexandra demanded. "Remove your veil and tell us who you really are!"

Kit already knew. The impossible hunch she'd developed from Gertie's description had become undeniable fact the moment she heard that horrible little giggle from the other side of the dining room door.

The stranger complied, reaching her left hand up to pluck the corner of the gauze. Her right hand remained tight upon the hatchet still at her side. Every movement careful, delicate, deliberate, she pinched and peeled away the veil from her face, exposing features Kit knew all too well.

"Patience Wheeler," Phoebe announced.

CHAPTER TWENTY-EIGHT

Patience Wheeler stood her ground. Five pairs of eyes upon her were not enough to disturb her. She'd always relished attention.

Kit stared at her in frank disbelief. She recalled the cook's words—her own glimpses of the veiled figure—the disappearance of her letters—of the photographic plate which would have proved Patience's presence in the house—

All this time, she'd been haunted by a living person.

But Patience didn't have so much as a glance to spare for Kit. Her cold blue eyes had fixed upon Vivian. A smile spread across her cherubic cheeks.

"Good evening, my darling," she said.

Kit glanced towards Vivian and saw no recognition in his astonished gaze.

Patience, however, seemed to see exactly what she wanted. "Did you enjoy your dinner?"

The blotchy blush flared to life all over Kit's face and neck. At last Patience glanced her way, just for a moment, and her angelic smile became, for the merest instant, a satisfied smirk.

"What," Alexandra said, her clear voice filling the foyer, "are you doing in our house?"

Patience arched her thin eyebrows. "It's my house, too, dear sister."

"The Devil it is!" Alexandra snapped. Her teeth gleamed white against her blood-red lips, as ferocious as the jaws of any wolf.

Patience replied in a tone as sweet and light as if Alexandra had merely wished her good-day. "It became my house the moment I became your brother's chosen bride." Her ice-blue eyes flitted over to Vivian. "Isn't that right, my dear?"

"Vivian," Alexandra growled. "Explain."

"I—I cannot!" Vivian protested. "Miss Wheeler, I'm gratified by your attentions, I'm sure, but I'm afraid I'm already married. To Catherine," he added as an afterthought, one hand groping towards Kit without looking at her. Kit stepped closer to assist him in winding his arm through her elbow.

Patience scoffed. "Don't you know her friends call her 'Kit'?"

Kit had wondered the same thing ever since Vivian had first proposed, but had never dared say as much aloud.

Patience continued. "You care nothing for her. I don't chide you for it—I commend you on your taste. You required her money, and so made a marriage of convenience. But you have never lain with her. I would have seen it."

A chill ran down Kit's spine. How much had Patience seen—from where had she watched—to what had she borne witness?

"At first," Patience went on, "I thought it was an expression of your superior taste. You would never lower yourself to lay with such an unnatural woman. A commendable sentiment. But then..."

The first inkling of displeasure came into Patience's china-doll face. A shadow of a sneer marred her smooth brow and twisted her smiling lip.

"Then I saw you with the thing in the attic."

Kit's blood ran cold. Alexandra's hand clenched in her own. If Patience had seen the two men together, they were as good as doomed. Her testimony would be enough to send Vivian to prison. Gareth would never survive the trial, much less punishment.

"But you may rest easy," Patience declared. In the space of a wink, her tone had shifted back to honeysuckle and light. "The issue is solved."

The simplicity of her announcement belied its dark implications. A shadow came over Kit's heart, in no way lessened by the bright and bubbly voice that had delivered it.

But it was Vivian who staggered forward.

"What," he said softly, expressing as much or more disbelief as Kit.

"You needn't worry about the thing in the attic anymore," she continued, her words syrupy-sweet. "I've taken care of it. Enough laudanum to put it out of its misery at last. One more night's sleep, and it need never wake. You'll be free of it, thanks to me."

Vivian gaped at her in horror.

"That wretched hunchback," Patience continued, beaming, oblivious, "won't come between us ever again. You'll be safe in my bed at last. I'll make a natural man of you. I'll cure you. You'll see, Vivian, my darling."

She spread her arms wide, ready to envelop him in her smothering embrace, the hatchet loosely held in her delicate little hand.

Vivian staggered towards her. One step. Two. Kit stared in mute disbelief.

Then he broke into a run.

Not, as Kit had first supposed, towards Patience. He leapt past her, bolting towards the grand staircase. His long legs stretched to take the steps two at a time.

But Patience proved faster.

She darted forward like a cobra—and struck with just as much violence. Her arm swung through the air, the hatchet in her hand, and buried the blade in Vivian's shin with a sickening crunch.

All this, in less time than it took Kit to blink.

Vivian collapsed with a cry of alarm, as much startled as pained. Alexandra's scream of outrage overpowered it. She flew past Kit—who only just managed to grab her wrist, to be dragged along beside her—towards her fallen brother.

Patience, meanwhile, had danced back from her victim and darted up the grand staircase. Halfway up, she stopped, and leaned over the railing to address those below. Her delicate little hand still clenched the bloodied hatchet. As she balanced it upon the railing, crimson drops fell from its blade to spatter on the foyer floorboards.

"Forgive me, my love!" she cried, her voice still just as sweet as finishing school elocution demanded. "I have erred grievously. I should have known the temptation would be far too great while the creature still lived, even if it were doomed. But I understand you, now, and shall remedy the issue directly."

She stroked the hatchet in a way which made her meaning quite plain.

Kit's heart leapt into her throat as she thought of Gareth—alone, utterly ignorant of what evils occurred in the house beneath him, and helpless to escape—then Vivian's groan of pain distracted her.

Alexandra had shaken off Kit's grip and was now on her knees beside Phoebe, who'd come to tend her newest patient. Already she'd taken his cravat and wrapped it around the wound as a bandage. A red stain seeped through the white cloth, but not so much as Kit had feared upon seeing the attack inflicted.

"Phoebe!" Kit whispered urgently. "How bad is it?"

"None so bad now," Phoebe replied without looking up from her work, "but I don't doubt it'll be much worse if she comes down again with that damned hatchet."

"Can you leave him?" Kit begged.

Phoebe paused dressing the wound to fix Kit with a curious look.

"There's another way upstairs," Kit rushed to explain. "If I lead you up to the attic, you could still save—!"

"Oi!"

Kit whirled towards the shout and discovered the cook—Gertie—with one foot upon the bottom step of the grand staircase, her one hand clenched in a fist by her side, and her jaw set tight as she glared up at Patience Wheeler.

"That's my hatchet, you two-penny harlot!" Gertie shook her hook as a gentleman might shake his fist. "Drop it! Now!"

Despite the harsh words and menacing gesture, Patience appeared nonplussed. She straightened up and lifted her chin coolly. "If you persist in speaking thusly to your mistress, Gertrude, I shall be forced to dismiss you without a character."

"Drop it," Gertie snarled, "or I'll take it back by force!"

"Ungrateful wench!" Patience snapped. "How dare you—!"

But Gertie had already leapt up the stairs to grapple with her.

Kit tore her eyes away from the battle and returned to her cousin. She opened her mouth to continue her explanation, but before she could speak, Vivian's voice cut her off.

"Catherine!" he cried.

Kit stared down at him in disbelief.

"Kit!" he added.

She continued staring, marveling at how he could suppose that was the source of her confusion, and not that he would call out for her when he lay bleeding out upon the floor of his own foyer, attended by his sister.

"Please!" he begged, his face white as milk. "I've no right to ask—I've been a dreadful husband to you, I know—but if what you say is true—if there's any way you can save—!"

He cut himself off, still unable to voice the name of one he'd kept secret for so long.

Kit understood perfectly. She turned to Alexandra. "If you can manage—"

"I've kept my brother alive this long," Alexandra replied. "A few more minutes won't change that."

Kit would've argued that the last few minutes had proved utterly unlike any that had come before, but she knew it would make no difference.

Instead, she kissed her.

Alexandra's mouth opened in astonishment beneath her lips. Kit wanted nothing more than to take the opportunity to deepen the kiss, to prolong this parting moment.

Yet she pulled back.

Alexandra's expression in that moment—shocked, pleading, wanting, desperate—tore Kit's heart in two. The last thing in the world she wanted to do was to leave her beloved in the clutches of her finishing school nightmare.

Nevertheless, Kit stood up. Phoebe followed suit.

"This way," said Kit, and led her cousin towards the dining room.

A strangled cry came from the staircase. Kit didn't dare look back. She leapt over the threshold and ran to the other side of the room, snatching the still-lit silver candelabra from the center of the table as she went. Then she forced herself to slow down as she ran her fingertips over the wainscoting, seeking the hidden passage. Phoebe, ever-observant, required no explanation to join her in her search.

"Here," Phoebe whispered at last. "A crack."

Kit's heart soared. Together, the cousins pulled the door open, revealing the narrow staircase.

"Mind the missing step," Kit warned, and, candelabra aloft, led the way up the stair.

The way was musty, dark, and silent. The candelabra's flames caught on cobwebs, incinerating them in rapid bursts. Kit wanted to run, knew every second they delayed was a second closer to disaster, but forced herself to take slow, deliberate steps, careful to illuminate the way before she put her foot down. Another sprained ankle would hardly help their mission. Halfway up, she found the very step she'd broken in her first climb. She stretched her long legs over it and continued her ascent.

The staircase terminated at a worn wooden door. It had no lock. Kit cautiously pushed it open a crack. Peering through, she saw vague white shapes—the sheet-covered furniture of the attic. Hearing nothing above her own panicked pulse, she opened the door. She paused again, waiting, watching, listening for any sign of Patience's approach. There were none.

"This way," she told Phoebe and strode boldly forward.

The unfamiliar entrance had her turned around for a moment, but she quickly re-oriented herself and found the door to Gareth's sickroom.

It was ajar.

Heart in her throat, Kit pushed the door fully open and braced herself for a ghastly sight.

There upon the bed lay Gareth. Where before he had formed the picture of perfect repose, now his body had twisted and tangled in the sheets, limbs contorted at odd angles, mouth open, eyes shut.

Kit quickly stepped into the room, out of her cousin's way. "Phoebe!"

"Right," Phoebe grunted, apparently unperturbed by the sight of grotesque suffering. "Come along, Kit. I require a nurse."

So saying, she approached the bed and set her black leather bag upon the nightstand. She opened it, slipped a hand into its unfathomable depths, and emerged with a stethoscope, which she wasted no time in putting to use upon her patient. Kit, who'd come up to stand beside her in the interim, awaited the result with bated breath.

"He's breathing," Phoebe pronounced after a few moments.

Kit let out a sigh of relief.

Phoebe bent down and picked up something from the floor. She brought it to her eye level for inspection, and Kit recognized it as the bottle of laudanum. From the way Phoebe handled it now, she knew it to be empty.

"It was nearly empty before," Kit blurted, eager to offer any information that might help her cousin in their quest.

"How nearly?" Phoebe asked, setting the bottle down. "A few teaspoons? Tablespoons?"

"Less than that," Kit replied. "Far less. Only a few more doses, I should think. It went more quickly once Alexandra had to dose myself as well as him."

Phoebe didn't so much as raise an eyebrow at this revelation. "And no doubt he's built up a tolerance in the meantime, based on your description. He might well have a chance yet." She cast a cursory glance over the nightstand and surrounding surfaces. "Patience didn't have any morphia to hand—I wouldn't be able to pull it out of his veins if she had—but laudanum, that we might yet be able to do something about."

Kit had a hundred other questions besides. She set down the candelabra beside Phoebe's bag and opened her mouth to ask them.

A creak interrupted her.

It sounded far off, but loud enough to ring through the attic like a gunshot. Kit, terrified, looked to her cousin. Phoebe continued treating her patient, apparently unaware of the noise beyond the sickroom.

"I'm going to go check the door," Kit said.

Phoebe frowned at her, puzzled, but before she could ask after Kit's purpose, Kit had already reached the door, and peered over the threshold.

The white sheets draped over the discarded furniture had never looked more ghostly. Kit tried to remember how it had all appeared when last she saw it, scant moments ago, so she could tell if anything had moved or changed. She could, of course, recall nothing specific, and cursed her own inattention to detail.

Another creak echoed up into the attic.

Kit stepped out and quietly shut the sickroom door behind herself. The footsteps continued their approach. She set out to meet them, past the ghostly furniture, around the corner of the fireplace. A glance down the secret passage showed no one. She quickly moved on to the narrow stair. It, too, appeared abandoned. She descended to the door, and, finding it unlocked, opened it.

The hallway remained empty as ever.

Yet the patter of footsteps echoed nearer and nearer with every passing moment.

Perhaps Gertie had triumphed over Patience on the grand staircase in the foyer. Perhaps Alexandra had come up to tell Kit of their victory.

But she knew her hopes were futile, even before she glimpsed a fluttering yellow skirt coming around the corner.

Kit shut the attic door behind herself just as Patience Wheeler came into the hall.

Patience came to a halt mid-step, her little foot slamming sharply into the floorboards. She gawked at Kit in frank disbelief. "You!"

"Me," Kit replied, not knowing how else to respond to such an exclamation.

Patience recovered herself with a sneer. "I suppose you intend to save the crippled thing?"

Kit caught her tongue before she answered with an honest affirmation. She knew she couldn't argue Patience out of her murderous intent. She needed some other way to stop her from ascending the narrow stair and invading the sickroom.

"He's dead," said Kit.

Patience stared at her. At first Kit feared her wide-eyed expression bespoke disbelief, but then her open mouth curled at its edges, and her lips peeled back from her perfect pearl-white teeth, Kit realized with growing horror that what Patience felt in that moment was pure astonished delight.

"Dead?" Patience replied in a hushed whisper.

Kit, her throat stopped with revulsion, could only nod.

Patience laughed, the beginnings of a girlish giggle escaping her throat before she put a ladylike hand over her mouth, just as finishing school had taught her. The other hand still held her gory hatchet.

Though her lie was evidently believed, Kit felt only short-lived relief. There was still every chance that Patience might glimpse Phoebe at her work. Kit had to stall her, distract her, convince her that it wouldn't be worth her while to check the sick-room.

"Why are you doing this?" Kit asked. "Why now? You've been here all this time. You could have made yourself known at any moment. Why tonight?"

"You think I have been wasting my time here at Heatherhurst?" Patience replied archly. "Shows what little you know. Every day I've worked towards my pending nuptials with Vivian—my just reward for all my labors. I've been dosing that thing ever since I arrived. A few more weeks and it would have slipped quietly away without attracting anyone's notice."

Kit's stomach turned in revulsion.

Patience cast a cool look over her person. "But my hand was forced. Just this afternoon, I heard my dear Vivian talking to that thing. He spoke of plans to leave England. To leave this house. To leave me! I won't be left behind a second time. I refuse."

Kit could muster no argument. She had no confidence in her powers of reason against the unreasonable.

Patience narrowed her eyes. "I also heard him say it was all your idea."

It was the first stroke of luck Kit had all evening. At last, an opportunity to draw Patience's ire away from the innocent and towards herself—the one responsible for Patience's presence in the house. Kit allowed a small smile to grace her lips as she replied, "Indeed."

"You confess?" Patience appeared aghast. "You admit to being the orchestrator of all my miseries?"

"I do."

"You are not ashamed of this," Patience observed.

"I see no reason to feel so," Kit replied.

"You wouldn't," Patience muttered darkly. She brought the hatchet to her bosom, closed both hands around it, her fingertips tapping its wooden handle as if playing a flute. Her eyes no longer met Kit's, her attention far from the present moment, intent upon some dark inner musings. "You're shameless. You can't even begin to understand what you've done."

With every word, her volume rose, until she was snarling.

Kit, wary of Patience's attention wandering back to her intended victim, tried to bring focus back to herself. "Tell me what I've done."

"It's not fair!" Patience screamed, her voice shrill and ragged, a child's tantrum tearing her throat. "What have you done to deserve this? You've no grace, no eloquence! You learnt nothing at finishing school! You're an overgrown weed! Someone ought to have cut you down years ago, but instead you sprouted up and got plucked into a bouquet! Crabgrass amongst roses! How could anyone—how could he—possibly choose you over me?! I'm modest—gentle—charming—beautiful—! I've trained for years to become the perfect lady! And even then, after he's taken leave of his senses and picked you to be his bride, you care nothing for him! You've made no efforts to draw him into your bed! You've done nothing to make yourself pleasing to him—to entice him away from that wretched creature in the attic! You have the perfect man all to yourself, and you don't even want him! You're the most unnatural creature to ever walk the earth!"

Her words stung, yet none so severely as those Kit had heard from her lips and from others at school. Then, she had crumpled under them, surviving only with Lucy's presence to soothe her wounds. Now, she had her husband, her cousin, and her beloved beside her, all under her own roof, which Patience had invaded like the Vikings before her. Kit would drive her out.

"You're not a woman!" Patience snapped. "You're a monster!"

Kit stared her down. "Come and slay me, then."

In the space of a blink, Patience pounced upon her.

Kit had braced for attack before she ever spoke the words, yet still found herself surprised at the speed and ferocity of her attacker. She just barely brought her arms up to block the first downward swing of the hatchet, her forearms forming a cross against Patience's elbow, and turning a skull-cracking strike into a mere glancing blow. The blade scraped against her forehead. Blood dripped from the wound, sticky and cold, just over her left eye, blurring her vision. Taller and more sturdily built than her opponent, Kit still struggled to hold her defensive position, her arms shaking against the fury of Patience's determined assault.

Then Patience reared back—the loss of opposing force sent Kit hurtling forward—she grabbed wildly for the hatchet, for Patience's arm, for anything—missed all—Patience swung again—Kit caught her wrist—it wasn't enough—the blade struck her skull—an explosion atop her head—like fire raining down—her vision went white—her ears rang—

Kit staggered back, blinking, shaking her head, trying desperately to clear her senses even as the floor tilted underfoot and the walls swam around her.

"Kit!"

The singular shriek of her own name formed an anchor in the swirling void. She clung to it, let it pull her down, down, down, back into her body, back into reality, to the hallway, to—

Her vision cleared, and at the end of the hall, she beheld the most welcome sight in all the world.

Alexandra stood before her.

Unfortunately, Patience Wheeler remained between them, with her hatchet raised above her head in both fists.

Kit darted to the side. The hatchet thudded into the floorboards where she'd been, missing her flesh but pinning her skirt to the floor. The sudden motion sent her head spinning again. She had to get up, to run to Alexandra, to join forces with her and together they could—

Patience yanked the hatchet out of the floorboards. The flat of its head cracked into Kit's ear.

Black spots swarmed her eyes like flies. She fell back into nothingness. Over the ringing in her ears, she heard Alexandra's shriek of anguish, and between the black spots, she saw Alexandra flying towards her.

If Alexandra's beautiful face proved the last sight she ever beheld, Kit could be content with that.

CHAPTER TWENTY-NINE

Alexandra watched Kit flee the foyer with her cousin in tow. Her heart ached to lose her. But she had no time for self-pity. Not in these dire circumstances. with her servant locked in combat with a madwoman, her wounded brother in her arms and his blood seeping into the floorboards.

A strangled cry came from the staircase. Alexandra glanced up just in time to see Gertie clutch at her face, blood streaming between her fingers, and fall. She tumbled down the staircase in the same instant that Patience Wheeler, crimson-coated hatchet still in hand, darted up.

Alexandra abandoned her brother to see to Gertie, who had landed prone at the base of the stair. Even as Alexandra approached her, she raised herself on one trembling elbow and looked about wildly.

"Where has she gone?" Gertie croaked, heedless of Alexandra falling to her knees at her side.

"Upstairs," Alexandra gasped. She reached for Gertie's face, to brush away the hair pulled loose in the fight and see to whatever wound the hatchet had wrought.

Gertie slapped her hand away. "Get after her, then! I'll be along!"

So saying, she made as if to sit up, but her eyes rolled to white and she fell back again, blinking as if stunned.

"Stay here," Alexandra begged her. She glanced over her shoulder at her brother, and found he'd crawled after her, and now lay within arm's reach. "I need you both to stay together, understand?"

"Safety in numbers, is it?" Vivian said wryly.

There could be no possible safety whilst Patience Wheeler lurked in their ancestral halls—and the realization of just how long she'd crept through the shadows amongst them, watching them, listening to them, plotting their demise, had only just begun to settle upon Alexandra's mind, leaving her with a horrible crawling sensation like a thousand spiders running over her skin.

Alexandra shook her head to clear it. She had no time for horror. She had to act. To save Gareth. Kit and Dr. Morgan, going up by the servants' stair, would reach the attic before Patience—but she would reach it eventually, and what would happen then, Alexandra dared not consider.

More determined than ever that Patience should not reach the attic, Alexandra stood.

"Stay here," she said again, and alighted the staircase without another backwards glance.

Patience had a head start on her. Alexandra took the steps two at a time to gain it back. Even so, she had not yet caught up with her by the time she made the landing. The pitter-patter of Patience's footsteps echoed ahead. She followed, already knowing where they would lead her. There were only so many paths to the attic.

Then the pattering of Patience's footsteps ceased and became voices raised in conversation. First, Patience's shrill whine, and then Kit's more measured tones.

The sound sent Alexandra's heart leaping into her throat.

She ran on, not stopping until she reached the hallway with the attic door at its end. She wouldn't have stopped there, either, had her attention not been arrested by the sight of Patience and Kit locked in mortal combat.

They struggled—seemed evenly matched—and then, as Alexandra watched, paralyzed with horror, the hatchet struck.

"Kit!"

The cry burst from Alexandra's throat on pure instinct.

And for one beautiful moment, Kit rallied.

Until the hatchet struck again, and she fell to the floorboards, and lay still.

All the good kindled in the past few hours—the joy of knowing Kit loved her as much as she loved Kit, the relief of divulging all the wretched secrets that had tied her to the past, their magnificent scheme of leaving Heatherhurst Hall behind and traveling to a new world full of new possibilities, hopes, dreams—all of it shattered like so much stained glass. Their whole future reduced to shards.

Seeing Kit fight had frozen her; seeing her fall spurred her into motion once more. Alexandra flew towards her, heedless to all danger.

Her movement greatly surprised Patience, who, having successfully freed her hatchet from the floorboards, had apparently intended to continue her assault, but stood stock still at Alexandra's approach, hatchet raised, eyes wide, mouth agape in disbelief.

Alexandra ignored her. She fell to her knees at Kit's side, screaming her name, clutching at her, searching her throat for a pulse, searching her face for any sign of life, begging for her to open her eyes, pleading with her to speak.

None of which provoked any response from Kit.

Blood streamed down her soft cheeks and stained her hair, turning it from gold to copper. It mixed with the scalding-hot tears pouring from Alexandra's eyes as screams poured from her throat. She looked up for guidance.

And found Patience Wheeler, hatchet in stand, still staring at her.

At the sight of her lover's murderer, all Alexandra's grief turned to rage. She let go of Kit. She began to rise.

Patience bolted up into the attic.

Alexandra tore after her.

Up the narrow stair, across the floorboards, past the abandoned furniture—Alexandra ran as she'd never run in her life, headlong, flying, like the Furies hot upon Patience's heels, fueled by a rage unknown to her until now, a rage that pounded in her ears and behind her eyes and threatened to burst forth from her ribcage in a torrent of boiling blood. Step by step, she gained, until she caught sight of the train of her mother's wedding gown vanishing down the servants' passage.

Alexandra dove into the darkness. She took the stairs in leaps, plunging with only her hands clawing the walls for support. Her luck held—she passed over the missing stair—she had hoped Patience might fall through it, and good riddance—but no, Patience reached the end of the passage without incident and bounded forward through the dining room.

Alexandra snatched the carving knife from the table as she darted after her.

The foyer afforded enough uninterrupted space to offer Alexandra a full view of her quarry. Patience ran ahead, past her first two victims, and slammed against the oaken doors to the courtyard.

Gertie had staggered to her feet, but could do little more than gape as Patience darted past her. Vivian, still lying on the floor at the foot of the grand staircase, could hardly be expected to do more. He shouted Alexandra's name as she ran through the foyer. She didn't spare him so much as a glance. Her eyes were fixed upon Patience.

Patience, meanwhile, had managed to pry open the oaken doors and slipped outside.

Alexandra yanked the door further open with all the fury of blind Samson and erupted into the courtyard.

Patience was nowhere to be seen.

The flat open moors held no natural hiding place. Alexandra turned her gaze to the unnatural—to the machines Vivian had dragged out into the sun.

To a curl of smoke coming from the chimney of the engine.

Alexandra clenched the carving-knife's handle as she watched the machines shudder to life. Their roar was nothing against the deafening shriek of agony tearing through her mind.

It would, however, cover the sound of her approach.

She crept forward, keeping close to the wall of the house as she moved, her eyes tracing back and forth for any sign of Patience Wheeler. Nothing at first—no motion save the juttering of the machines, the spinning of their wheels and cogs and the long leather belt that formed a figure-eight between the steam engine and the thresher it powered.

Then, amongst all the cast iron, a soft flicker of yellow fabric.

Alexandra dashed forward. There, crouched behind the thresher, was her lover's murderer.

"I have you!" Alexandra hadn't meant to scream, but she found herself roaring to rival the machines, swinging the carving knife above her head as she ran at Patience. "I will flay you! I will eviscerate you! I will carve the eyes from your head! Do you hear me? I will take your eyes! *I will have your eyes!*"

Patience had begun scrambling up the side of the thresher the moment Alexandra had moved. By the time Alexandra announced her intentions, Patience stood atop it. From here, she delivered her retort.

"I should have been your sister!" Patience howled.

Of all the things Patience might have chosen to say in that moment, this was, perhaps, the worst possible choice.

Alexandra leapt up to slash at her ankles with the carving knife. Patience shrieked and scampered back, running across the machine to its far side, taking a circuitous route to avoid the whirling wheels of jagged metal teeth designed to crush stalks of wheat and tear the grain from the fibers.

"My *sister?*" Alexandra snarled, slashing again with every word. "Did you miss me? Come and kiss me." *The Goblin Market* came to her lips unbidden, the memory of reading it aloud to Kit in her convalescence—*She clung about her sister, Kiss'd and kiss'd and kiss'd her*—the verses bubbled up out of order, out of all reason. "Never mind my bruises! Hug me, kiss me—"

Patience was shouting something back, something about her love for Vivian, something Alexandra couldn't hear above the shriek of the boiler-valve letting off steam, above the grief-stricken wailing of her own thoughts, for Kit was dead, dead, dead, and nothing else in this world mattered, and nothing would ever matter again.

"Must your light like mine be hidden?" Alexandra muttered to herself, every word of the poem rushing through her lips like the bitterest prayer. She withdrew the carving knife and set herself to climbing up the wheel of the thresher, clawing her way to its roof. "Your young life like mine be wasted?"

"I am your sister!" cried Patience, her expression horror-stricken as Alexandra pulled herself up into view.

"Undone in my undoing!" Alexandra shot back, finally on level ground with her lover's murderer. She lunged forward with her knife. Its blade came within inches of Patience's breast.

Patience staggered back, teetering on the far edge of the thresher. The whirling wheels of jagged teeth remained between them, grinding, growling, as hungry for blood as Alexandra herself. She would have it. She would paint the walls of Heatherhurst crimson with it. She would take the eyes that had watched them all this time—

"And ruin'd in my ruin!"

With this final scream, Alexandra leapt across the thresher, the carving-knife in both fists above her head, ready to plunge into Patience's withered and pathetic heart.

Patience flung up her hatchet to block the blow.

Yet as Alexandra's arms came down, and the knife dove closer to her prey, Patience fell away from it, back and down, far further down than the thresher allowed.

For, in staggering back out of Alexandra's reach, she had stumbled off the edge of it entirely.

In an instant which seemed to stretch on for an age, Alexandra watched her fall. She struck an exposed cog on the way down—it flung her into the spinning belt—the figure-eight loop twined around her throat—

And with a sickening crack of her neck, Patience's limp body struck the side of the steam engine. She hung suspended from the belt, its wheels shrieking in their efforts to move despite her weight.

Alexandra, robbed of her revenge, had hardly time to blink.

Then she, too, was abruptly yanked backwards.

Something clawed at her skirts—she fell—threw out her arms to catch herself lest she smash face-first into the roof of the thresher—dropped the carving-knife—scrambled backwards against her will—

Something bit her left foot—and continued chewing.

She had just begun to understand the sharp, repetitive pressure as pain when it leapt up to her ankle. Her right leg she'd already tucked up underneath herself, out of danger, but for how long she could keep it so, she didn't know.

What she did know, was that the train of her skirt had caught in the toothed wheels of the thresher, and as the wheels spun, pulling her further and further into it, her foot bent at unnatural angles, then snapped into pieces.

The pain was nothing next to the agony in her heart, yet it shot white-hot through her red haze, bringing the world into awful clarity for the briefest moment. She howled, half for herself, more for Kit.

The thresher devoured her ankle, shattering it to shards of bone and sprays of gore, and began work on her calf.

This would be the end, then. Devoured by her brother's hubris, divine punishment for her murderous impulse, denied even the bitterest satisfaction of destroying her lover's killer.

She knew she ought to struggle to free herself. The carving knife lay just beyond her reach. If she made the attempt, she could very well grasp it, and use its blade to slash through her own skirts, to escape the roiling iron teeth.

But without Kit, it seemed a futile effort.

Alexandra collapsed atop the thresher. Already the blood pumping from her crushed leg had sapped her strength. She waited for the machine to consume her and her suffering both. The thresher rumbled beneath her, hungry, insatiable, relentless.

Then, all at once, it shuddered to a halt.

Even the sweet release of death, it seemed, would be denied her. She raised her head to search for whatever cruel hand had stopped the mechanism. Perhaps Vivian had overcome his injuries and run outside to ensure the preservation of his precious engineering experiments.

But as she looked up, she saw no sign of her brother. Nor of Gertie. Nor even of Dr. Morgan. Her eyes rolled wildly in her head as she examined her surroundings.

A thud, then the whole thresher rocked from side-to-side, as if someone had scrambled up onto it. Then hands on her shoulders, turning her up towards the sky. Alexandra would've fought them, had she not felt so weak. She fell limply into the arms of her unknown rescuer.

And looked up into Kit's eyes.

Alexandra stared in mute disbelief. There were the soft brown doe-eyes, brimming with tears. There was the strong chin, crumpled and trembling. There were the long golden tresses cascading down like sunbeams, still with a copper streak of blood, haloing the most beautiful face Alexandra had ever seen.

"Alex?" Kit whispered.

"Angel," Alexandra murmured in reply.

Kit's brow furrowed. She opened her mouth, as if to say something, but Alexandra spoke over her.

"Whether you've come to guide me to Heaven or Hell, I care not. So long as I go with you."

"Alex—" Kit said, as if in protest.

But Alexandra, falling backwards into all-consuming darkness, heard no more of it.

CHAPTER THIRTY

Alexandra awoke.

This alone seemed an extraordinary circumstance. Her surroundings rendered it still more extraordinary, for she awoke not in the mechanical thresher, nor in a coffin, but in her own bed, in her own room, in Heatherhurst Hall. There was her dressing table, with her old ebony hairbrush and hair-receiver upon it. There was her nightstand, with a bottle of laudanum beside her well-worn copy of *Carmilla*. There were the four posts of her cherry-wood bed, with its midnight-blue curtains pulled back to let in the sunshine...

...and there was Kit, sleeping on the counterpane beside her.

Alexandra stared at her. With her expression softened, her long lashes shut, and her golden tresses spilling over the pillow like a shimmering tide, Kit looked every bit an angel in repose. There was no trace of the horrible wound dealt to her skull.

This, then, was Heaven.

Alexandra could not hope for a more perfect eternity than one spent beside her beloved. She lay contented for some time, watching Kit's bosom rise and fall with her sweet breaths, marveling at the sharp line of her jaw contrasted against her soft cheek, gazing at her rose-pink lips.

Yet even Heaven wasn't free of temptation, and soon Alexandra could resist it no further. She sat up—her head swimming as she did so—and kissed those perfect lips.

Kit's doe eyes fluttered open.

"Oh!" she said softly. "You're awake!"

So saying, she too sat up. Her hair fell into her face, and she tucked it out of the way behind her ear.

Revealing a white linen bandage underneath.

Alexandra furrowed her brow at this. Surely in Heaven all wounds were healed, or so her nursemaid had told her as a child.

Kit kissed her again, which almost drove the mystery from Alexandra's mind. Almost.

"How are you feeling?" Kit pulled away to ask. "Are you hungry at all?"

Hunger, like injury, was supposed to be banished from the blissful afterlife. Alexandra began to suspect a flaw in her initial conclusion.

"Where's Patience Wheeler?" she asked.

Kit's face fell. A moment passed before she replied, "She's dead."

Alexandra remembered that much—the whip-crack of Patience's neck audible even above the crunching of her own bones—but if Kit spoke of Patience as merely dead rather than in Hell, then it must follow that...

"We're not dead," Alexandra observed.

A faint smile returned to Kit's lips. "No, we're not."

"I'm glad of that," said Alexandra, and pulled her down for another kiss.

Though, as they parted for breath, she couldn't help remembering her own injuries in the furious battle that had culminated in Patience's death. She glanced past Kit down the length of her own body, trying to determine from the lumps under the counterpane where her legs began and ended. Growing quickly frustrated with the dearth of information, she grabbed the edge of the counterpane and flung it off herself.

Someone had dressed her in a flowing nightgown. Amongst the delicate muslin folds, she found her left leg ended at the knee, wrapped in linen bandages.

Alexandra blinked at its absence, then turned to Kit, catching her mid-wince.

"It's not so bad," Kit spoke before Alexandra could say anything. Then, wincing again at her own words, she added in haste, "Your skirts will cover it. No one will ever have to know. Besides, I've got legs enough for two."

Alexandra continued staring at her in disbelief.

The adorable strawberry blush broke out over Kit's face and throat, lending a charming warmth to her features. "I'm sorry—"

Whatever further apology she intended was cut off by Alexandra's burst of whooping laughter. The astonished look Kit gave her in response only made her laugh all the more.

"It's worth it," Alexandra said when she caught her breath, "to have you here with me."

This statement did nothing to halt Kit's blush. Alexandra, kissing her again, couldn't find it in herself to repent.

"And Vivian?" she asked when Kit paused to breathe.

"Doing very well," Kit gasped, then gathered herself to reply in stronger tones. "Better than any of the rest of us. Gareth is recovering wonderfully. And Gertie refuses to stay in bed."

"She would," Alexandra mused, recalling Gertie's reaction to the amputation of her hand.

"As do some other patients I could mention," said a new voice.

Both Alexandra and Kit whipped their heads around to regard Dr. Phoebe Morgan standing upon the threshold, her surgical bag in hand.

Dr. Morgan looked from her cousin to Alexandra and back again with a disinterested expression, her displeasure expressed only in the small wrinkle of annoyance between her brows. "Go back to bed, Kit."

Kit worried her bottom lip between her teeth. "Must I?"

"Doctor's orders," Dr. Morgan insisted.

"She's not doing me any harm," Alexandra pointed out.

Dr. Morgan raised an eyebrow at her. "Maybe so, but she may very well be doing harm to herself by refusing to rest."

"Could we not compromise?" Kit pleaded. "I'll stay in bed, just as quiet as you like—only let me stay in this bed in particular."

Dr. Morgan leveled a long considering look at her cousin. At last, she sighed. "Fine."

Kit beamed like the sun itself.

Dr. Morgan proceeded to examine each of her patients in turn, and, finding nothing worrisome in either case, didn't stay longer than necessary to measure out their respective doses of medicine.

"Rest," she intoned gravely, pausing on the threshold on her way out of the room. "And don't let me catch you out of bed again."

Kit assured her cousin she would obey, and Dr. Morgan departed.

"If memory serves," Alexandra said, "she'll have a Devil of a time getting Vivian to keep away from Gareth's bedside."

"His case is far less concerning than our own, from what I understand," Kit replied easily. "A clean blow and a clean break."

"Your cousin told you?"

"Yes, and I saw him myself besides."

Alexandra couldn't help a pang of jealousy. "You left your bed to see him?"

"No," Kit replied. "He left his bed to see you."

Alexandra blinked in surprise—then, realization turned her expression from astonishment to affection. "And you were already here."

Kit blushed anew. Alexandra laughed and pulled her into an embrace. Cheek-to-cheek, she could feel the warmth of Kit's blush against her own flesh.

"We talked while you were asleep," Kit confessed. "About where we'll all go once we've recovered. We thought we might start out in New Bedford—I've still got my parents' house there—and then see how it suits us. He seems far more amenable to the idea now. Gareth is all for it, which helped his change of heart along, I think. That, and seeing his own dear sister mangled by his machines."

Alexandra doubted fraternal affection had motivated him where his love for Gareth could not, but her doubts were immaterial in the face of the promised reality. "We'll leave the very minute your cousin lets me out of this damned bed."

Kit grinned in reply. "And catch the very first steamer across the Atlantic?"

"Between my peg-leg and Gertie's hook," Alexandra observed, "we'll make quite the piratical crew."

Kit laughed. She quickly clapped a hand over her mouth to stifle it, but Alexandra caught her wrist and pulled it away for a kiss.

THE END

Lightning Source UK Ltd.
Milton Keynes UK
UKHW010637030221
378167UK00002B/391